G.I. JOE

ORIGINS

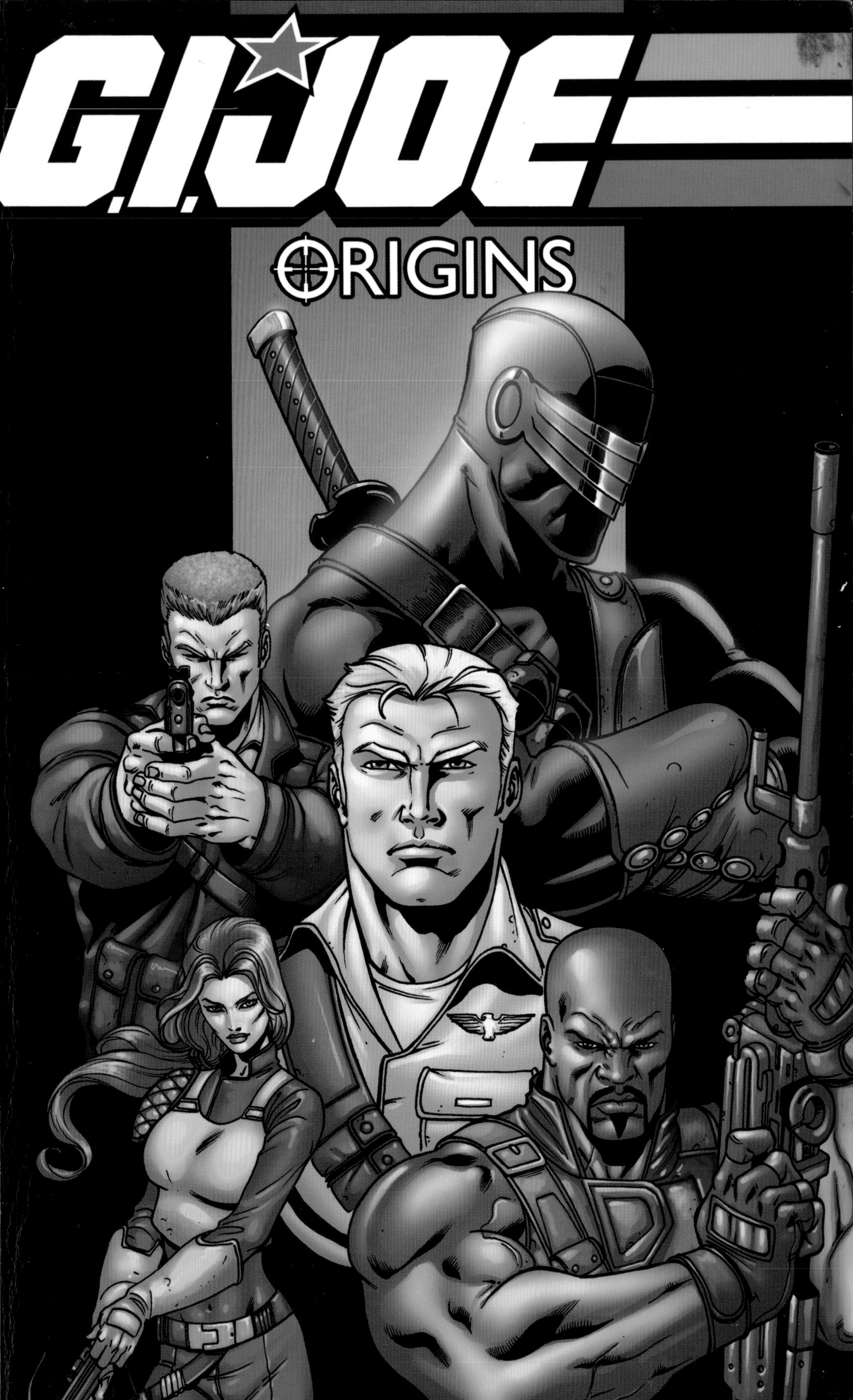

LARRY HAMA ★ MIKE HAWTHORNE

G.I. JOE

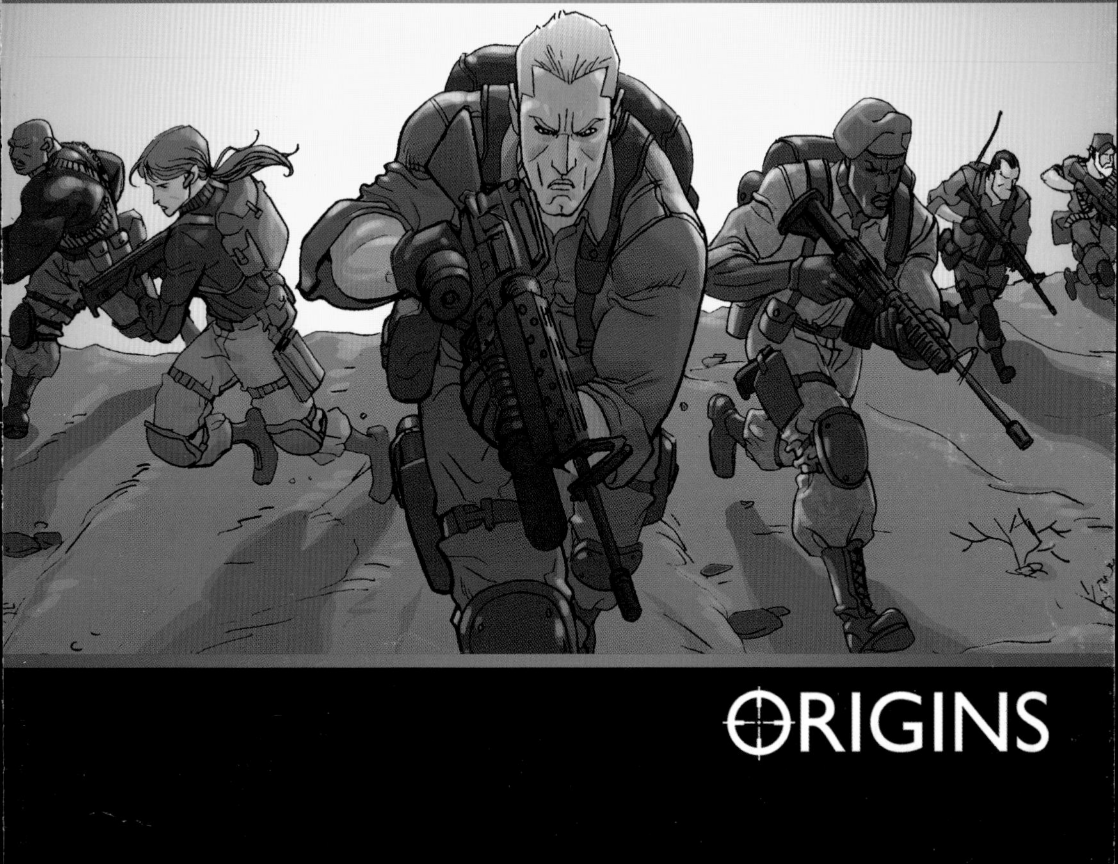

ORIGINS

G.I. JOE: ORIGINS

WRITTEN BY **LARRY HAMA**

ART & COLOR BY **MIKE HAWTHORNE** AND **TOM FEISTER**

COLOR ASSISTS BY **ERIK SWANSON**

LETTERING BY **ROBBIE ROBBINS, CHRIS MOWRY** AND **NEIL UYETAKE**

ORIGINAL SERIES EDITS BY **ANDY SCHMIDT**

COLLECTION EDITS BY **JUSTIN EISINGER**

COLLECTION DESIGN BY **NEIL UYETAKE**

ISBN: 978-1-60010-497-8

12 11 10 09   1 2 3 4

Special thanks to Hasbro's Aaron Archer, Michael Kelly, Amie Lozanski, Ed Lane, Joe Furfaro, Sarah Baskin, Jos Huxley, Michael Ritchie, Samantha Lomow, and Michael Verrecchia for their invaluable assistance.

Licensed By:

To discuss this issue of **G.I. JOE**, join the IDW Insiders, and for exclusive offers, check out our Web site:

www.IDWPUBLISHING.com

IDW Publishing
Operations:
Ted Adams, Chief Executive Officer
Greg Goldstein, Chief Operating Officer
Matthew Ruzicka, CPA, Chief Financial Officer
Alan Payne, VP of Sales
Lorelei Bunjes, Dir. of Digital Services
AnnaMaria White, Marketing & PR Manager
Marci Hubbard, Executive Assistant
Alonzo Simon, Shipping Manager
Angela Loggins, Staff Accountant

Editorial:
Chris Ryall, Publisher/Editor-in-Chief
Scott Dunbier, Editor, Special Projects
Andy Schmidt, Senior Editor
Justin Eisinger, Editor
Kris Oprisko, Editor/Foreign Lic.
Denton J. Tipton, Editor
Tom Waltz, Editor
Mariah Huehner, Associate Editor
Carlos Guzman, Editorial Assistant

Design:
Robbie Robbins, EVP/Sr. Graphic Artist
Neil Uyetake, Art Director
Chris Mowry, Graphic Artist
Amauri Osorio, Graphic Artist
Gilberto Lazcano, Production Assistant

CHAPTER ONE

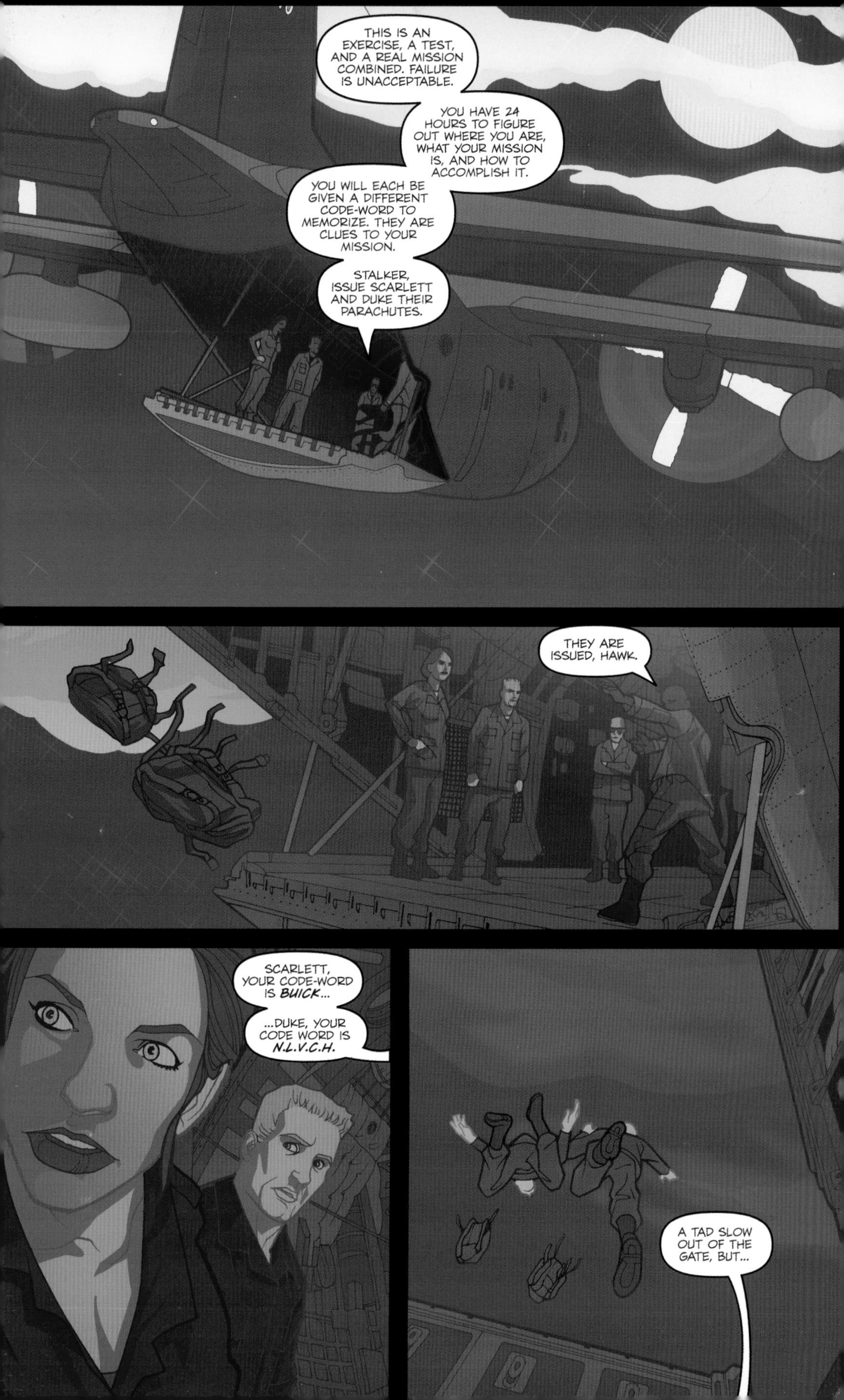
THIS IS AN EXERCISE, A TEST, AND A REAL MISSION COMBINED. FAILURE IS UNACCEPTABLE.
YOU HAVE 24 HOURS TO FIGURE OUT WHERE YOU ARE, WHAT YOUR MISSION IS, AND HOW TO ACCOMPLISH IT.
YOU WILL EACH BE GIVEN A DIFFERENT CODE-WORD TO MEMORIZE. THEY ARE CLUES TO YOUR MISSION.
STALKER, ISSUE SCARLETT AND DUKE THEIR PARACHUTES.
THEY ARE ISSUED, HAWK.
SCARLETT, YOUR CODE-WORD IS *BUICK*...
...DUKE, YOUR CODE WORD IS *N.L.V.C.H.*
A TAD SLOW OUT OF THE GATE, BUT...

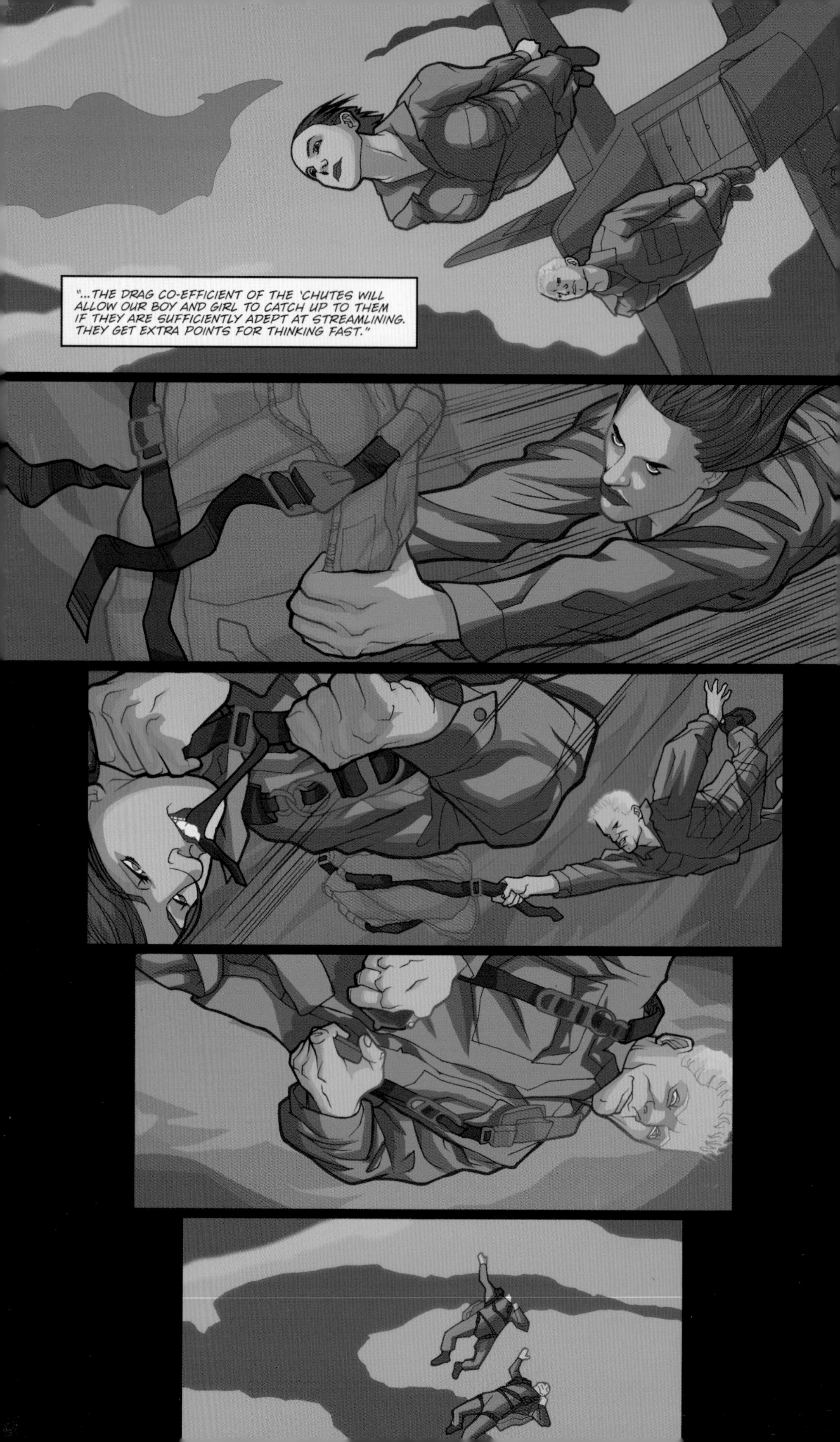
"...THE DRAG CO-EFFICIENT OF THE 'CHUTES WILL ALLOW OUR BOY AND GIRL TO CATCH UP TO THEM IF THEY ARE SUFFICIENTLY ADEPT AT STREAMLINING. THEY GET EXTRA POINTS FOR THINKING FAST."

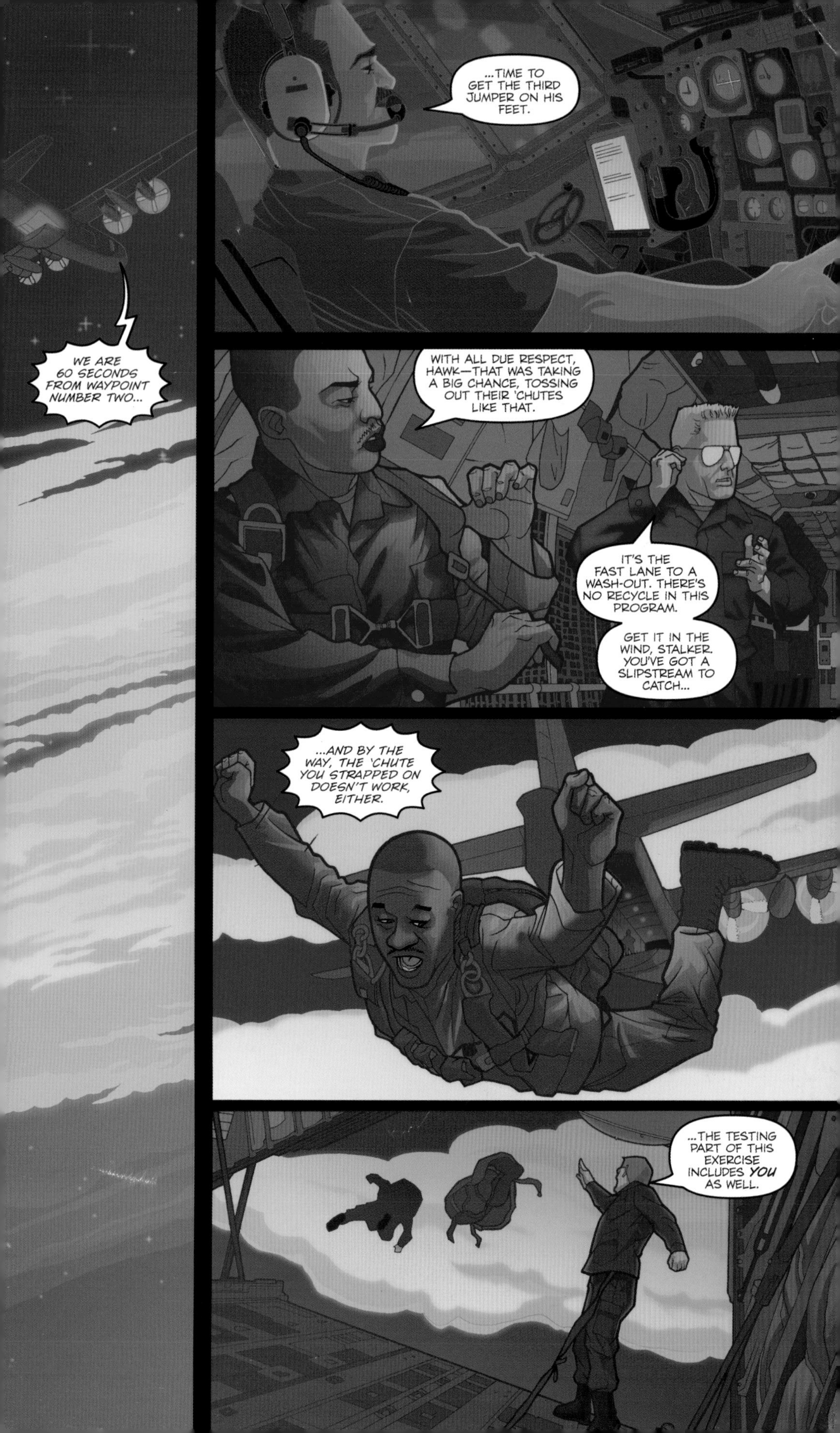
...TIME TO GET THE THIRD JUMPER ON HIS FEET.
WE ARE 60 SECONDS FROM WAYPOINT NUMBER TWO...
WITH ALL DUE RESPECT, HAWK—THAT WAS TAKING A BIG CHANCE, TOSSING OUT THEIR 'CHUTES LIKE THAT.
IT'S THE FAST LANE TO A WASH-OUT. THERE'S NO RECYCLE IN THIS PROGRAM.
GET IT IN THE WIND, STALKER. YOU'VE GOT A SLIPSTREAM TO CATCH...
...AND BY THE WAY, THE 'CHUTE YOU STRAPPED ON DOESN'T WORK, EITHER.
...THE TESTING PART OF THIS EXERCISE INCLUDES *YOU* AS WELL.

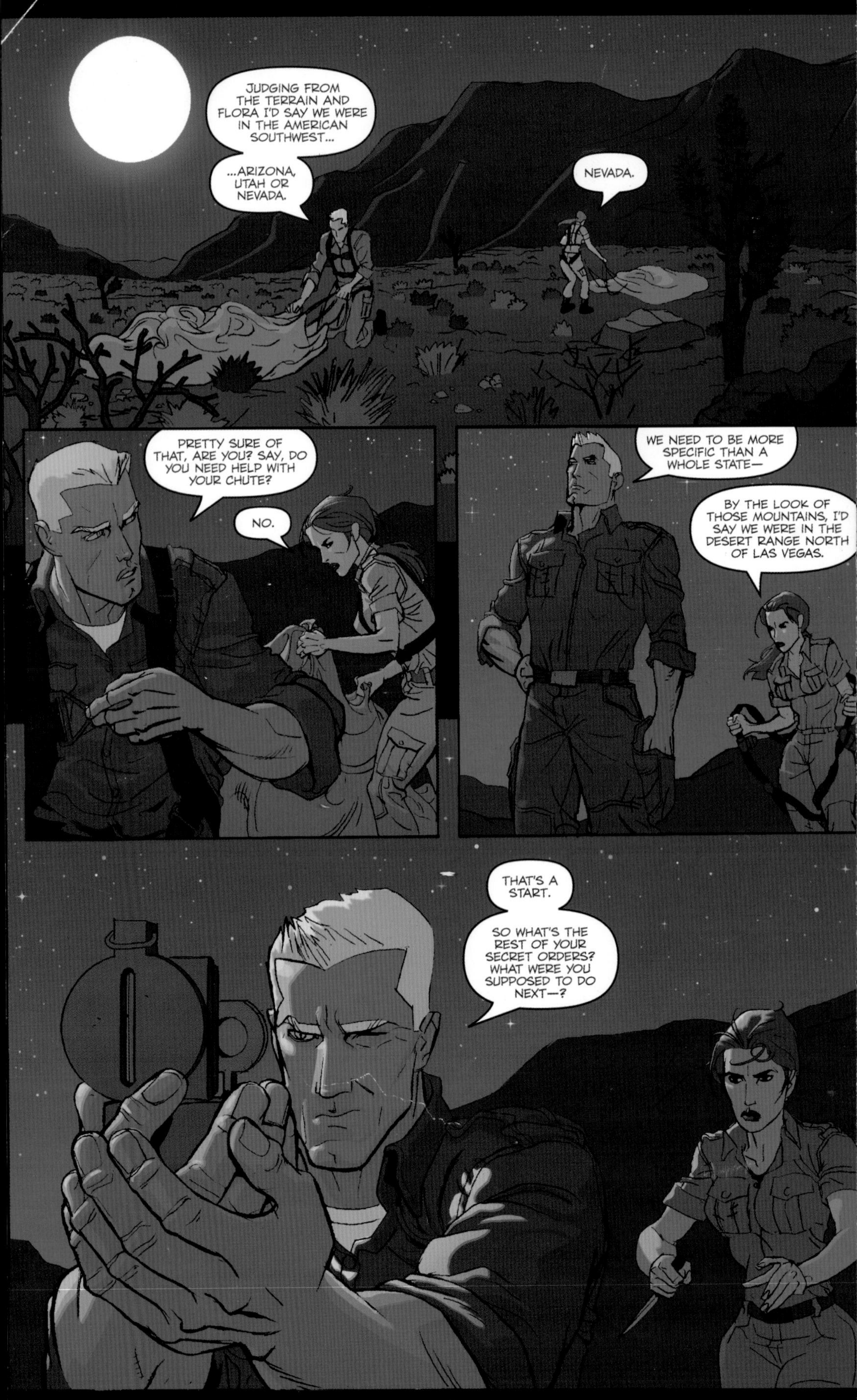
JUDGING FROM THE TERRAIN AND FLORA I'D SAY WE WERE IN THE AMERICAN SOUTHWEST...
...ARIZONA, UTAH OR NEVADA.
NEVADA.
PRETTY SURE OF THAT, ARE YOU? SAY, DO YOU NEED HELP WITH YOUR CHUTE?
NO.
WE NEED TO BE MORE SPECIFIC THAN A WHOLE STATE—
BY THE LOOK OF THOSE MOUNTAINS, I'D SAY WE WERE IN THE DESERT RANGE NORTH OF LAS VEGAS.
THAT'S A START.
SO WHAT'S THE REST OF YOUR SECRET ORDERS? WHAT WERE YOU SUPPOSED TO DO NEXT—?

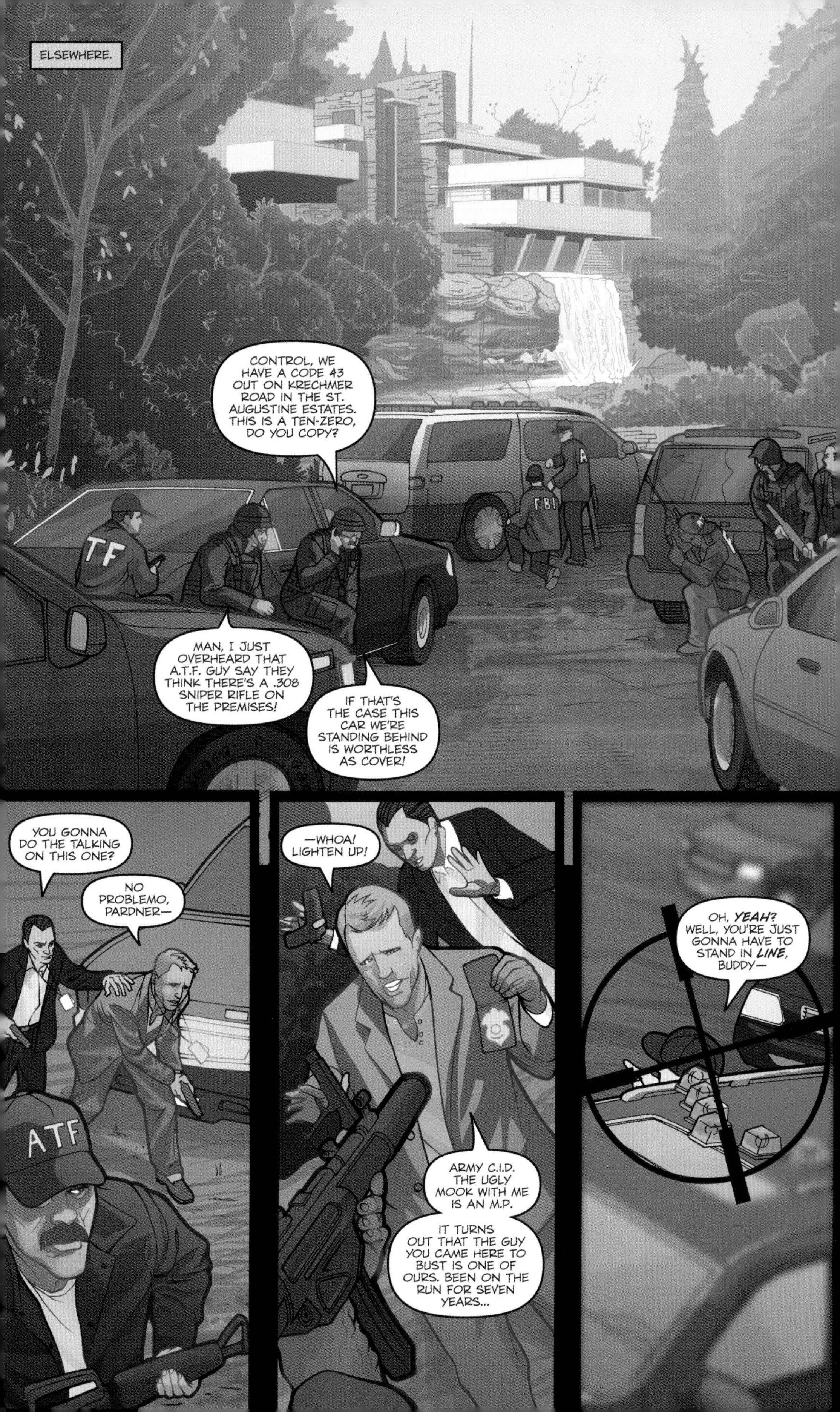
ELSEWHERE.
CONTROL, WE HAVE A CODE 43 OUT ON KRECHMER ROAD IN THE ST. AUGUSTINE ESTATES. THIS IS A TEN-ZERO, DO YOU COPY?
MAN, I JUST OVERHEARD THAT A.T.F. GUY SAY THEY THINK THERE'S A .308 SNIPER RIFLE ON THE PREMISES!
IF THAT'S THE CASE THIS CAR WE'RE STANDING BEHIND IS WORTHLESS AS COVER!
YOU GONNA DO THE TALKING ON THIS ONE?
NO PROBLEMO, PARDNER—
—WHOA! LIGHTEN UP!
ARMY C.I.D. THE UGLY MOOK WITH ME IS AN M.P.
IT TURNS OUT THAT THE GUY YOU CAME HERE TO BUST IS ONE OF OURS. BEEN ON THE RUN FOR SEVEN YEARS...
OH, YEAH? WELL, YOU'RE JUST GONNA HAVE TO STAND IN LINE, BUDDY—

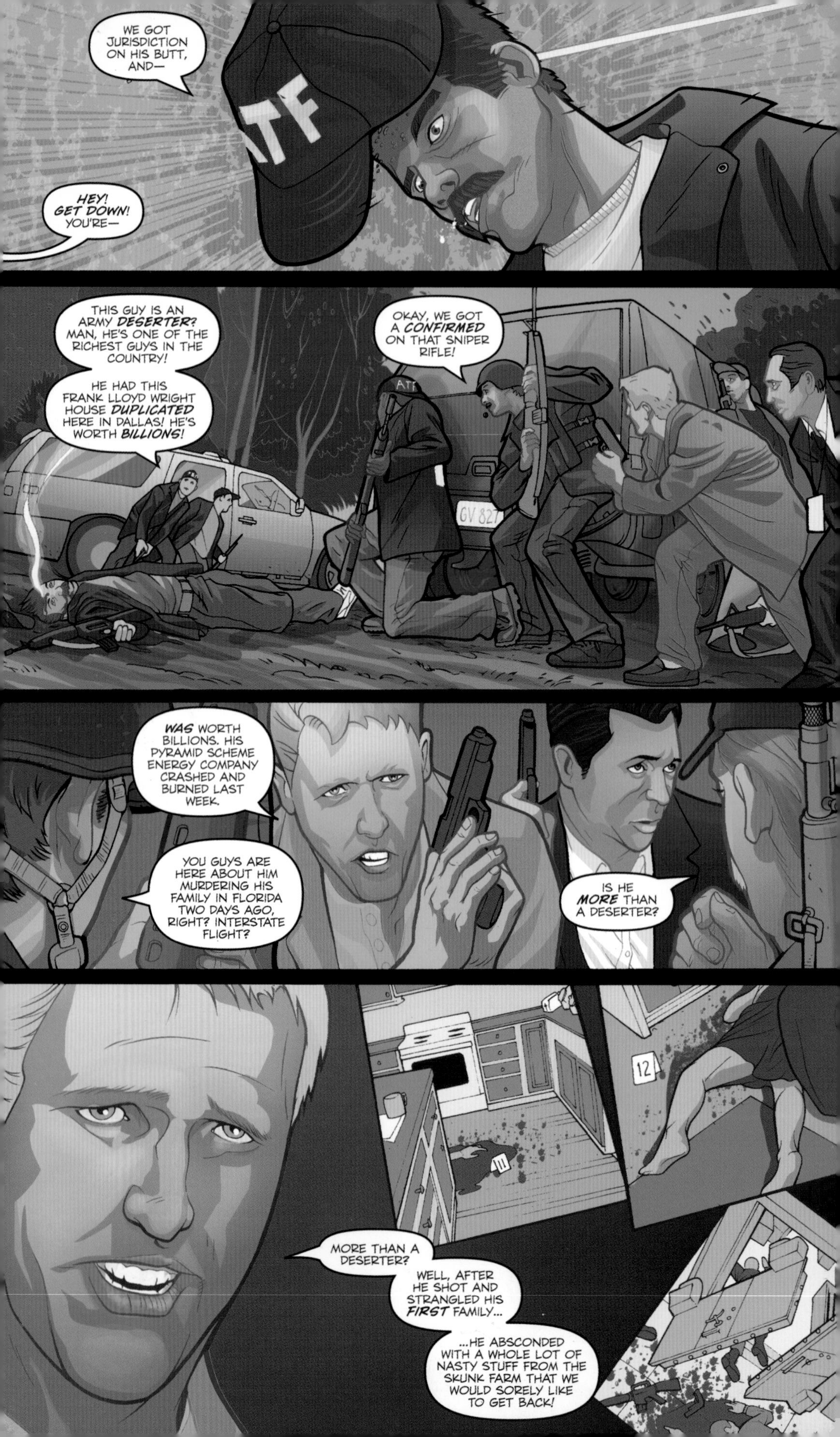
WE GOT JURISDICTION ON HIS BUTT, AND—
HEY! GET DOWN! YOU'RE—
THIS GUY IS AN ARMY DESERTER? MAN, HE'S ONE OF THE RICHEST GUYS IN THE COUNTRY!
HE HAD THIS FRANK LLOYD WRIGHT HOUSE DUPLICATED HERE IN DALLAS! HE'S WORTH BILLIONS!
OKAY, WE GOT A CONFIRMED ON THAT SNIPER RIFLE!
WAS WORTH BILLIONS. HIS PYRAMID SCHEME ENERGY COMPANY CRASHED AND BURNED LAST WEEK.
YOU GUYS ARE HERE ABOUT HIM MURDERING HIS FAMILY IN FLORIDA TWO DAYS AGO, RIGHT? INTERSTATE FLIGHT?
IS HE MORE THAN A DESERTER?
MORE THAN A DESERTER?
WELL, AFTER HE SHOT AND STRANGLED HIS FIRST FAMILY...
...HE ABSCONDED WITH A WHOLE LOT OF NASTY STUFF FROM THE SKUNK FARM THAT WE WOULD SORELY LIKE TO GET BACK!

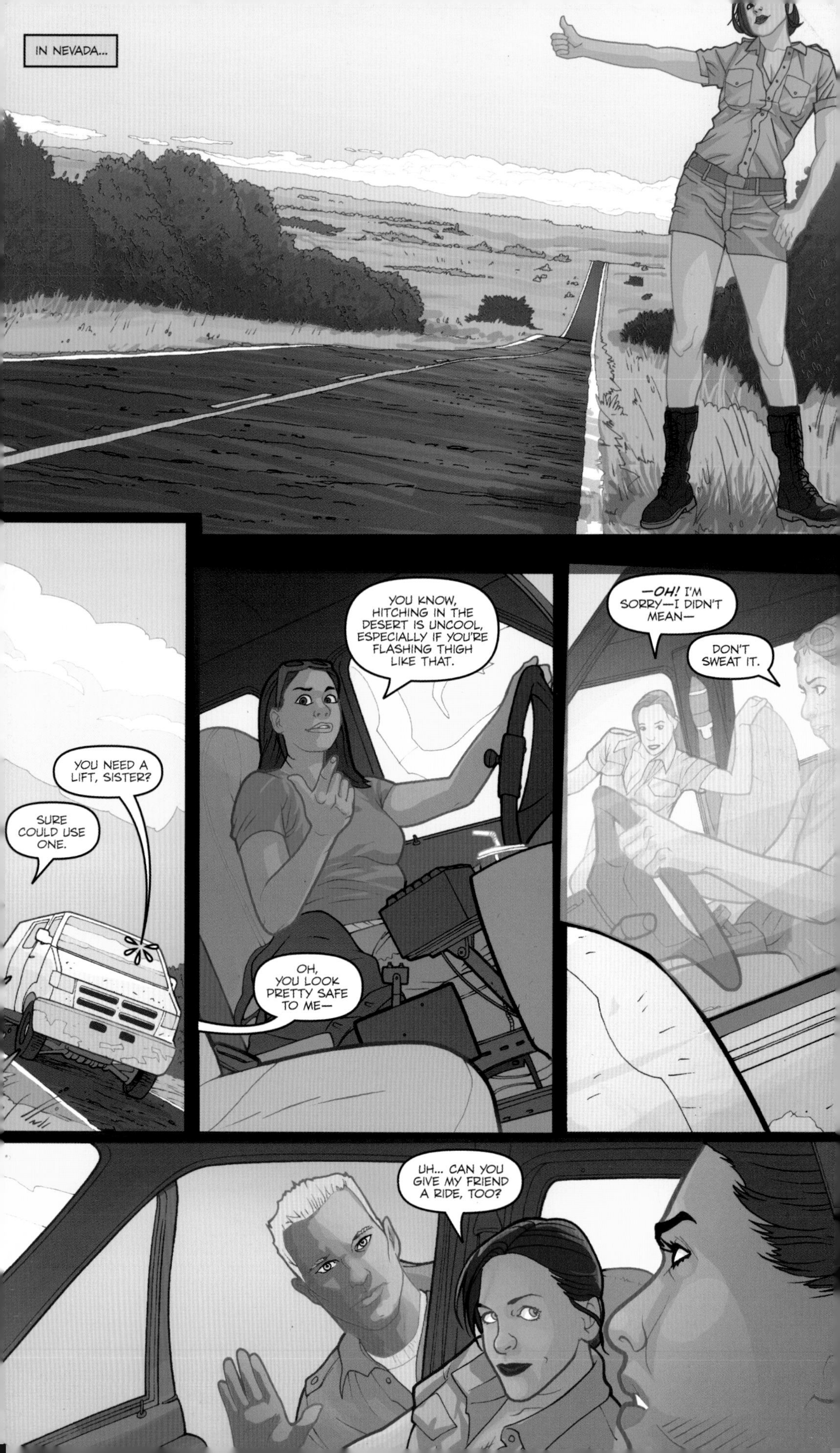
IN NEVADA...
YOU NEED A LIFT, SISTER?
SURE COULD USE ONE.
YOU KNOW, HITCHING IN THE DESERT IS UNCOOL, ESPECIALLY IF YOU'RE FLASHING THIGH LIKE THAT.
OH, YOU LOOK PRETTY SAFE TO ME—
—OH! I'M SORRY—I DIDN'T MEAN—
DON'T SWEAT IT.
UH... CAN YOU GIVE MY FRIEND A RIDE, TOO?

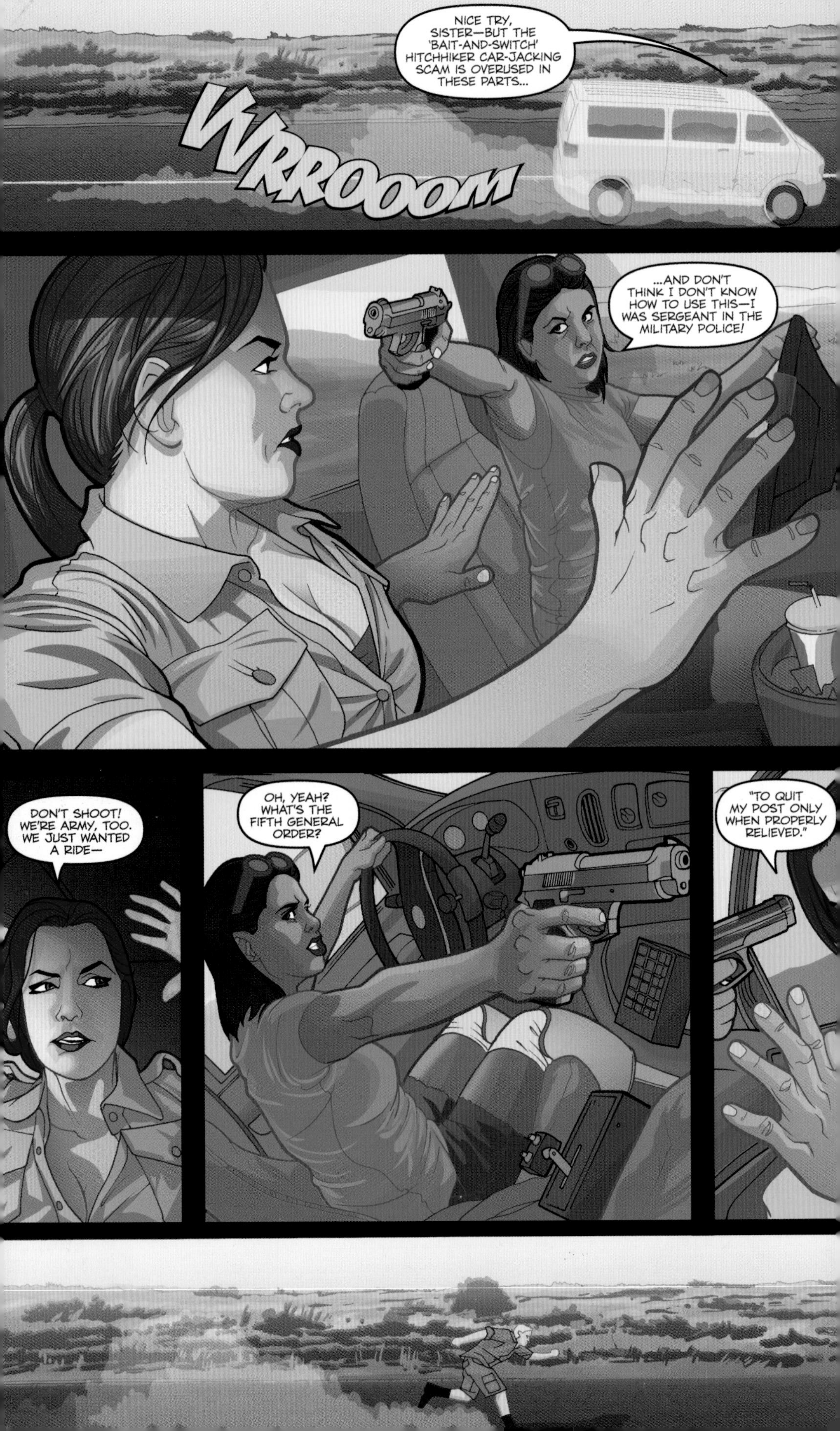
NICE TRY, SISTER—BUT THE 'BAIT-AND-SWITCH' HITCHHIKER CAR-JACKING SCAM IS OVERUSED IN THESE PARTS...
WRROOOOM
...AND DON'T THINK I DON'T KNOW HOW TO USE THIS—I WAS SERGEANT IN THE MILITARY POLICE!
DON'T SHOOT! WE'RE ARMY, TOO. WE JUST WANTED A RIDE—
OH, YEAH? WHAT'S THE FIFTH GENERAL ORDER?
"TO QUIT MY POST ONLY WHEN PROPERLY RELIEVED."

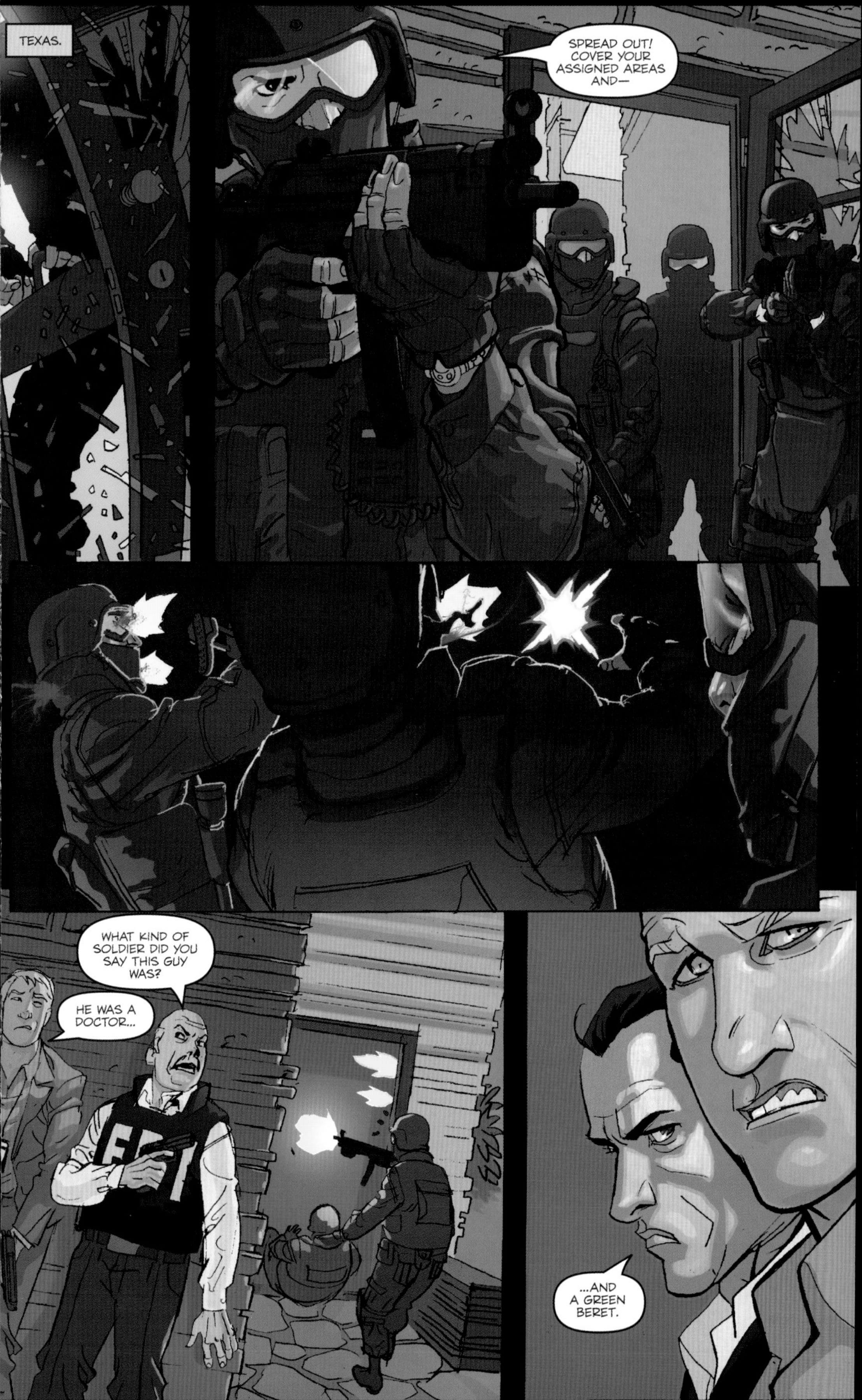
TEXAS.
SPREAD OUT! COVER YOUR ASSIGNED AREAS AND—
WHAT KIND OF SOLDIER DID YOU SAY THIS GUY WAS?
HE WAS A DOCTOR...
...AND A GREEN BERET.

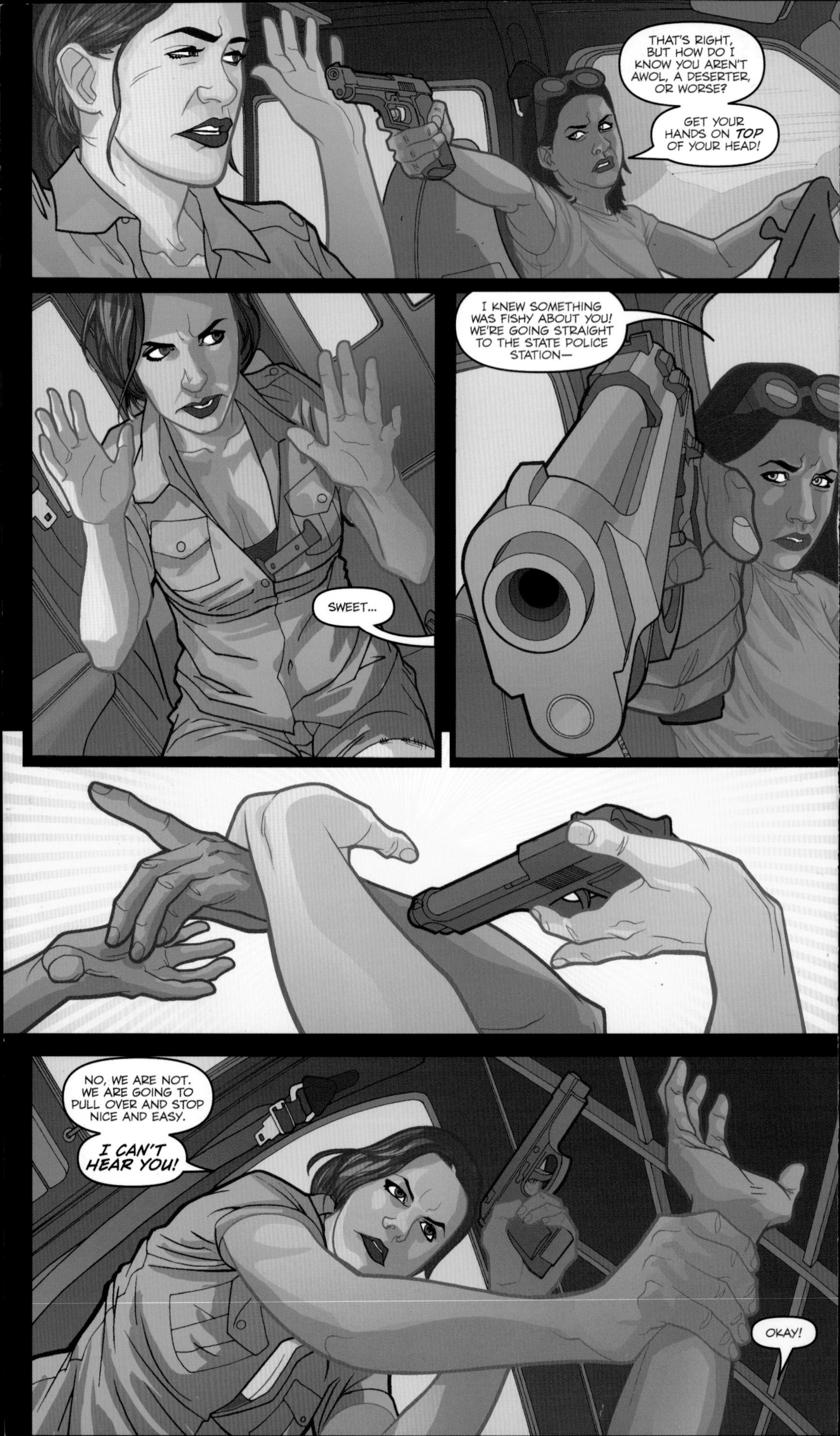

THAT'S RIGHT, BUT HOW DO I KNOW YOU AREN'T AWOL, A DESERTER, OR WORSE?
GET YOUR HANDS ON *TOP* OF YOUR HEAD!
SWEET...
I KNEW SOMETHING WAS FISHY ABOUT YOU! WE'RE GOING STRAIGHT TO THE STATE POLICE STATION—
NO, WE ARE NOT. WE ARE GOING TO PULL OVER AND STOP NICE AND EASY.
I CAN'T HEAR YOU!
OKAY!

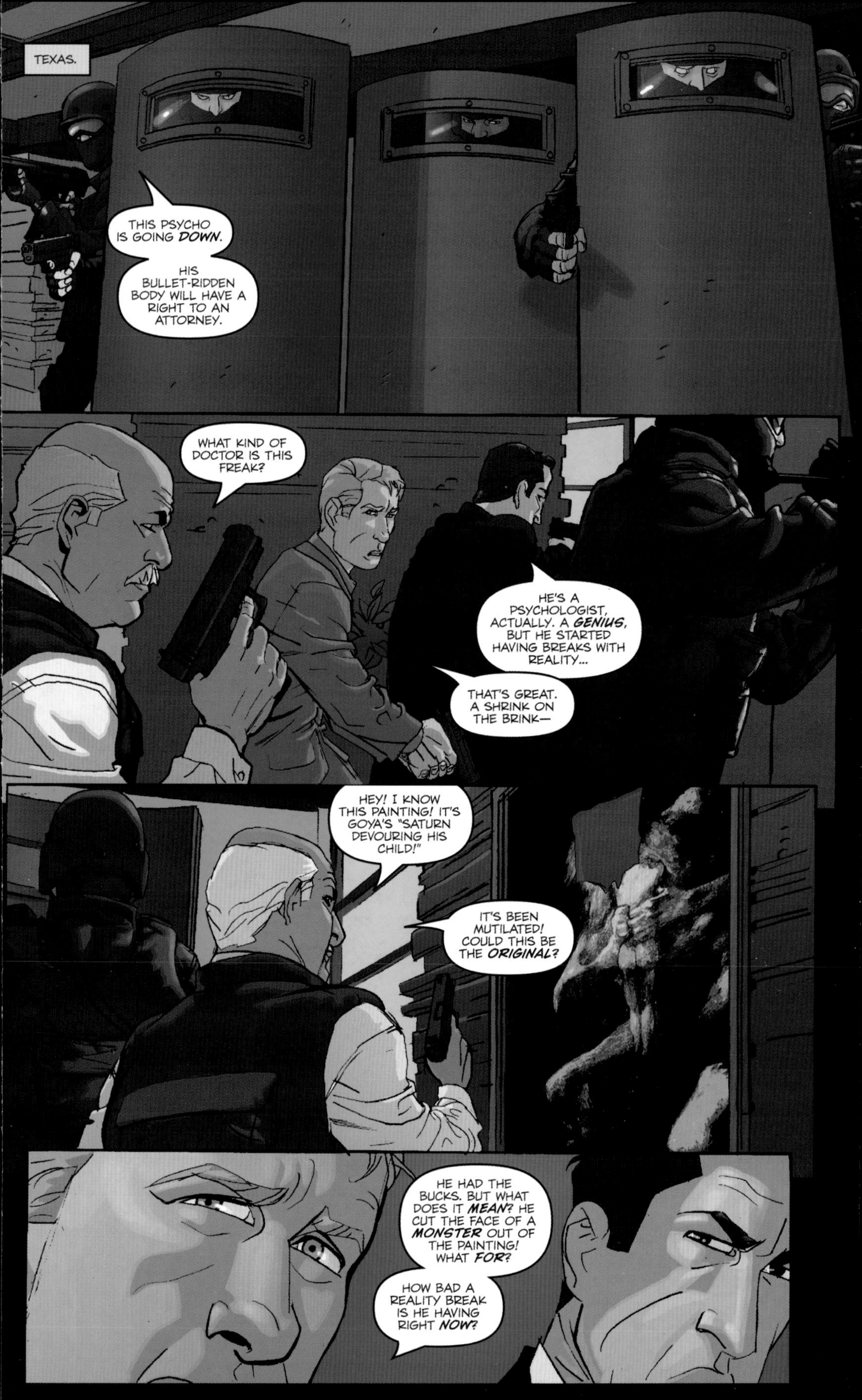
TEXAS.
THIS PSYCHO IS GOING *DOWN*.
HIS BULLET-RIDDEN BODY WILL HAVE A RIGHT TO AN ATTORNEY.
WHAT KIND OF DOCTOR IS THIS FREAK?
HE'S A PSYCHOLOGIST, ACTUALLY. A *GENIUS*, BUT HE STARTED HAVING BREAKS WITH REALITY...
THAT'S GREAT. A SHRINK ON THE BRINK—
HEY! I KNOW THIS PAINTING! IT'S GOYA'S "SATURN DEVOURING HIS CHILD!"
IT'S BEEN MUTILATED! COULD THIS BE THE *ORIGINAL*?
HE HAD THE BUCKS. BUT WHAT DOES IT *MEAN*? HE CUT THE FACE OF A *MONSTER* OUT OF THE PAINTING! WHAT *FOR*?
HOW BAD A REALITY BREAK IS HE HAVING RIGHT *NOW*?

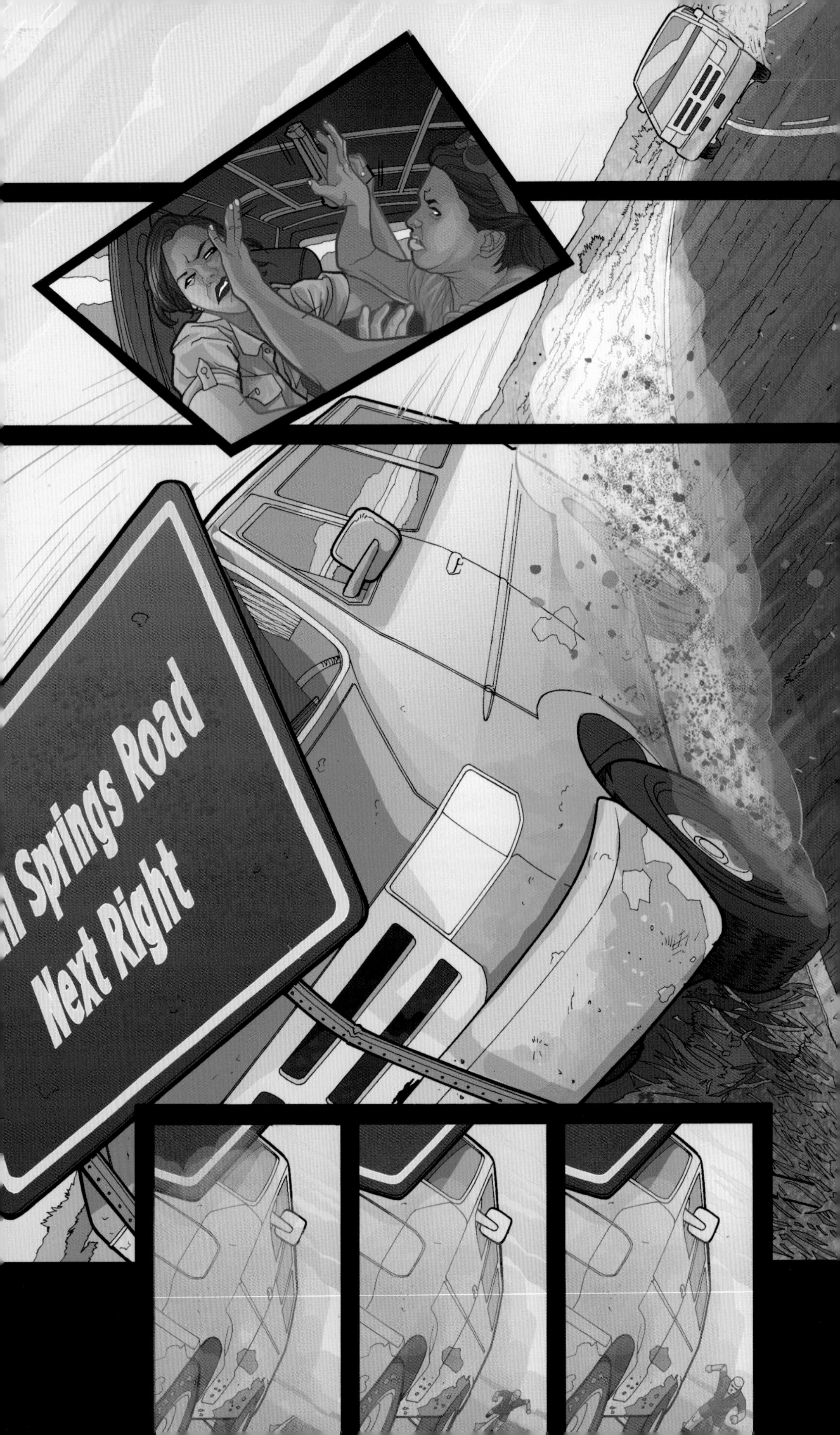
Springs Road
Next Right

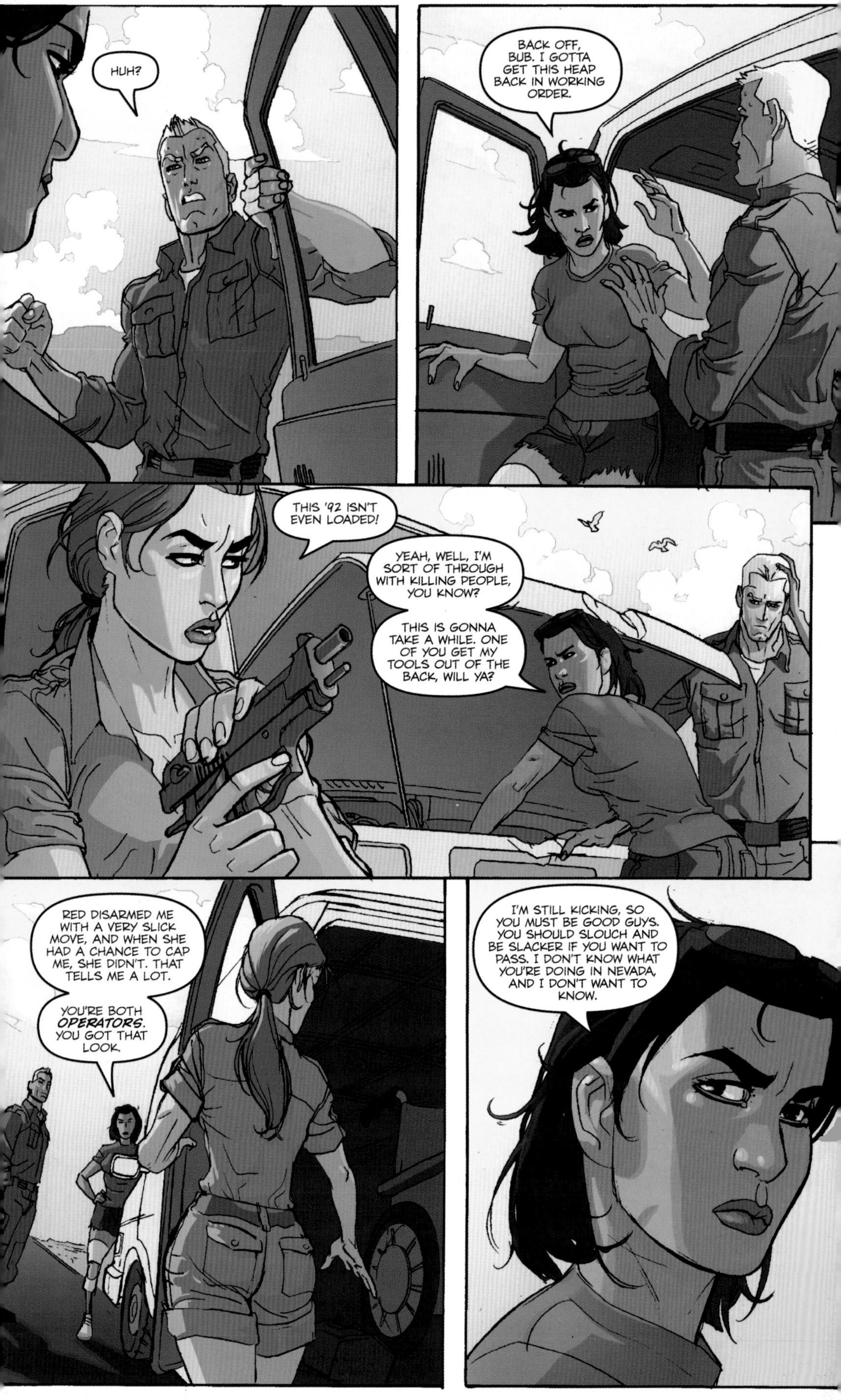
HUH?
BACK OFF, BUB. I GOTTA GET THIS HEAP BACK IN WORKING ORDER.
THIS '92 ISN'T EVEN LOADED!
YEAH, WELL, I'M SORT OF THROUGH WITH KILLING PEOPLE, YOU KNOW?
THIS IS GONNA TAKE A WHILE. ONE OF YOU GET MY TOOLS OUT OF THE BACK, WILL YA?
RED DISARMED ME WITH A VERY SLICK MOVE, AND WHEN SHE HAD A CHANCE TO CAP ME, SHE DIDN'T. THAT TELLS ME A LOT.
YOU'RE BOTH *OPERATORS*. YOU GOT THAT LOOK.
I'M STILL KICKING, SO YOU MUST BE GOOD GUYS. YOU SHOULD SLOUCH AND BE SLACKER IF YOU WANT TO PASS. I DON'T KNOW WHAT YOU'RE DOING IN NEVADA, AND I DON'T WANT TO KNOW.

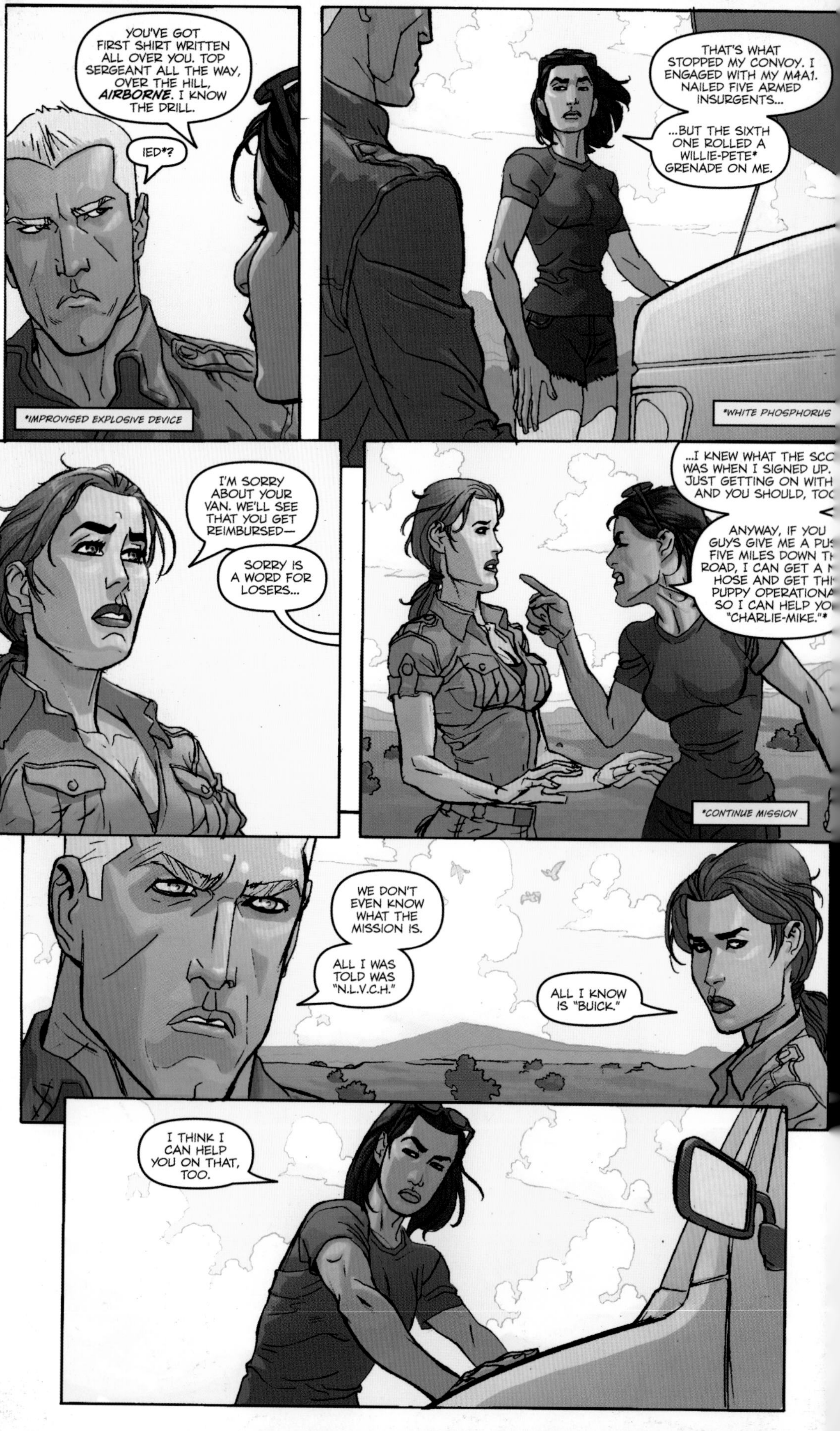

YOU'VE GOT FIRST SHIRT WRITTEN ALL OVER YOU. TOP SERGEANT ALL THE WAY, OVER THE HILL, AIRBORNE. I KNOW THE DRILL.
IED*?
*IMPROVISED EXPLOSIVE DEVICE
THAT'S WHAT STOPPED MY CONVOY. I ENGAGED WITH MY M4A1. NAILED FIVE ARMED INSURGENTS...
...BUT THE SIXTH ONE ROLLED A WILLIE-PETE* GRENADE ON ME.
*WHITE PHOSPHORUS
I'M SORRY ABOUT YOUR VAN. WE'LL SEE THAT YOU GET REIMBURSED—
SORRY IS A WORD FOR LOSERS...
...I KNEW WHAT THE SC WAS WHEN I SIGNED UP. JUST GETTING ON WITH AND YOU SHOULD, TOO
ANYWAY, IF YOU GUYS GIVE ME A PU FIVE MILES DOWN T ROAD, I CAN GET A HOSE AND GET TH PUPPY OPERATION SO I CAN HELP YO "CHARLIE-MIKE."*
*CONTINUE MISSION
WE DON'T EVEN KNOW WHAT THE MISSION IS.
ALL I WAS TOLD WAS "N.L.V.C.H."
ALL I KNOW IS "BUICK."
I THINK I CAN HELP YOU ON THAT, TOO.

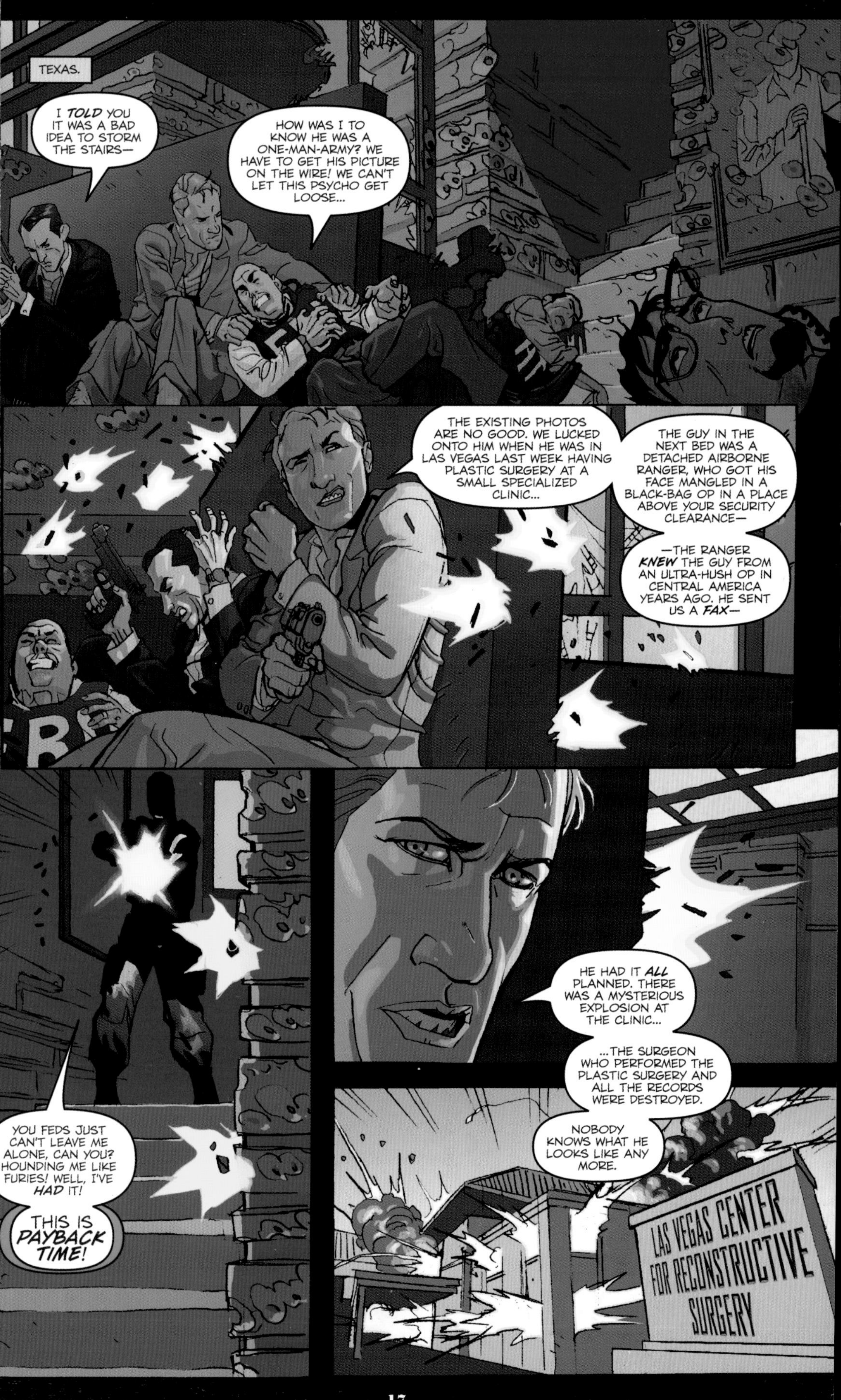
TEXAS.
I *TOLD* YOU IT WAS A BAD IDEA TO STORM THE STAIRS—
HOW WAS I TO KNOW HE WAS A ONE-MAN-ARMY? WE HAVE TO GET HIS PICTURE ON THE WIRE! WE CAN'T LET THIS PSYCHO GET LOOSE...
THE EXISTING PHOTOS ARE NO GOOD. WE LUCKED ONTO HIM WHEN HE WAS IN LAS VEGAS LAST WEEK HAVING PLASTIC SURGERY AT A SMALL SPECIALIZED CLINIC...
THE GUY IN THE NEXT BED WAS A DETACHED AIRBORNE RANGER, WHO GOT HIS FACE MANGLED IN A BLACK-BAG OP IN A PLACE ABOVE YOUR SECURITY CLEARANCE—
—THE RANGER *KNEW* THE GUY FROM AN ULTRA-HUSH OP IN CENTRAL AMERICA YEARS AGO. HE SENT US A *FAX*—
YOU FEDS JUST CAN'T LEAVE ME ALONE, CAN YOU? HOUNDING ME LIKE FURIES! WELL, I'VE *HAD* IT!
THIS IS *PAYBACK TIME!*
HE HAD IT *ALL* PLANNED. THERE WAS A MYSTERIOUS EXPLOSION AT THE CLINIC...
...THE SURGEON WHO PERFORMED THE PLASTIC SURGERY AND ALL THE RECORDS WERE DESTROYED.
NOBODY KNOWS WHAT HE LOOKS LIKE ANY MORE.
LAS VEGAS CENTER FOR RECONSTRUCTIVE SURGERY

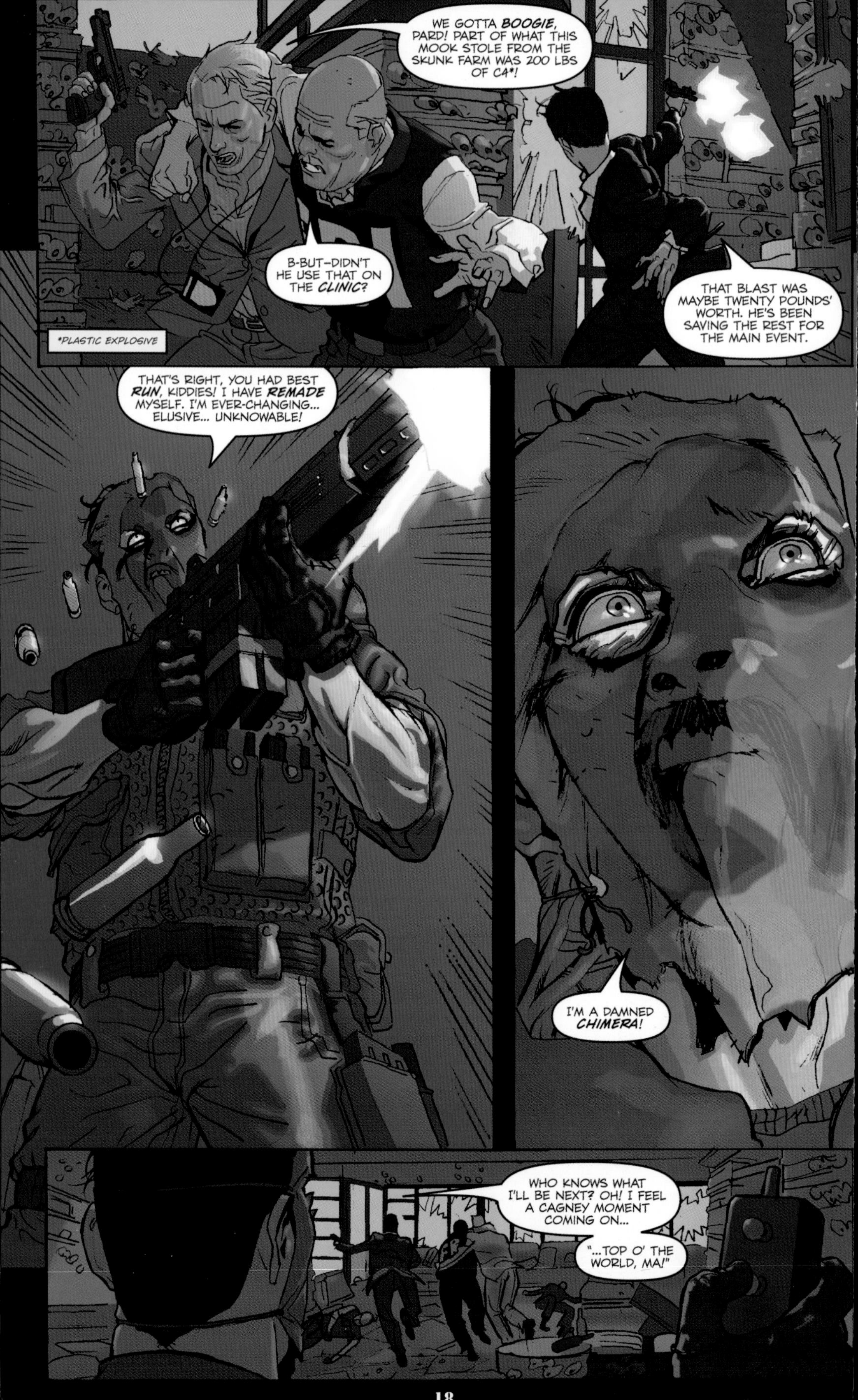
WE GOTTA BOOGIE, PARD! PART OF WHAT THIS MOOK STOLE FROM THE SKUNK FARM WAS 200 LBS OF C4*!
B-BUT–DIDN'T HE USE THAT ON THE CLINIC?
THAT BLAST WAS MAYBE TWENTY POUNDS' WORTH. HE'S BEEN SAVING THE REST FOR THE MAIN EVENT.
*PLASTIC EXPLOSIVE
THAT'S RIGHT, YOU HAD BEST RUN, KIDDIES! I HAVE REMADE MYSELF. I'M EVER-CHANGING... ELUSIVE... UNKNOWABLE!
I'M A DAMNED CHIMERA!
WHO KNOWS WHAT I'LL BE NEXT? OH! I FEEL A CAGNEY MOMENT COMING ON...
"...TOP O' THE WORLD, MA!"

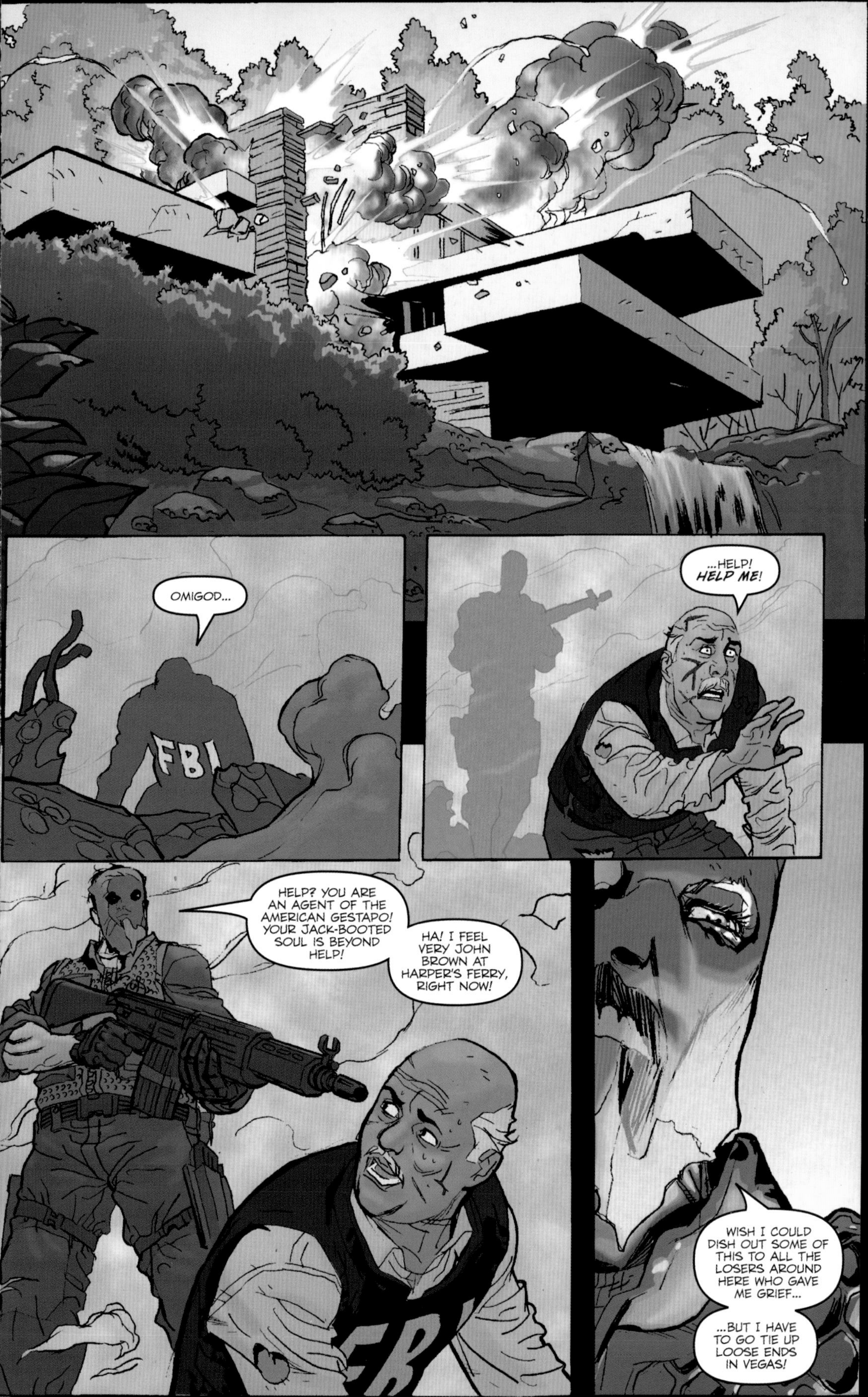
OMIGOD...
...HELP! HELP ME!
HELP? YOU ARE AN AGENT OF THE AMERICAN GESTAPO! YOUR JACK-BOOTED SOUL IS BEYOND HELP!
HA! I FEEL VERY JOHN BROWN AT HARPER'S FERRY, RIGHT NOW!
WISH I COULD DISH OUT SOME OF THIS TO ALL THE LOSERS AROUND HERE WHO GAVE ME GRIEF...
...BUT I HAVE TO GO TIE UP LOOSE ENDS IN VEGAS!
FBI

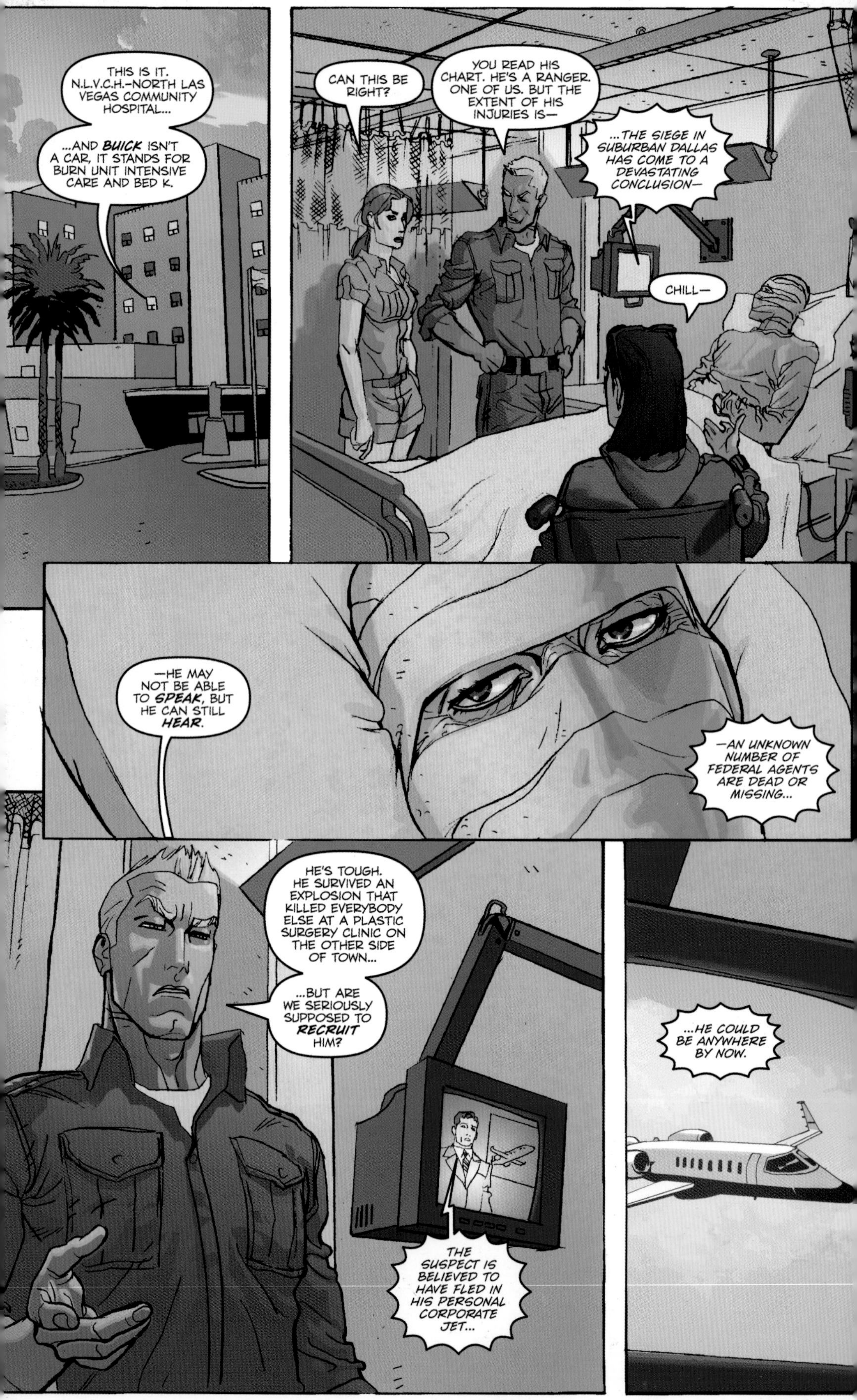
THIS IS IT. N.L.V.C.H.–NORTH LAS VEGAS COMMUNITY HOSPITAL...
...AND BUICK ISN'T A CAR, IT STANDS FOR BURN UNIT INTENSIVE CARE AND BED K.
CAN THIS BE RIGHT?
YOU READ HIS CHART. HE'S A RANGER. ONE OF US. BUT THE EXTENT OF HIS INJURIES IS—
...THE SIEGE IN SUBURBAN DALLAS HAS COME TO A DEVASTATING CONCLUSION—
CHILL—
—HE MAY NOT BE ABLE TO SPEAK, BUT HE CAN STILL HEAR.
—AN UNKNOWN NUMBER OF FEDERAL AGENTS ARE DEAD OR MISSING...
HE'S TOUGH. HE SURVIVED AN EXPLOSION THAT KILLED EVERYBODY ELSE AT A PLASTIC SURGERY CLINIC ON THE OTHER SIDE OF TOWN...
...BUT ARE WE SERIOUSLY SUPPOSED TO RECRUIT HIM?
THE SUSPECT IS BELIEVED TO HAVE FLED IN HIS PERSONAL CORPORATE JET...
...HE COULD BE ANYWHERE BY NOW.

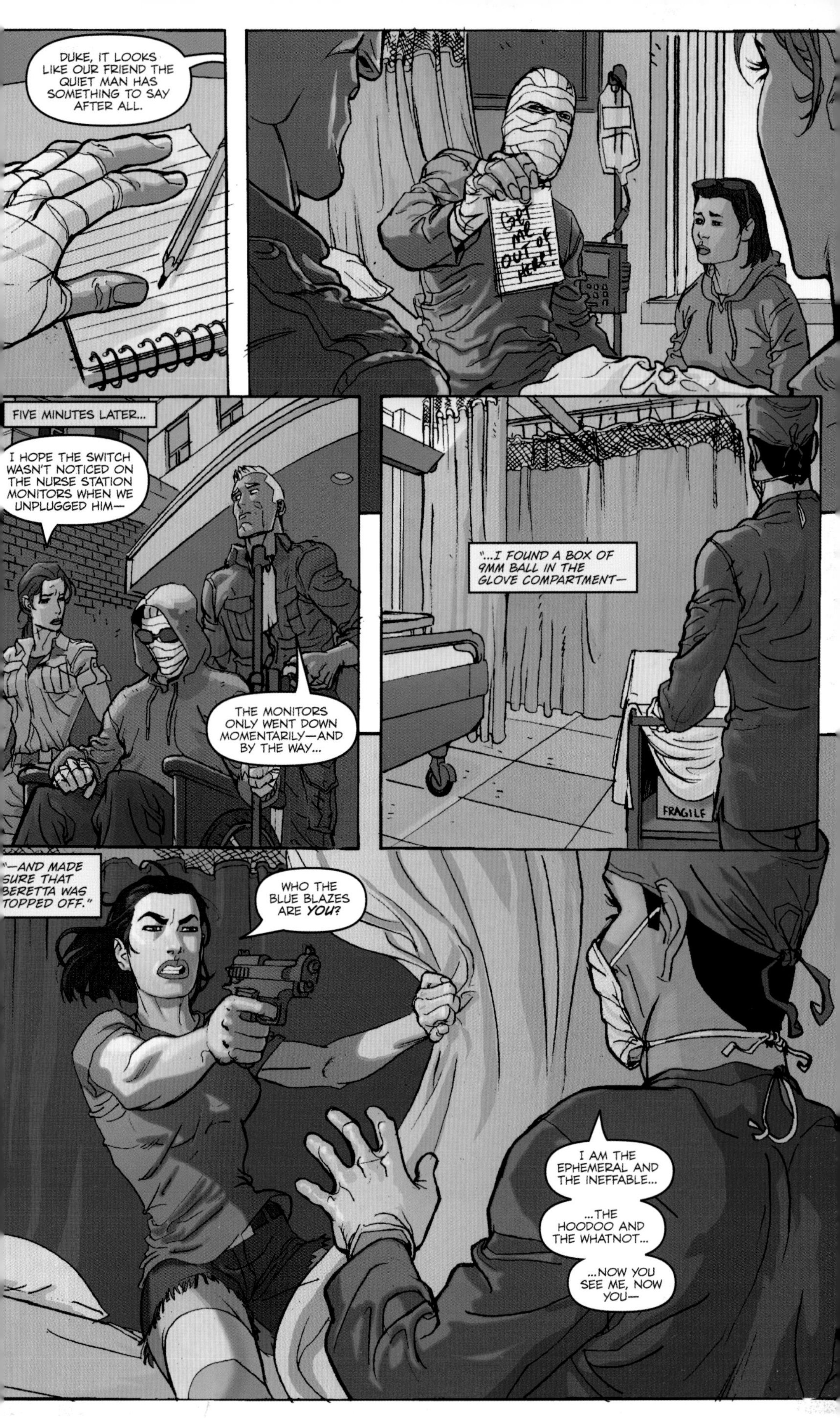

DUKE, IT LOOKS LIKE OUR FRIEND THE QUIET MAN HAS SOMETHING TO SAY AFTER ALL.
GET ME OUT OF HERE!
FIVE MINUTES LATER...
I HOPE THE SWITCH WASN'T NOTICED ON THE NURSE STATION MONITORS WHEN WE UNPLUGGED HIM—
THE MONITORS ONLY WENT DOWN MOMENTARILY—AND BY THE WAY...
"...I FOUND A BOX OF 9MM BALL IN THE GLOVE COMPARTMENT—
FRAGILE
"—AND MADE SURE THAT BERETTA WAS TOPPED OFF."
WHO THE BLUE BLAZES ARE *YOU*?
I AM THE EPHEMERAL AND THE INEFFABLE...
...THE HOODOO AND THE WHATNOT...
...NOW YOU SEE ME, NOW YOU—

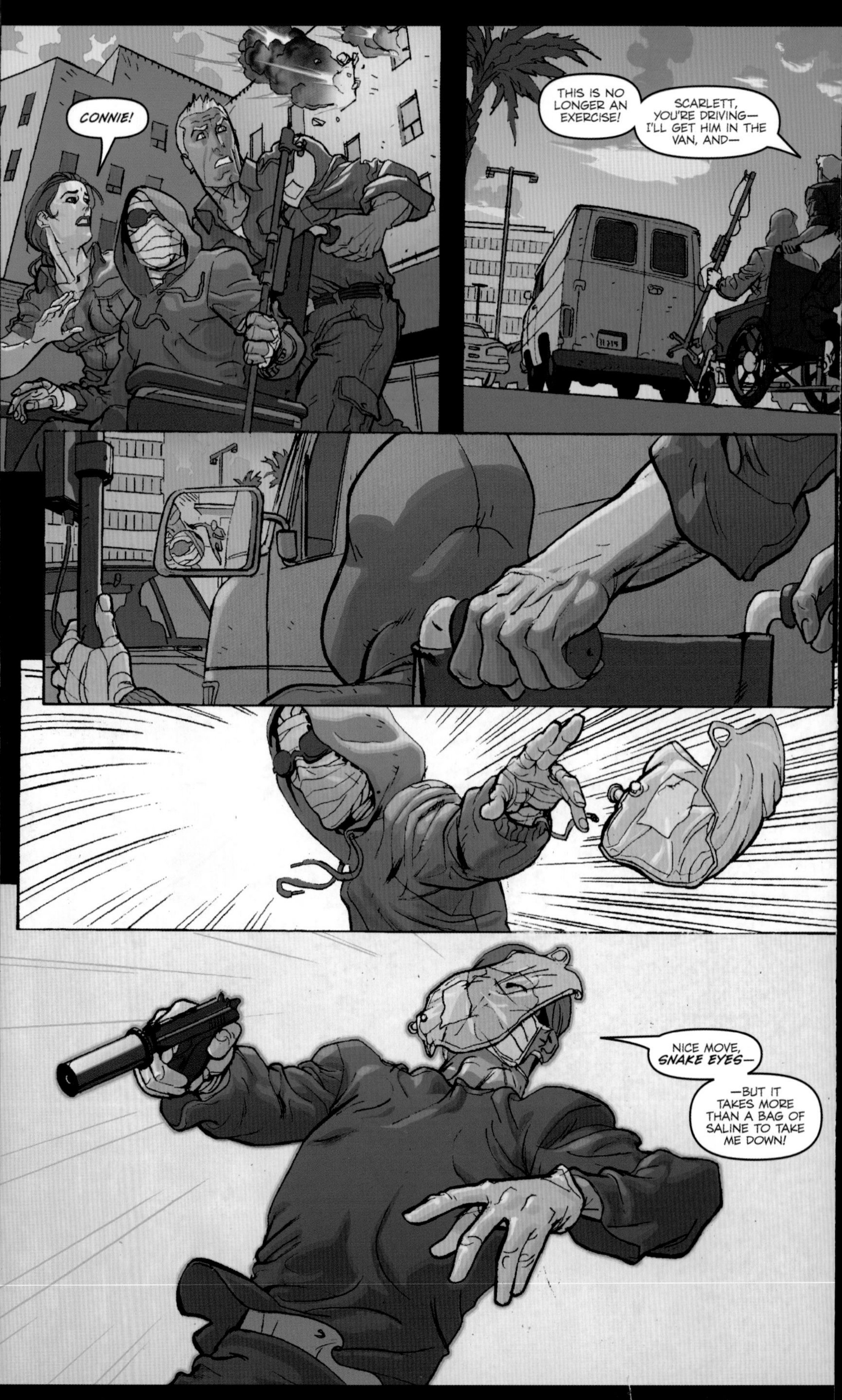
CONNIE!
THIS IS NO LONGER AN EXERCISE!
SCARLETT, YOU'RE DRIVING— I'LL GET HIM IN THE VAN, AND—
NICE MOVE, SNAKE EYES—
—BUT IT TAKES MORE THAN A BAG OF SALINE TO TAKE ME DOWN!

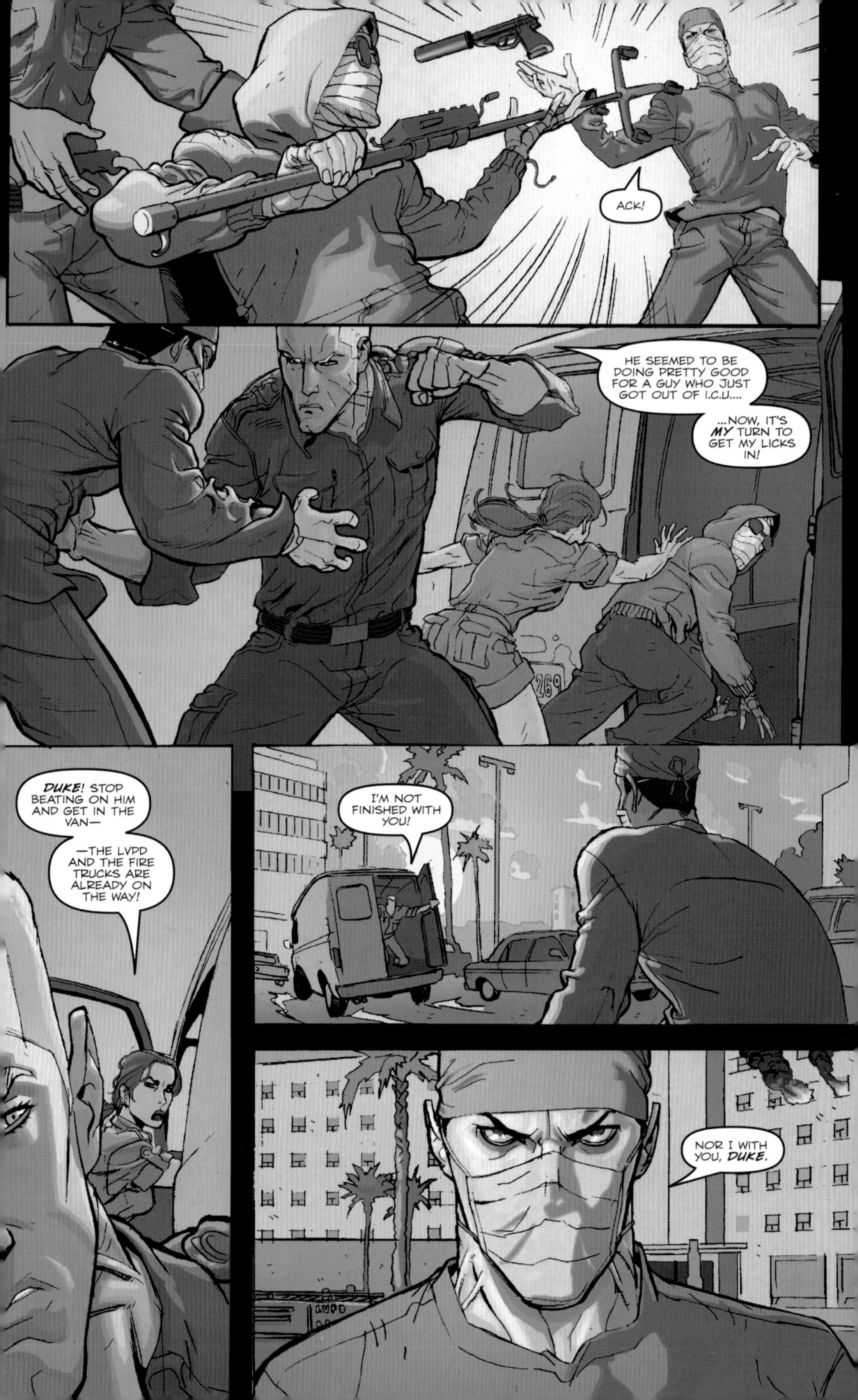
ACK!
HE SEEMED TO BE DOING PRETTY GOOD FOR A GUY WHO JUST GOT OUT OF I.C.U....
...NOW, IT'S MY TURN TO GET MY LICKS IN!
DUKE! STOP BEATING ON HIM AND GET IN THE VAN—
—THE LVPD AND THE FIRE TRUCKS ARE ALREADY ON THE WAY!
I'M NOT FINISHED WITH YOU!
NOR I WITH YOU, DUKE.

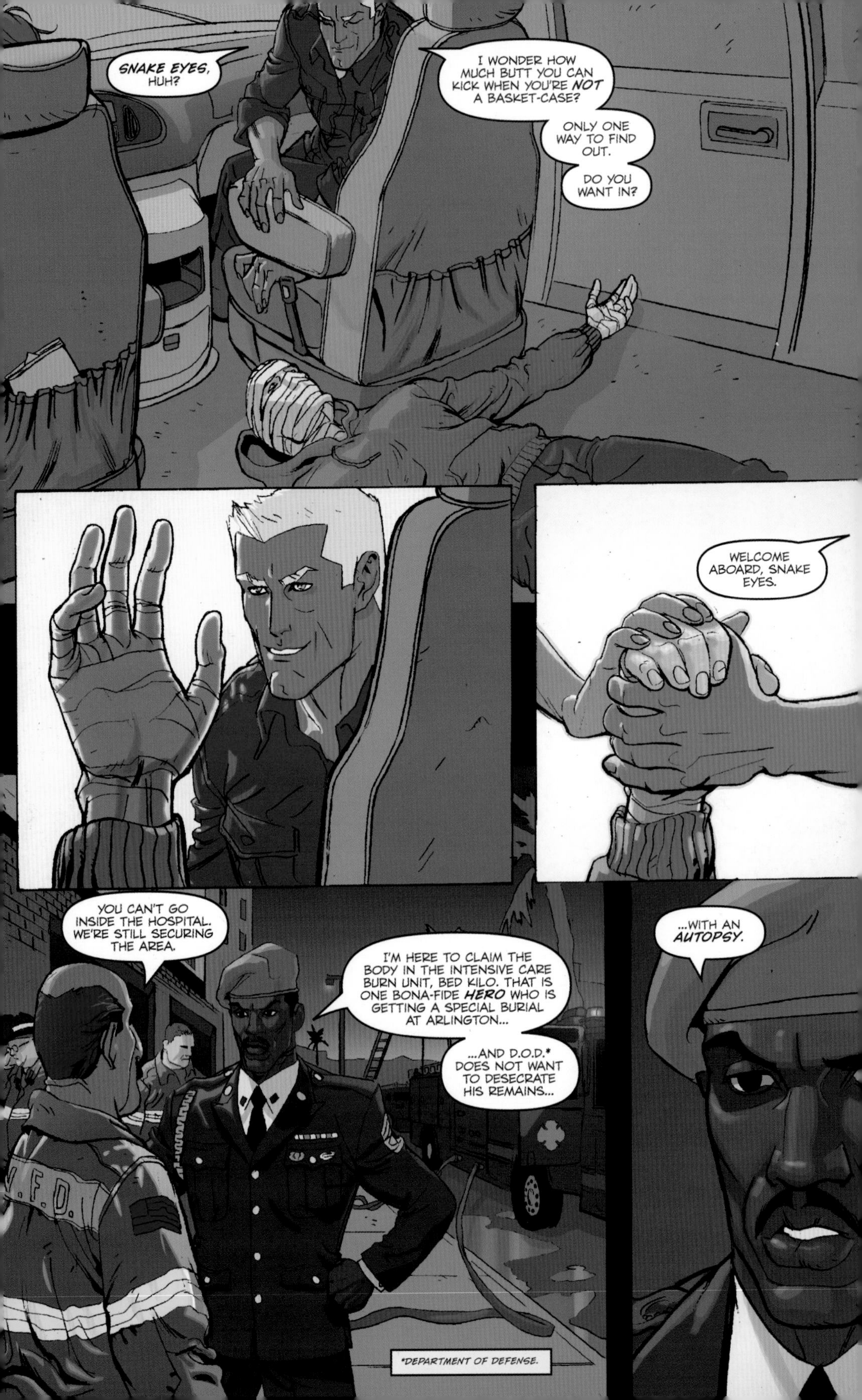
SNAKE EYES, HUH?
I WONDER HOW MUCH BUTT YOU CAN KICK WHEN YOU'RE NOT A BASKET-CASE?
ONLY ONE WAY TO FIND OUT.
DO YOU WANT IN?
WELCOME ABOARD, SNAKE EYES.
YOU CAN'T GO INSIDE THE HOSPITAL. WE'RE STILL SECURING THE AREA.
I'M HERE TO CLAIM THE BODY IN THE INTENSIVE CARE BURN UNIT, BED KILO. THAT IS ONE BONA-FIDE HERO WHO IS GETTING A SPECIAL BURIAL AT ARLINGTON...
...AND D.O.D.* DOES NOT WANT TO DESECRATE HIS REMAINS...
...WITH AN AUTOPSY.
*DEPARTMENT OF DEFENSE.

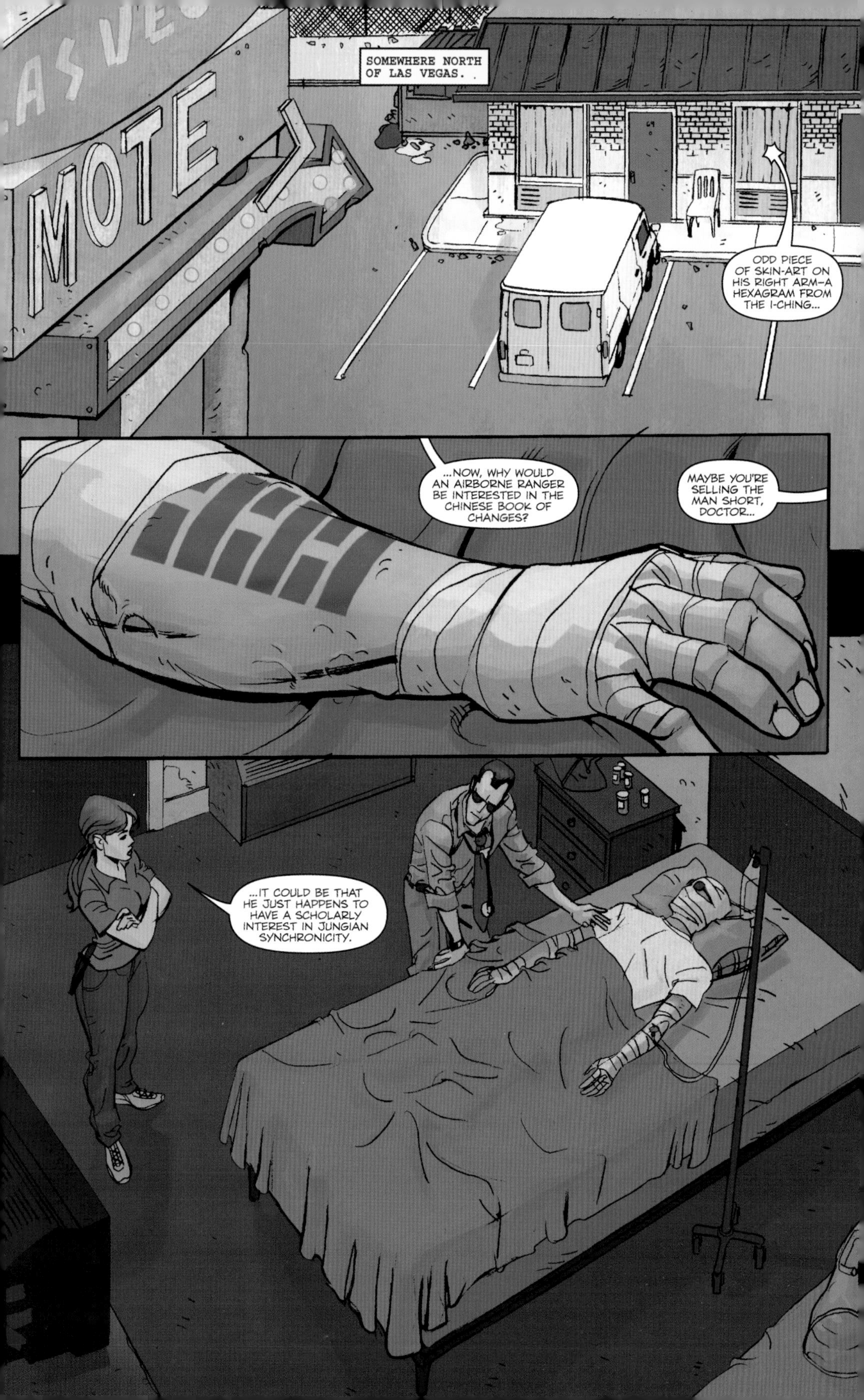

SOMEWHERE NORTH OF LAS VEGAS. .
MOTE
ODD PIECE OF SKIN-ART ON HIS RIGHT ARM--A HEXAGRAM FROM THE I-CHING...
...NOW, WHY WOULD AN AIRBORNE RANGER BE INTERESTED IN THE CHINESE BOOK OF CHANGES?
MAYBE YOU'RE SELLING THE MAN SHORT, DOCTOR...
...IT COULD BE THAT HE JUST HAPPENS TO HAVE A SCHOLARLY INTEREST IN JUNGIAN SYNCHRONICITY.

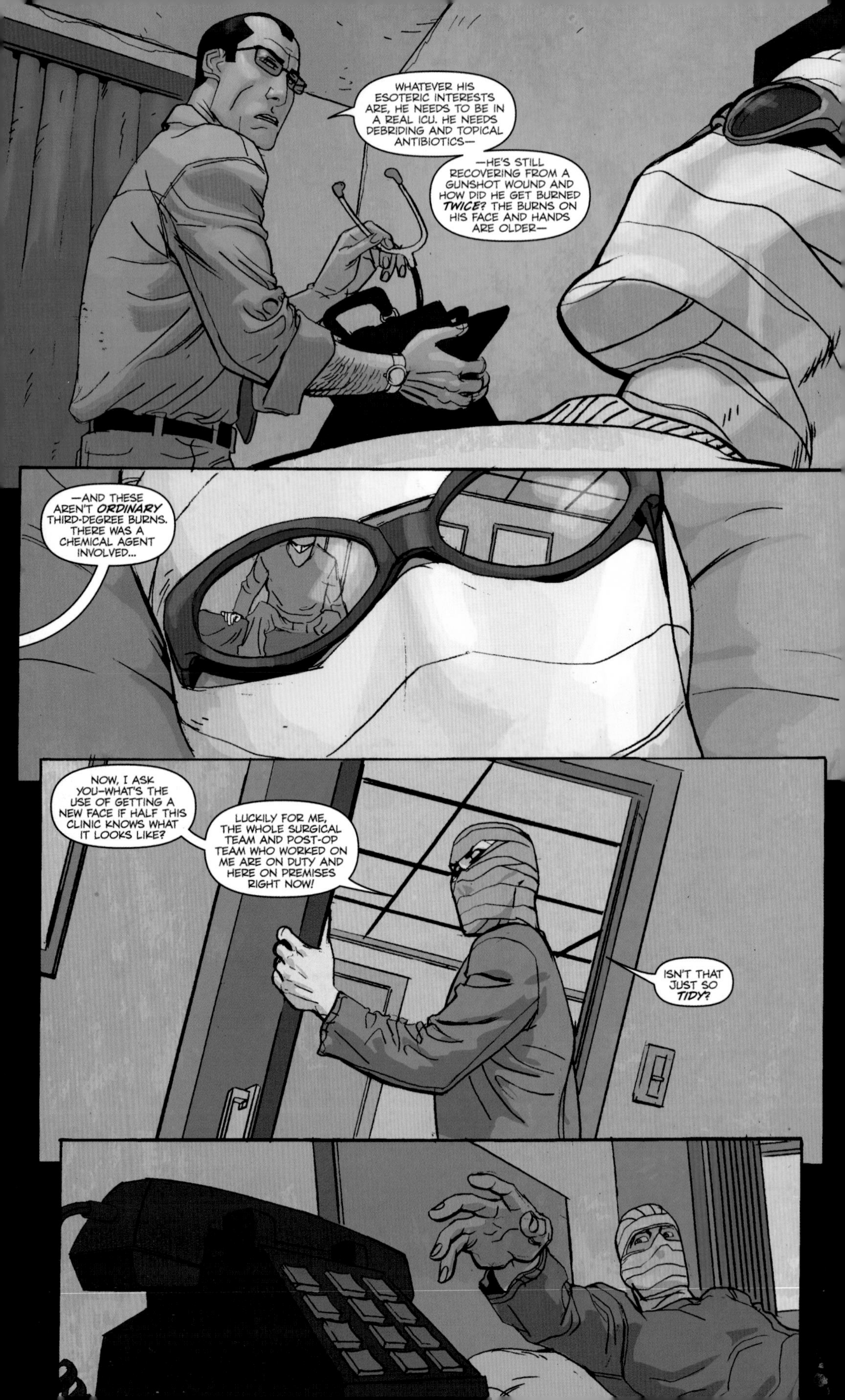
WHATEVER HIS ESOTERIC INTERESTS ARE, HE NEEDS TO BE IN A REAL ICU. HE NEEDS DEBRIDING AND TOPICAL ANTIBIOTICS—
—HE'S STILL RECOVERING FROM A GUNSHOT WOUND AND HOW DID HE GET BURNED TWICE? THE BURNS ON HIS FACE AND HANDS ARE OLDER—
—AND THESE AREN'T ORDINARY THIRD-DEGREE BURNS. THERE WAS A CHEMICAL AGENT INVOLVED...
NOW, I ASK YOU—WHAT'S THE USE OF GETTING A NEW FACE IF HALF THIS CLINIC KNOWS WHAT IT LOOKS LIKE?
LUCKILY FOR ME, THE WHOLE SURGICAL TEAM AND POST-OP TEAM WHO WORKED ON ME ARE ON DUTY AND HERE ON PREMISES RIGHT NOW!
ISN'T THAT JUST SO TIDY?

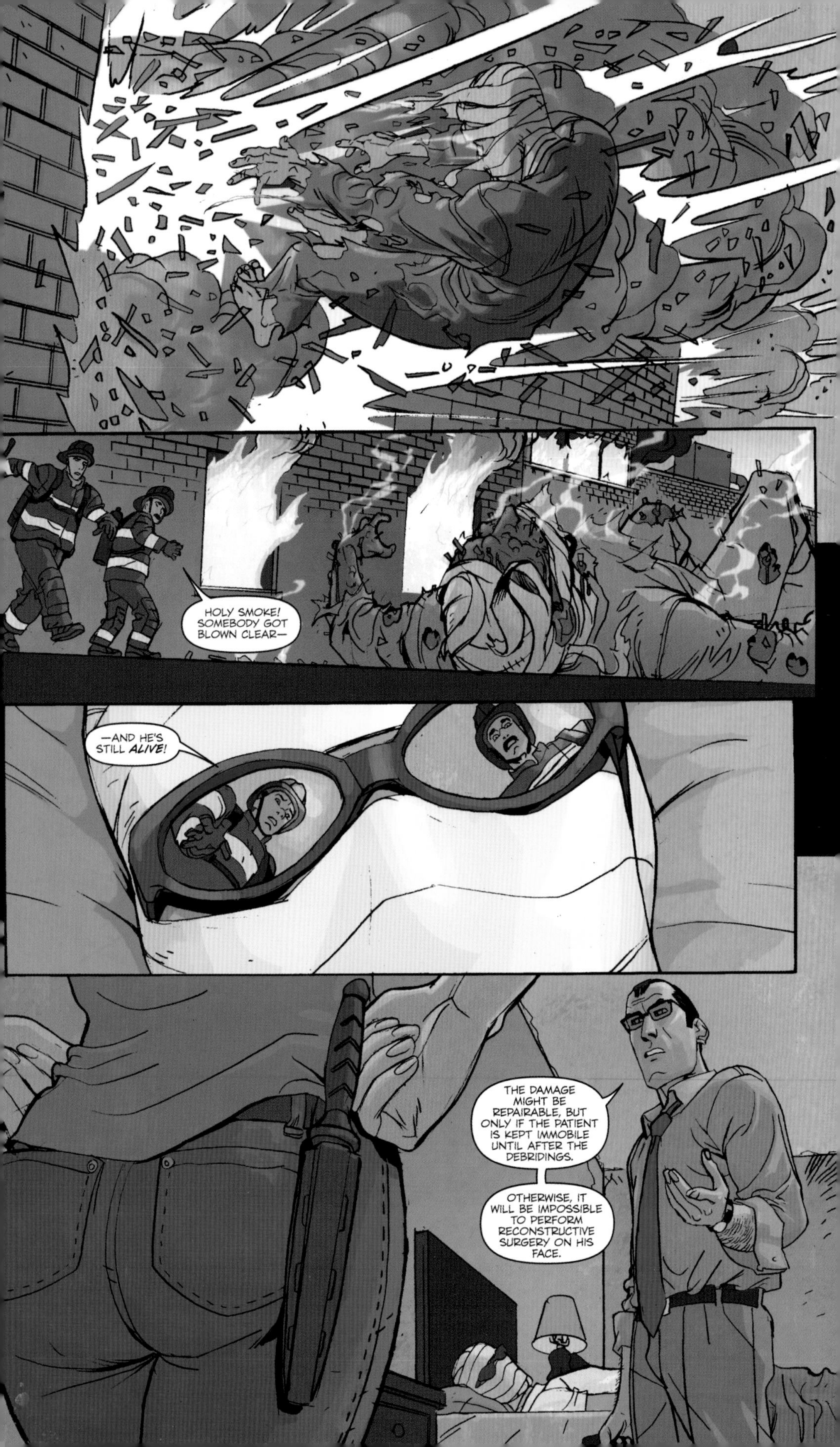
HOLY SMOKE! SOMEBODY GOT BLOWN CLEAR—
—AND HE'S STILL *ALIVE*!
THE DAMAGE MIGHT BE REPAIRABLE, BUT ONLY IF THE PATIENT IS KEPT IMMOBILE UNTIL AFTER THE DEBRIDINGS.
OTHERWISE, IT WILL BE IMPOSSIBLE TO PERFORM RECONSTRUCTIVE SURGERY ON HIS FACE.

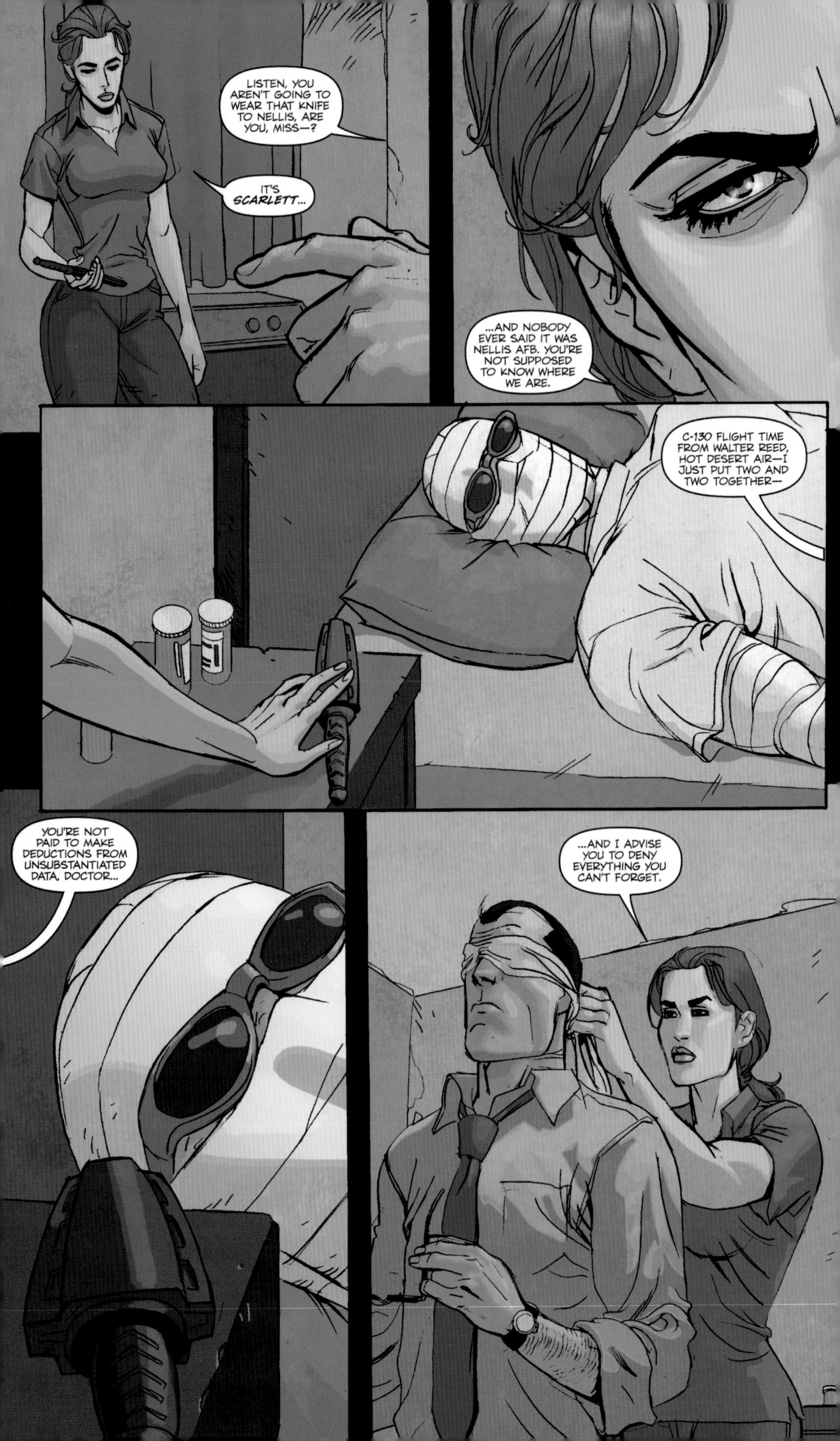
LISTEN, YOU AREN'T GOING TO WEAR THAT KNIFE TO NELLIS, ARE YOU, MISS—?
IT'S SCARLETT...
...AND NOBODY EVER SAID IT WAS NELLIS AFB. YOU'RE NOT SUPPOSED TO KNOW WHERE WE ARE.
C-130 FLIGHT TIME FROM WALTER REED, HOT DESERT AIR—I JUST PUT TWO AND TWO TOGETHER—
YOU'RE NOT PAID TO MAKE DEDUCTIONS FROM UNSUBSTANTIATED DATA, DOCTOR...
...AND I ADVISE YOU TO DENY EVERYTHING YOU CAN'T FORGET.

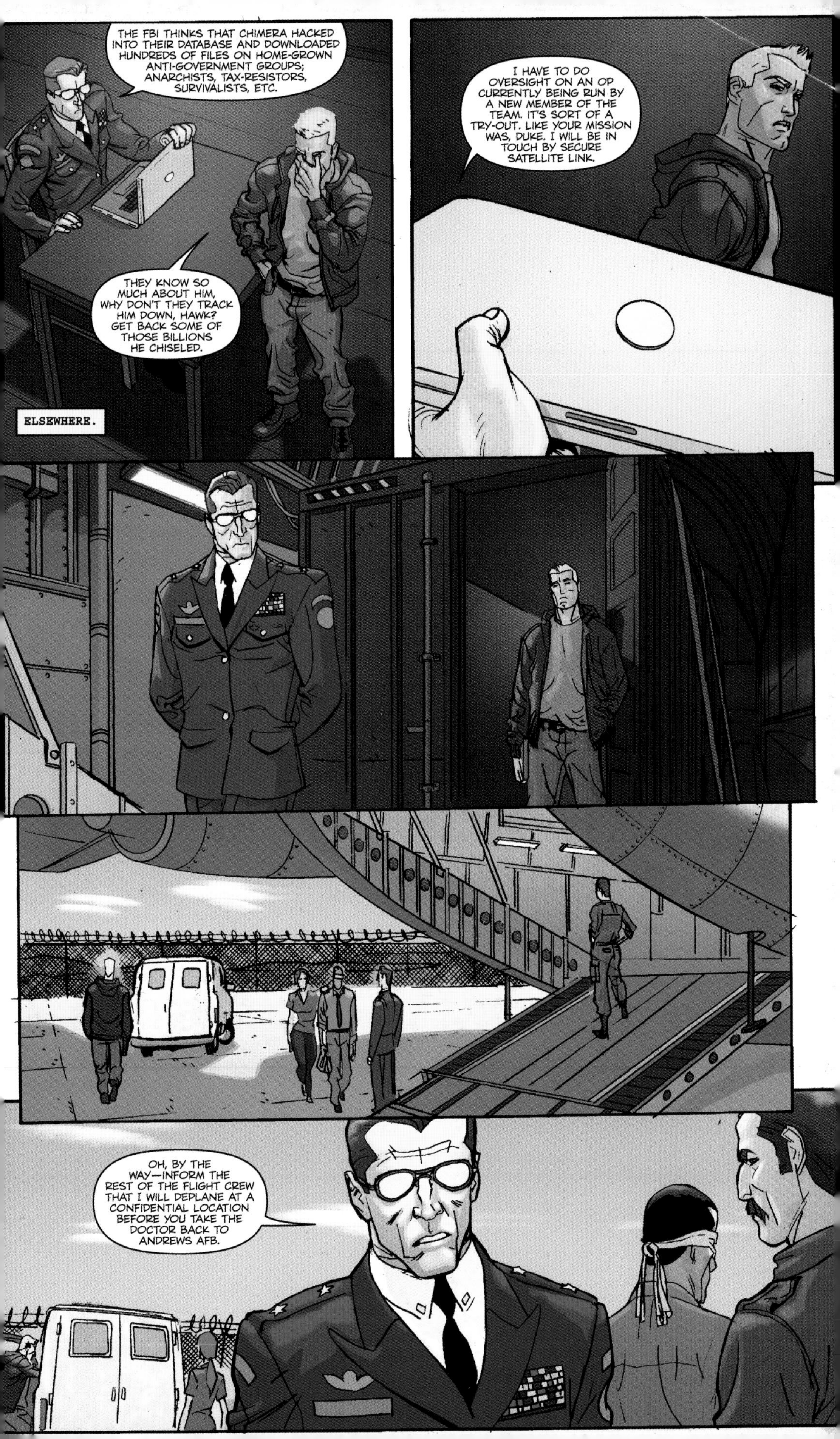
THE FBI THINKS THAT CHIMERA HACKED INTO THEIR DATABASE AND DOWNLOADED HUNDREDS OF FILES ON HOME-GROWN ANTI-GOVERNMENT GROUPS; ANARCHISTS, TAX-RESISTORS, SURVIVALISTS, ETC.
THEY KNOW SO MUCH ABOUT HIM, WHY DON'T THEY TRACK HIM DOWN, HAWK? GET BACK SOME OF THOSE BILLIONS HE CHISELED.
ELSEWHERE.
I HAVE TO DO OVERSIGHT ON AN OP CURRENTLY BEING RUN BY A NEW MEMBER OF THE TEAM. IT'S SORT OF A TRY-OUT. LIKE YOUR MISSION WAS, DUKE. I WILL BE IN TOUCH BY SECURE SATELLITE LINK.
OH, BY THE WAY—INFORM THE REST OF THE FLIGHT CREW THAT I WILL DEPLANE AT A CONFIDENTIAL LOCATION BEFORE YOU TAKE THE DOCTOR BACK TO ANDREWS AFB.

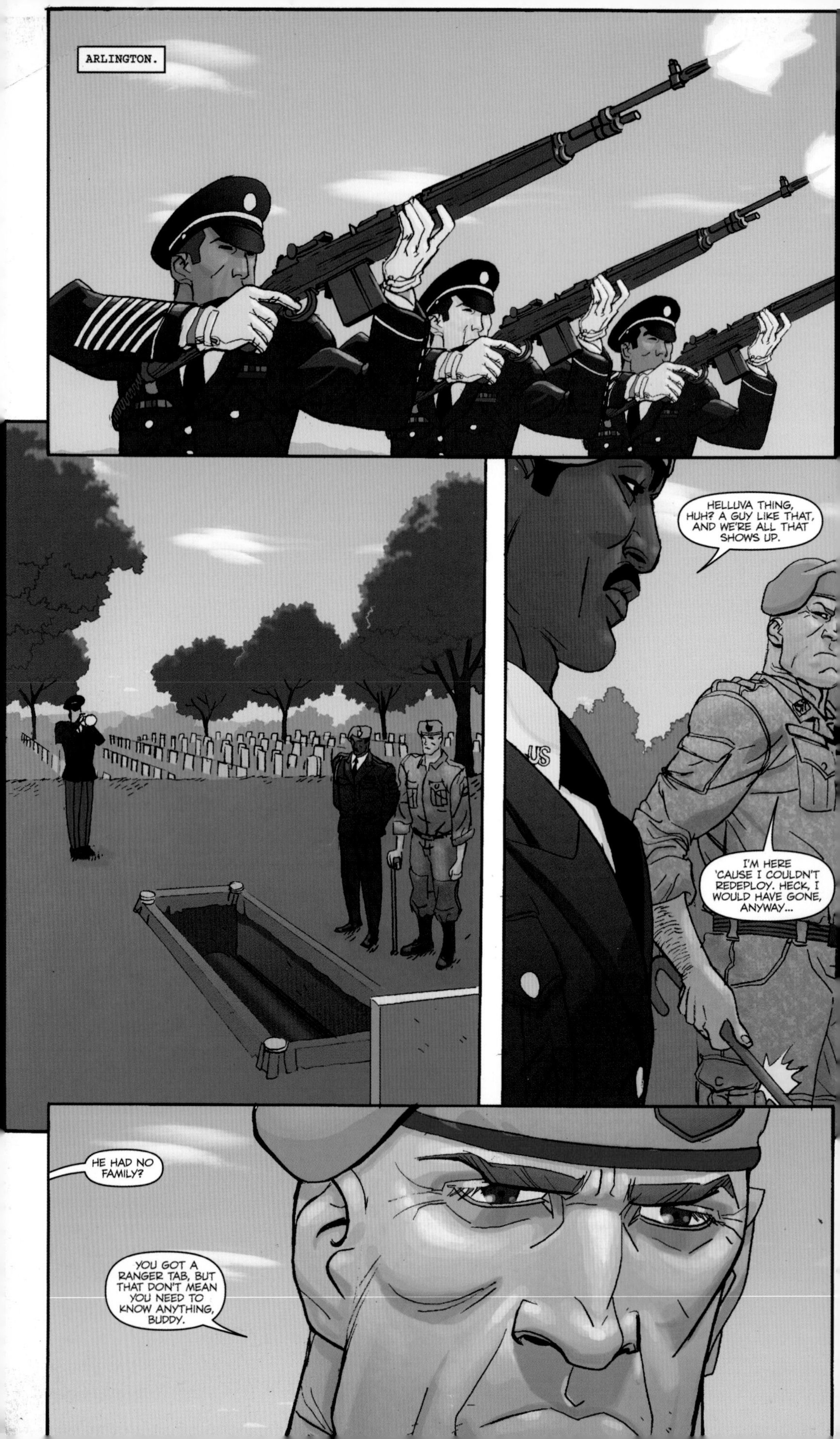
ARLINGTON.
HELLUVA THING, HUH? A GUY LIKE THAT, AND WE'RE ALL THAT SHOWS UP.
I'M HERE 'CAUSE I COULDN'T REDEPLOY. HECK, I WOULD HAVE GONE, ANYWAY...
HE HAD NO FAMILY?
YOU GOT A RANGER TAB, BUT THAT DON'T MEAN YOU NEED TO KNOW ANYTHING, BUDDY.

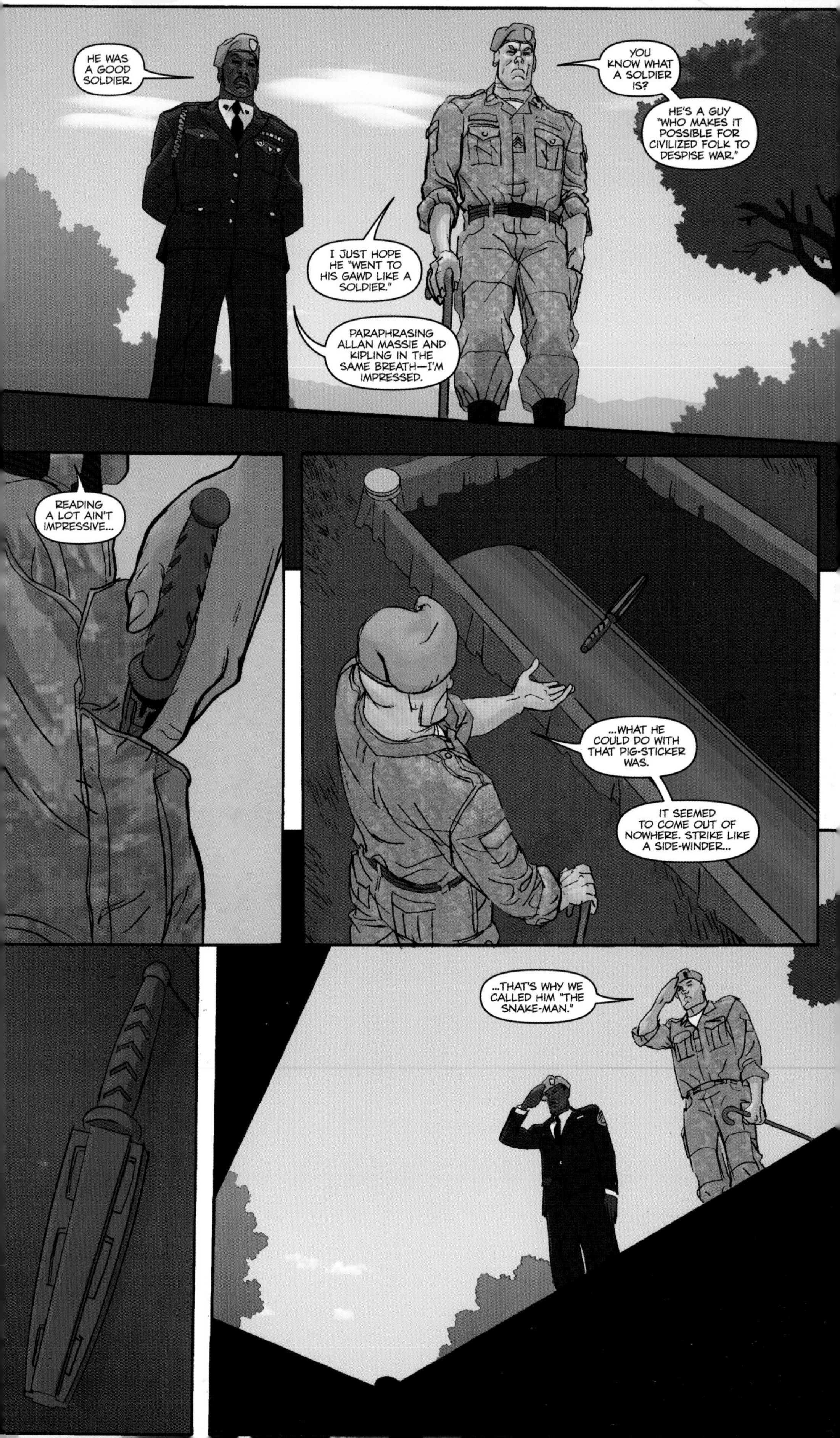
HE WAS A GOOD SOLDIER.
YOU KNOW WHAT A SOLDIER IS?
HE'S A GUY "WHO MAKES IT POSSIBLE FOR CIVILIZED FOLK TO DESPISE WAR."
I JUST HOPE HE "WENT TO HIS GAWD LIKE A SOLDIER."
PARAPHRASING ALLAN MASSIE AND KIPLING IN THE SAME BREATH—I'M IMPRESSED.
READING A LOT AIN'T IMPRESSIVE...
...WHAT HE COULD DO WITH THAT PIG-STICKER WAS.
IT SEEMED TO COME OUT OF NOWHERE. STRIKE LIKE A SIDE-WINDER...
...THAT'S WHY WE CALLED HIM "THE SNAKE-MAN."

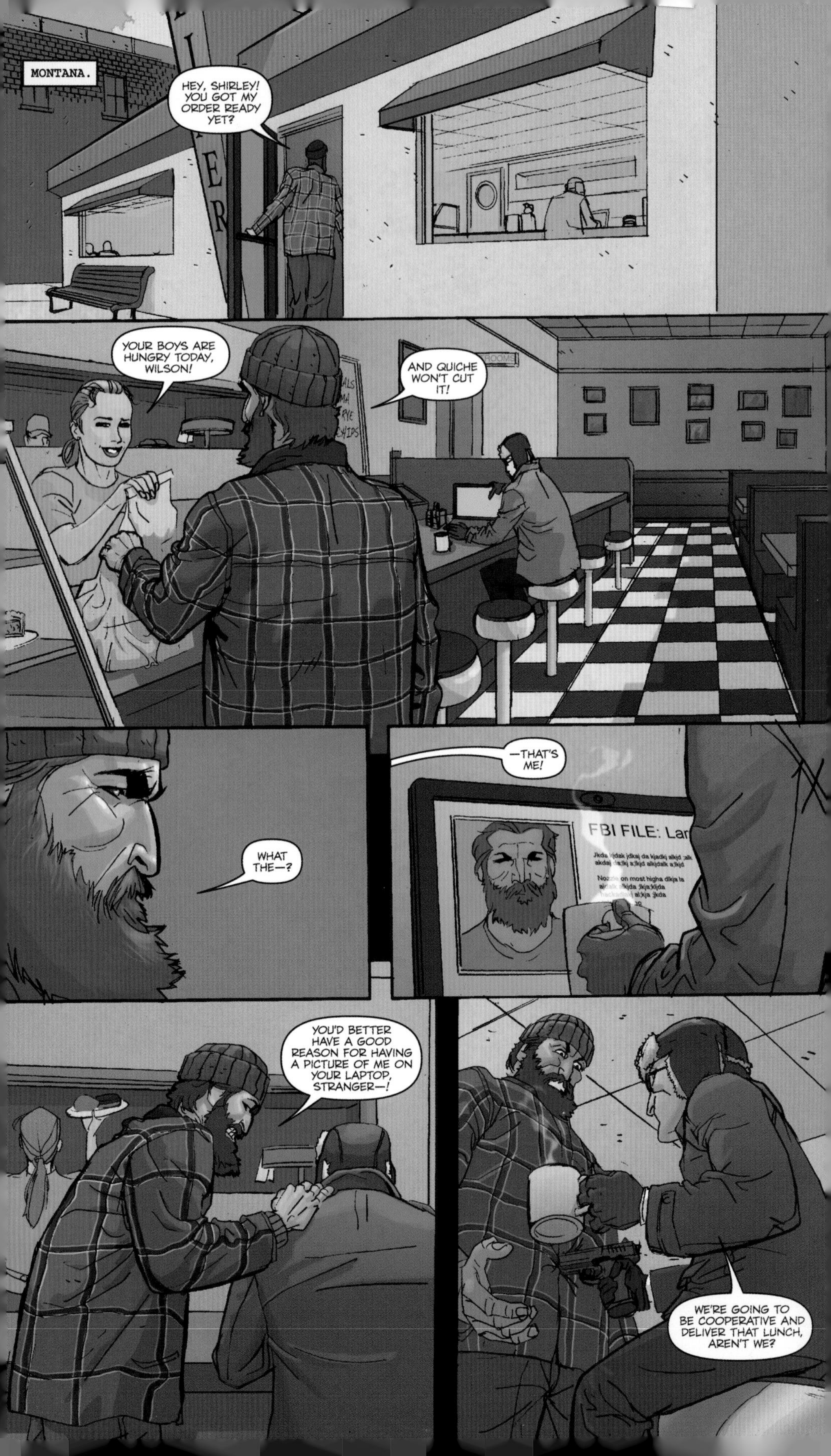
MONTANA.
HEY, SHIRLEY! YOU GOT MY ORDER READY YET?
YOUR BOYS ARE HUNGRY TODAY, WILSON!
AND QUICHE WON'T CUT IT!
WHAT THE—?
—THAT'S ME!
FBI FILE:
YOU'D BETTER HAVE A GOOD REASON FOR HAVING A PICTURE OF ME ON YOUR LAPTOP, STRANGER—!
WE'RE GOING TO BE COOPERATIVE AND DELIVER THAT LUNCH, AREN'T WE?

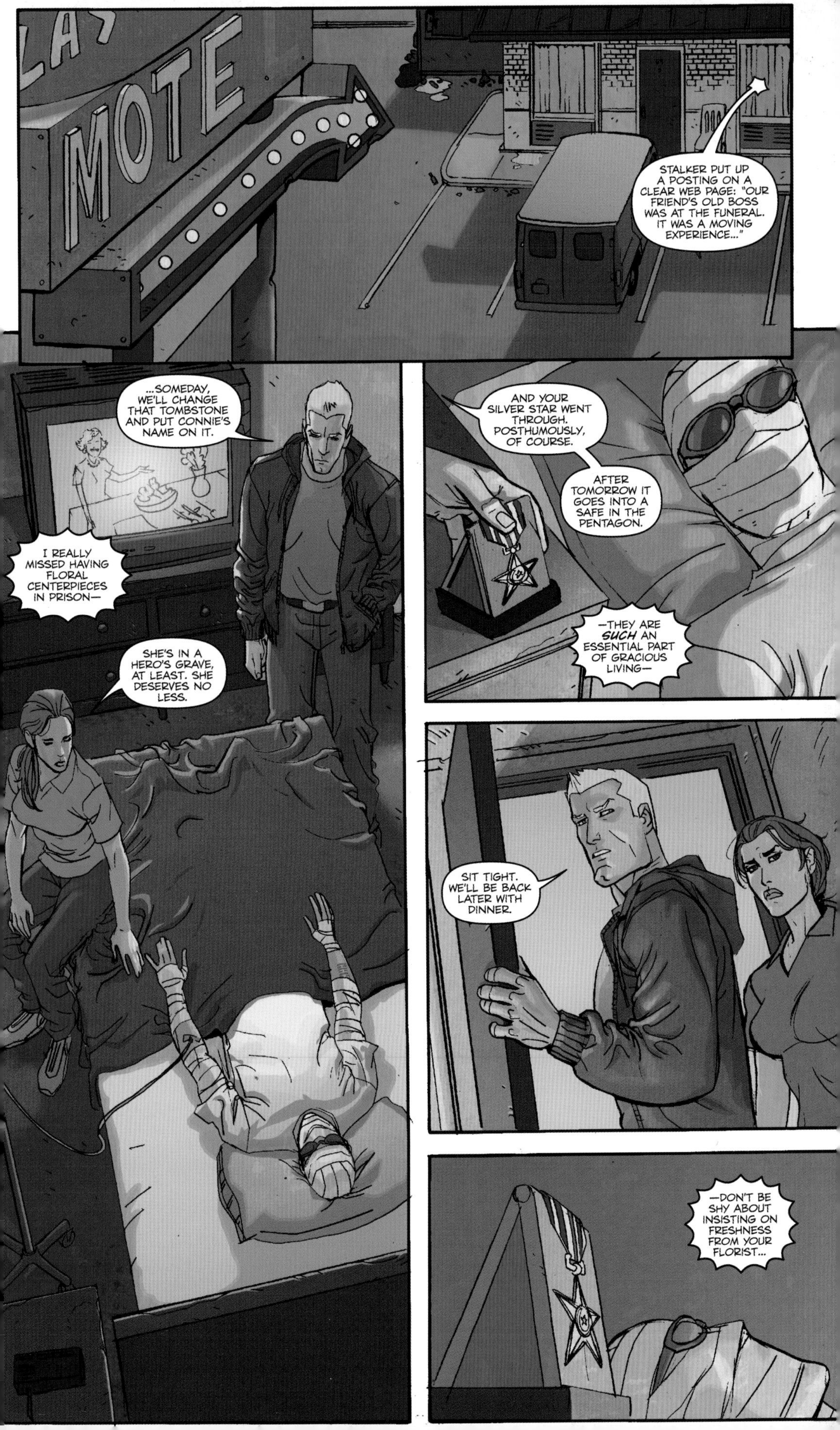
MOTE
STALKER PUT UP A POSTING ON A CLEAR WEB PAGE: "OUR FRIEND'S OLD BOSS WAS AT THE FUNERAL. IT WAS A MOVING EXPERIENCE..."
...SOMEDAY, WE'LL CHANGE THAT TOMBSTONE AND PUT CONNIE'S NAME ON IT.
I REALLY MISSED HAVING FLORAL CENTERPIECES IN PRISON—
SHE'S IN A HERO'S GRAVE, AT LEAST. SHE DESERVES NO LESS.
AND YOUR SILVER STAR WENT THROUGH. POSTHUMOUSLY, OF COURSE.
AFTER TOMORROW IT GOES INTO A SAFE IN THE PENTAGON.
—THEY ARE *SUCH* AN ESSENTIAL PART OF GRACIOUS LIVING—
SIT TIGHT. WE'LL BE BACK LATER WITH DINNER.
—DON'T BE SHY ABOUT INSISTING ON FRESHNESS FROM YOUR FLORIST...

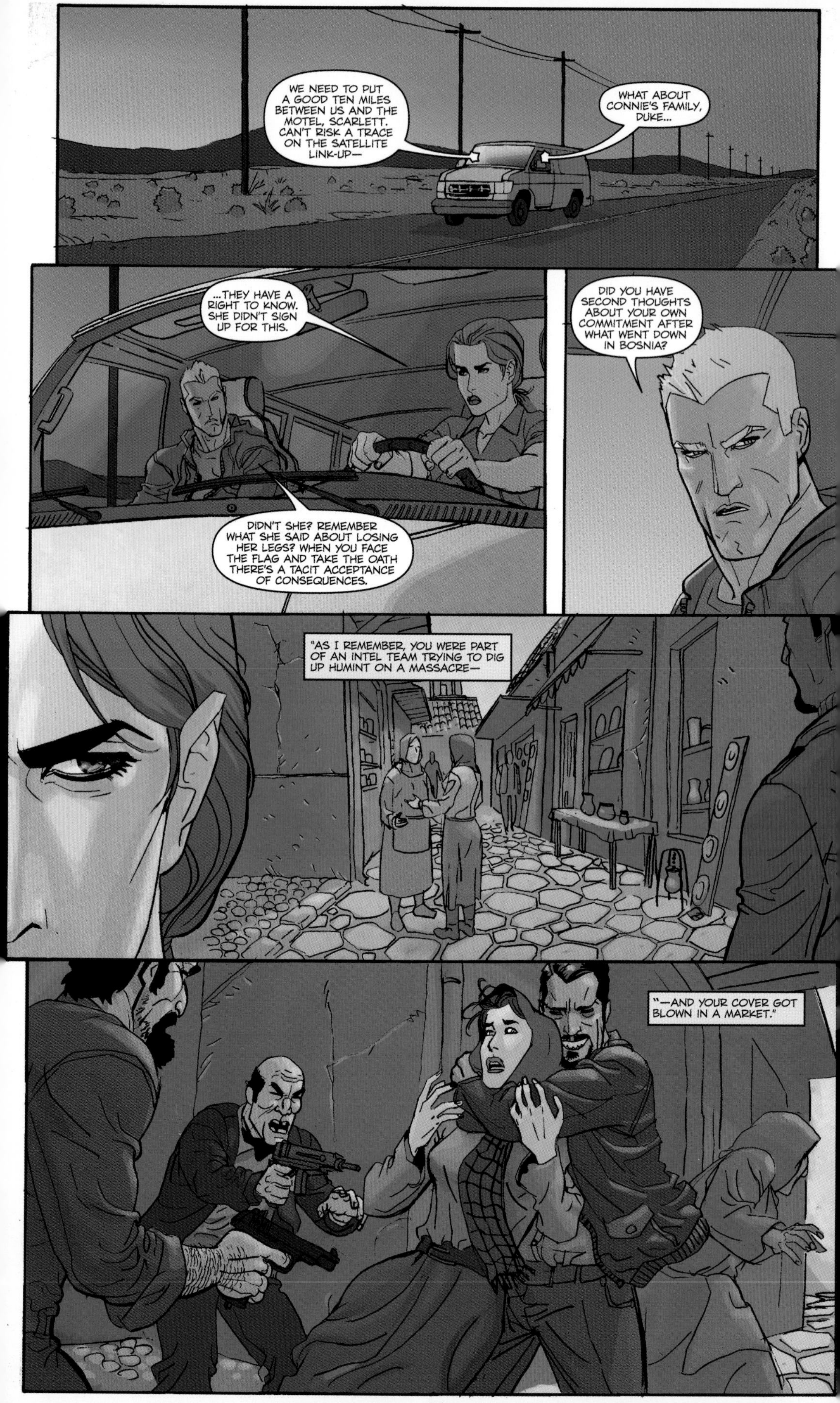
WE NEED TO PUT A GOOD TEN MILES BETWEEN US AND THE MOTEL, SCARLETT. CAN'T RISK A TRACE ON THE SATELLITE LINK-UP—
WHAT ABOUT CONNIE'S FAMILY, DUKE...
...THEY HAVE A RIGHT TO KNOW. SHE DIDN'T SIGN UP FOR THIS.
DIDN'T SHE? REMEMBER WHAT SHE SAID ABOUT LOSING HER LEGS? WHEN YOU FACE THE FLAG AND TAKE THE OATH THERE'S A TACIT ACCEPTANCE OF CONSEQUENCES.
DID YOU HAVE SECOND THOUGHTS ABOUT YOUR OWN COMMITMENT AFTER WHAT WENT DOWN IN BOSNIA?
"AS I REMEMBER, YOU WERE PART OF AN INTEL TEAM TRYING TO DIG UP HUMINT ON A MASSACRE—
"—AND YOUR COVER GOT BLOWN IN A MARKET."

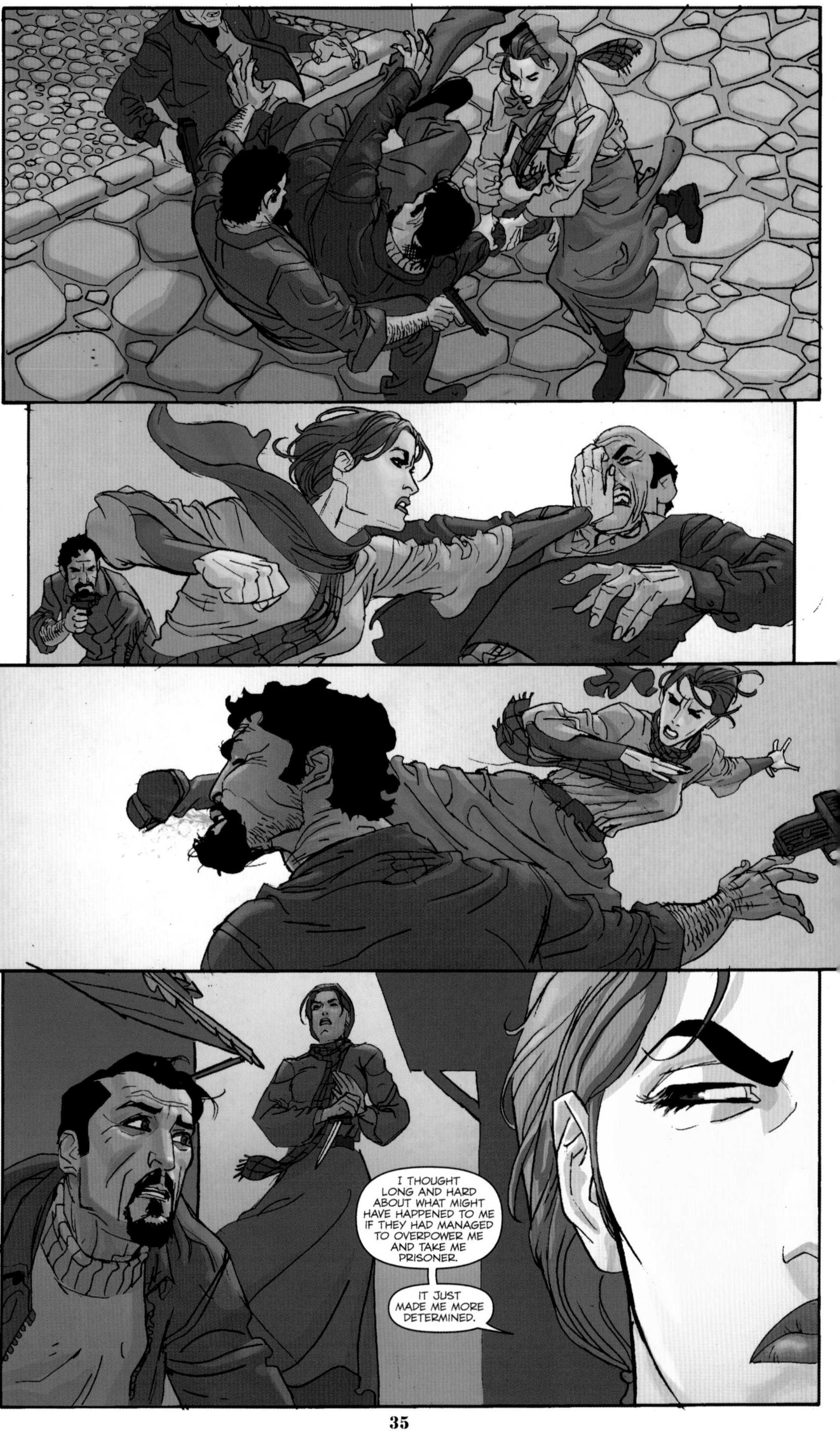
I THOUGHT LONG AND HARD ABOUT WHAT MIGHT HAVE HAPPENED TO ME IF THEY HAD MANAGED TO OVERPOWER ME AND TAKE ME PRISONER.
IT JUST MADE ME MORE DETERMINED.

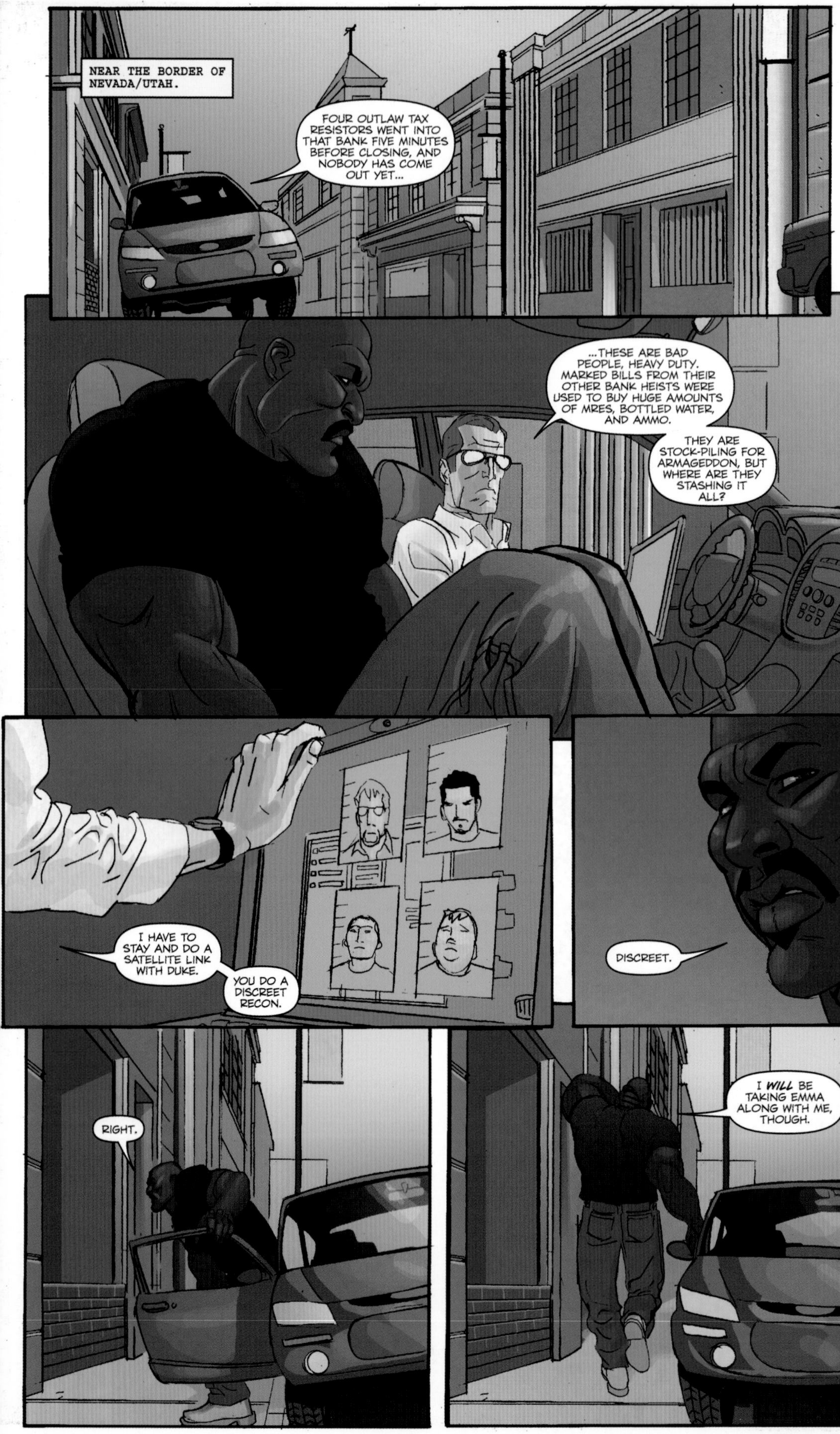
NEAR THE BORDER OF NEVADA/UTAH.
FOUR OUTLAW TAX RESISTORS WENT INTO THAT BANK FIVE MINUTES BEFORE CLOSING, AND NOBODY HAS COME OUT YET...
...THESE ARE BAD PEOPLE, HEAVY DUTY. MARKED BILLS FROM THEIR OTHER BANK HEISTS WERE USED TO BUY HUGE AMOUNTS OF MRES, BOTTLED WATER, AND AMMO.
THEY ARE STOCK-PILING FOR ARMAGEDDON, BUT WHERE ARE THEY STASHING IT ALL?
I HAVE TO STAY AND DO A SATELLITE LINK WITH DUKE.
YOU DO A DISCREET RECON.
DISCREET.
RIGHT.
I ***WILL*** BE TAKING EMMA ALONG WITH ME, THOUGH.

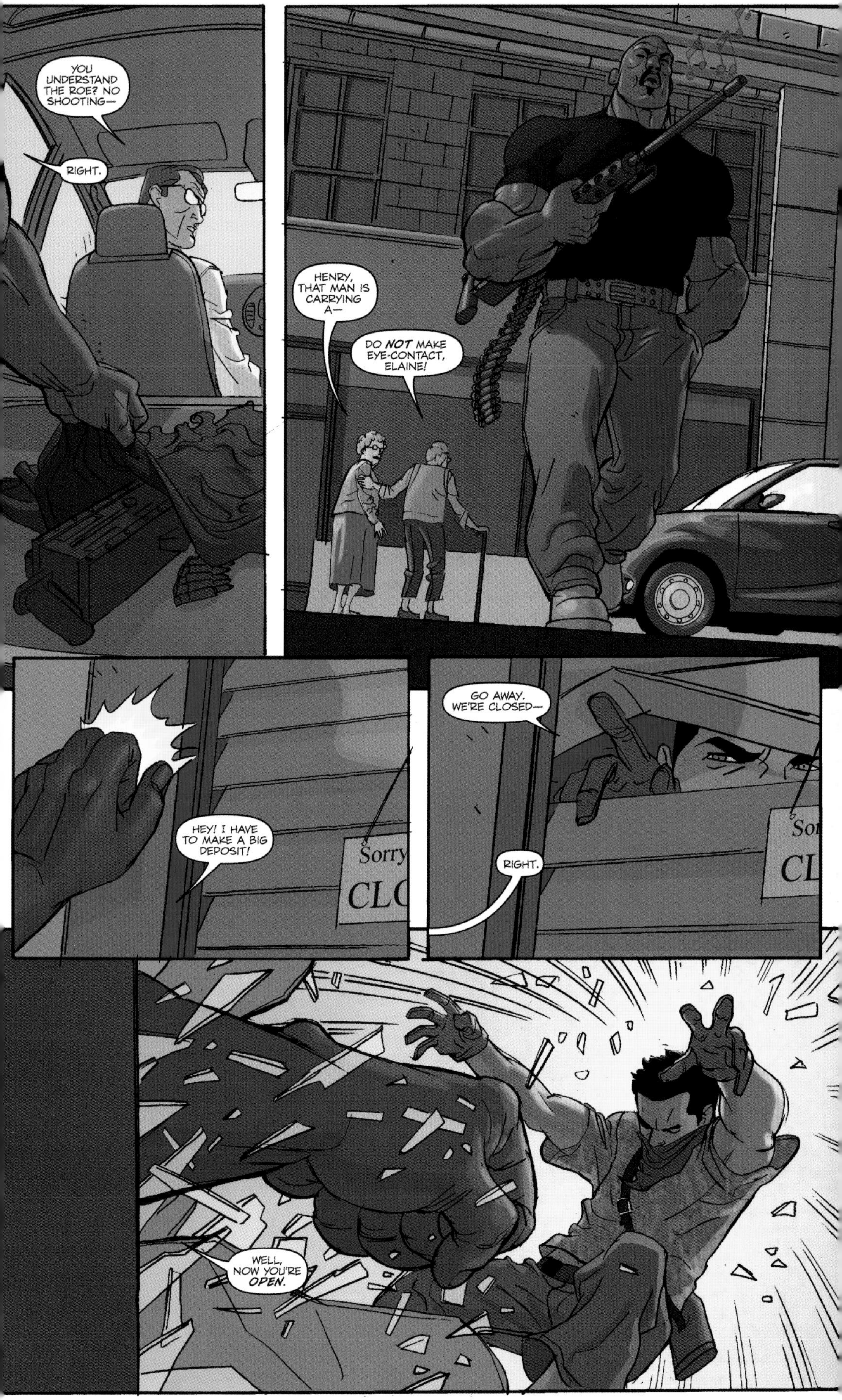
YOU UNDERSTAND THE ROE? NO SHOOTING—
RIGHT.
HENRY, THAT MAN IS CARRYING A—
DO *NOT* MAKE EYE-CONTACT, ELAINE!
HEY! I HAVE TO MAKE A BIG DEPOSIT!
Sorry
CL
GO AWAY. WE'RE CLOSED—
RIGHT.
WELL, NOW YOU'RE *OPEN*.

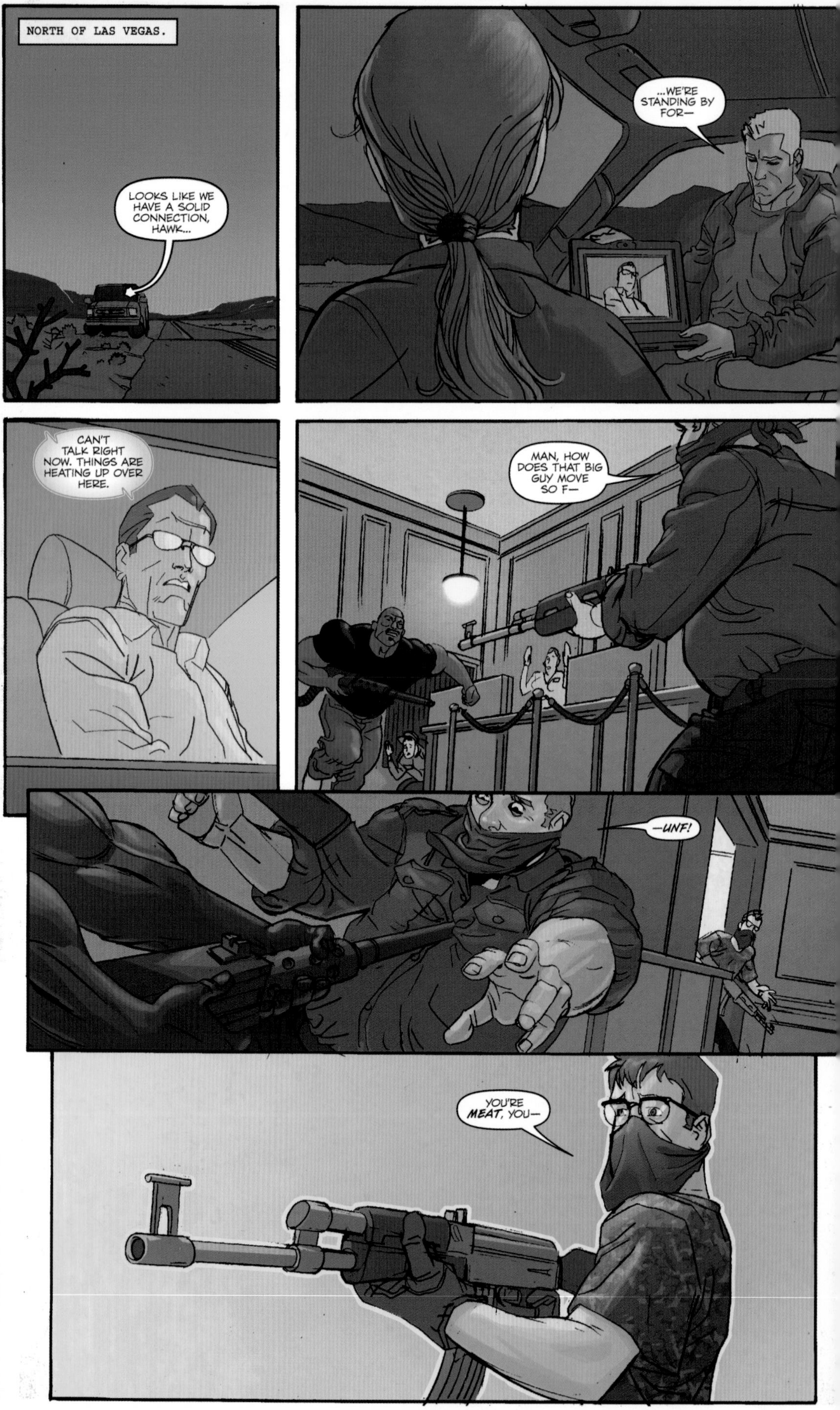
NORTH OF LAS VEGAS.
LOOKS LIKE WE HAVE A SOLID CONNECTION, HAWK...
...WE'RE STANDING BY FOR—
CAN'T TALK RIGHT NOW. THINGS ARE HEATING UP OVER HERE.
MAN, HOW DOES THAT BIG GUY MOVE SO F—
—UNF!
YOU'RE MEAT, YOU—

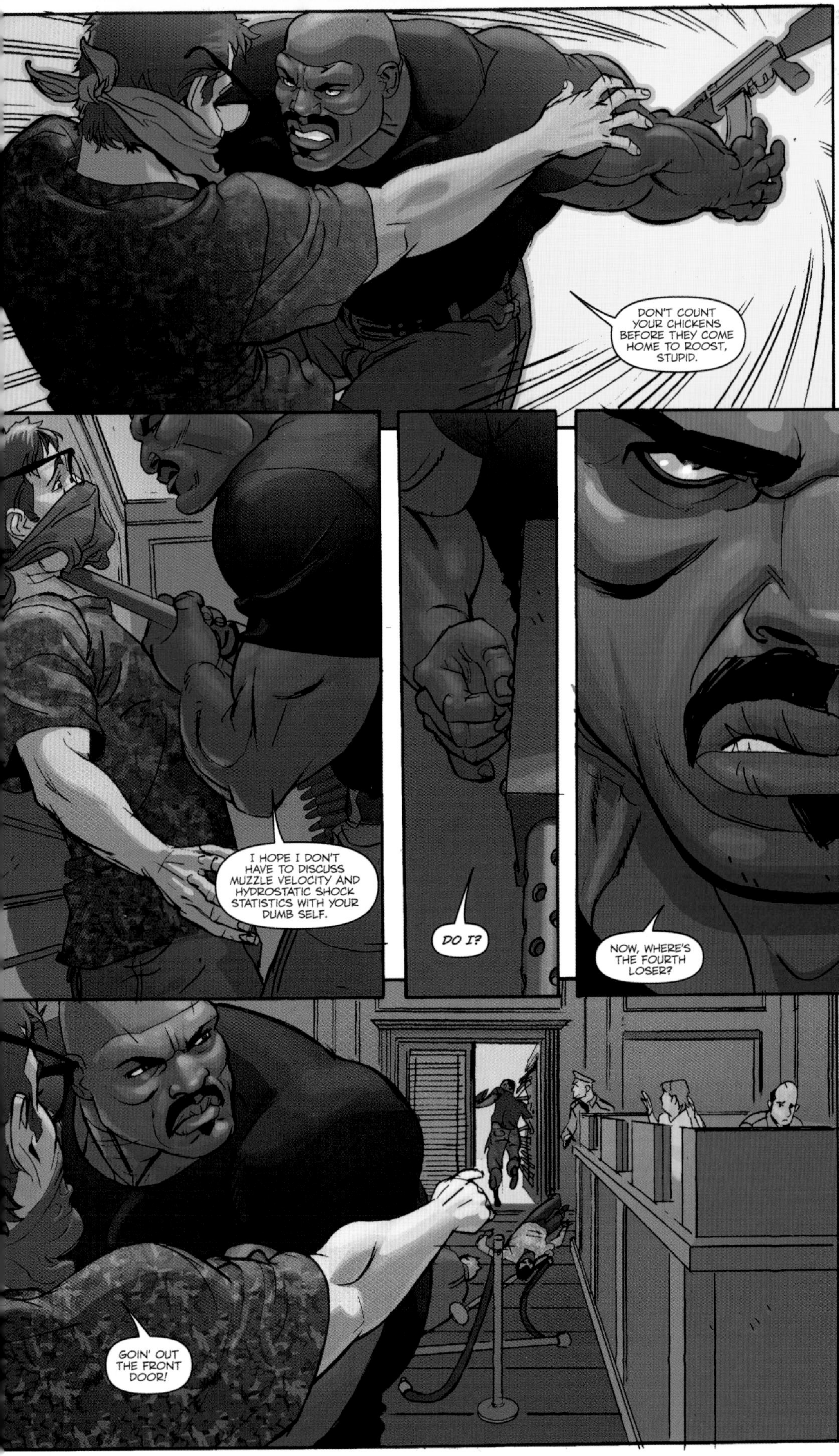
DON'T COUNT YOUR CHICKENS BEFORE THEY COME HOME TO ROOST, STUPID.
I HOPE I DON'T HAVE TO DISCUSS MUZZLE VELOCITY AND HYDROSTATIC SHOCK STATISTICS WITH YOUR DUMB SELF.
DO I?
NOW, WHERE'S THE FOURTH LOSER?
GOIN' OUT THE FRONT DOOR!

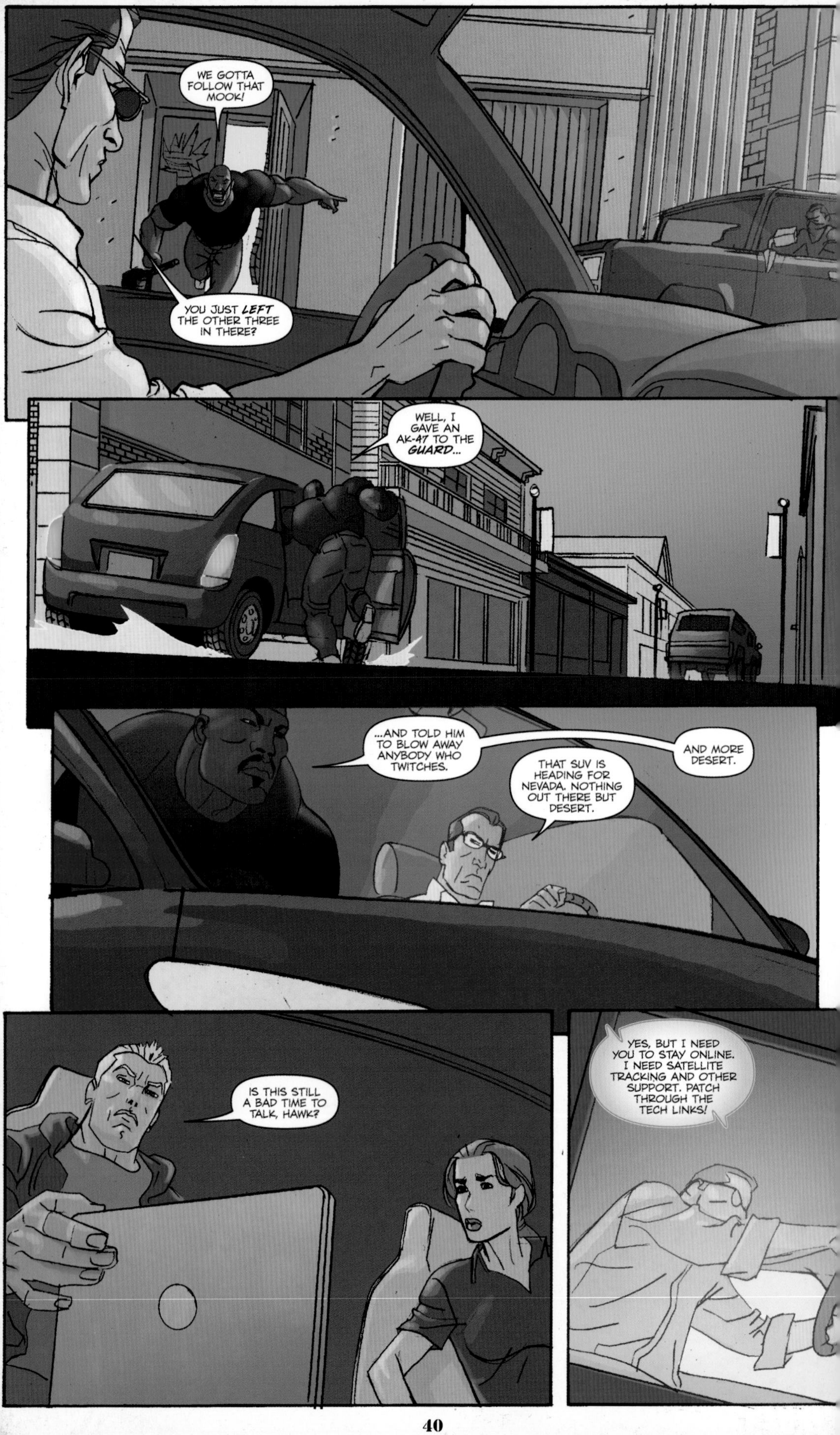

WE GOTTA FOLLOW THAT MOOK!
YOU JUST LEFT THE OTHER THREE IN THERE?
WELL, I GAVE AN AK-47 TO THE GUARD...
...AND TOLD HIM TO BLOW AWAY ANYBODY WHO TWITCHES.
THAT SUV IS HEADING FOR NEVADA. NOTHING OUT THERE BUT DESERT.
AND MORE DESERT.
IS THIS STILL A BAD TIME TO TALK, HAWK?
YES, BUT I NEED YOU TO STAY ONLINE. I NEED SATELLITE TRACKING AND OTHER SUPPORT. PATCH THROUGH THE TECH LINKS!

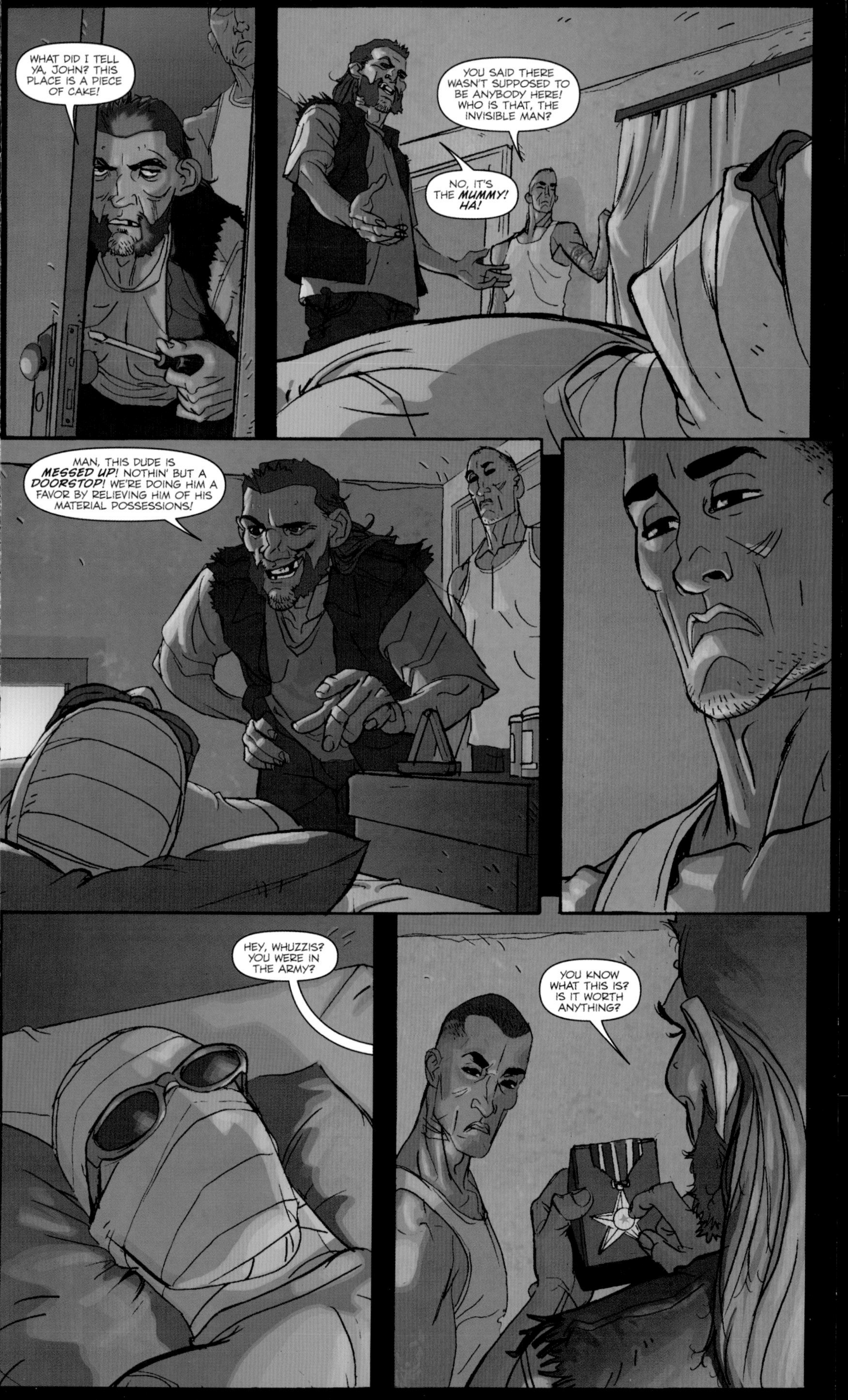
WHAT DID I TELL YA, JOHN? THIS PLACE IS A PIECE OF CAKE!
YOU SAID THERE WASN'T SUPPOSED TO BE ANYBODY HERE! WHO IS THAT, THE INVISIBLE MAN?
NO, IT'S THE MUMMY! HA!
MAN, THIS DUDE IS MESSED UP! NOTHIN' BUT A DOORSTOP! WE'RE DOING HIM A FAVOR BY RELIEVING HIM OF HIS MATERIAL POSSESSIONS!
HEY, WHUZZIS? YOU WERE IN THE ARMY?
YOU KNOW WHAT THIS IS? IS IT WORTH ANYTHING?

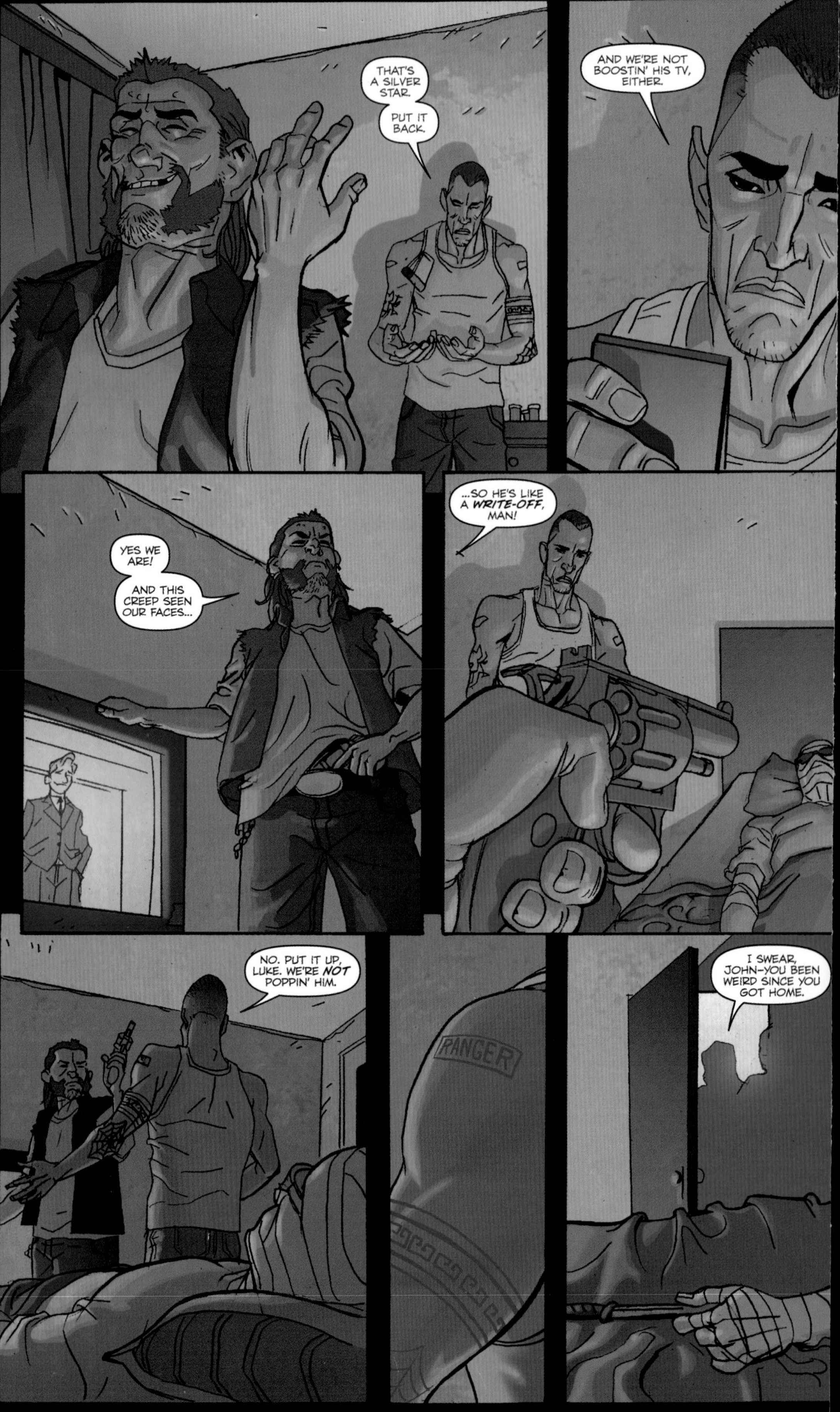
THAT'S A SILVER STAR.
PUT IT BACK.
AND WE'RE NOT BOOSTIN' HIS TV, EITHER.
YES WE ARE!
AND THIS CREEP SEEN OUR FACES...
...SO HE'S LIKE A WRITE-OFF, MAN!
NO. PUT IT UP, LUKE. WE'RE NOT POPPIN' HIM.
RANGER
I SWEAR, JOHN—YOU BEEN WEIRD SINCE YOU GOT HOME.

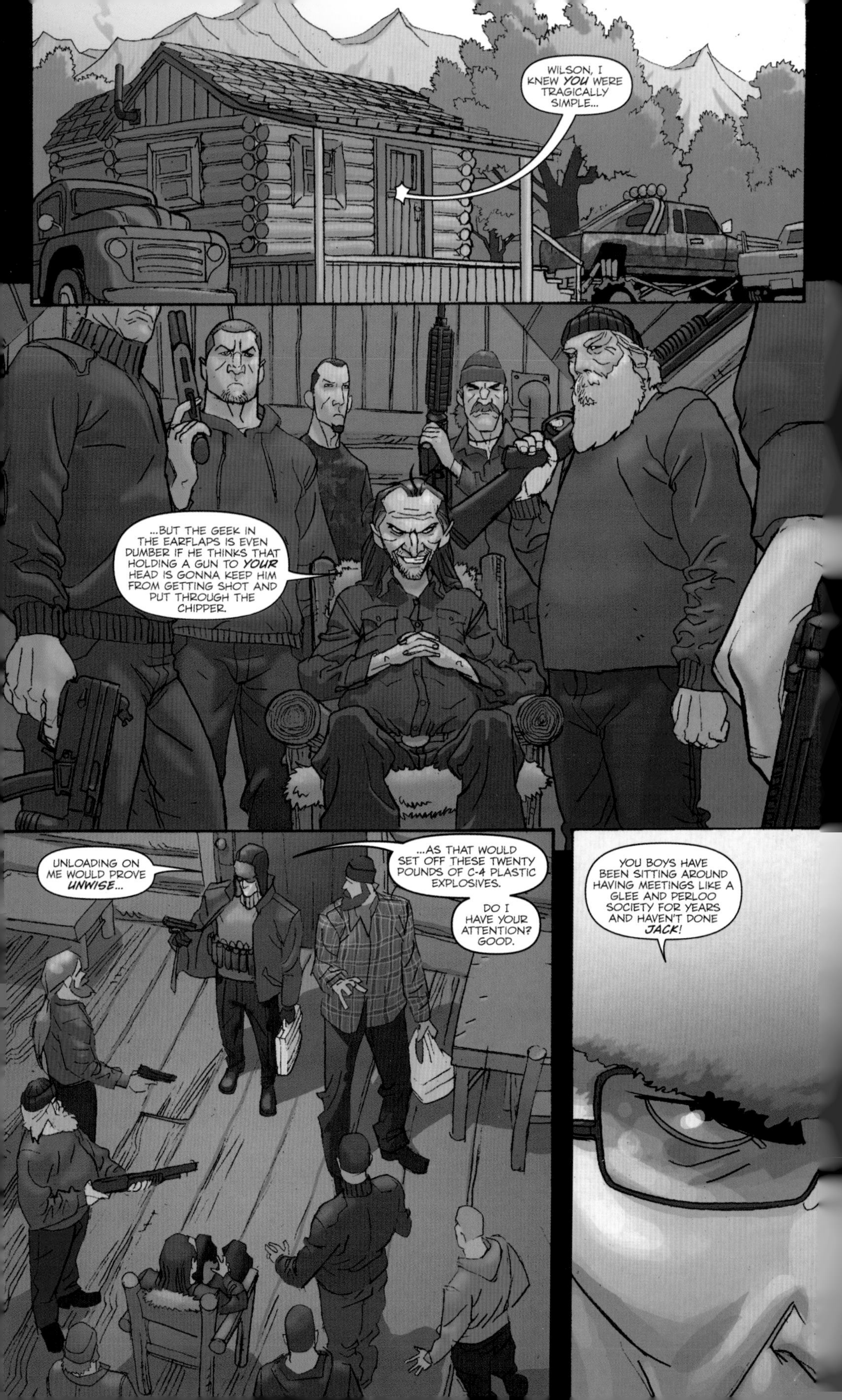

WILSON, I KNEW *YOU* WERE TRAGICALLY SIMPLE...
...BUT THE GEEK IN THE EARFLAPS IS EVEN DUMBER IF HE THINKS THAT HOLDING A GUN TO *YOUR* HEAD IS GONNA KEEP HIM FROM GETTING SHOT AND PUT THROUGH THE CHIPPER.
UNLOADING ON ME WOULD PROVE *UNWISE*...
...AS THAT WOULD SET OFF THESE TWENTY POUNDS OF C-4 PLASTIC EXPLOSIVES.
DO I HAVE YOUR ATTENTION? GOOD.
YOU BOYS HAVE BEEN SITTING AROUND HAVING MEETINGS LIKE A GLEE AND PERLOO SOCIETY FOR YEARS AND HAVEN'T DONE *JACK*!

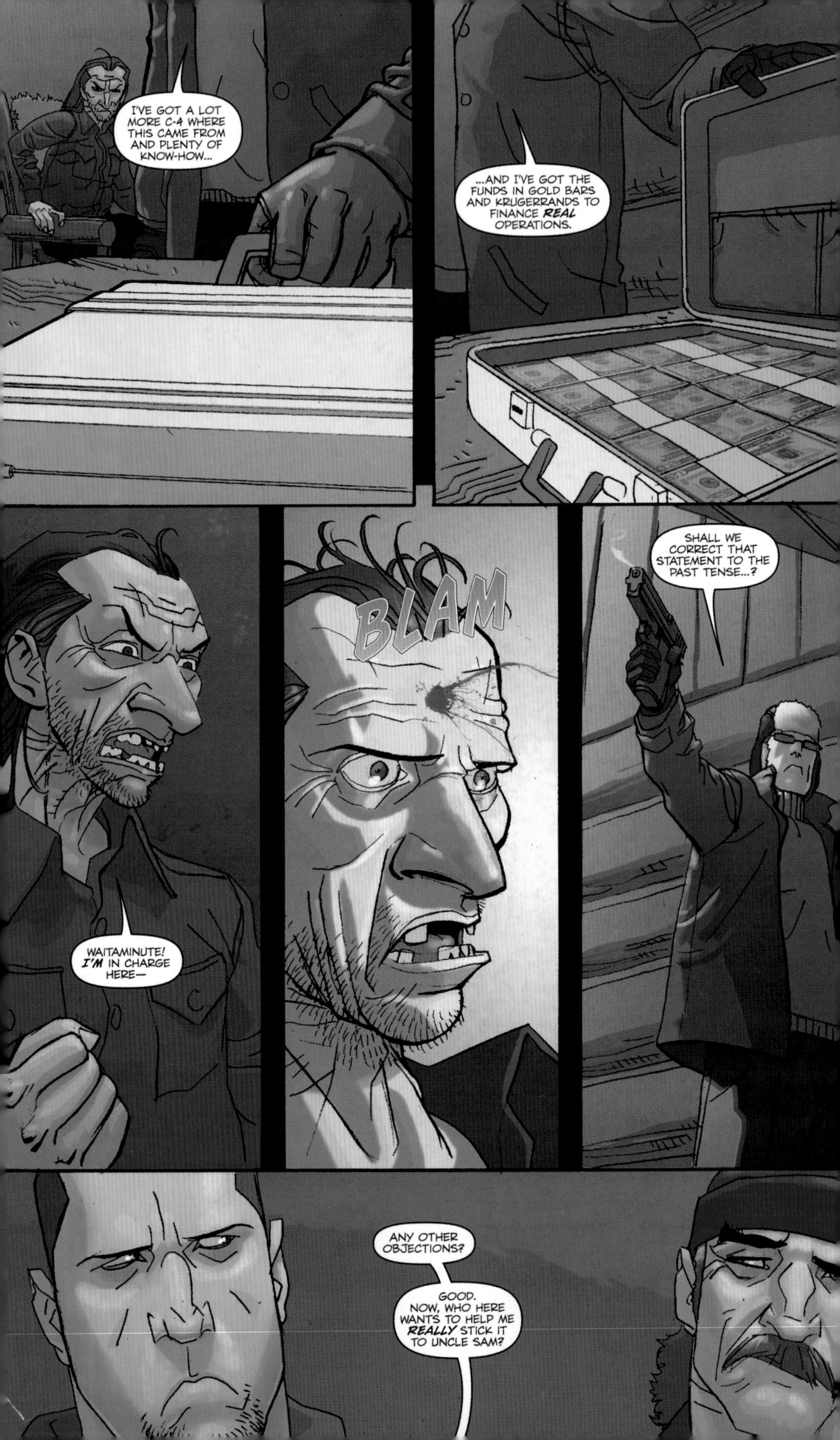

I'VE GOT A LOT MORE C-4 WHERE THIS CAME FROM AND PLENTY OF KNOW-HOW...
...AND I'VE GOT THE FUNDS IN GOLD BARS AND KRUGERRANDS TO FINANCE *REAL* OPERATIONS.
WAITAMINUTE! *I'M* IN CHARGE HERE—
BLAM
SHALL WE CORRECT THAT STATEMENT TO THE PAST TENSE...?
ANY OTHER OBJECTIONS?
GOOD. NOW, WHO HERE WANTS TO HELP ME *REALLY* STICK IT TO UNCLE SAM?

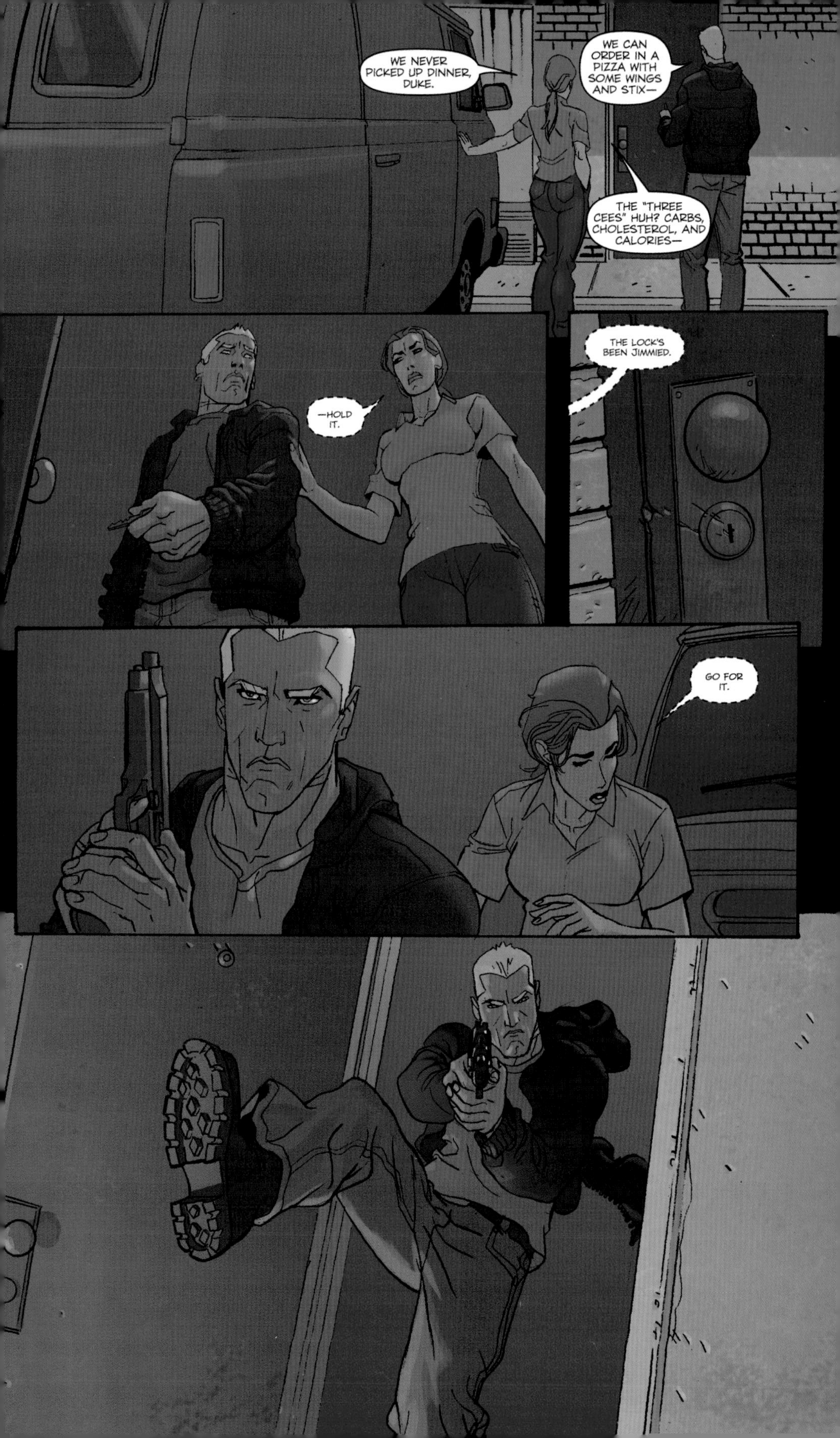
WE NEVER PICKED UP DINNER, DUKE.
WE CAN ORDER IN A PIZZA WITH SOME WINGS AND STIX—
THE "THREE CEES" HUH? CARBS, CHOLESTEROL, AND CALORIES—
—HOLD IT.
THE LOCK'S BEEN JIMMIED.
GO FOR IT.

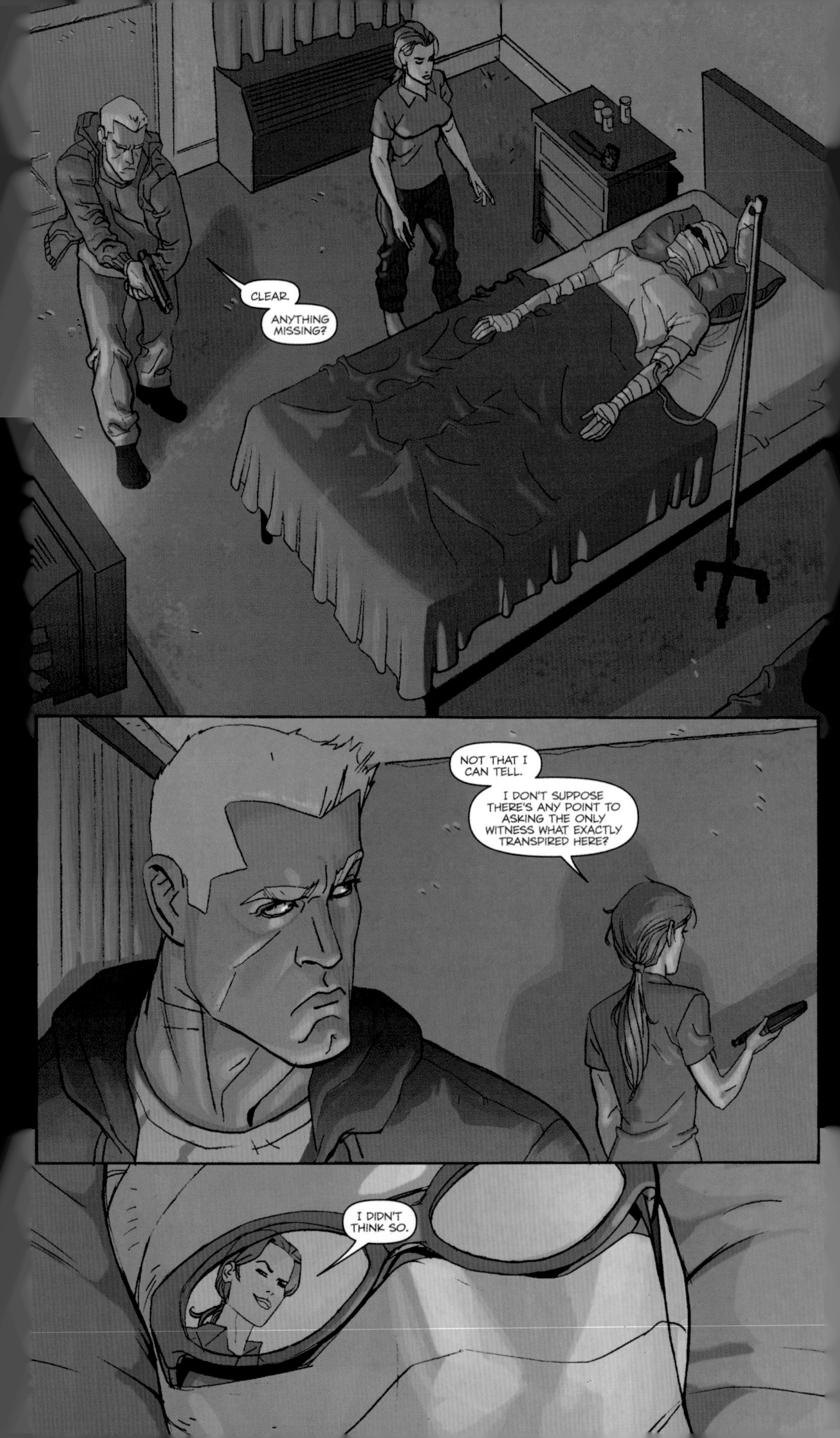
CLEAR.
ANYTHING MISSING?
NOT THAT I CAN TELL.
I DON'T SUPPOSE THERE'S ANY POINT TO ASKING THE ONLY WITNESS WHAT EXACTLY TRANSPIRED HERE?
I DIDN'T THINK SO.

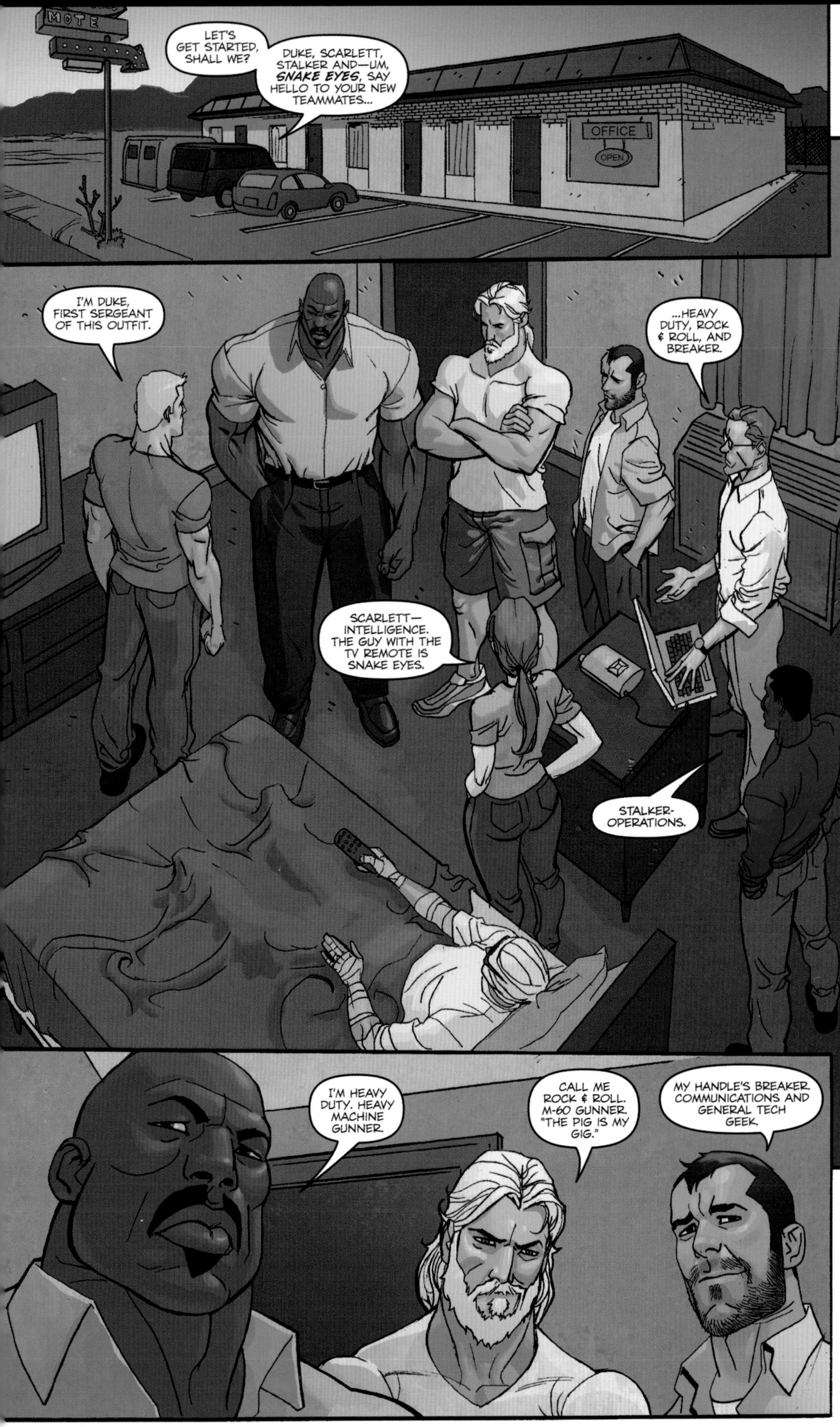
MOTE
LET'S GET STARTED, SHALL WE?
DUKE, SCARLETT, STALKER AND—UM, SNAKE EYES, SAY HELLO TO YOUR NEW TEAMMATES...
OFFICE
OPEN
I'M DUKE, FIRST SERGEANT OF THIS OUTFIT.
...HEAVY DUTY, ROCK & ROLL, AND BREAKER.
SCARLETT— INTELLIGENCE. THE GUY WITH THE TV REMOTE IS SNAKE EYES.
STALKER- OPERATIONS.
I'M HEAVY DUTY. HEAVY MACHINE GUNNER.
CALL ME ROCK & ROLL. M-60 GUNNER. "THE PIG IS MY GIG."
MY HANDLE'S BREAKER. COMMUNICATIONS AND GENERAL TECH GEEK.

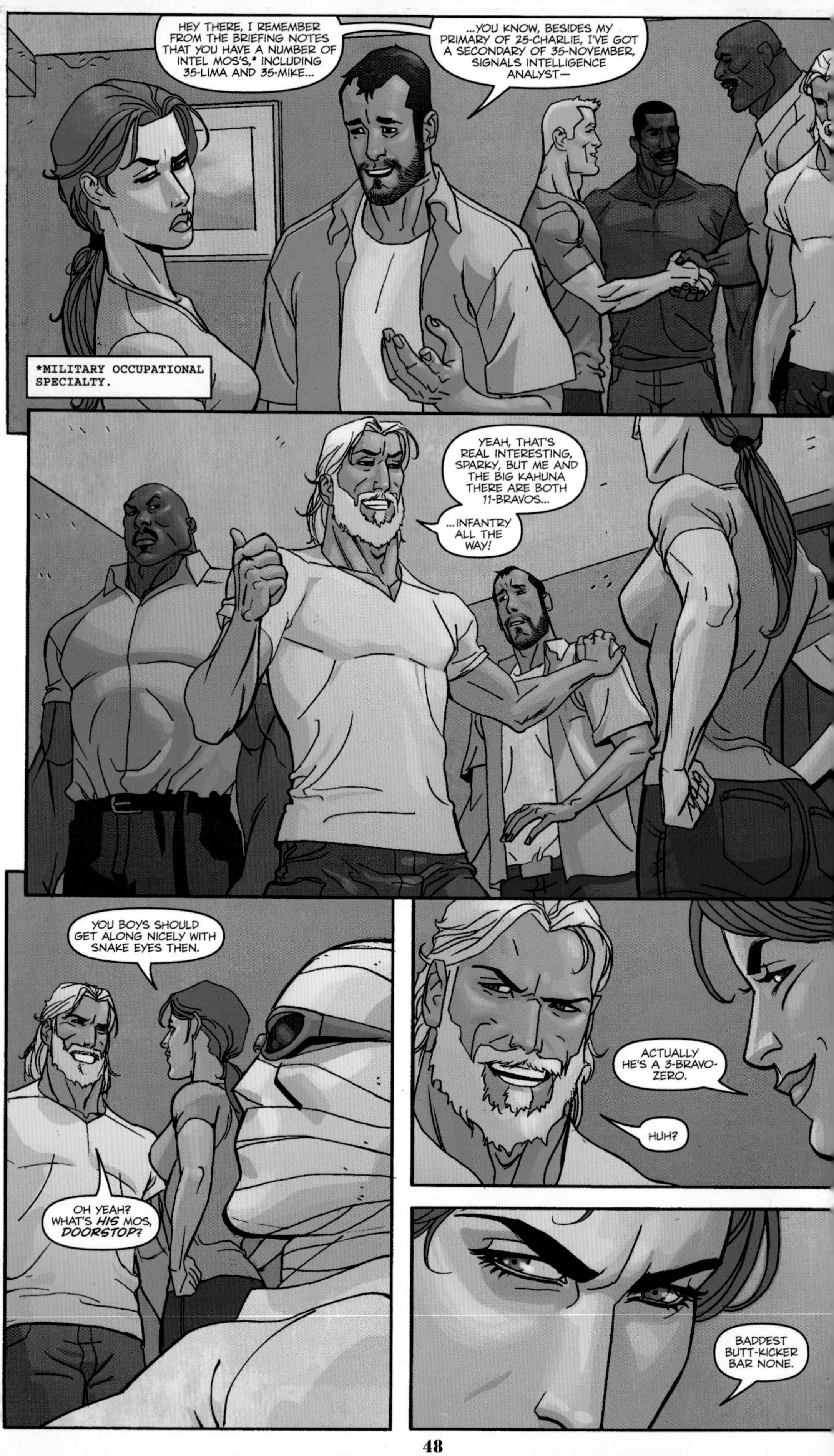
HEY THERE, I REMEMBER FROM THE BRIEFING NOTES THAT YOU HAVE A NUMBER OF INTEL MOS'S,* INCLUDING 35-LIMA AND 35-MIKE...
...YOU KNOW, BESIDES MY PRIMARY OF 25-CHARLIE, I'VE GOT A SECONDARY OF 35-NOVEMBER, SIGNALS INTELLIGENCE ANALYST—
*MILITARY OCCUPATIONAL SPECIALTY.
YEAH, THAT'S REAL INTERESTING, SPARKY, BUT ME AND THE BIG KAHUNA THERE ARE BOTH 11-BRAVOS...
...INFANTRY ALL THE WAY!
YOU BOYS SHOULD GET ALONG NICELY WITH SNAKE EYES THEN.
OH YEAH? WHAT'S *HIS* MOS, *DOORSTOP*?
ACTUALLY HE'S A 3-BRAVO-ZERO.
HUH?
BADDEST BUTT-KICKER BAR NONE.

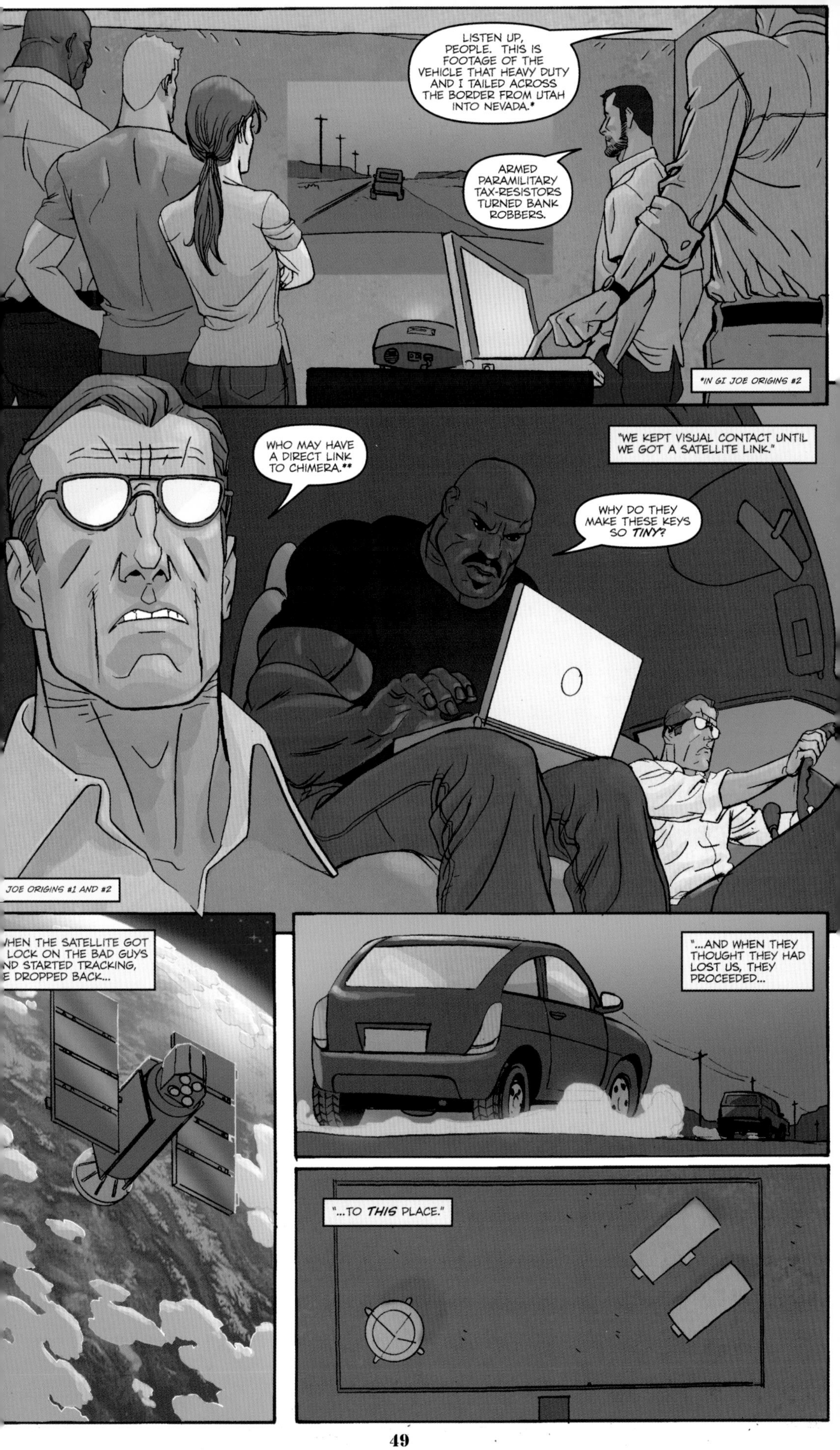
LISTEN UP, PEOPLE. THIS IS FOOTAGE OF THE VEHICLE THAT HEAVY DUTY AND I TAILED ACROSS THE BORDER FROM UTAH INTO NEVADA.*
ARMED PARAMILITARY TAX-RESISTORS TURNED BANK ROBBERS.
*IN GI JOE ORIGINS #2
WHO MAY HAVE A DIRECT LINK TO CHIMERA.**
"WE KEPT VISUAL CONTACT UNTIL WE GOT A SATELLITE LINK."
WHY DO THEY MAKE THESE KEYS SO TINY?
JOE ORIGINS #1 AND #2
"...AND WHEN THEY THOUGHT THEY HAD LOST US, THEY PROCEEDED...
"...TO THIS PLACE."

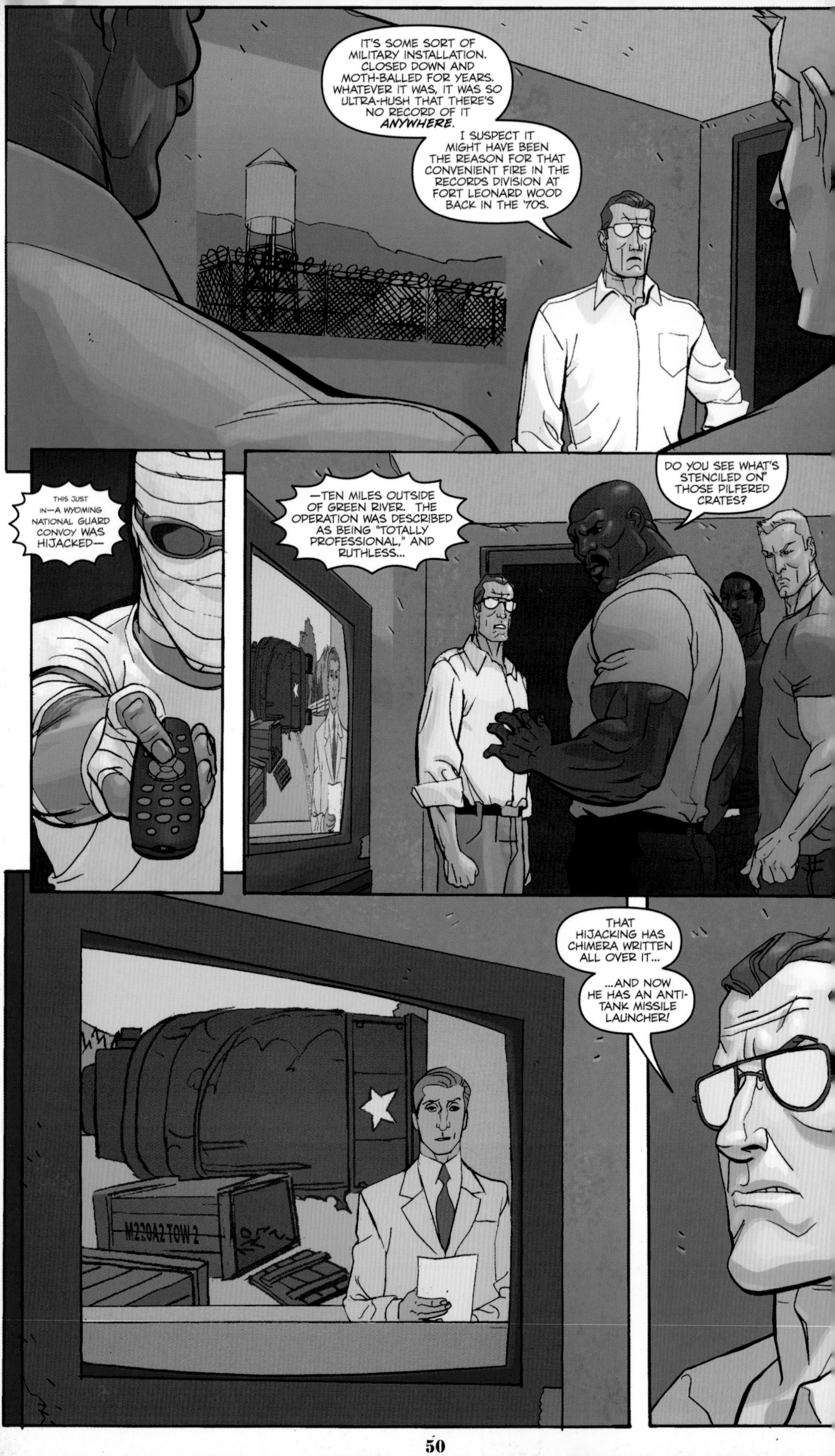
IT'S SOME SORT OF MILITARY INSTALLATION. CLOSED DOWN AND MOTH-BALLED FOR YEARS. WHATEVER IT WAS, IT WAS SO ULTRA-HUSH THAT THERE'S NO RECORD OF IT ANYWHERE.
I SUSPECT IT MIGHT HAVE BEEN THE REASON FOR THAT CONVENIENT FIRE IN THE RECORDS DIVISION AT FORT LEONARD WOOD BACK IN THE '70S.
THIS JUST IN—A WYOMING NATIONAL GUARD CONVOY WAS HIJACKED—
—TEN MILES OUTSIDE OF GREEN RIVER. THE OPERATION WAS DESCRIBED AS BEING "TOTALLY PROFESSIONAL," AND RUTHLESS...
DO YOU SEE WHAT'S STENCILED ON THOSE PILFERED CRATES?
M220A2 TOW 2
THAT HIJACKING HAS CHIMERA WRITTEN ALL OVER IT...
...AND NOW HE HAS AN ANTI-TANK MISSILE LAUNCHER!

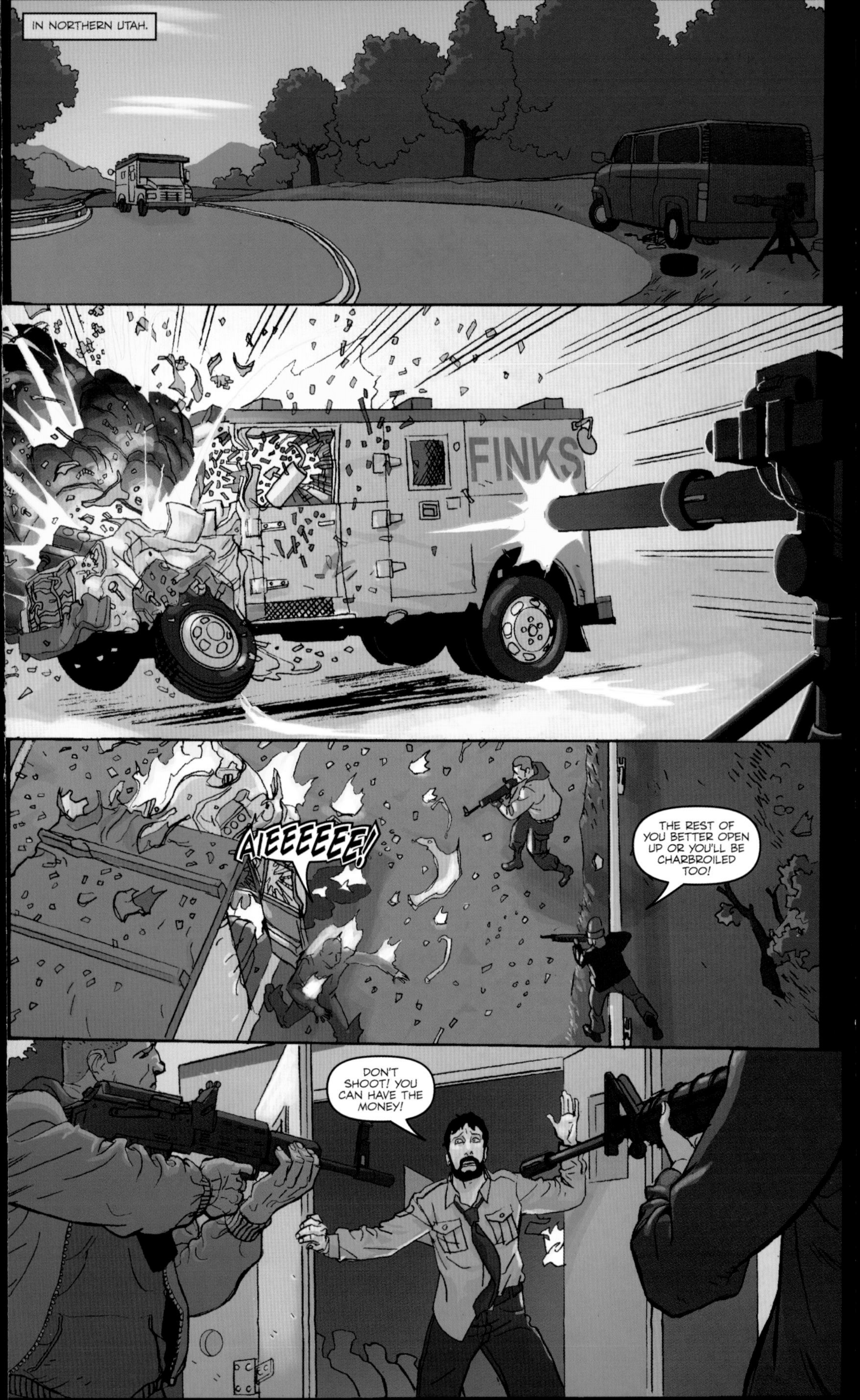
IN NORTHERN UTAH.
FINKS
AIEEEEEE!
THE REST OF YOU BETTER OPEN UP OR YOU'LL BE CHARBROILED TOO!
DON'T SHOOT! YOU CAN HAVE THE MONEY!

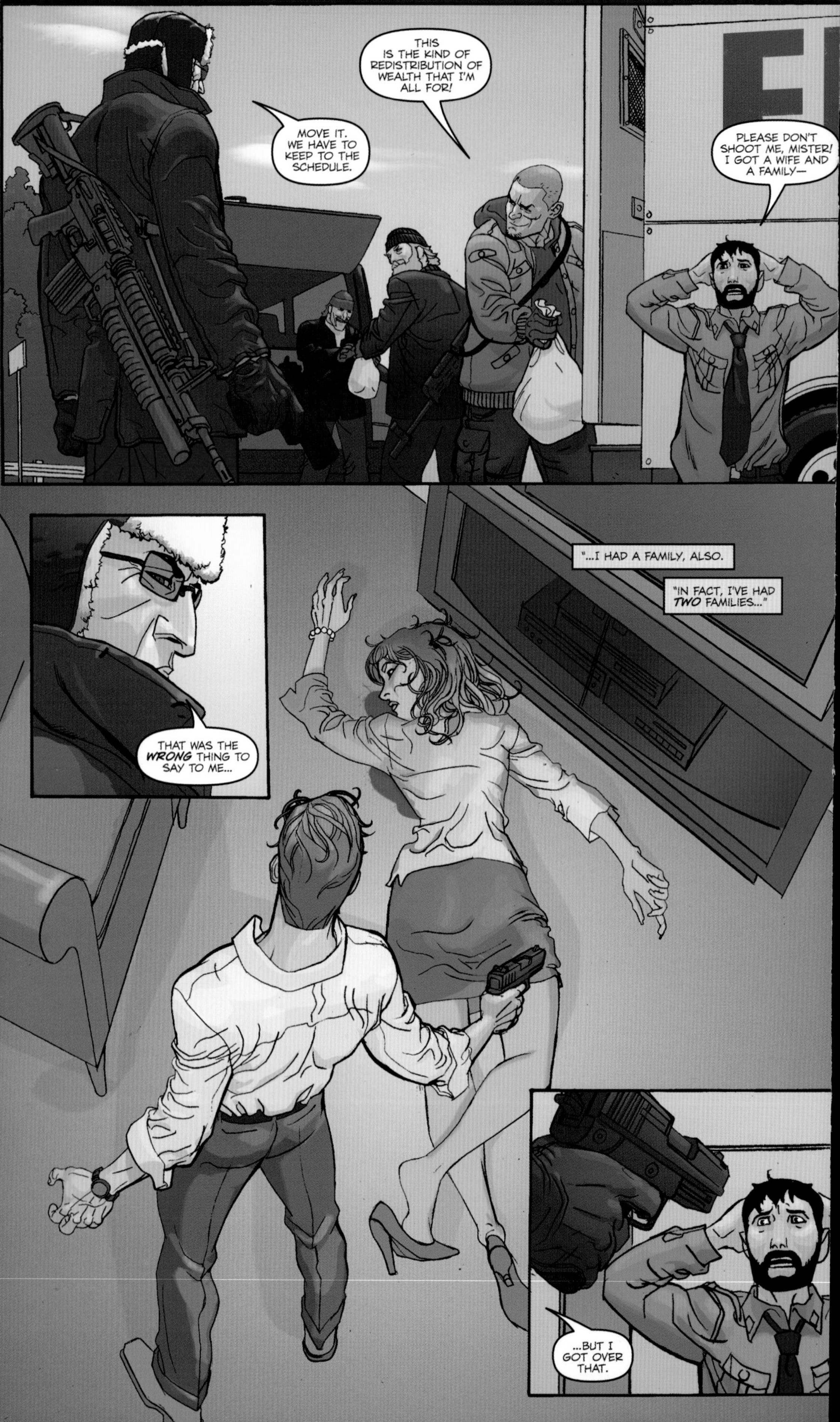
MOVE IT. WE HAVE TO KEEP TO THE SCHEDULE.
THIS IS THE KIND OF REDISTRIBUTION OF WEALTH THAT I'M ALL FOR!
PLEASE DON'T SHOOT ME, MISTER! I GOT A WIFE AND A FAMILY—
THAT WAS THE WRONG THING TO SAY TO ME...
"...I HAD A FAMILY, ALSO.
"IN FACT, I'VE HAD TWO FAMILIES..."
...BUT I GOT OVER THAT.

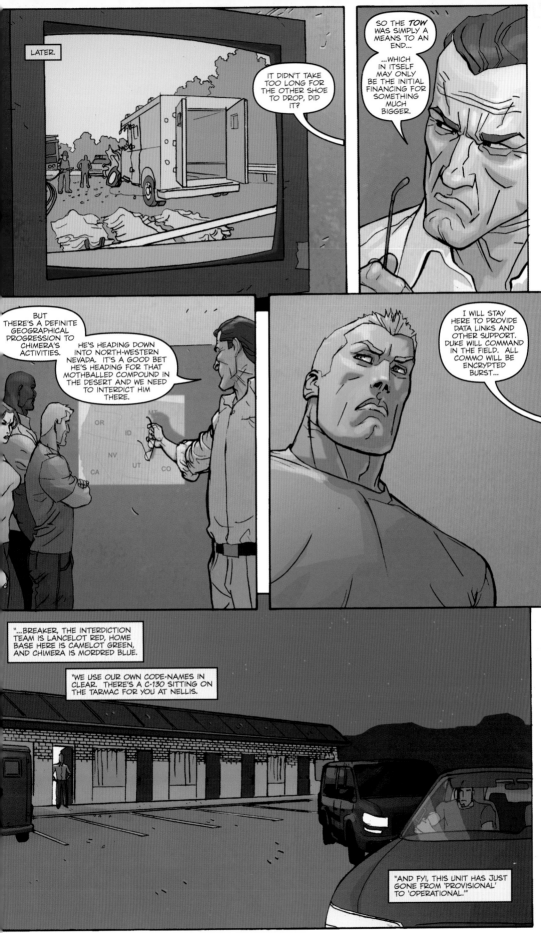

LATER.

IT DIDN'T TAKE TOO LONG FOR THE OTHER SHOE TO DROP, DID IT?

SO THE *TOW* WAS SIMPLY A MEANS TO AN END...

...WHICH IN ITSELF MAY ONLY BE THE INITIAL FINANCING FOR SOMETHING MUCH BIGGER.

BUT THERE'S A DEFINITE GEOGRAPHICAL PROGRESSION TO CHIMERA'S ACTIVITIES.

HE'S HEADING DOWN INTO NORTH-WESTERN NEVADA. IT'S A GOOD BET HE'S HEADING FOR THAT MOTHBALLED COMPOUND IN THE DESERT AND WE NEED TO INTERDICT HIM THERE.

I WILL STAY HERE TO PROVIDE DATA LINKS AND OTHER SUPPORT. DUKE WILL COMMAND IN THE FIELD. ALL COMMO WILL BE ENCRYPTED BURST...

"...BREAKER, THE INTERDICTION TEAM IS LANCELOT RED, HOME BASE HERE IS CAMELOT GREEN, AND CHIMERA IS MORDRED BLUE.

"WE USE OUR OWN CODE-NAMES IN CLEAR. THERE'S A C-130 SITTING ON THE TARMAC FOR YOU AT NELLIS.

"AND FYI, THIS UNIT HAS JUST GONE FROM 'PROVISIONAL' TO 'OPERATIONAL.'"

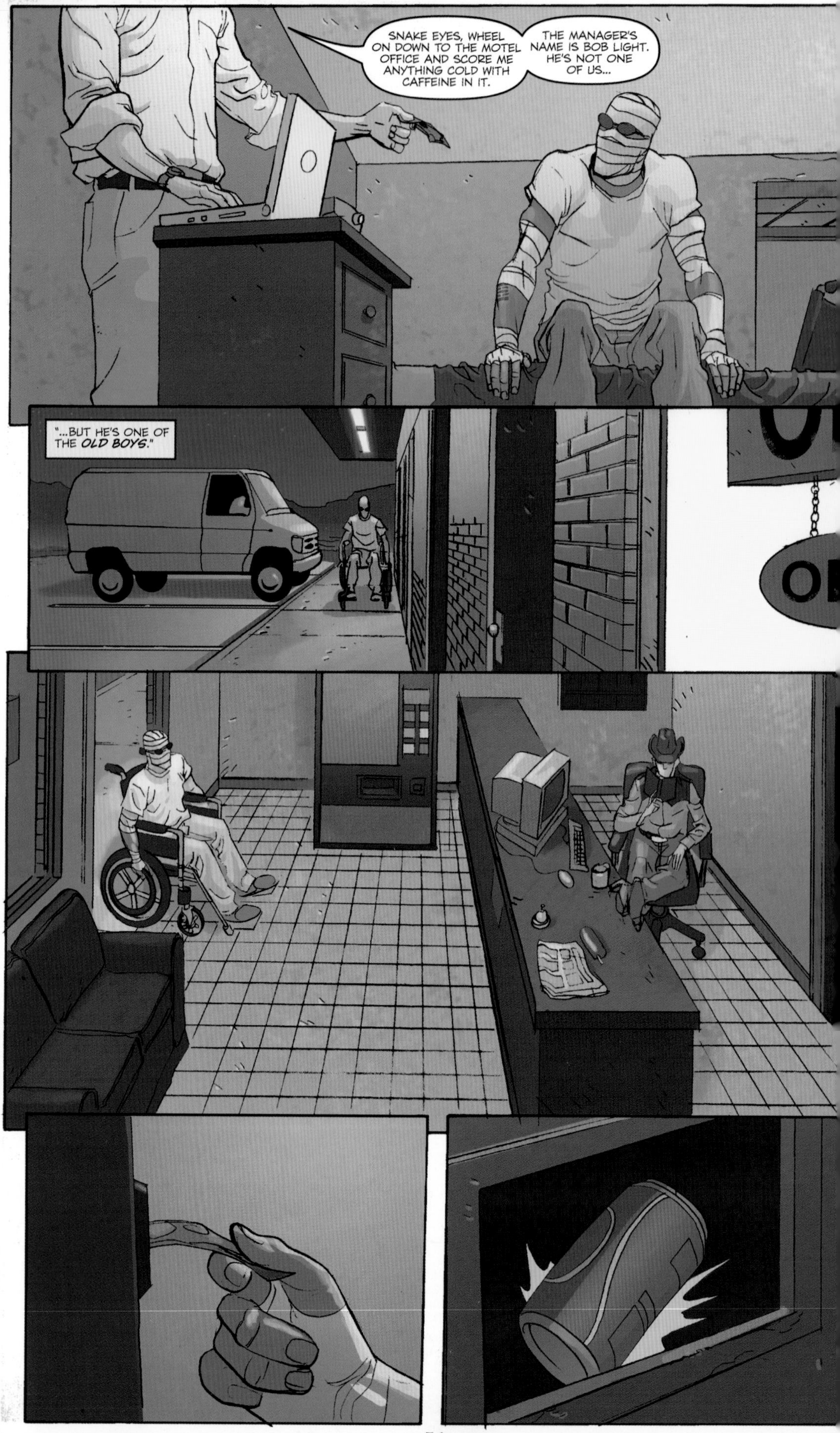
SNAKE EYES, WHEEL ON DOWN TO THE MOTEL OFFICE AND SCORE ME ANYTHING COLD WITH CAFFEINE IN IT.
THE MANAGER'S NAME IS BOB LIGHT. HE'S NOT ONE OF US...
"...BUT HE'S ONE OF THE *OLD BOYS*."

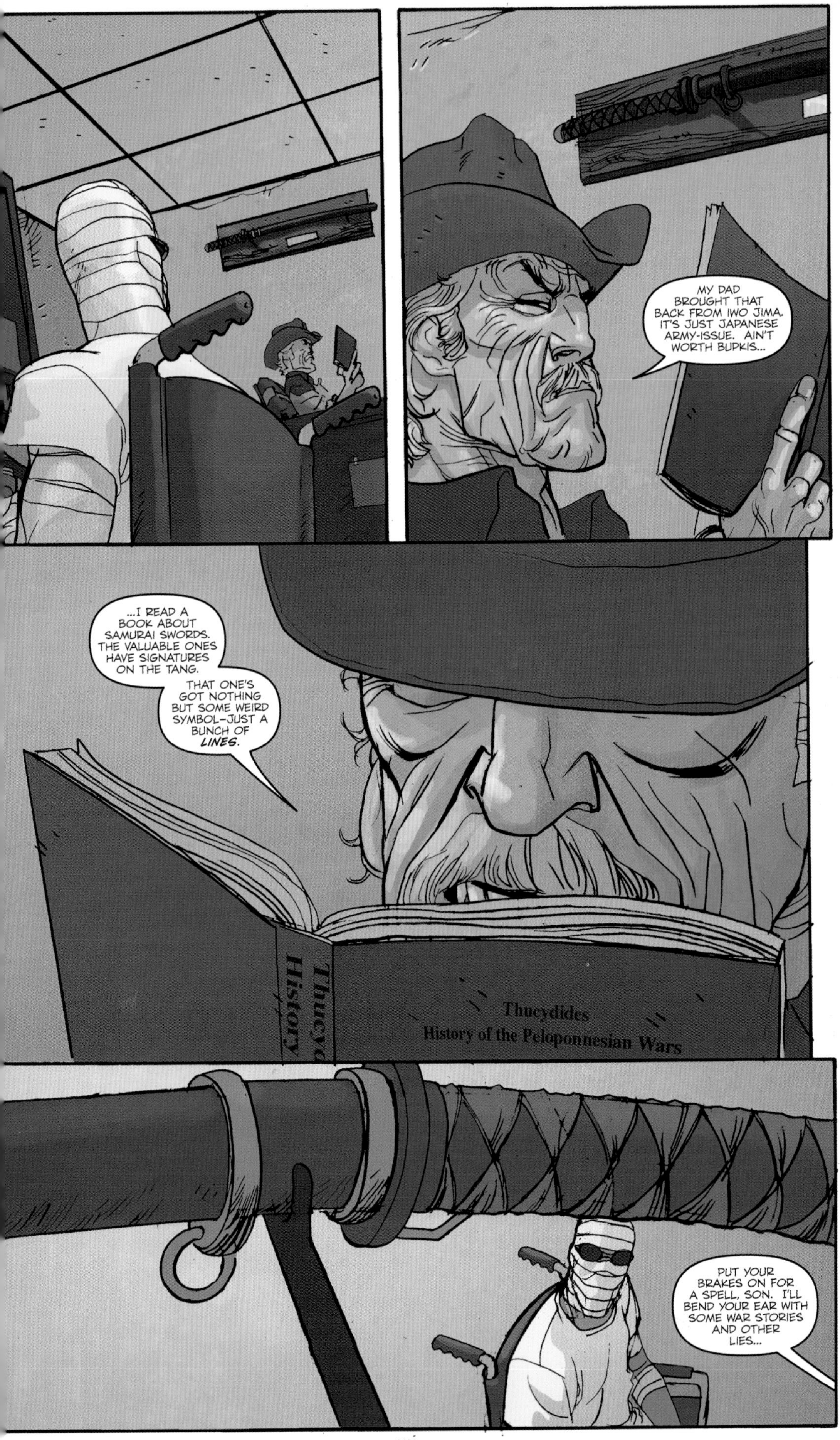
MY DAD BROUGHT THAT BACK FROM IWO JIMA. IT'S JUST JAPANESE ARMY-ISSUE. AIN'T WORTH BUPKIS...
...I READ A BOOK ABOUT SAMURAI SWORDS. THE VALUABLE ONES HAVE SIGNATURES ON THE TANG.
THAT ONE'S GOT NOTHING BUT SOME WEIRD SYMBOL–JUST A BUNCH OF LINES.
Thucydides History
Thucydides
History of the Peloponnesian Wars
PUT YOUR BRAKES ON FOR A SPELL, SON. I'LL BEND YOUR EAR WITH SOME WAR STORIES AND OTHER LIES...

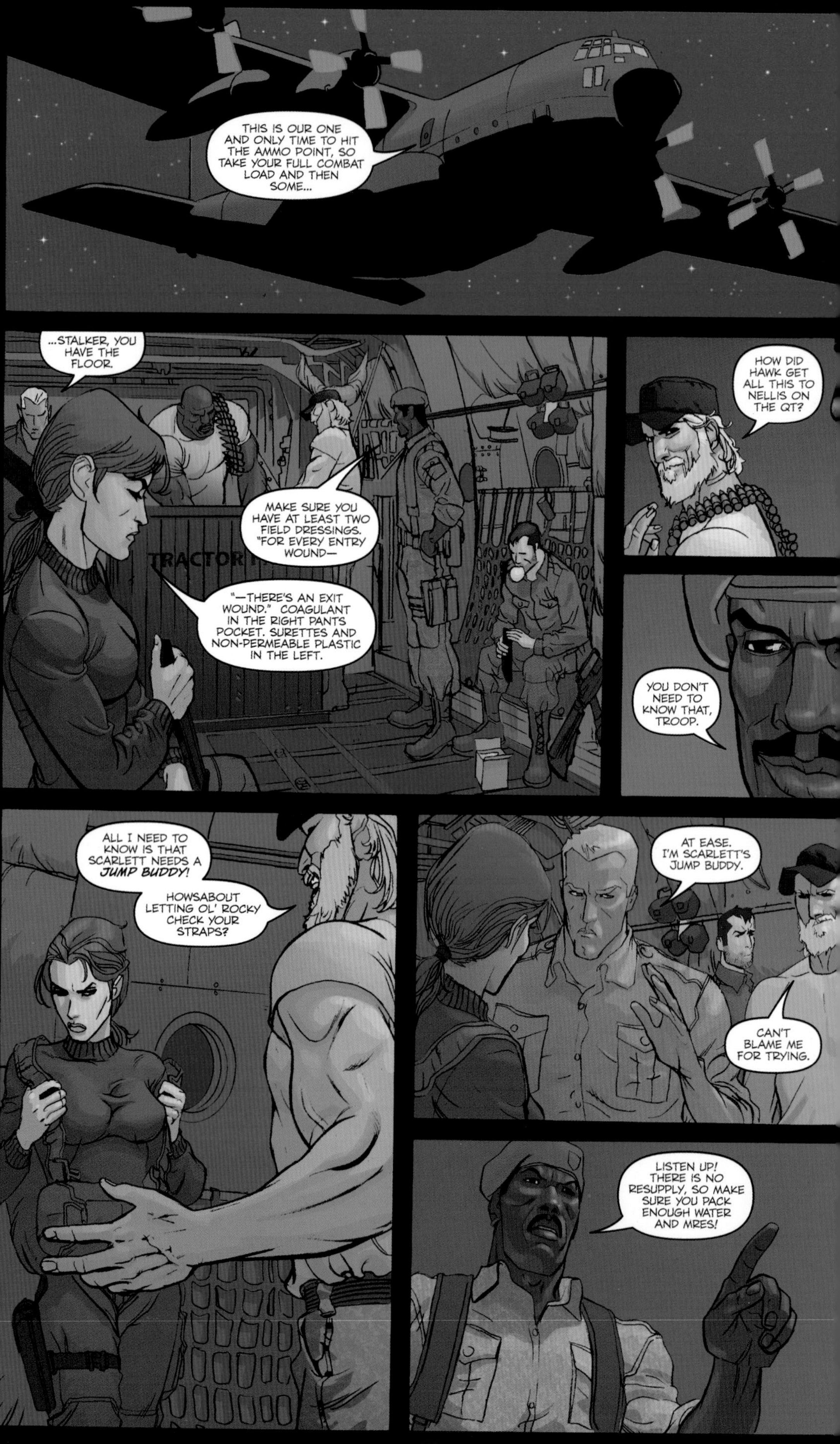
THIS IS OUR ONE AND ONLY TIME TO HIT THE AMMO POINT, SO TAKE YOUR FULL COMBAT LOAD AND THEN SOME...
...STALKER, YOU HAVE THE FLOOR.
MAKE SURE YOU HAVE AT LEAST TWO FIELD DRESSINGS. "FOR EVERY ENTRY WOUND—
"—THERE'S AN EXIT WOUND." COAGULANT IN THE RIGHT PANTS POCKET. SURETTES AND NON-PERMEABLE PLASTIC IN THE LEFT.
TRACTOR
HOW DID HAWK GET ALL THIS TO NELLIS ON THE QT?
YOU DON'T NEED TO KNOW THAT, TROOP.
ALL I NEED TO KNOW IS THAT SCARLETT NEEDS A *JUMP BUDDY*!
HOWSABOUT LETTING OL' ROCKY CHECK YOUR STRAPS?
AT EASE. I'M SCARLETT'S JUMP BUDDY.
CAN'T BLAME ME FOR TRYING.
LISTEN UP! THERE IS NO RESUPPLY, SO MAKE SURE YOU PACK ENOUGH WATER AND MRES!

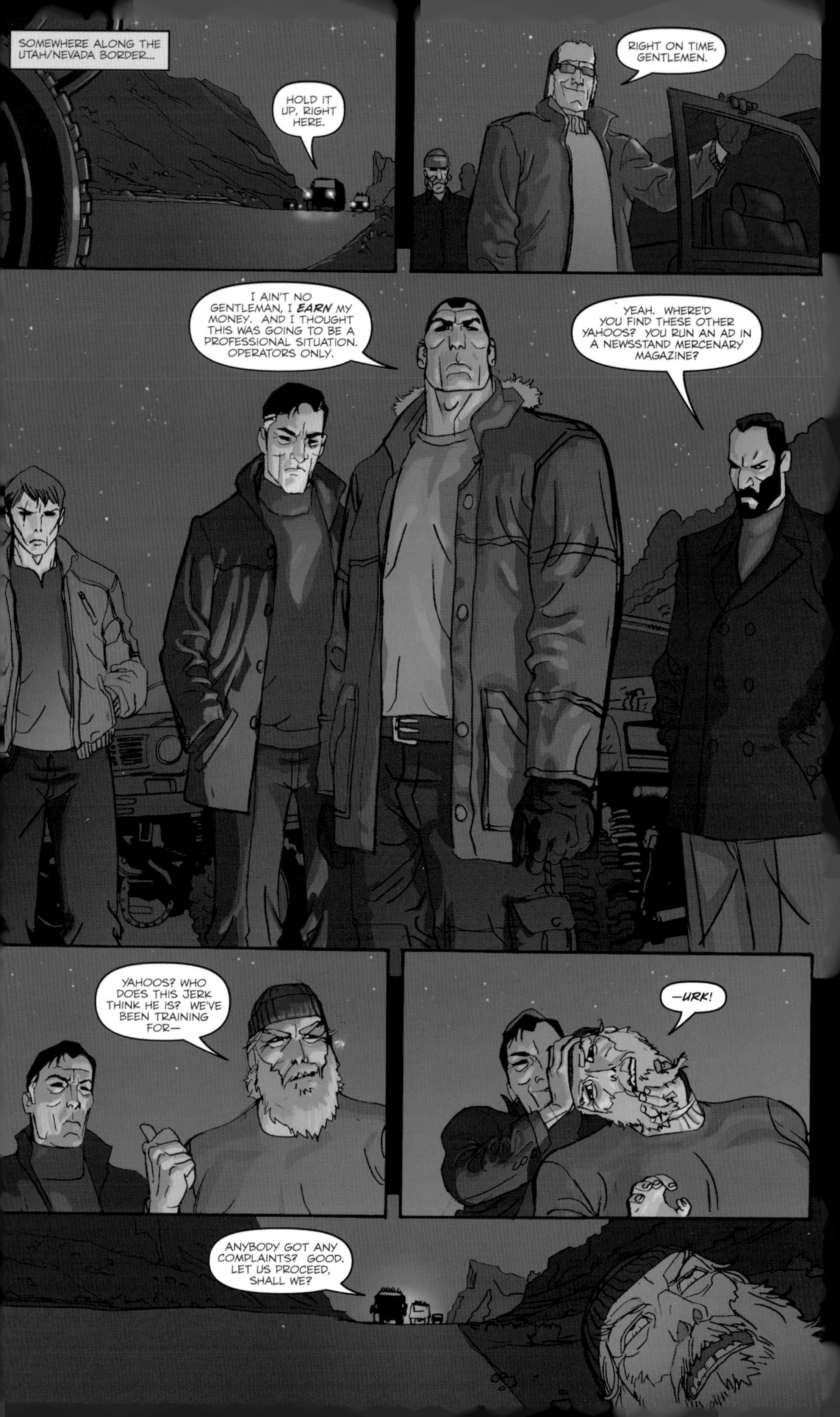

SOMEWHERE ALONG THE UTAH/NEVADA BORDER...
HOLD IT UP, RIGHT HERE.
RIGHT ON TIME, GENTLEMEN.
I AIN'T NO GENTLEMAN, I EARN MY MONEY. AND I THOUGHT THIS WAS GOING TO BE A PROFESSIONAL SITUATION. OPERATORS ONLY.
YEAH. WHERE'D YOU FIND THESE OTHER YAHOOS? YOU RUN AN AD IN A NEWSSTAND MERCENARY MAGAZINE?
YAHOOS? WHO DOES THIS JERK THINK HE IS? WE'VE BEEN TRAINING FOR—
—URK!
ANYBODY GOT ANY COMPLAINTS? GOOD. LET US PROCEED, SHALL WE?

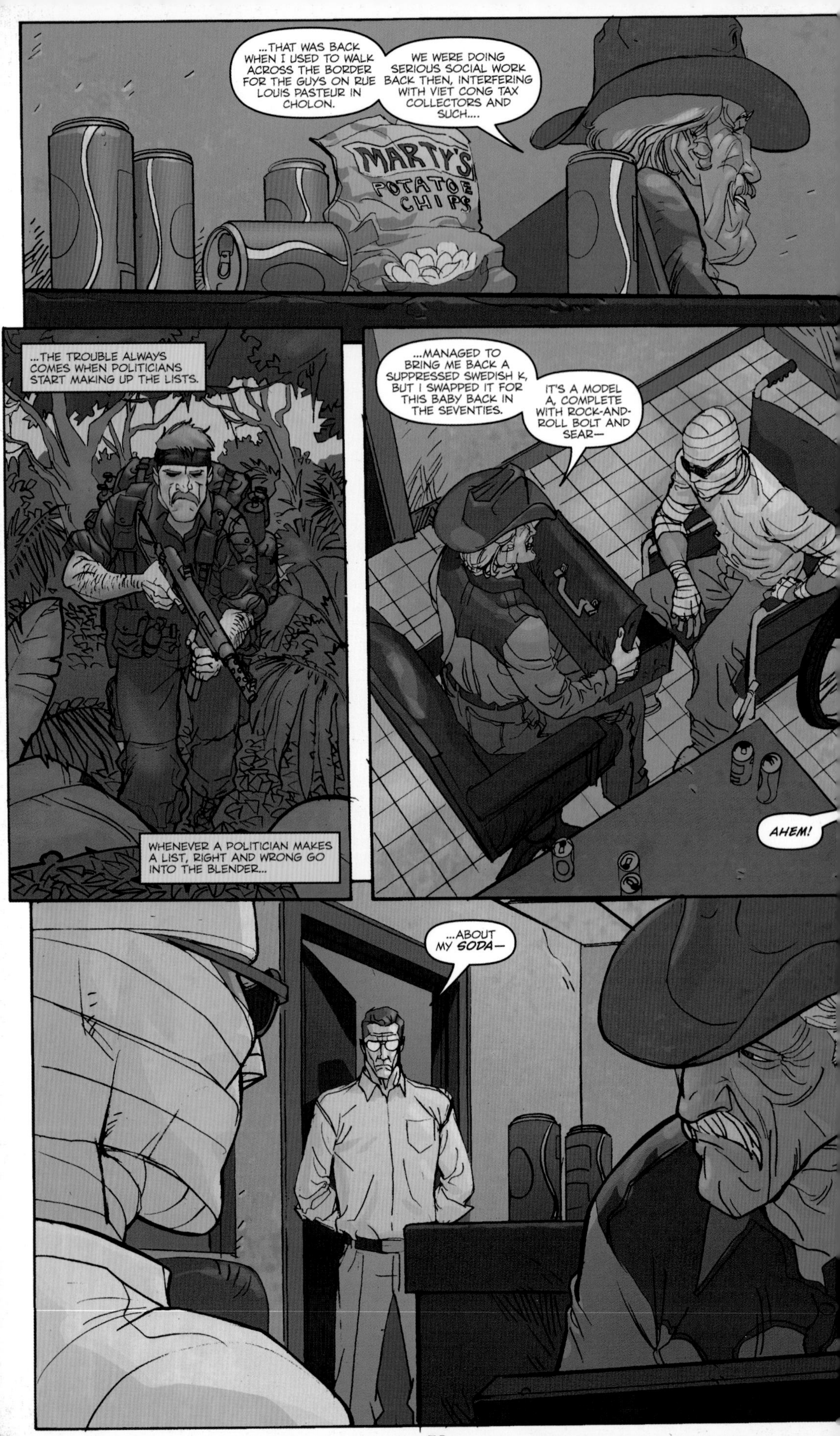
...THAT WAS BACK WHEN I USED TO WALK ACROSS THE BORDER FOR THE GUYS ON RUE LOUIS PASTEUR IN CHOLON.
WE WERE DOING SERIOUS SOCIAL WORK BACK THEN, INTERFERING WITH VIET CONG TAX COLLECTORS AND SUCH....
MARTY'S POTATOE CHIPS
...THE TROUBLE ALWAYS COMES WHEN POLITICIANS START MAKING UP THE LISTS.
WHENEVER A POLITICIAN MAKES A LIST, RIGHT AND WRONG GO INTO THE BLENDER...
...MANAGED TO BRING ME BACK A SUPPRESSED SWEDISH K, BUT I SWAPPED IT FOR THIS BABY BACK IN THE SEVENTIES.
IT'S A MODEL A, COMPLETE WITH ROCK-AND-ROLL BOLT AND SEAR—
AHEM!
...ABOUT MY SODA—

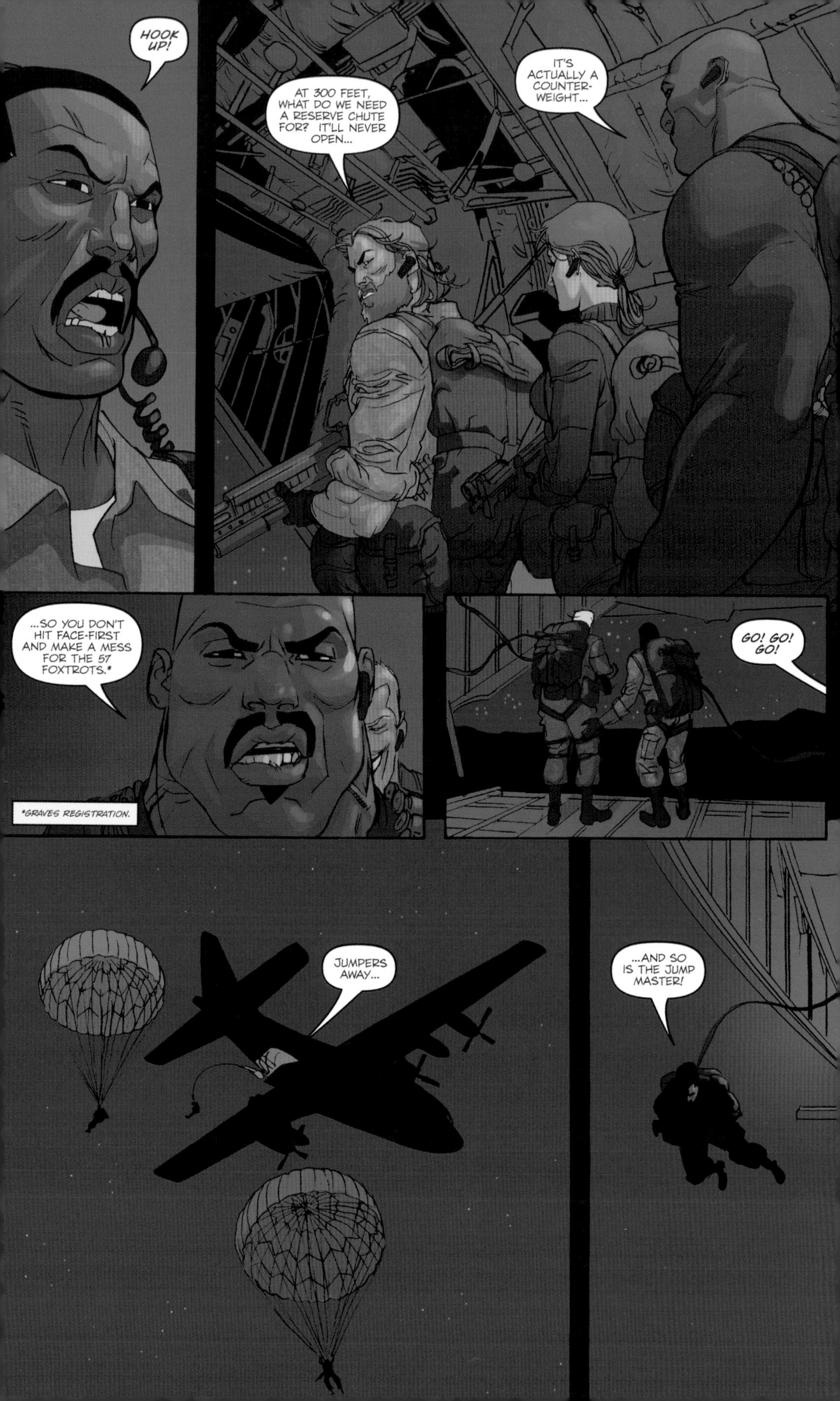
HOOK UP!
AT 300 FEET, WHAT DO WE NEED A RESERVE CHUTE FOR? IT'LL NEVER OPEN...
IT'S ACTUALLY A COUNTER-WEIGHT...
...SO YOU DON'T HIT FACE-FIRST AND MAKE A MESS FOR THE 57 FOXTROTS.*
*GRAVES REGISTRATION.
GO! GO! GO!
JUMPERS AWAY...
...AND SO IS THE JUMP MASTER!

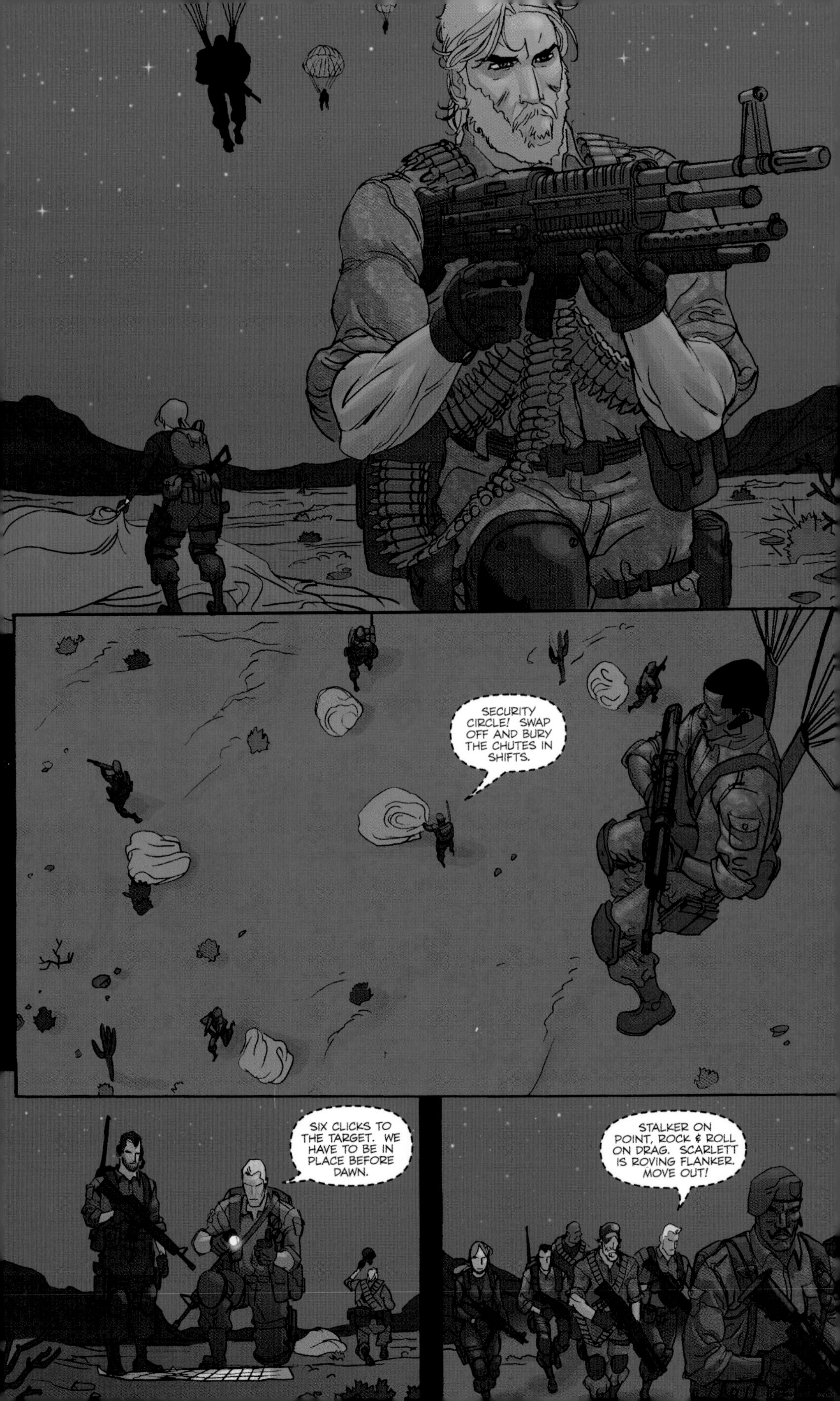
SECURITY CIRCLE! SWAP OFF AND BURY THE CHUTES IN SHIFTS.
SIX CLICKS TO THE TARGET. WE HAVE TO BE IN PLACE BEFORE DAWN.
STALKER ON POINT, ROCK & ROLL ON DRAG. SCARLETT IS ROVING FLANKER. MOVE OUT!

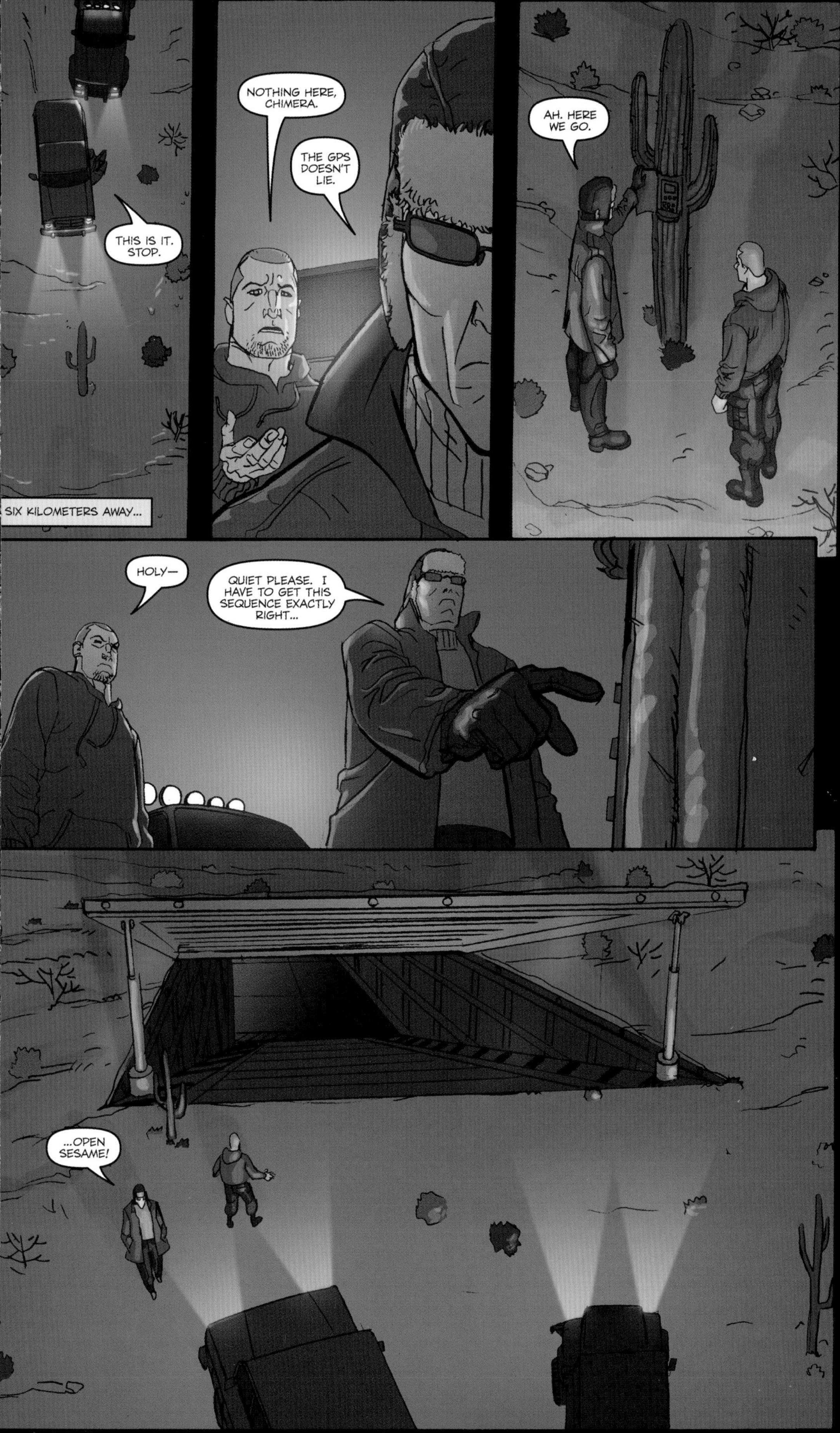
THIS IS IT. STOP.
SIX KILOMETERS AWAY...
NOTHING HERE, CHIMERA.
THE GPS DOESN'T LIE.
AH. HERE WE GO.
HOLY—
QUIET PLEASE. I HAVE TO GET THIS SEQUENCE EXACTLY RIGHT...
...OPEN SESAME!

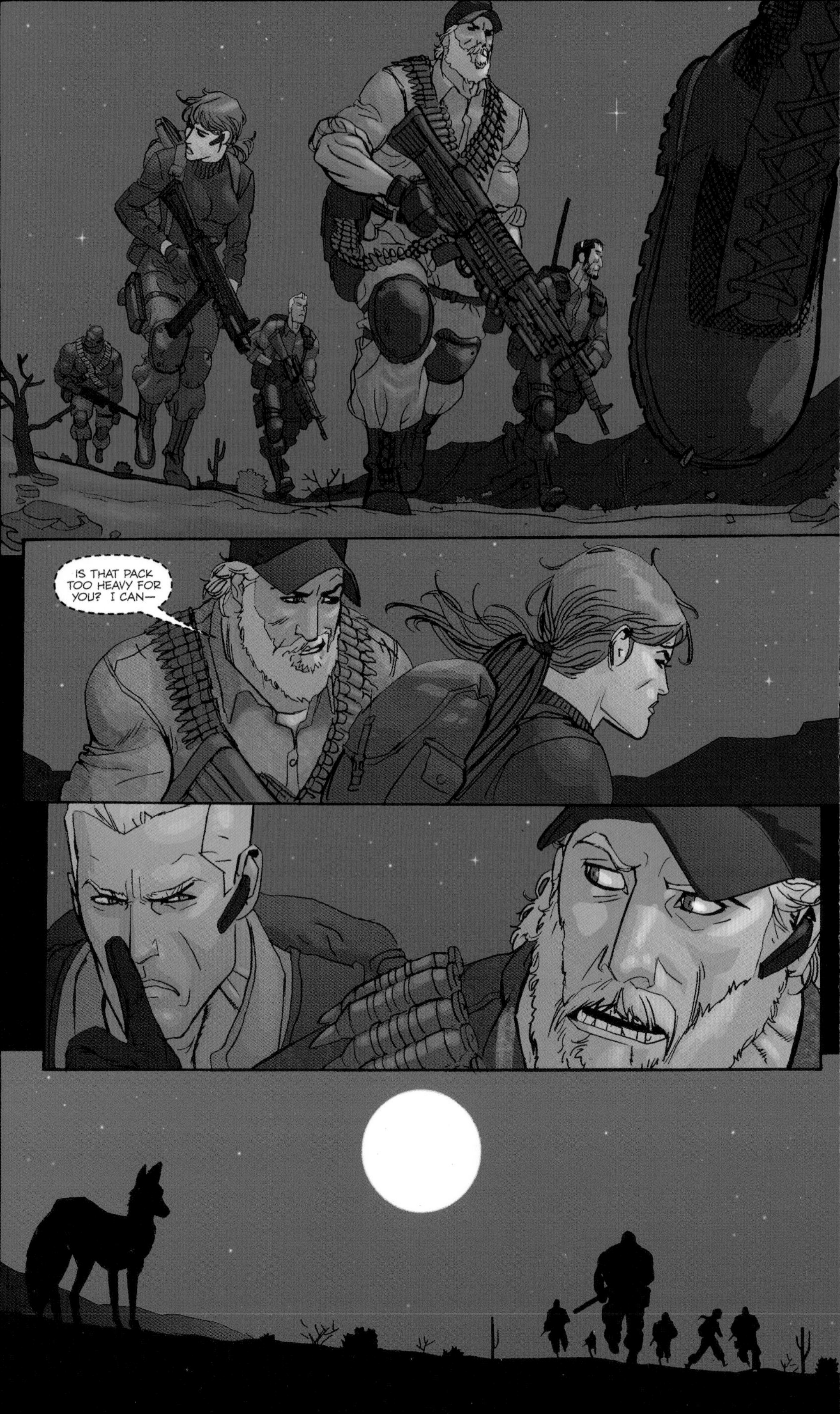
IS THAT PACK TOO HEAVY FOR YOU? I CAN—

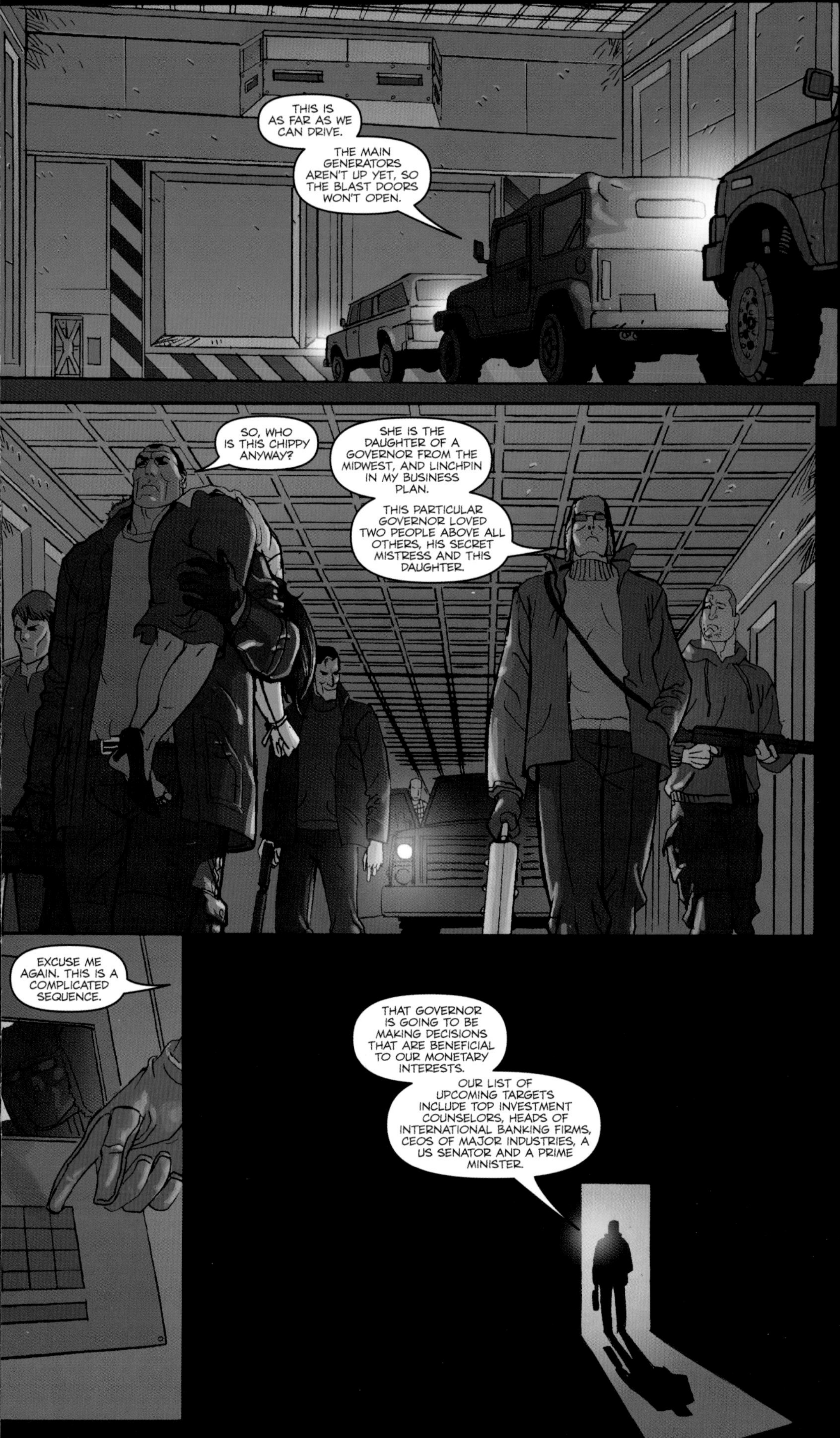
THIS IS AS FAR AS WE CAN DRIVE.
THE MAIN GENERATORS AREN'T UP YET, SO THE BLAST DOORS WON'T OPEN.
SO, WHO IS THIS CHIPPY ANYWAY?
SHE IS THE DAUGHTER OF A GOVERNOR FROM THE MIDWEST, AND LINCHPIN IN MY BUSINESS PLAN.
THIS PARTICULAR GOVERNOR LOVED TWO PEOPLE ABOVE ALL OTHERS, HIS SECRET MISTRESS AND THIS DAUGHTER.
EXCUSE ME AGAIN. THIS IS A COMPLICATED SEQUENCE.
THAT GOVERNOR IS GOING TO BE MAKING DECISIONS THAT ARE BENEFICIAL TO OUR MONETARY INTERESTS.
OUR LIST OF UPCOMING TARGETS INCLUDE TOP INVESTMENT COUNSELORS, HEADS OF INTERNATIONAL BANKING FIRMS, CEOS OF MAJOR INDUSTRIES, A US SENATOR AND A PRIME MINISTER.

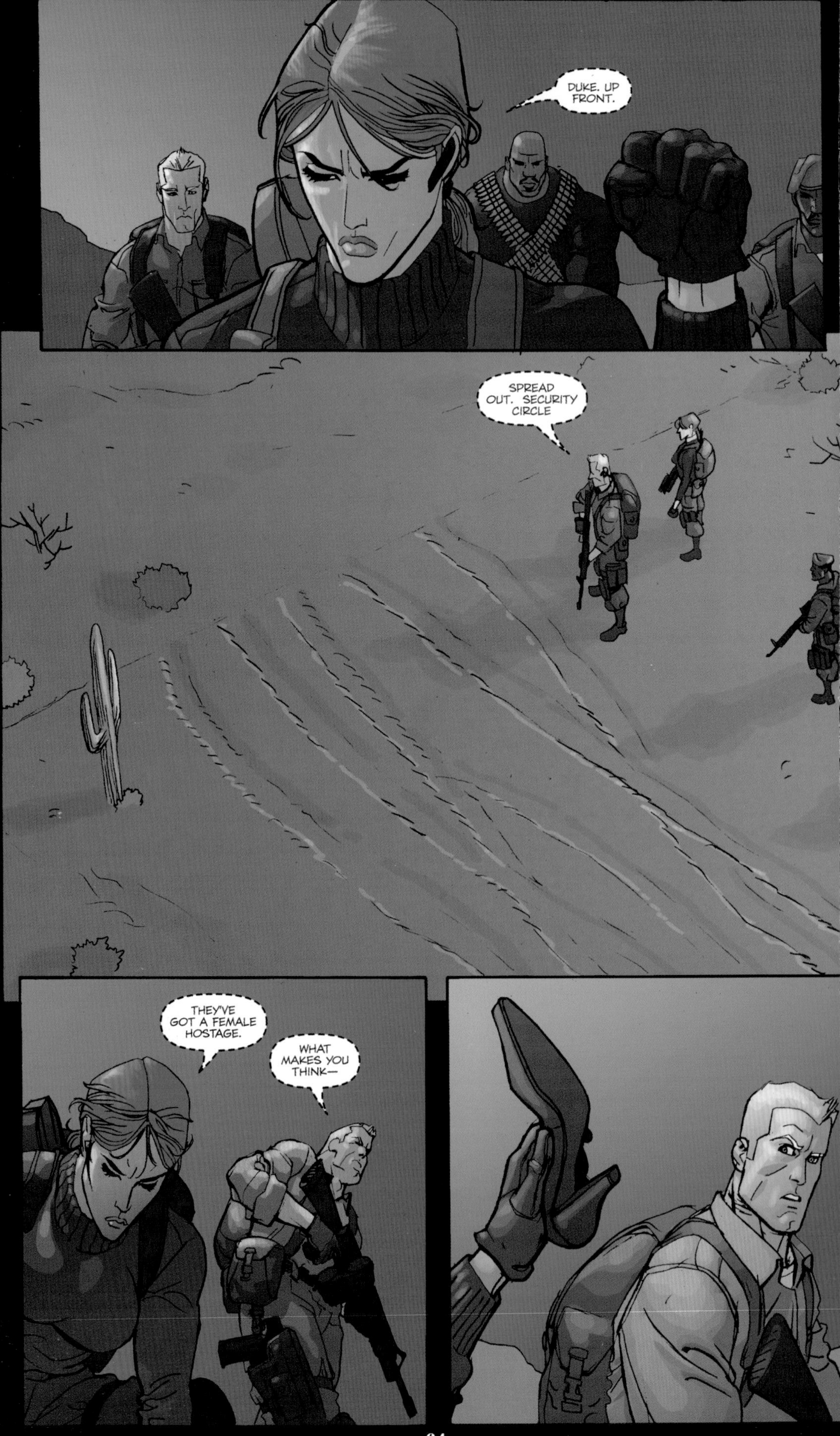
DUKE. UP FRONT.
SPREAD OUT. SECURITY CIRCLE
THEY'VE GOT A FEMALE HOSTAGE.
WHAT MAKES YOU THINK—

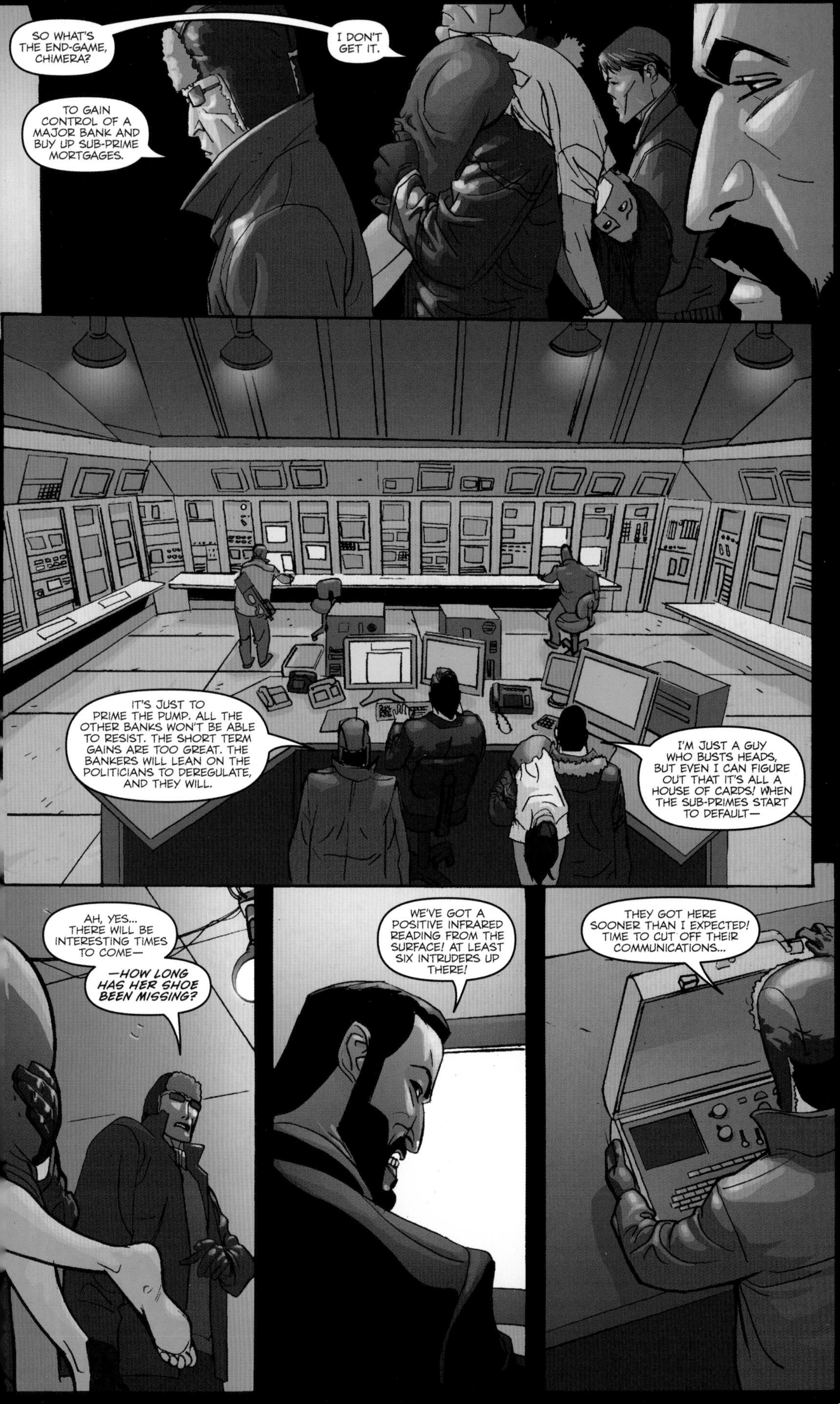
SO WHAT'S THE END-GAME, CHIMERA?
I DON'T GET IT.
TO GAIN CONTROL OF A MAJOR BANK AND BUY UP SUB-PRIME MORTGAGES.
IT'S JUST TO PRIME THE PUMP. ALL THE OTHER BANKS WON'T BE ABLE TO RESIST. THE SHORT TERM GAINS ARE TOO GREAT. THE BANKERS WILL LEAN ON THE POLITICIANS TO DEREGULATE, AND THEY WILL.
I'M JUST A GUY WHO BUSTS HEADS, BUT EVEN I CAN FIGURE OUT THAT IT'S ALL A HOUSE OF CARDS! WHEN THE SUB-PRIMES START TO DEFAULT—
AH, YES... THERE WILL BE INTERESTING TIMES TO COME—
—HOW LONG HAS HER SHOE BEEN MISSING?
WE'VE GOT A POSITIVE INFRARED READING FROM THE SURFACE! AT LEAST SIX INTRUDERS UP THERE!
THEY GOT HERE SOONER THAN I EXPECTED! TIME TO CUT OFF THEIR COMMUNICATIONS...

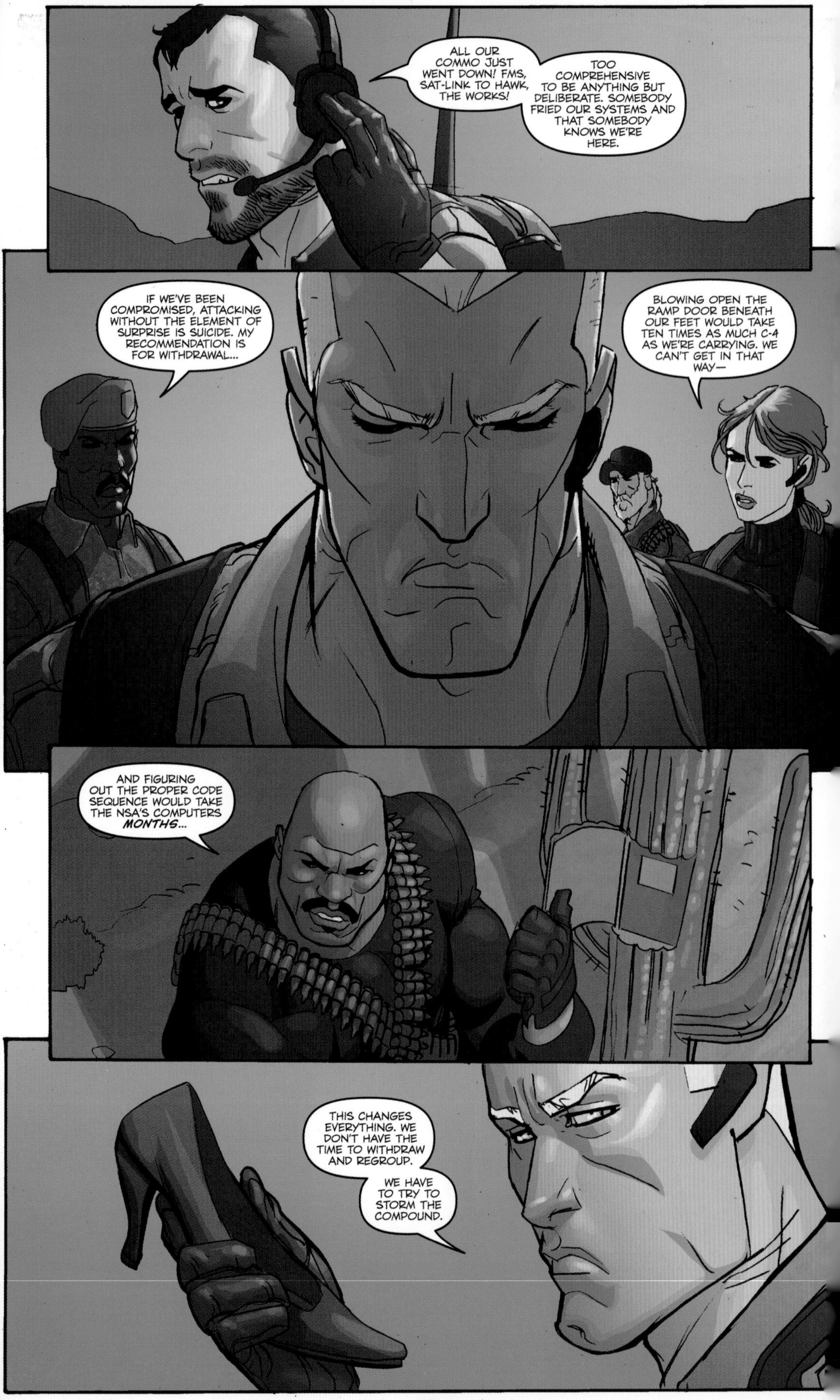
ALL OUR COMMO JUST WENT DOWN! FMS, SAT-LINK TO HAWK, THE WORKS!
TOO COMPREHENSIVE TO BE ANYTHING BUT DELIBERATE. SOMEBODY FRIED OUR SYSTEMS AND THAT SOMEBODY KNOWS WE'RE HERE.
IF WE'VE BEEN COMPROMISED, ATTACKING WITHOUT THE ELEMENT OF SURPRISE IS SUICIDE. MY RECOMMENDATION IS FOR WITHDRAWAL...
BLOWING OPEN THE RAMP DOOR BENEATH OUR FEET WOULD TAKE TEN TIMES AS MUCH C-4 AS WE'RE CARRYING. WE CAN'T GET IN THAT WAY—
AND FIGURING OUT THE PROPER CODE SEQUENCE WOULD TAKE THE NSA'S COMPUTERS ***MONTHS***...
THIS CHANGES EVERYTHING. WE DON'T HAVE THE TIME TO WITHDRAW AND REGROUP.
WE HAVE TO TRY TO STORM THE COMPOUND.

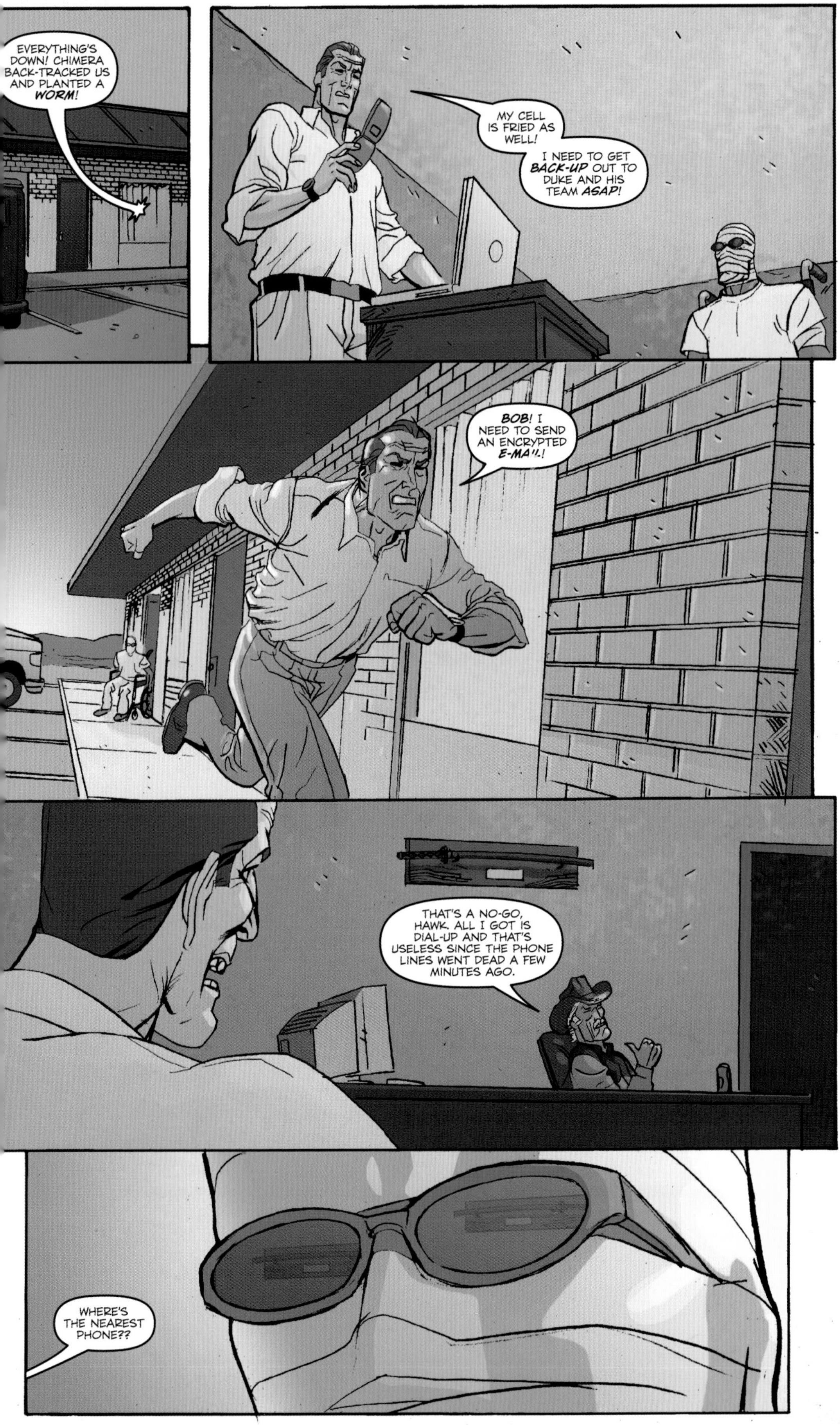
EVERYTHING'S DOWN! CHIMERA BACK-TRACKED US AND PLANTED A WORM!
MY CELL IS FRIED AS WELL!
I NEED TO GET BACK-UP OUT TO DUKE AND HIS TEAM ASAP!
BOB! I NEED TO SEND AN ENCRYPTED E-MAIL!
THAT'S A NO-GO, HAWK. ALL I GOT IS DIAL-UP AND THAT'S USELESS SINCE THE PHONE LINES WENT DEAD A FEW MINUTES AGO.
WHERE'S THE NEAREST PHONE??

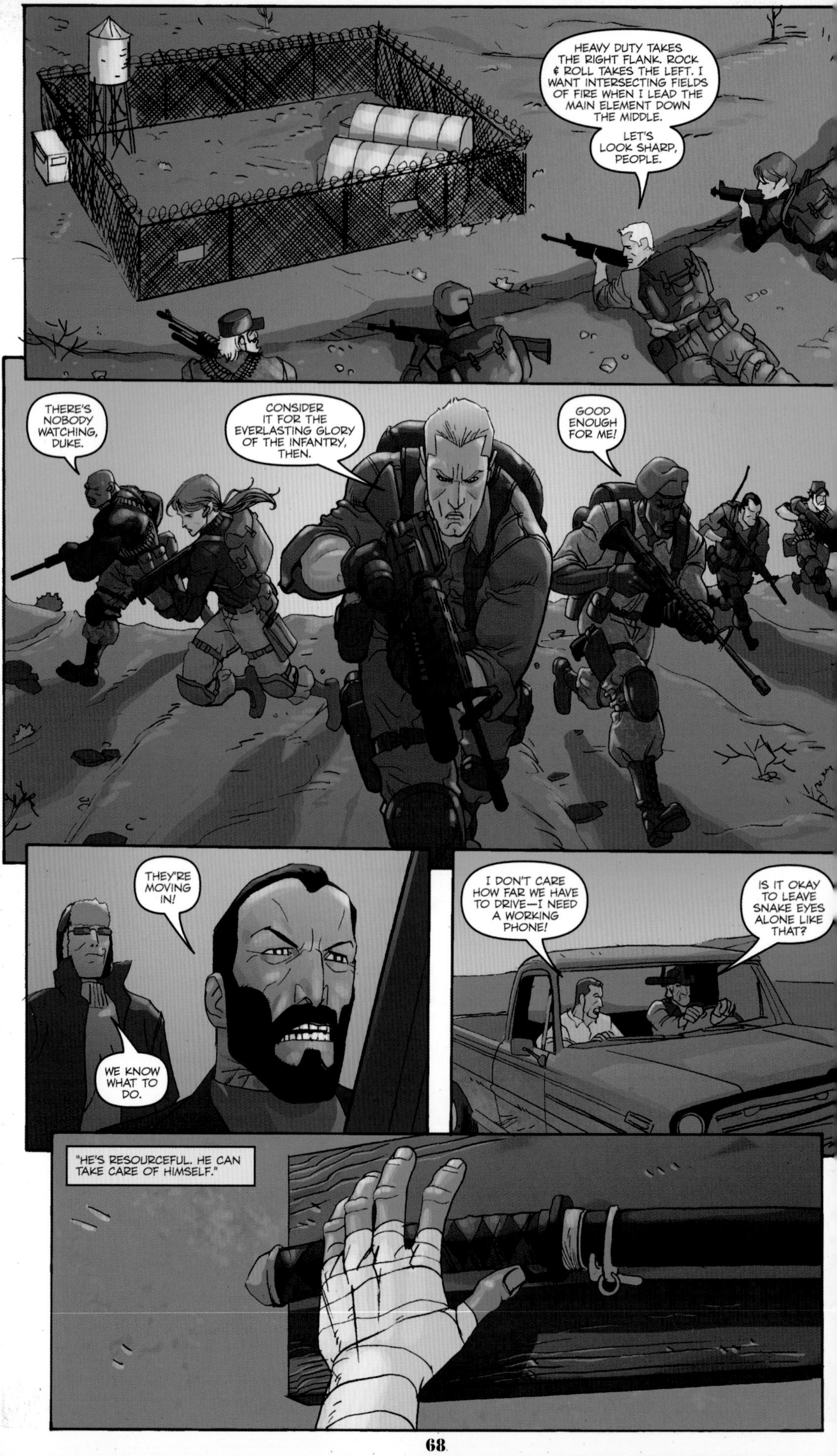
HEAVY DUTY TAKES THE RIGHT FLANK. ROCK & ROLL TAKES THE LEFT. I WANT INTERSECTING FIELDS OF FIRE WHEN I LEAD THE MAIN ELEMENT DOWN THE MIDDLE.
LET'S LOOK SHARP, PEOPLE.
THERE'S NOBODY WATCHING, DUKE.
CONSIDER IT FOR THE EVERLASTING GLORY OF THE INFANTRY, THEN.
GOOD ENOUGH FOR ME!
THEY'RE MOVING IN!
WE KNOW WHAT TO DO.
I DON'T CARE HOW FAR WE HAVE TO DRIVE—I NEED A WORKING PHONE!
IS IT OKAY TO LEAVE SNAKE EYES ALONE LIKE THAT?
"HE'S RESOURCEFUL. HE CAN TAKE CARE OF HIMSELF."

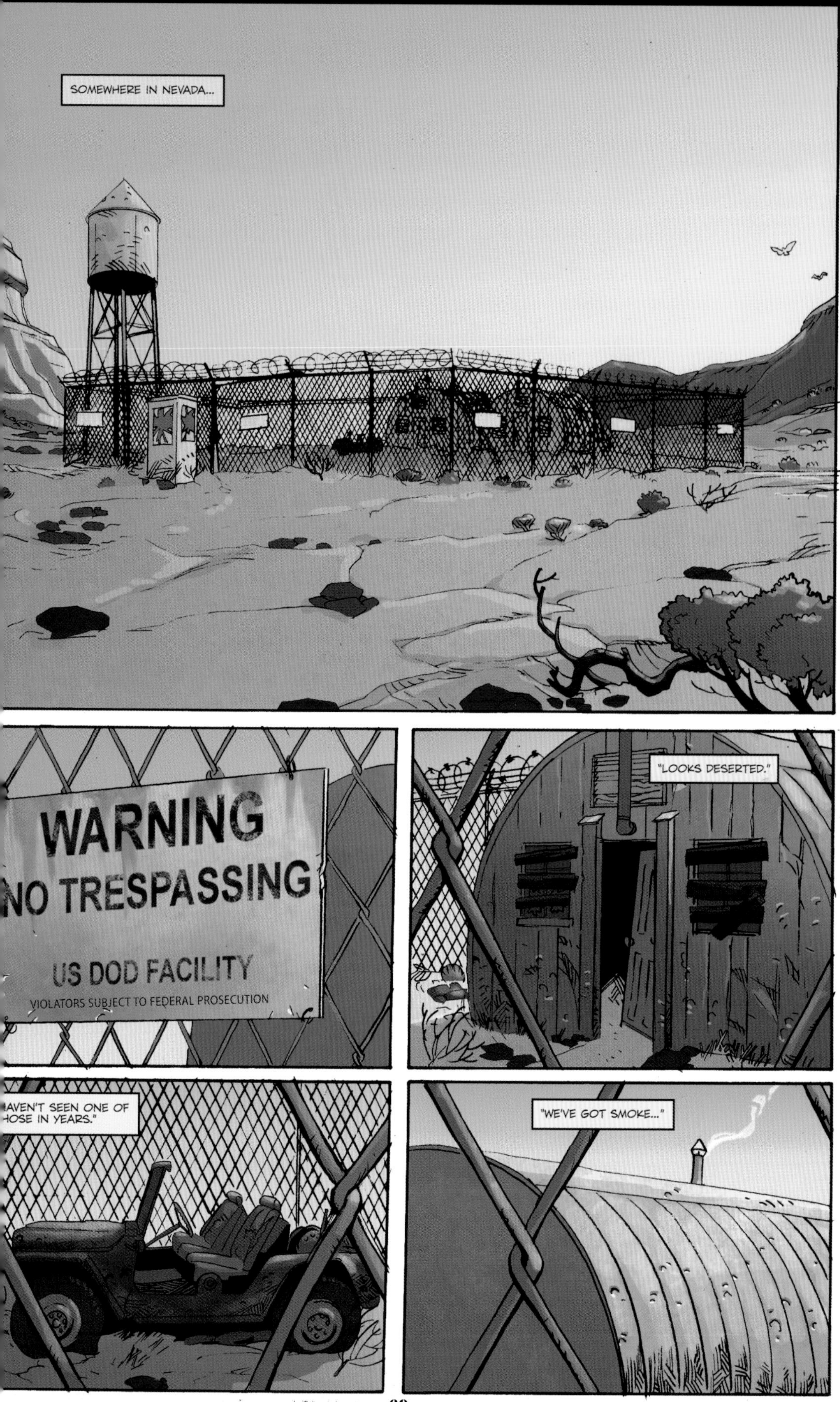
SOMEWHERE IN NEVADA...
WARNING
NO TRESPASSING
US DOD FACILITY
VIOLATORS SUBJECT TO FEDERAL PROSECUTION
"LOOKS DESERTED."
AVEN'T SEEN ONE OF
HOSE IN YEARS."
"WE'VE GOT SMOKE..."

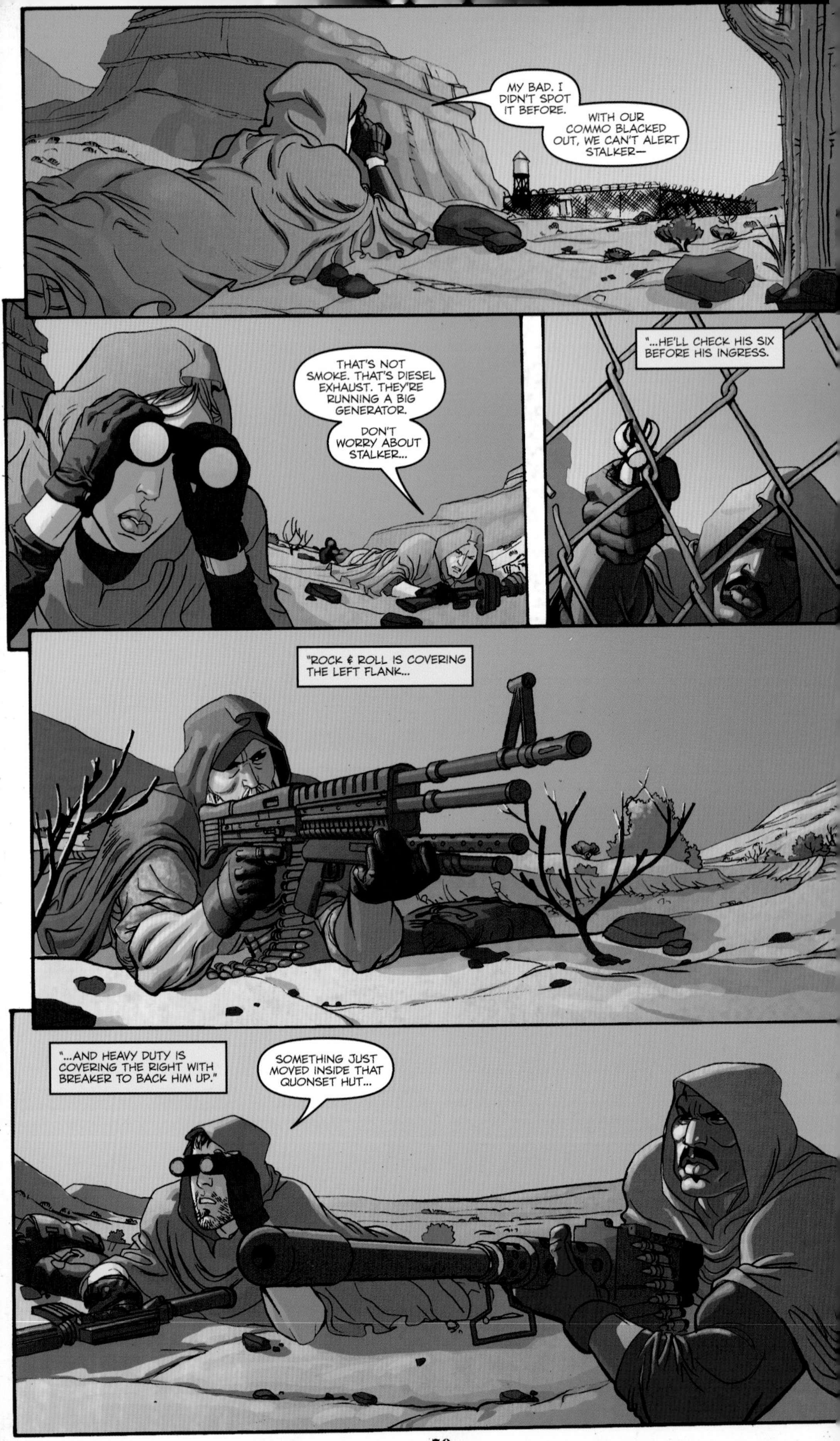
MY BAD. I DIDN'T SPOT IT BEFORE.
WITH OUR COMMO BLACKED OUT, WE CAN'T ALERT STALKER—
THAT'S NOT SMOKE. THAT'S DIESEL EXHAUST. THEY'RE RUNNING A BIG GENERATOR.
DON'T WORRY ABOUT STALKER...
"...HE'LL CHECK HIS SIX BEFORE HIS INGRESS.
"ROCK & ROLL IS COVERING THE LEFT FLANK...
"...AND HEAVY DUTY IS COVERING THE RIGHT WITH BREAKER TO BACK HIM UP."
SOMETHING JUST MOVED INSIDE THAT QUONSET HUT...

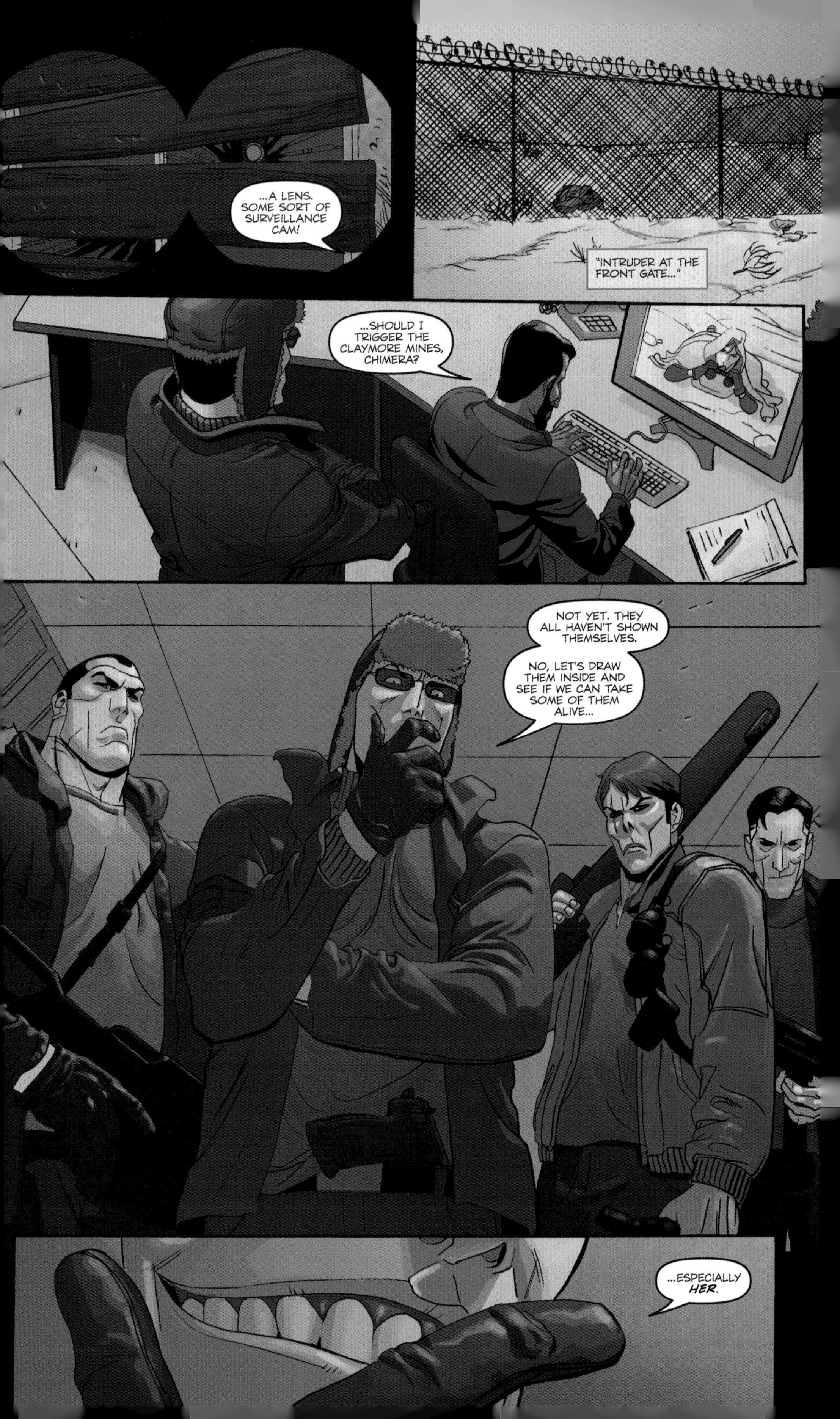
...A LENS. SOME SORT OF SURVEILLANCE CAM!
"INTRUDER AT THE FRONT GATE..."
...SHOULD I TRIGGER THE CLAYMORE MINES, CHIMERA?
NOT YET. THEY ALL HAVEN'T SHOWN THEMSELVES.
NO, LET'S DRAW THEM INSIDE AND SEE IF WE CAN TAKE SOME OF THEM ALIVE...
...ESPECIALLY *HER*.

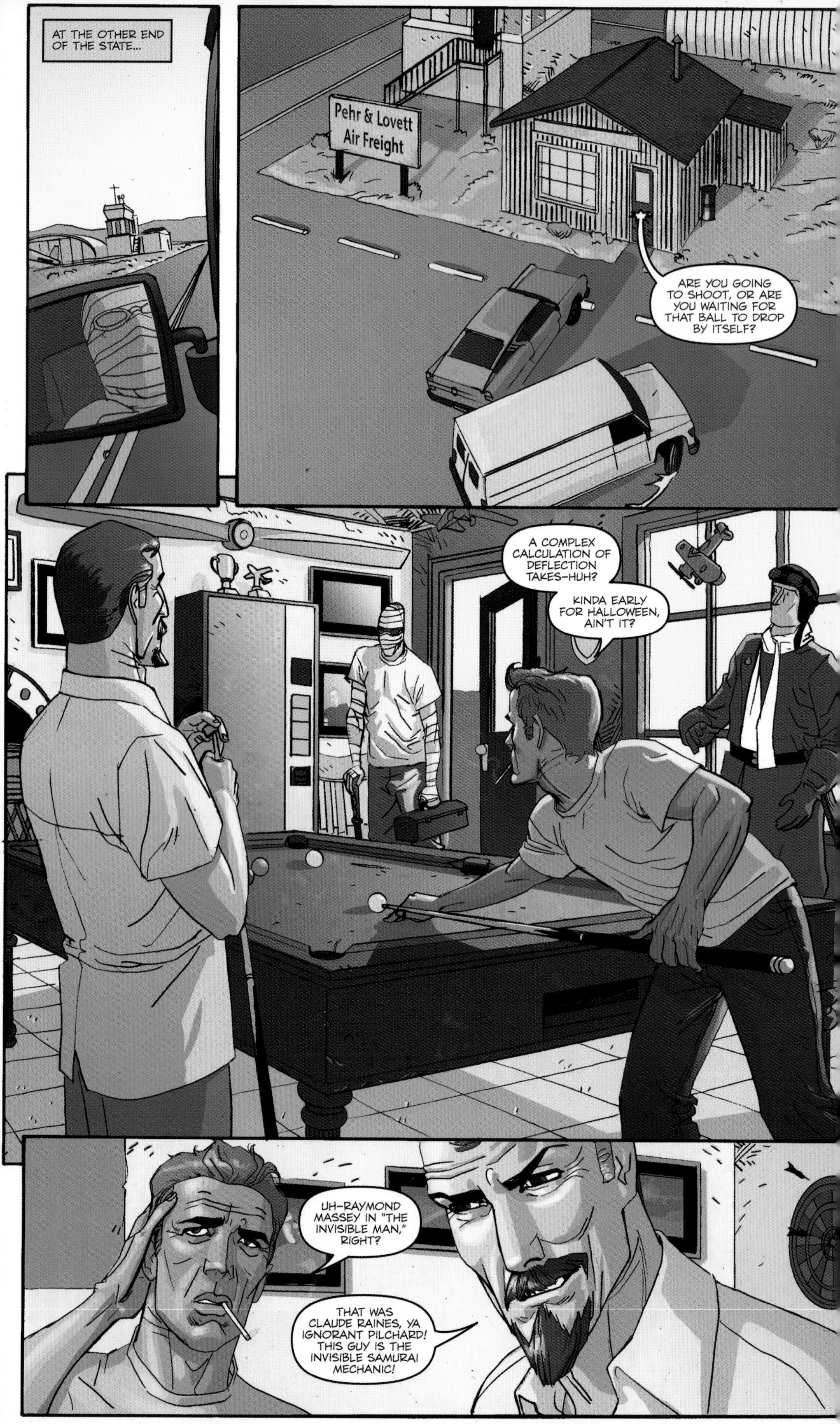
AT THE OTHER END OF THE STATE...
Pehr & Lovett Air Freight
ARE YOU GOING TO SHOOT, OR ARE YOU WAITING FOR THAT BALL TO DROP BY ITSELF?
A COMPLEX CALCULATION OF DEFLECTION TAKES–HUH?
KINDA EARLY FOR HALLOWEEN, AIN'T IT?
UH–RAYMOND MASSEY IN "THE INVISIBLE MAN," RIGHT?
THAT WAS CLAUDE RAINES, YA IGNORANT PILCHARD! THIS GUY IS THE INVISIBLE SAMURAI MECHANIC!

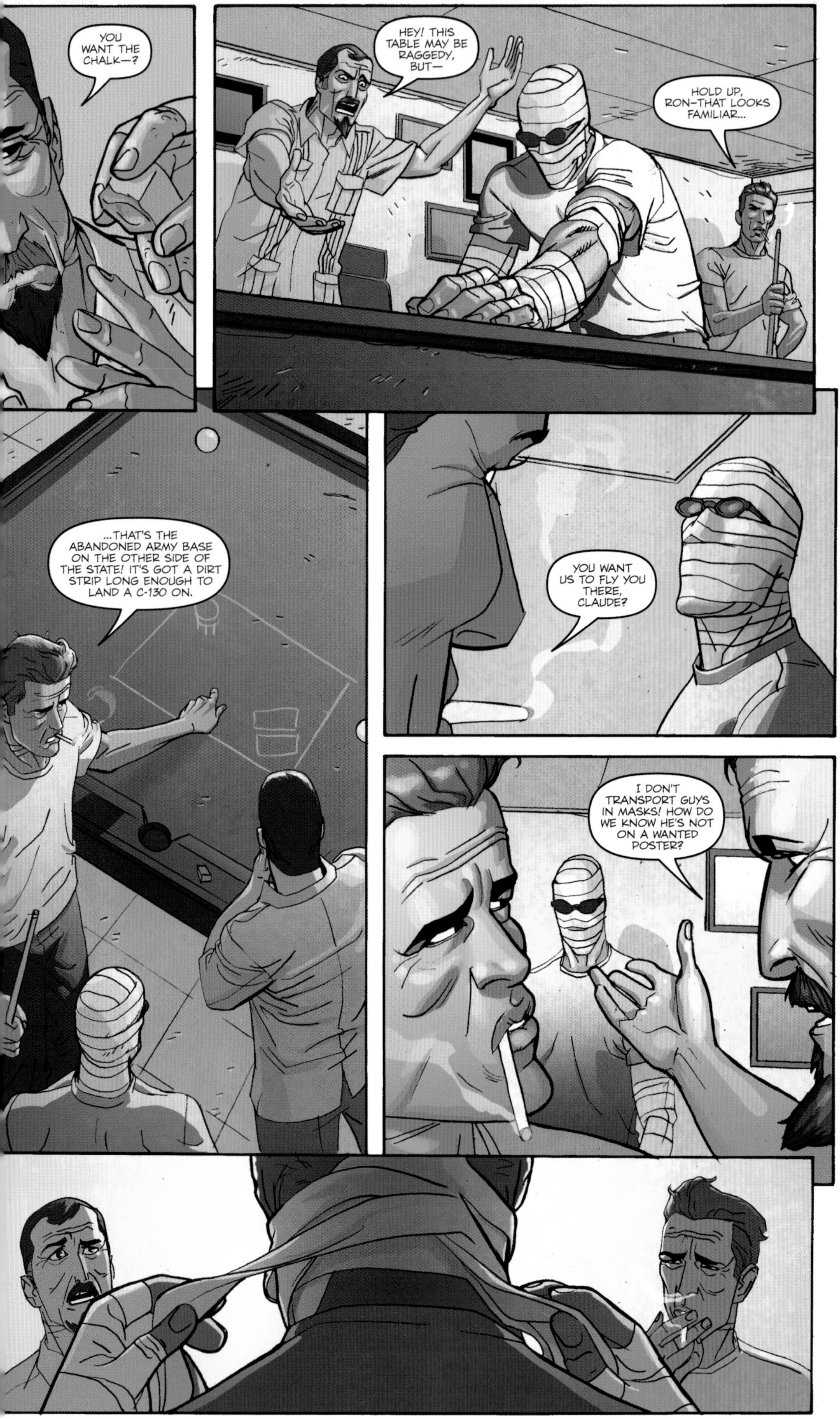
YOU WANT THE CHALK—?
HEY! THIS TABLE MAY BE RAGGEDY, BUT—
HOLD UP, RON—THAT LOOKS FAMILIAR...
...THAT'S THE ABANDONED ARMY BASE ON THE OTHER SIDE OF THE STATE! IT'S GOT A DIRT STRIP LONG ENOUGH TO LAND A C-130 ON.
YOU WANT US TO FLY YOU THERE, CLAUDE?
I DON'T TRANSPORT GUYS IN MASKS! HOW DO WE KNOW HE'S NOT ON A WANTED POSTER?

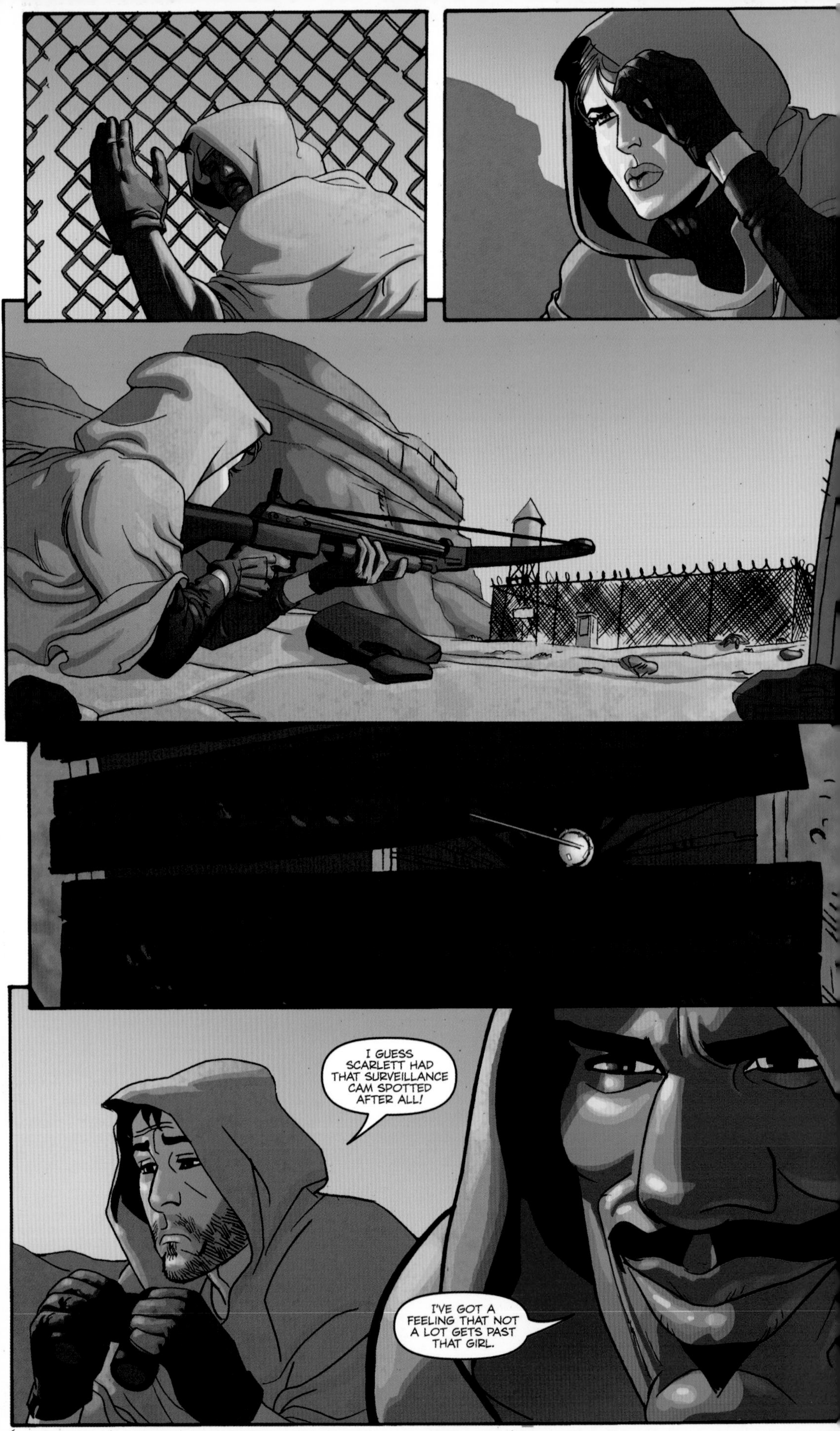
I GUESS SCARLETT HAD THAT SURVEILLANCE CAM SPOTTED AFTER ALL!
I'VE GOT A FEELING THAT NOT A LOT GETS PAST THAT GIRL.

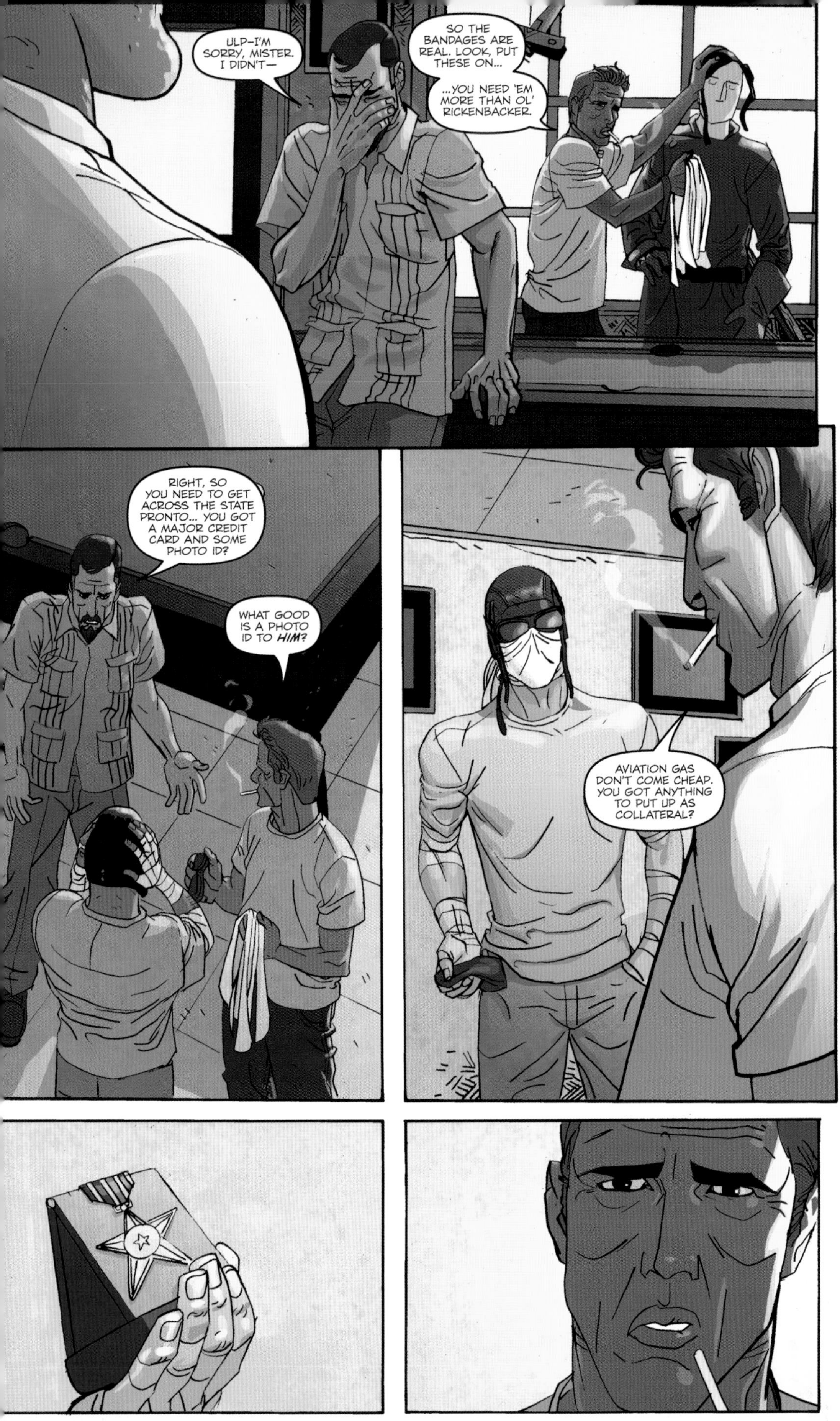
ULP—I'M SORRY, MISTER. I DIDN'T—
SO THE BANDAGES ARE REAL. LOOK, PUT THESE ON...
...YOU NEED 'EM MORE THAN OL' RICKENBACKER.
RIGHT, SO YOU NEED TO GET ACROSS THE STATE PRONTO... YOU GOT A MAJOR CREDIT CARD AND SOME PHOTO ID?
WHAT GOOD IS A PHOTO ID TO *HIM*?
AVIATION GAS DON'T COME CHEAP. YOU GOT ANYTHING TO PUT UP AS COLLATERAL?

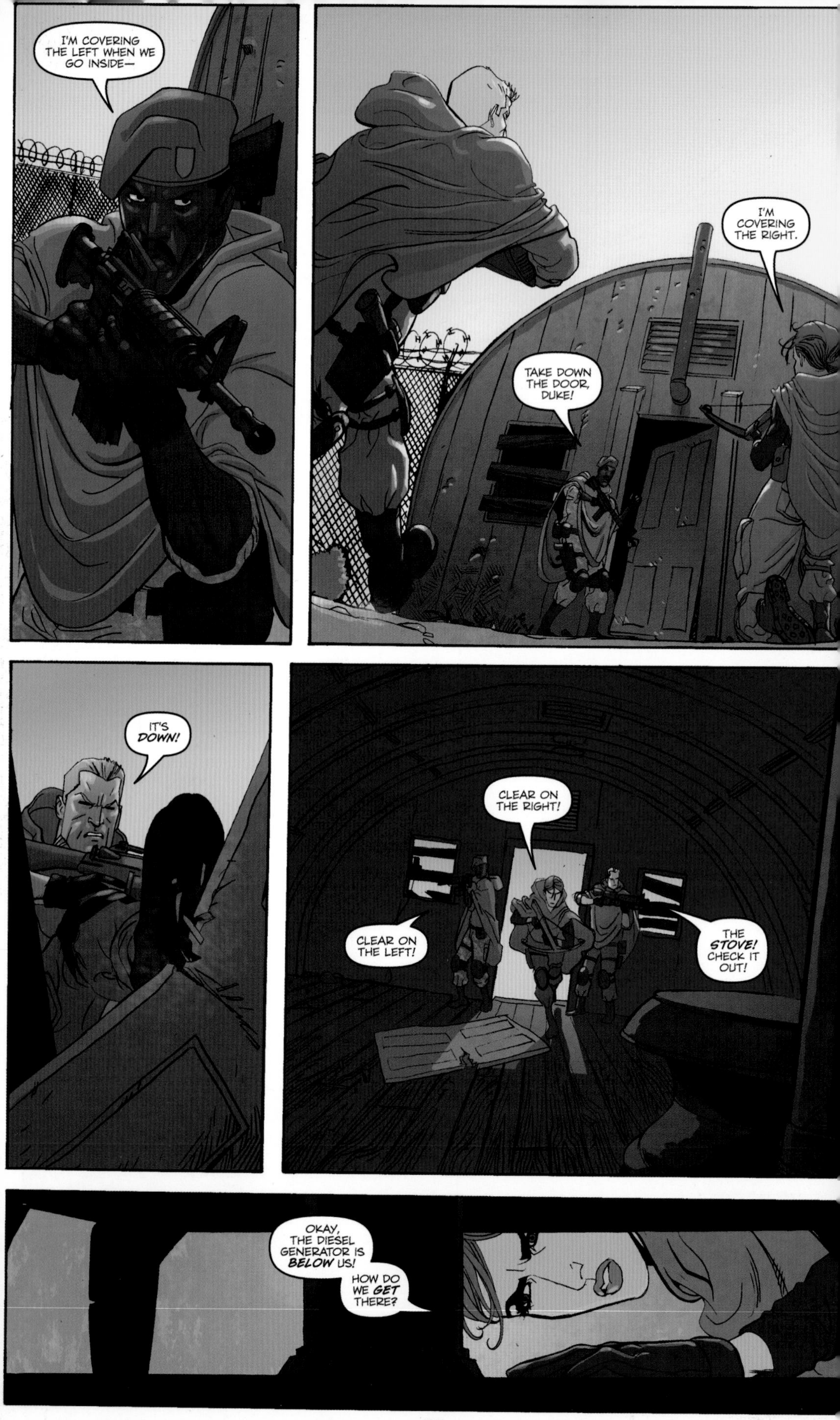
I'M COVERING THE LEFT WHEN WE GO INSIDE—
I'M COVERING THE RIGHT.
TAKE DOWN THE DOOR, DUKE!
IT'S DOWN!
CLEAR ON THE RIGHT!
CLEAR ON THE LEFT!
THE STOVE! CHECK IT OUT!
OKAY, THE DIESEL GENERATOR IS BELOW US!
HOW DO WE GET THERE?

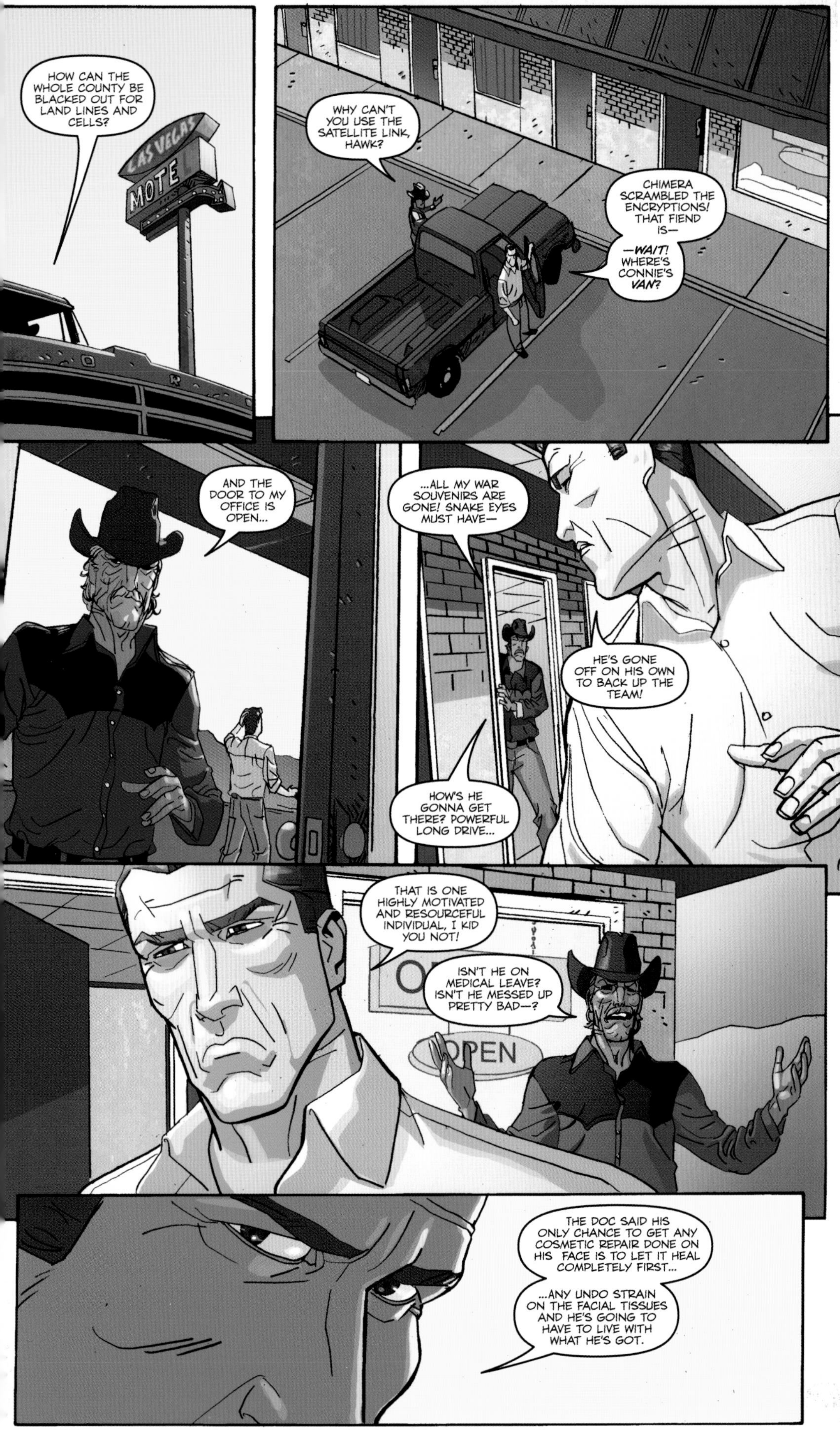
HOW CAN THE WHOLE COUNTY BE BLACKED OUT FOR LAND LINES AND CELLS?
LAS VEGAS
MOTE
WHY CAN'T YOU USE THE SATELLITE LINK, HAWK?
CHIMERA SCRAMBLED THE ENCRYPTIONS! THAT FIEND IS—
—*WAIT!* WHERE'S CONNIE'S *VAN?*
AND THE DOOR TO MY OFFICE IS OPEN...
...ALL MY WAR SOUVENIRS ARE GONE! SNAKE EYES MUST HAVE—
HE'S GONE OFF ON HIS OWN TO BACK UP THE TEAM!
HOW'S HE GONNA GET THERE? POWERFUL LONG DRIVE...
THAT IS ONE HIGHLY MOTIVATED AND RESOURCEFUL INDIVIDUAL, I KID YOU NOT!
ISN'T HE ON MEDICAL LEAVE? ISN'T HE MESSED UP PRETTY BAD—?
OPEN
THE DOC SAID HIS ONLY CHANCE TO GET ANY COSMETIC REPAIR DONE ON HIS FACE IS TO LET IT HEAL COMPLETELY FIRST...
...ANY UNDO STRAIN ON THE FACIAL TISSUES AND HE'S GOING TO HAVE TO LIVE WITH WHAT HE'S GOT.

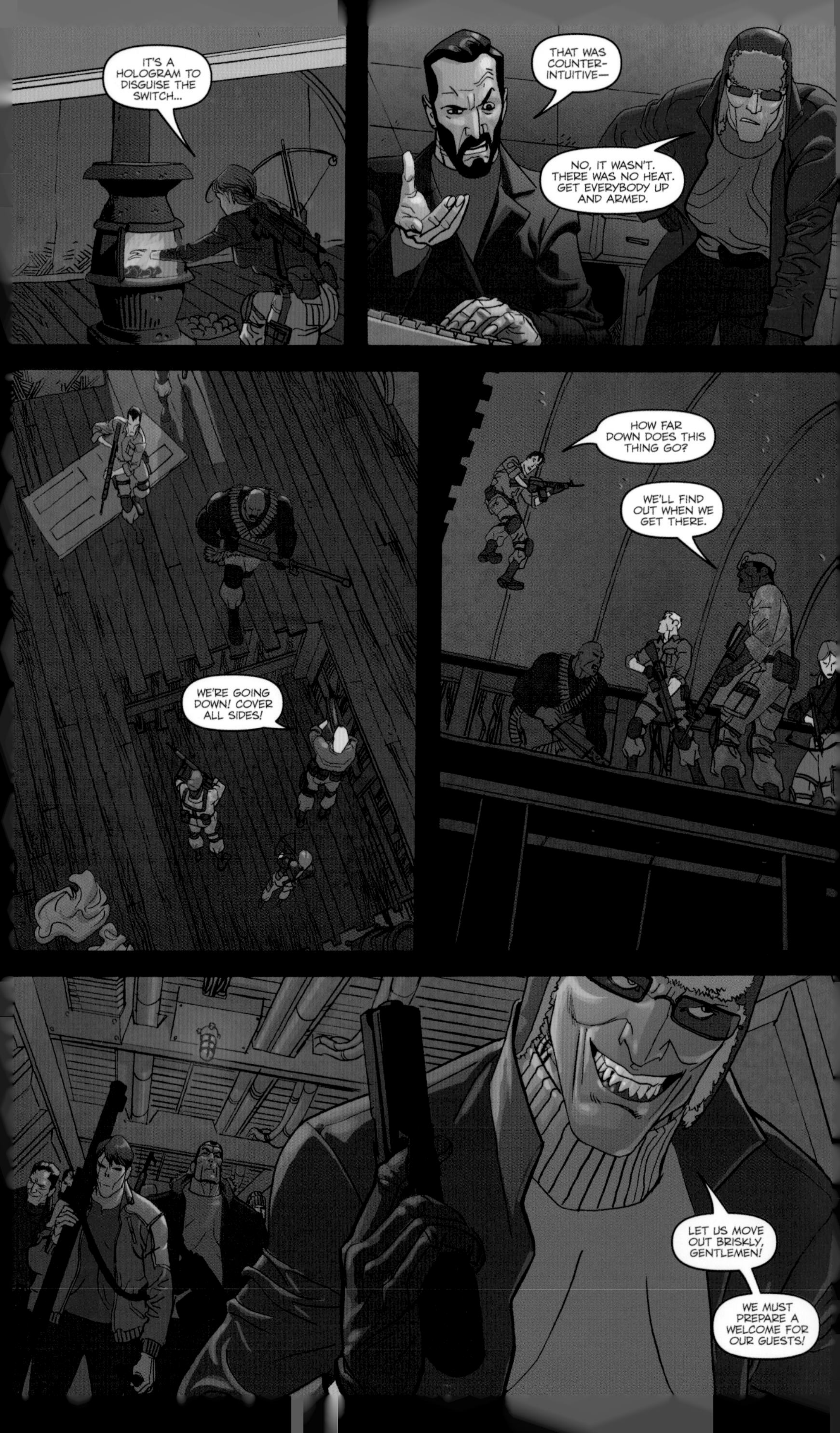
IT'S A HOLOGRAM TO DISGUISE THE SWITCH...
THAT WAS COUNTER-INTUITIVE—
NO, IT WASN'T. THERE WAS NO HEAT. GET EVERYBODY UP AND ARMED.
WE'RE GOING DOWN! COVER ALL SIDES!
HOW FAR DOWN DOES THIS THING GO?
WE'LL FIND OUT WHEN WE GET THERE.
LET US MOVE OUT BRISKLY, GENTLEMEN!
WE MUST PREPARE A WELCOME FOR OUR GUESTS!

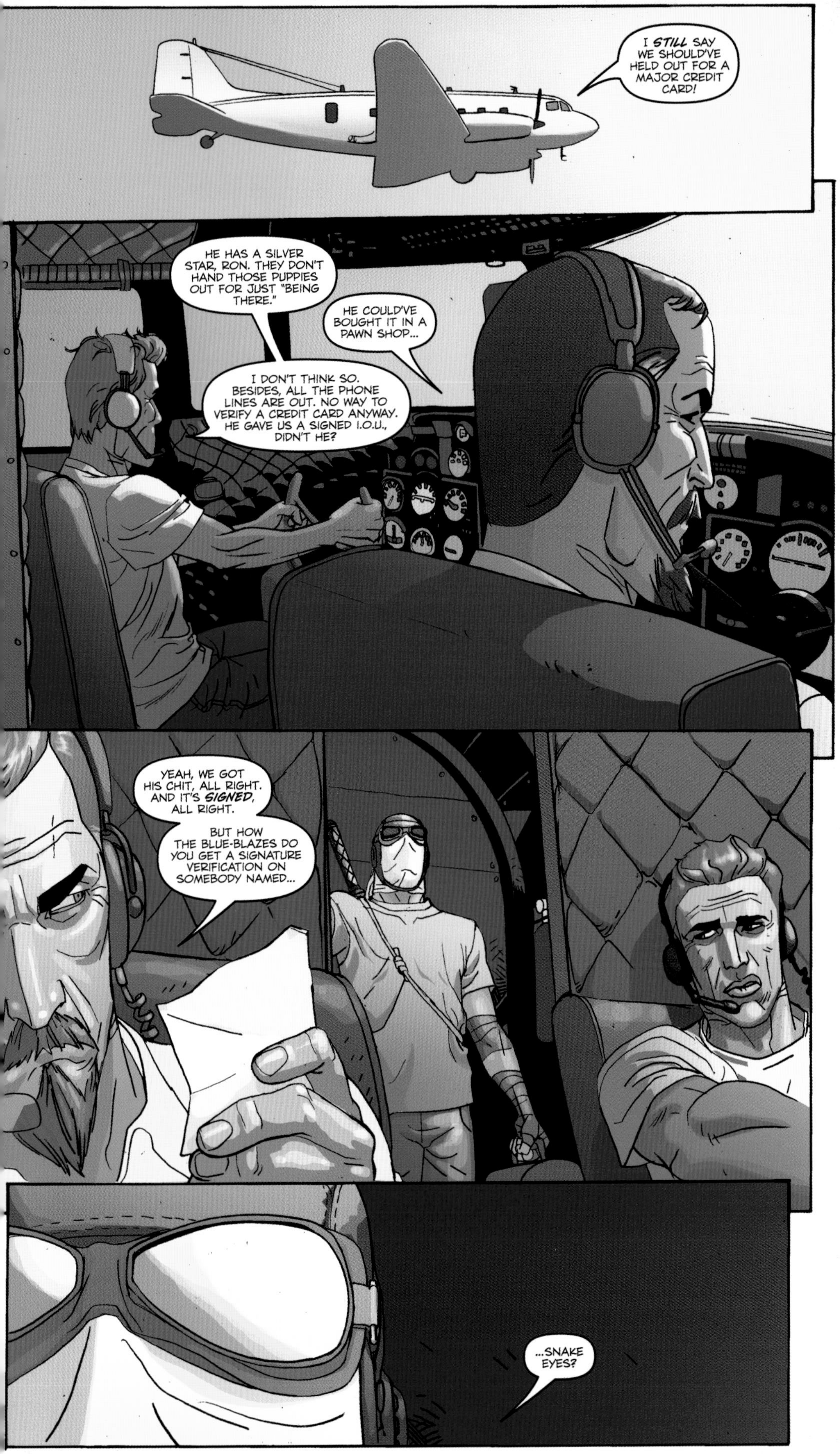
I STILL SAY WE SHOULD'VE HELD OUT FOR A MAJOR CREDIT CARD!
HE HAS A SILVER STAR, RON. THEY DON'T HAND THOSE PUPPIES OUT FOR JUST "BEING THERE."
HE COULD'VE BOUGHT IT IN A PAWN SHOP...
I DON'T THINK SO. BESIDES, ALL THE PHONE LINES ARE OUT. NO WAY TO VERIFY A CREDIT CARD ANYWAY. HE GAVE US A SIGNED I.O.U., DIDN'T HE?
YEAH, WE GOT HIS CHIT, ALL RIGHT. AND IT'S SIGNED, ALL RIGHT.
BUT HOW THE BLUE-BLAZES DO YOU GET A SIGNATURE VERIFICATION ON SOMEBODY NAMED...
...SNAKE EYES?

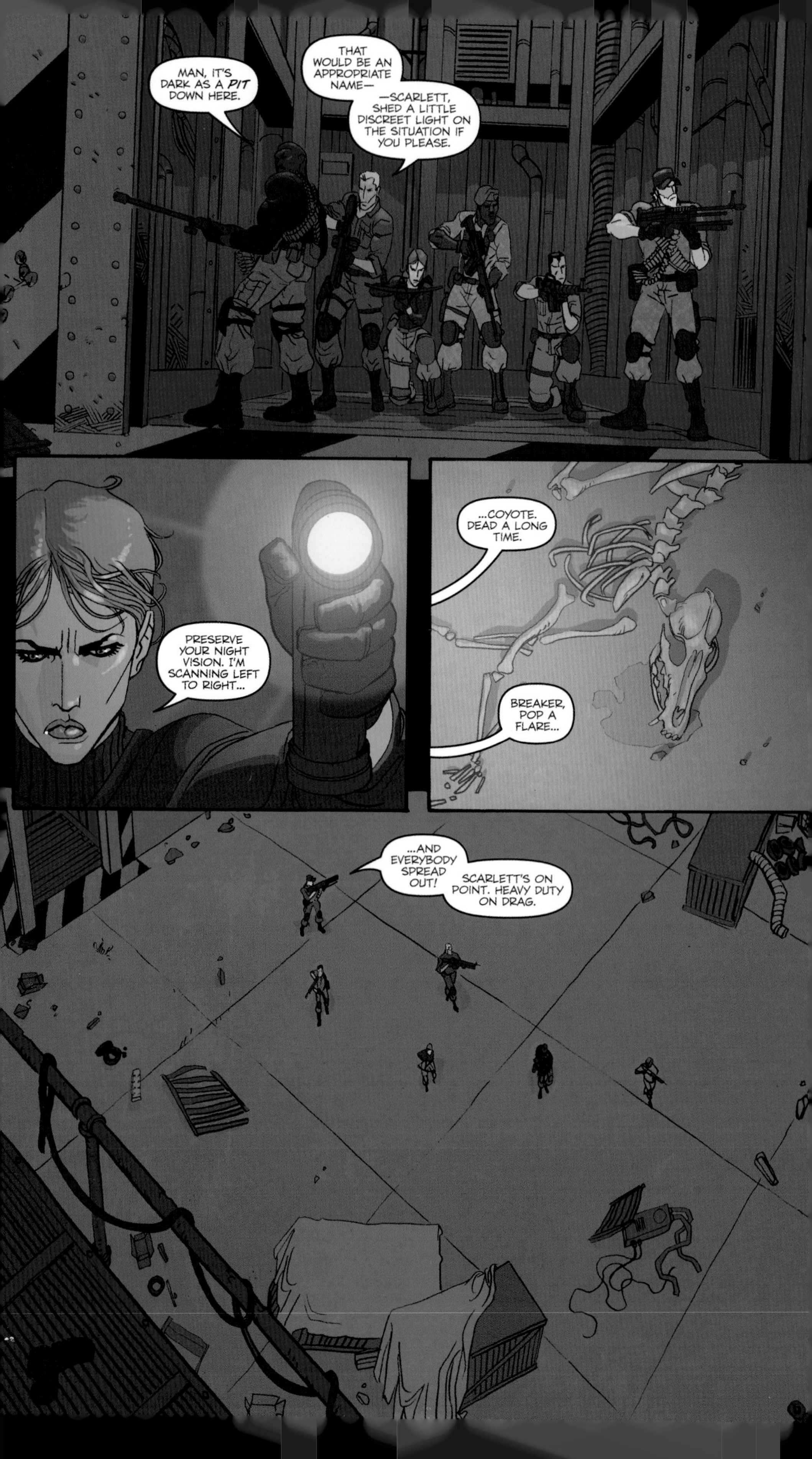
MAN, IT'S DARK AS A *PIT* DOWN HERE.
THAT WOULD BE AN APPROPRIATE NAME—
—SCARLETT, SHED A LITTLE DISCREET LIGHT ON THE SITUATION IF YOU PLEASE.
PRESERVE YOUR NIGHT VISION. I'M SCANNING LEFT TO RIGHT...
...COYOTE. DEAD A LONG TIME.
BREAKER, POP A FLARE...
...AND EVERYBODY SPREAD OUT!
SCARLETT'S ON POINT. HEAVY DUTY ON DRAG.

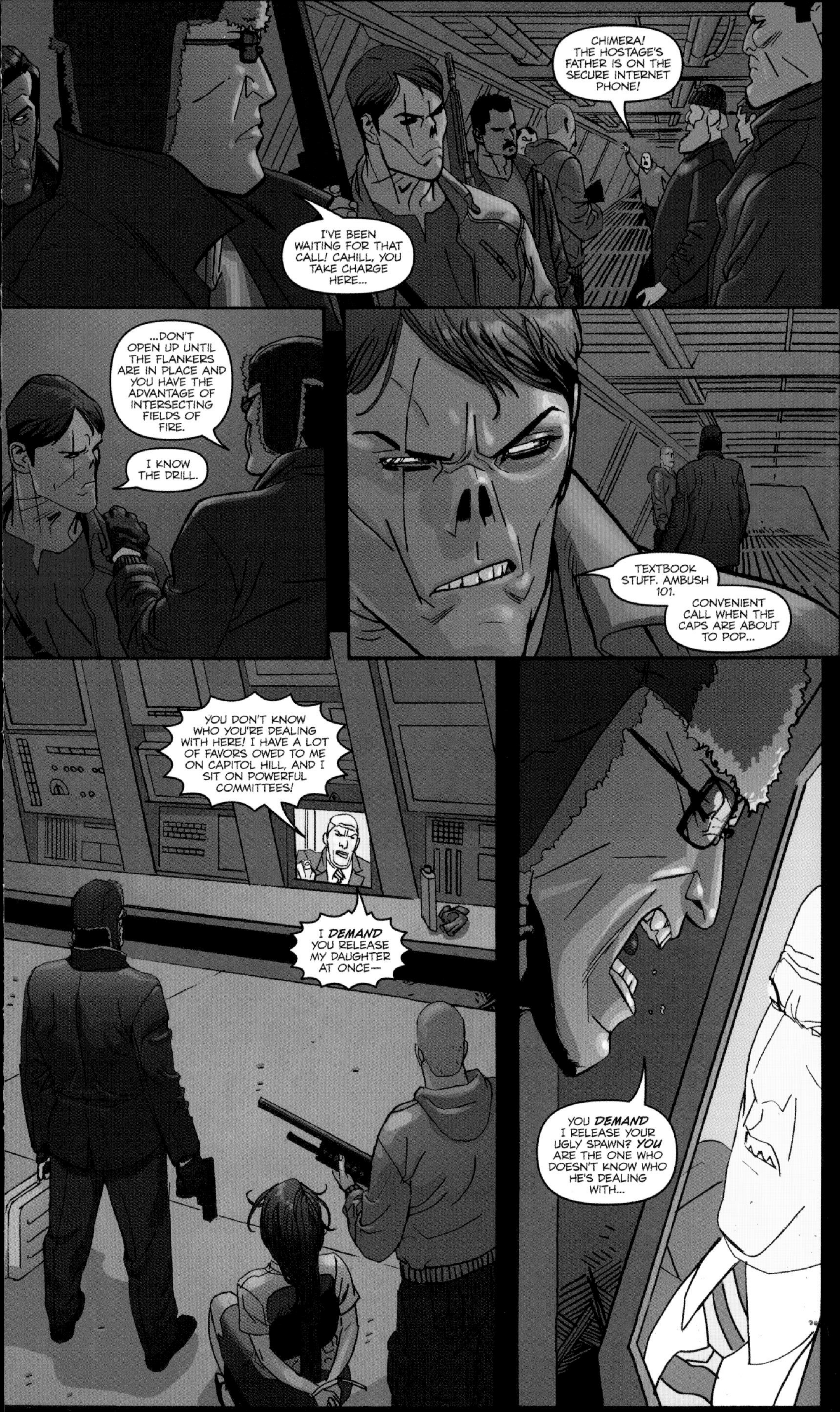
CHIMERA! THE HOSTAGE'S FATHER IS ON THE SECURE INTERNET PHONE!
I'VE BEEN WAITING FOR THAT CALL! CAHILL, YOU TAKE CHARGE HERE...
...DON'T OPEN UP UNTIL THE FLANKERS ARE IN PLACE AND YOU HAVE THE ADVANTAGE OF INTERSECTING FIELDS OF FIRE.
I KNOW THE DRILL.
TEXTBOOK STUFF. AMBUSH 101.
CONVENIENT CALL WHEN THE CAPS ARE ABOUT TO POP...
YOU DON'T KNOW WHO YOU'RE DEALING WITH HERE! I HAVE A LOT OF FAVORS OWED TO ME ON CAPITOL HILL, AND I SIT ON POWERFUL COMMITTEES!
I *DEMAND* YOU RELEASE MY DAUGHTER AT ONCE—
YOU *DEMAND* I RELEASE YOUR UGLY SPAWN? *YOU* ARE THE ONE WHO DOESN'T KNOW WHO HE'S DEALING WITH...

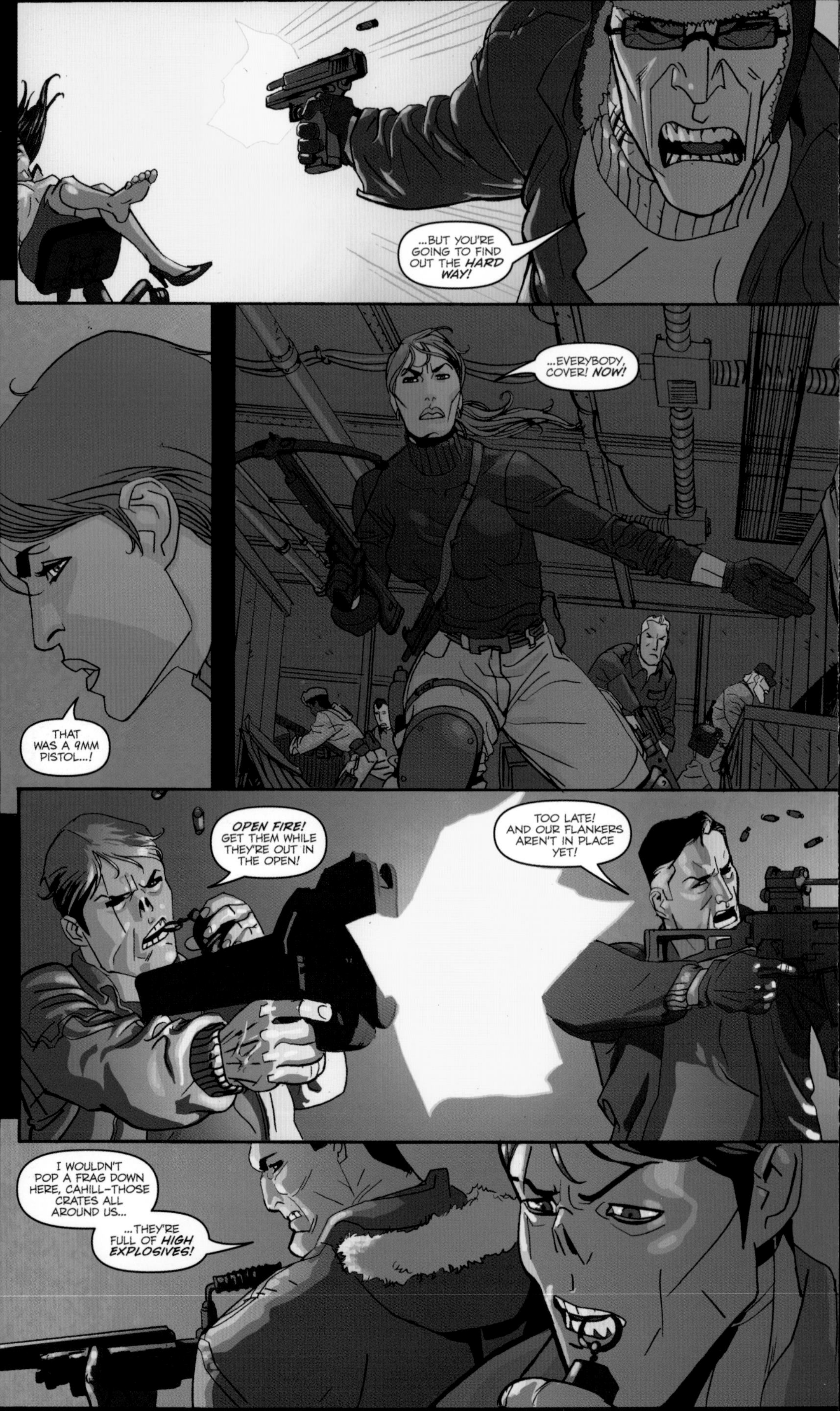
...BUT YOU'RE GOING TO FIND OUT THE *HARD WAY!*
THAT WAS A 9MM PISTOL...!
...EVERYBODY, COVER! *NOW!*
OPEN FIRE! GET THEM WHILE THEY'RE OUT IN THE OPEN!
TOO LATE! AND OUR FLANKERS AREN'T IN PLACE YET!
I WOULDN'T POP A FRAG DOWN HERE, CAHILL-THOSE CRATES ALL AROUND US...
...THEY'RE FULL OF *HIGH EXPLOSIVES!*

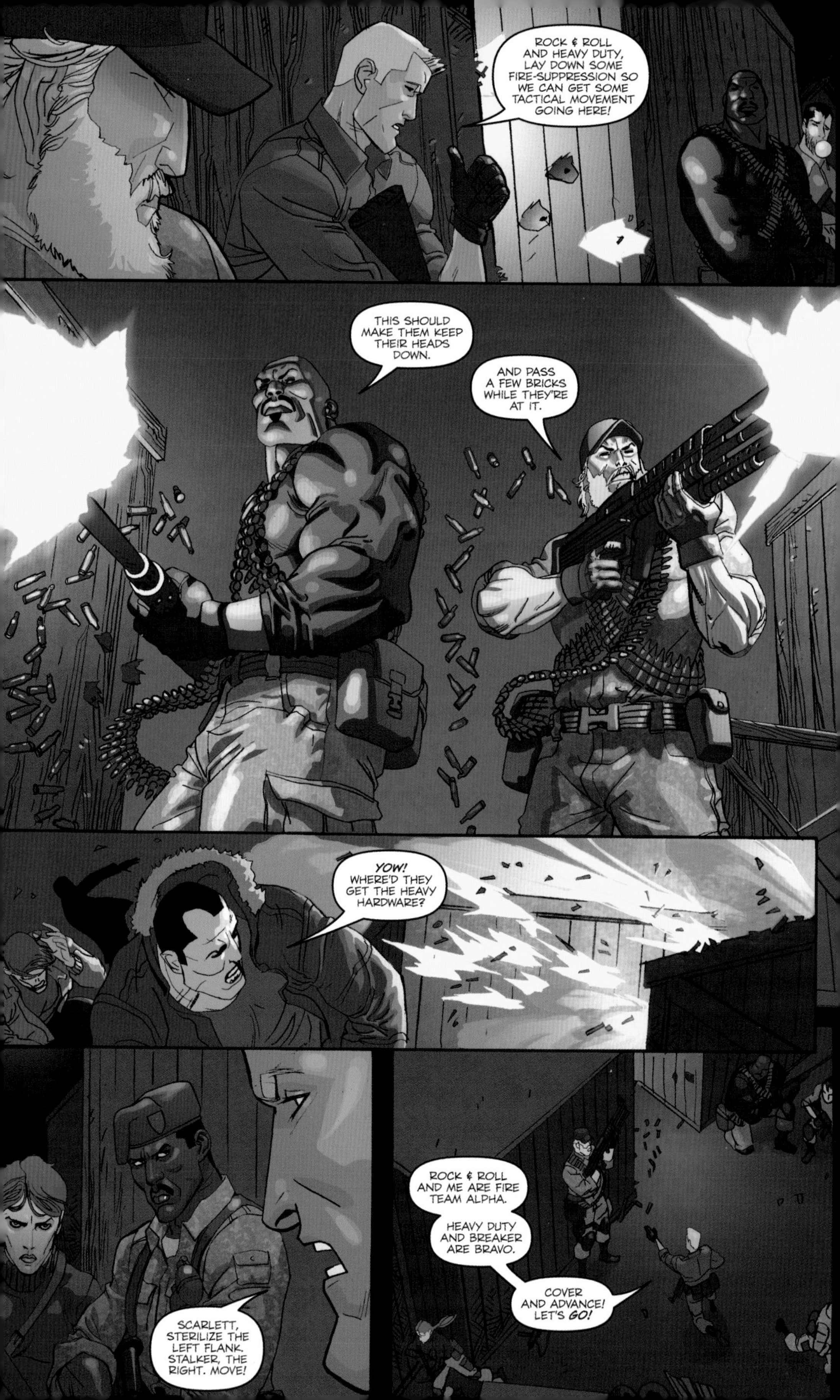
ROCK & ROLL AND HEAVY DUTY, LAY DOWN SOME FIRE-SUPPRESSION SO WE CAN GET SOME TACTICAL MOVEMENT GOING HERE!
THIS SHOULD MAKE THEM KEEP THEIR HEADS DOWN.
AND PASS A FEW BRICKS WHILE THEY'RE AT IT.
YOW! WHERE'D THEY GET THE HEAVY HARDWARE?
SCARLETT, STERILIZE THE LEFT FLANK. STALKER, THE RIGHT. MOVE!
ROCK & ROLL AND ME ARE FIRE TEAM ALPHA.
HEAVY DUTY AND BREAKER ARE BRAVO.
COVER AND ADVANCE! LET'S GO!

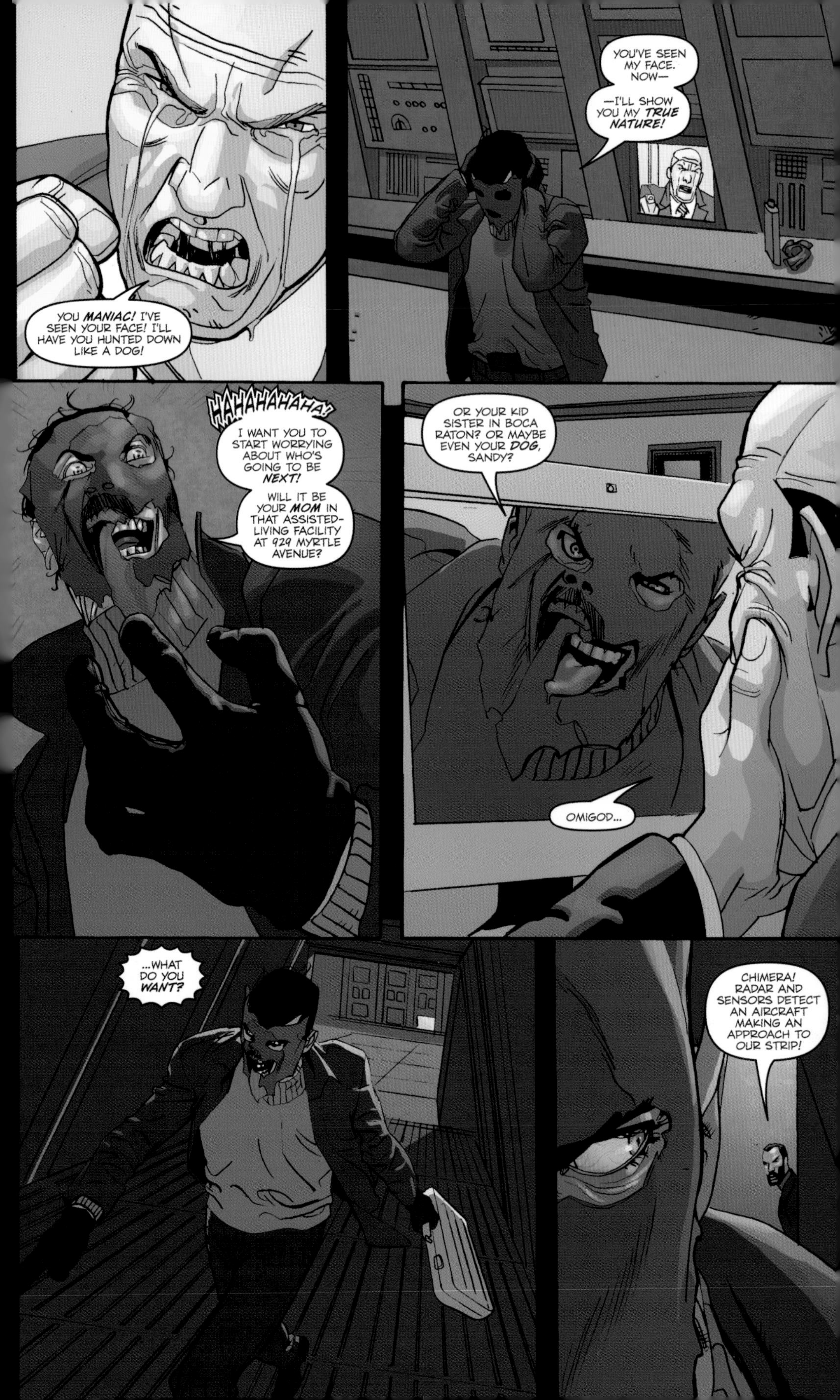
YOU MANIAC! I'VE SEEN YOUR FACE! I'LL HAVE YOU HUNTED DOWN LIKE A DOG!
YOU'VE SEEN MY FACE. NOW—
—I'LL SHOW YOU MY TRUE NATURE!
HAHAHAHAHA!
I WANT YOU TO START WORRYING ABOUT WHO'S GOING TO BE NEXT!
WILL IT BE YOUR MOM IN THAT ASSISTED-LIVING FACILITY AT 929 MYRTLE AVENUE?
OR YOUR KID SISTER IN BOCA RATON? OR MAYBE EVEN YOUR DOG, SANDY?
OMIGOD...
...WHAT DO YOU WANT?
CHIMERA! RADAR AND SENSORS DETECT AN AIRCRAFT MAKING AN APPROACH TO OUR STRIP!

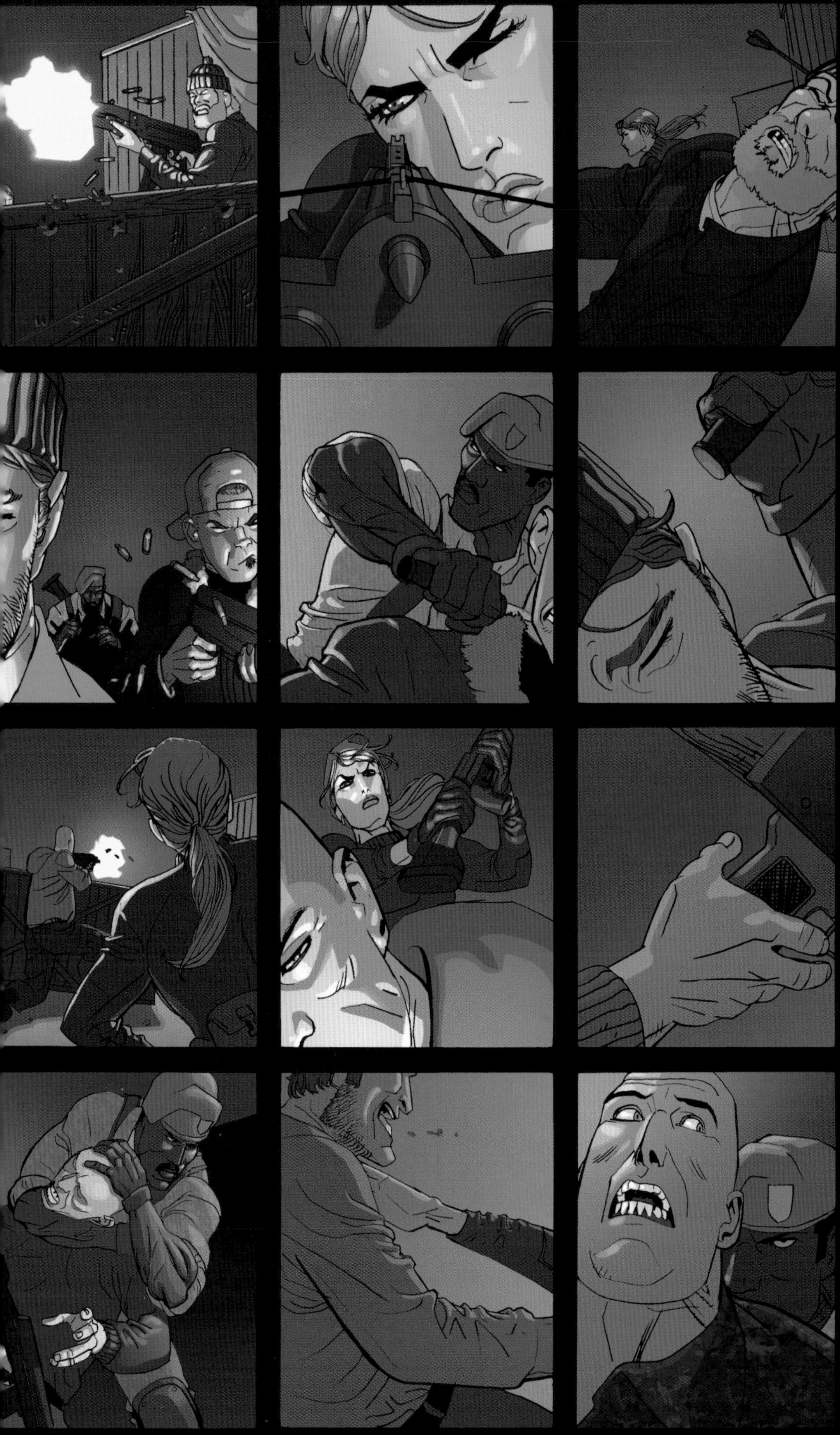

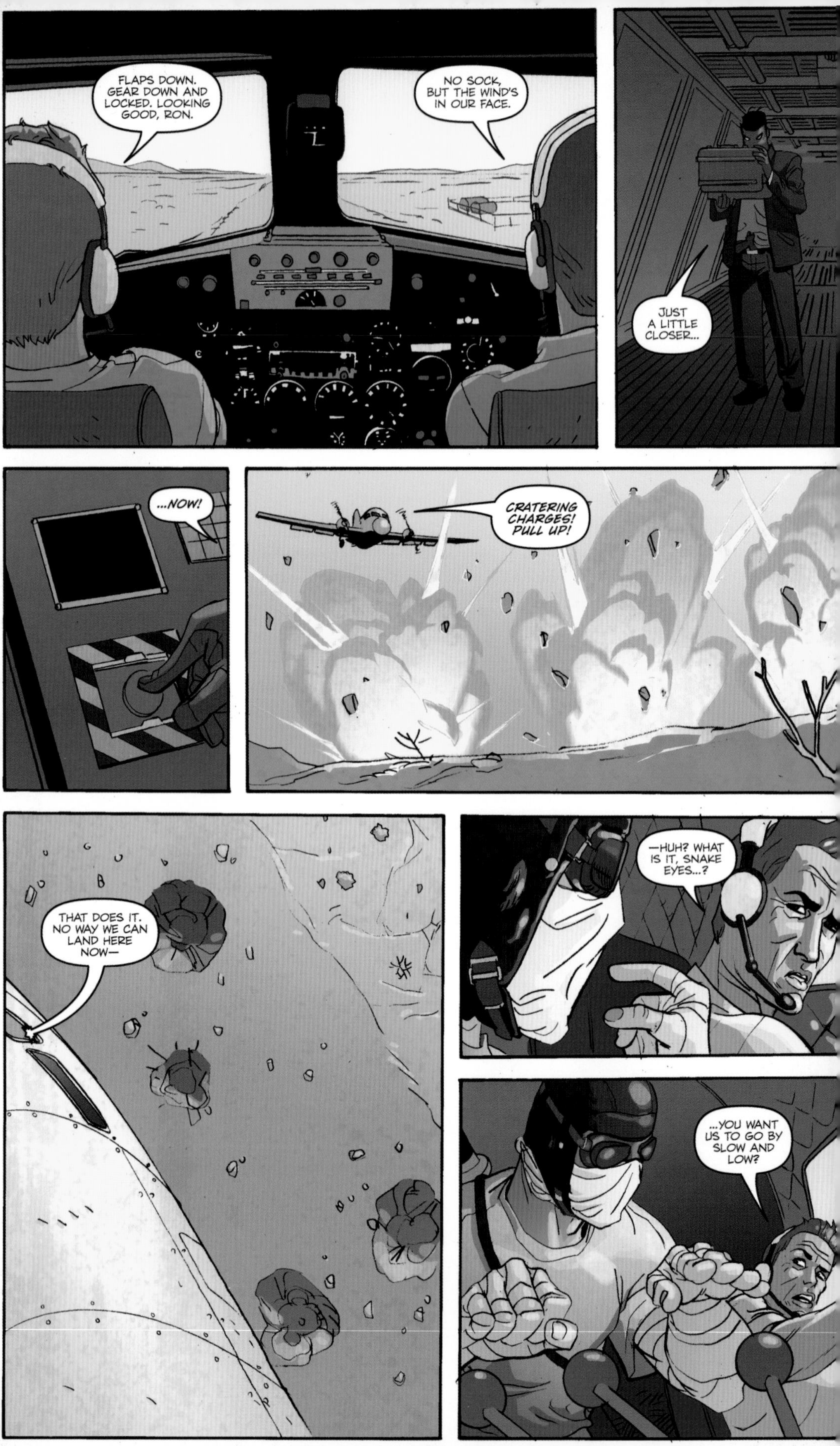
FLAPS DOWN. GEAR DOWN AND LOCKED. LOOKING GOOD, RON.
NO SOCK, BUT THE WIND'S IN OUR FACE.
JUST A LITTLE CLOSER...
...NOW!
CRATERING CHARGES! PULL UP!
THAT DOES IT. NO WAY WE CAN LAND HERE NOW—
—HUH? WHAT IS IT, SNAKE EYES...?
...YOU WANT US TO GO BY SLOW AND LOW?

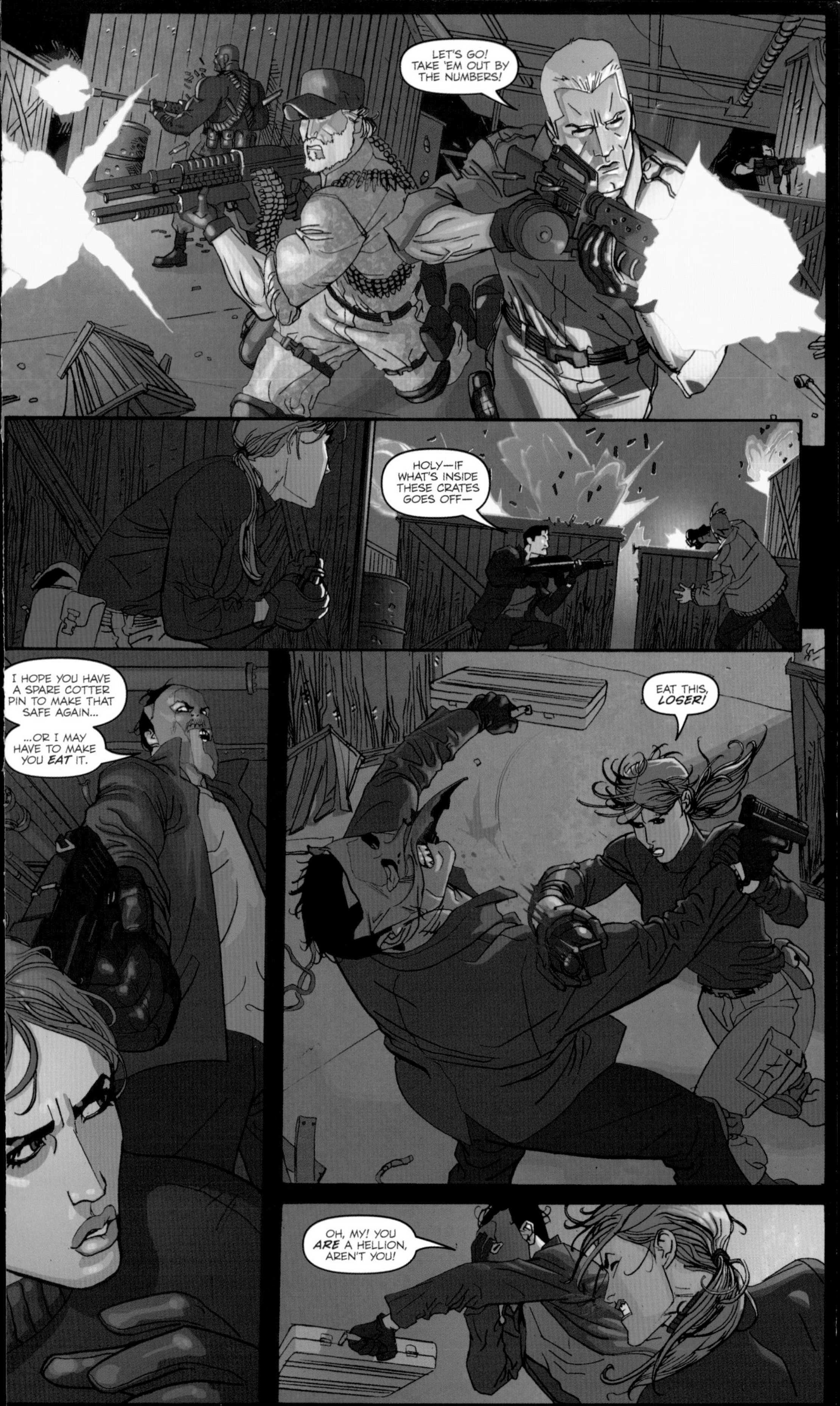
LET'S GO! TAKE 'EM OUT BY THE NUMBERS!
HOLY—IF WHAT'S INSIDE THESE CRATES GOES OFF—
I HOPE YOU HAVE A SPARE COTTER PIN TO MAKE THAT SAFE AGAIN...
...OR I MAY HAVE TO MAKE YOU EAT IT.
EAT THIS, LOSER!
OH, MY! YOU ARE A HELLION, AREN'T YOU!

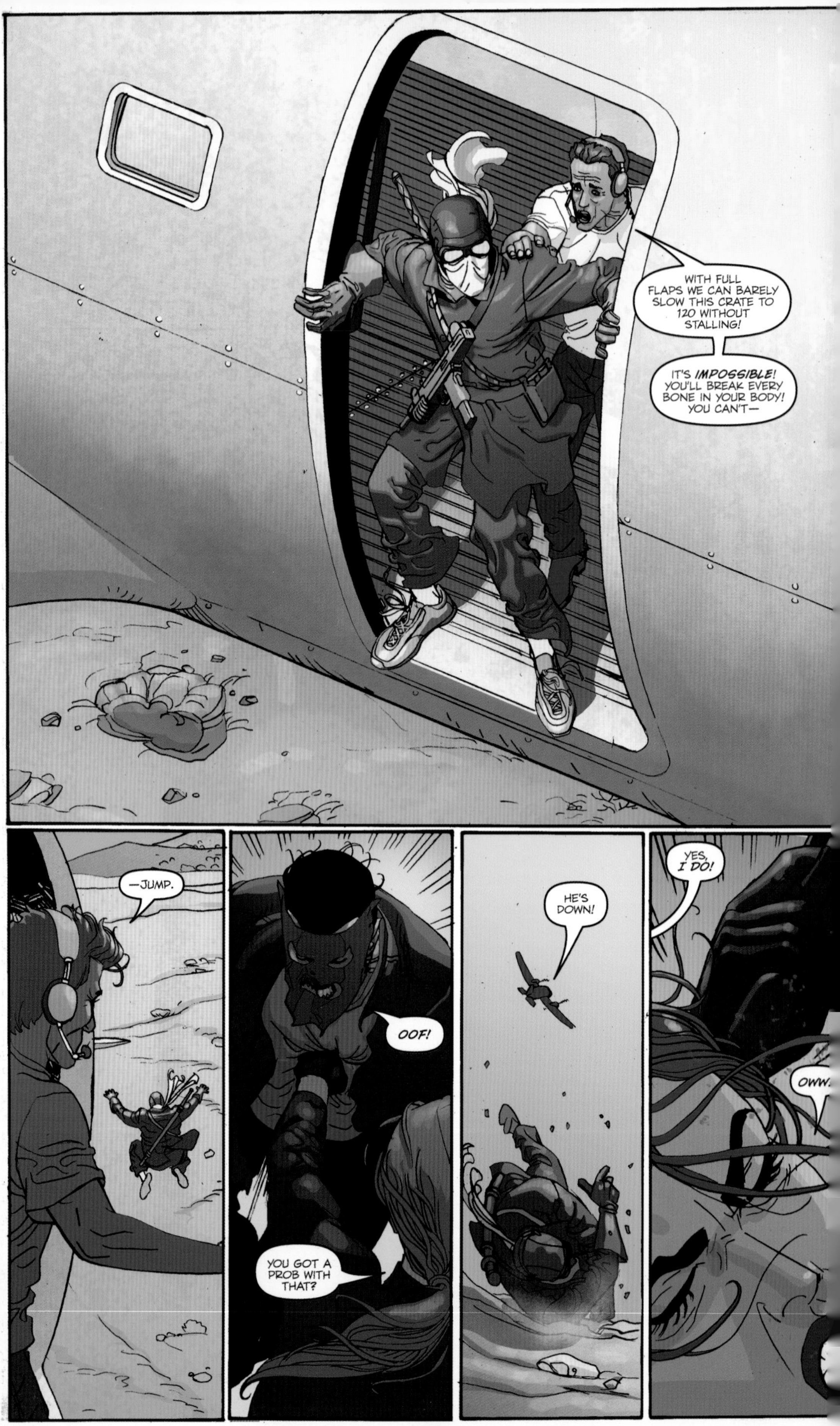
WITH FULL FLAPS WE CAN BARELY SLOW THIS CRATE TO 120 WITHOUT STALLING!
IT'S *IMPOSSIBLE!* YOU'LL BREAK EVERY BONE IN YOUR BODY! YOU CAN'T—
—JUMP.
OOF!
YOU GOT A PROB WITH THAT?
HE'S DOWN!
YES, *I DO!*
OWW

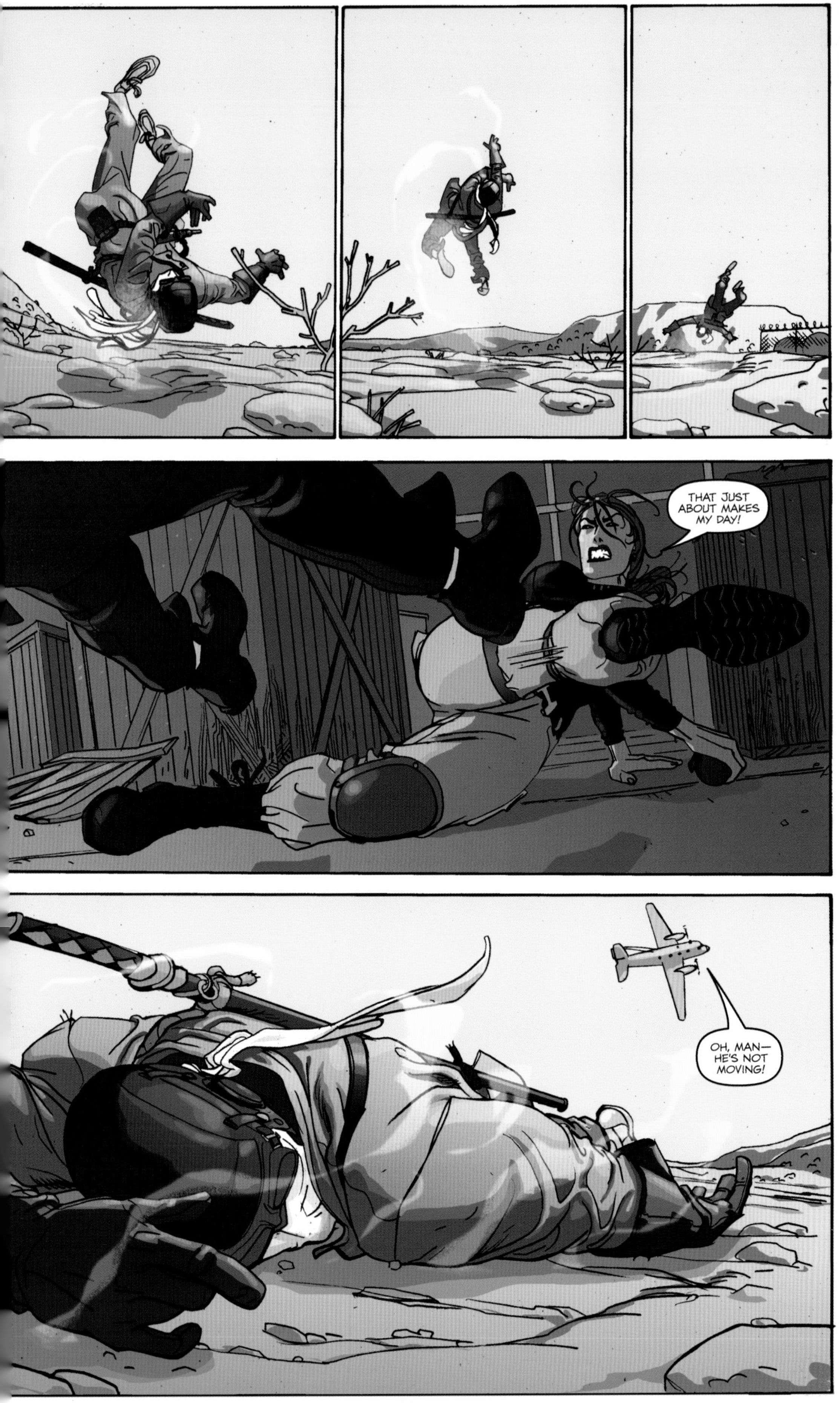
THAT JUST ABOUT MAKES MY DAY!
OH, MAN— HE'S NOT MOVING!

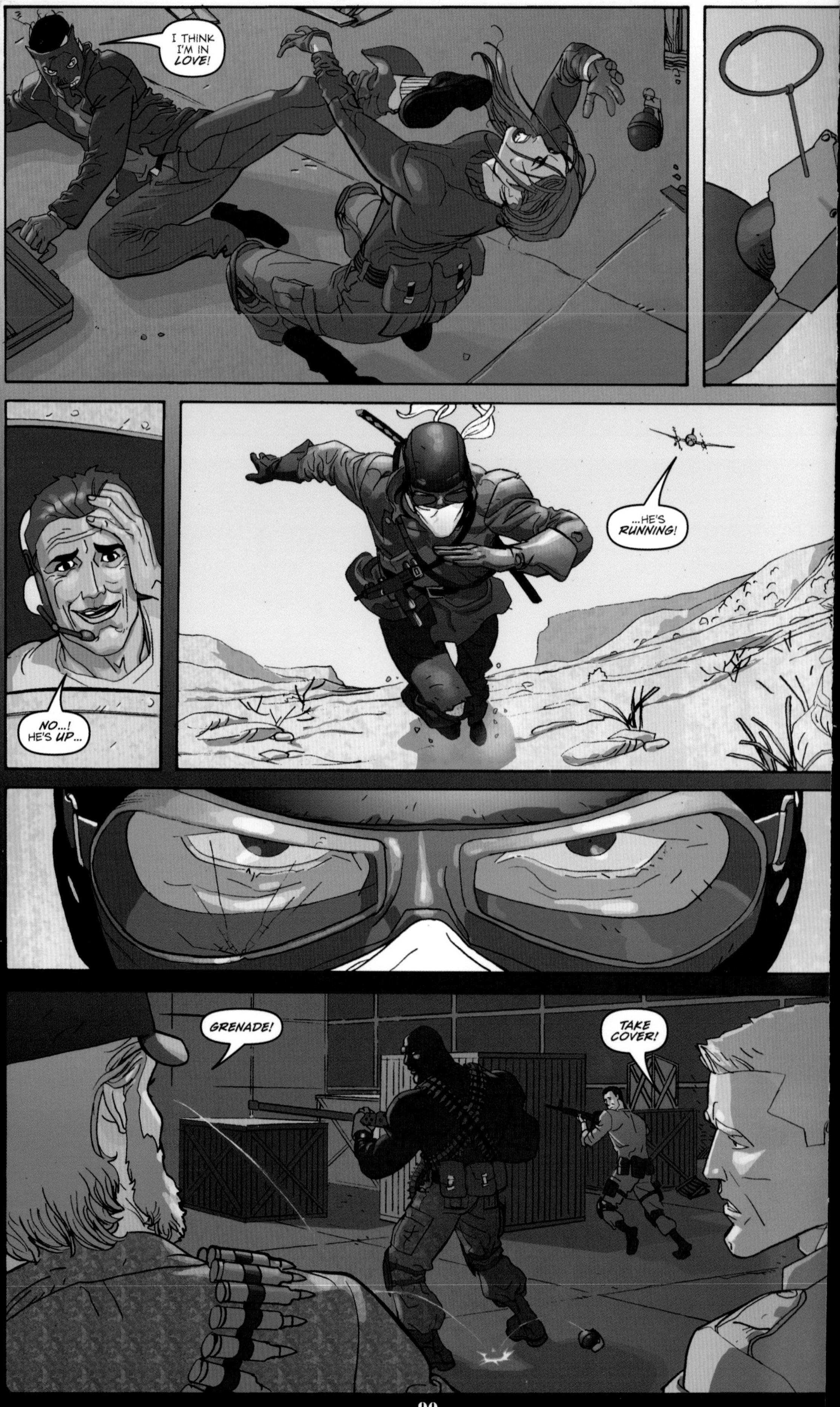
I THINK I'M IN LOVE!
NO...! HE'S UP...
...HE'S RUNNING!
GRENADE!
TAKE COVER!

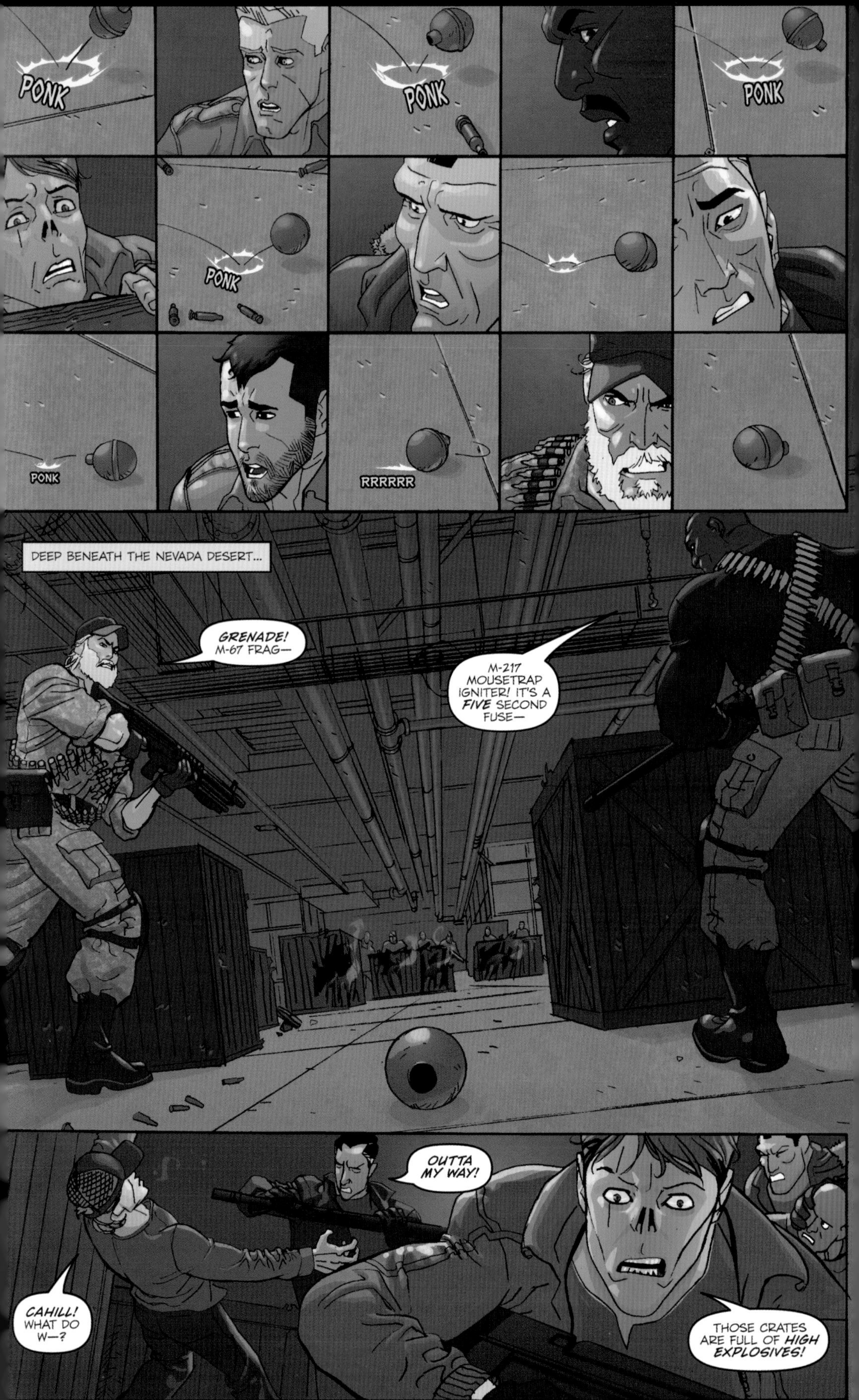
PONK
PONK
PONK
PONK
PONK
RRRRRR
DEEP BENEATH THE NEVADA DESERT...
GRENADE! M-67 FRAG—
M-217 MOUSETRAP IGNITER! IT'S A FIVE SECOND FUSE—
OUTTA MY WAY!
CAHILL! WHAT DO W—?
THOSE CRATES ARE FULL OF HIGH EXPLOSIVES!

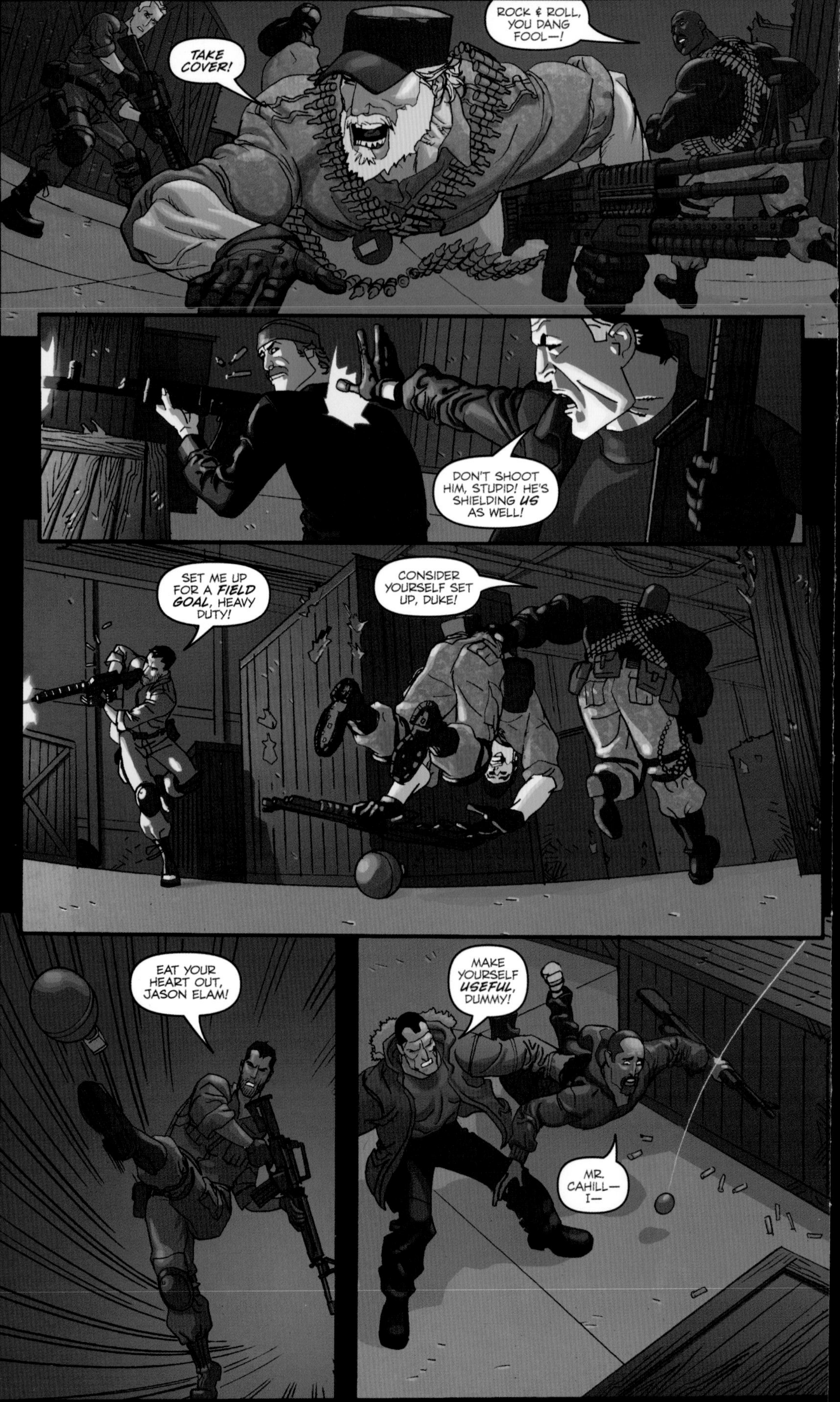
TAKE COVER!
ROCK & ROLL, YOU DANG FOOL—!
DON'T SHOOT HIM, STUPID! HE'S SHIELDING US AS WELL!
SET ME UP FOR A FIELD GOAL, HEAVY DUTY!
CONSIDER YOURSELF SET UP, DUKE!
EAT YOUR HEART OUT, JASON ELAM!
MAKE YOURSELF USEFUL, DUMMY!
MR. CAHILL— I—

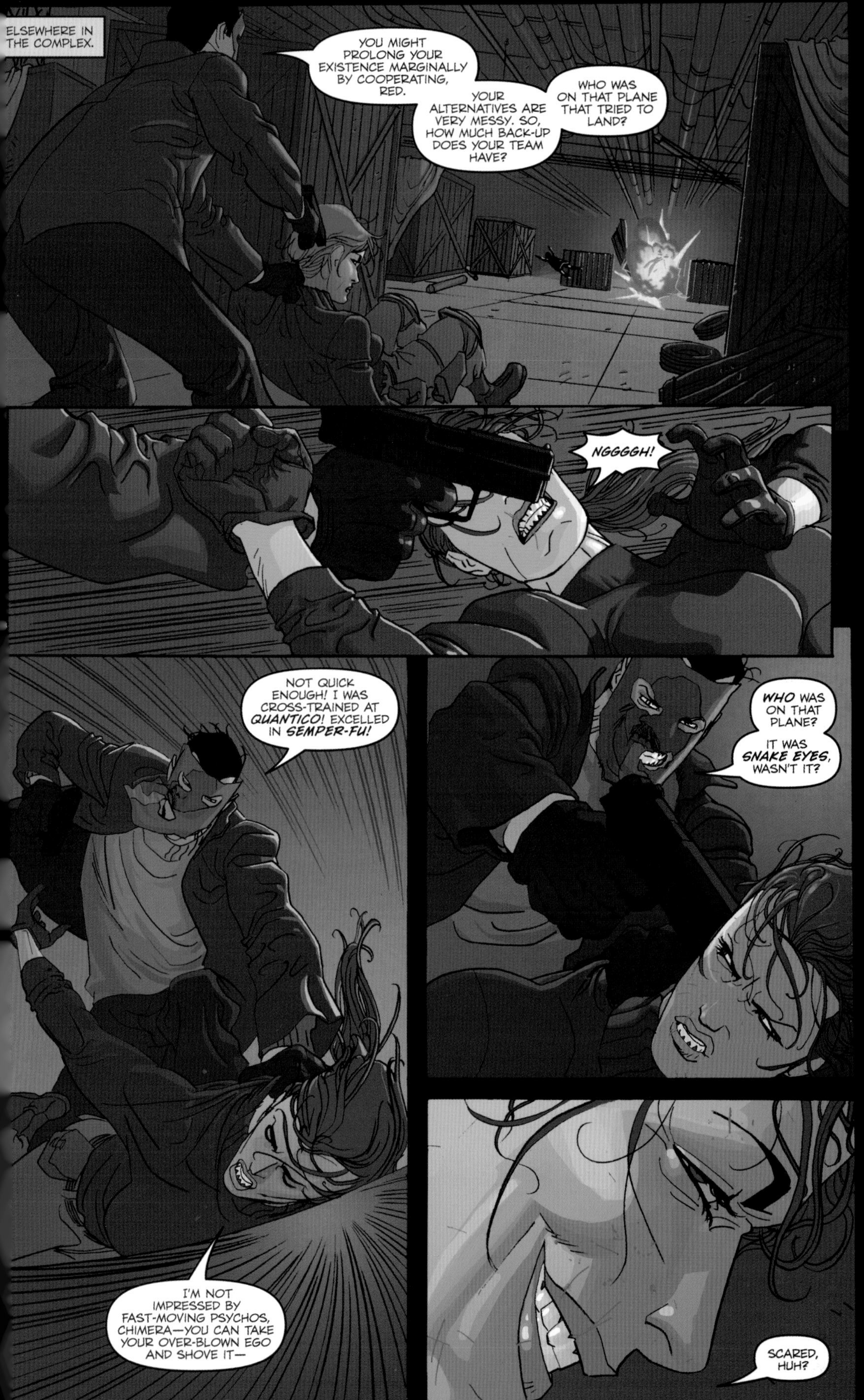

ELSEWHERE IN THE COMPLEX.
YOU MIGHT PROLONG YOUR EXISTENCE MARGINALLY BY COOPERATING, RED.
YOUR ALTERNATIVES ARE VERY MESSY. SO, HOW MUCH BACK-UP DOES YOUR TEAM HAVE?
WHO WAS ON THAT PLANE THAT TRIED TO LAND?
NGGGGH!
NOT QUICK ENOUGH! I WAS CROSS-TRAINED AT QUANTICO! EXCELLED IN SEMPER-FU!
I'M NOT IMPRESSED BY FAST-MOVING PSYCHOS, CHIMERA—YOU CAN TAKE YOUR OVER-BLOWN EGO AND SHOVE IT—
WHO WAS ON THAT PLANE?
IT WAS SNAKE EYES, WASN'T IT?
SCARED, HUH?

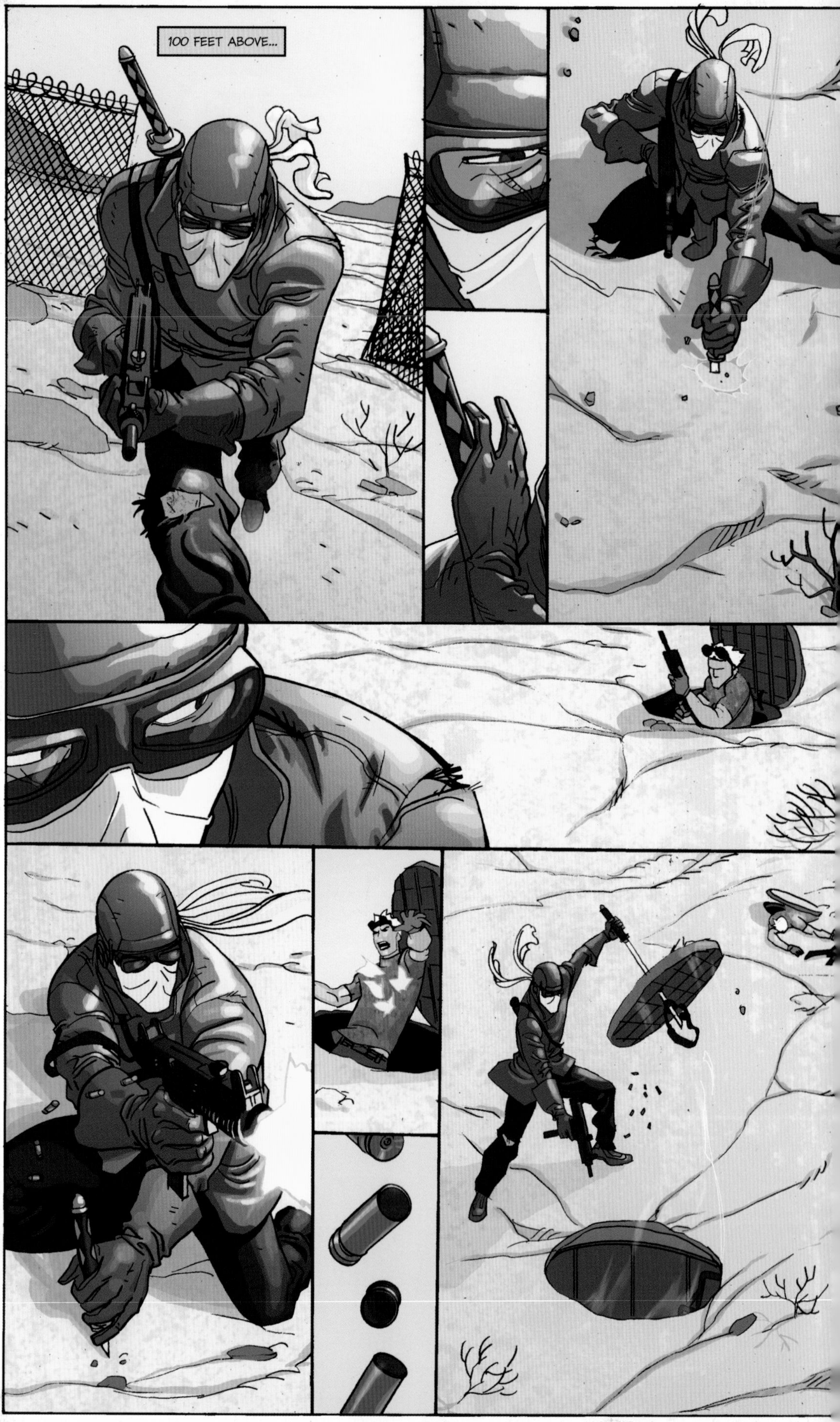
100 FEET ABOVE...

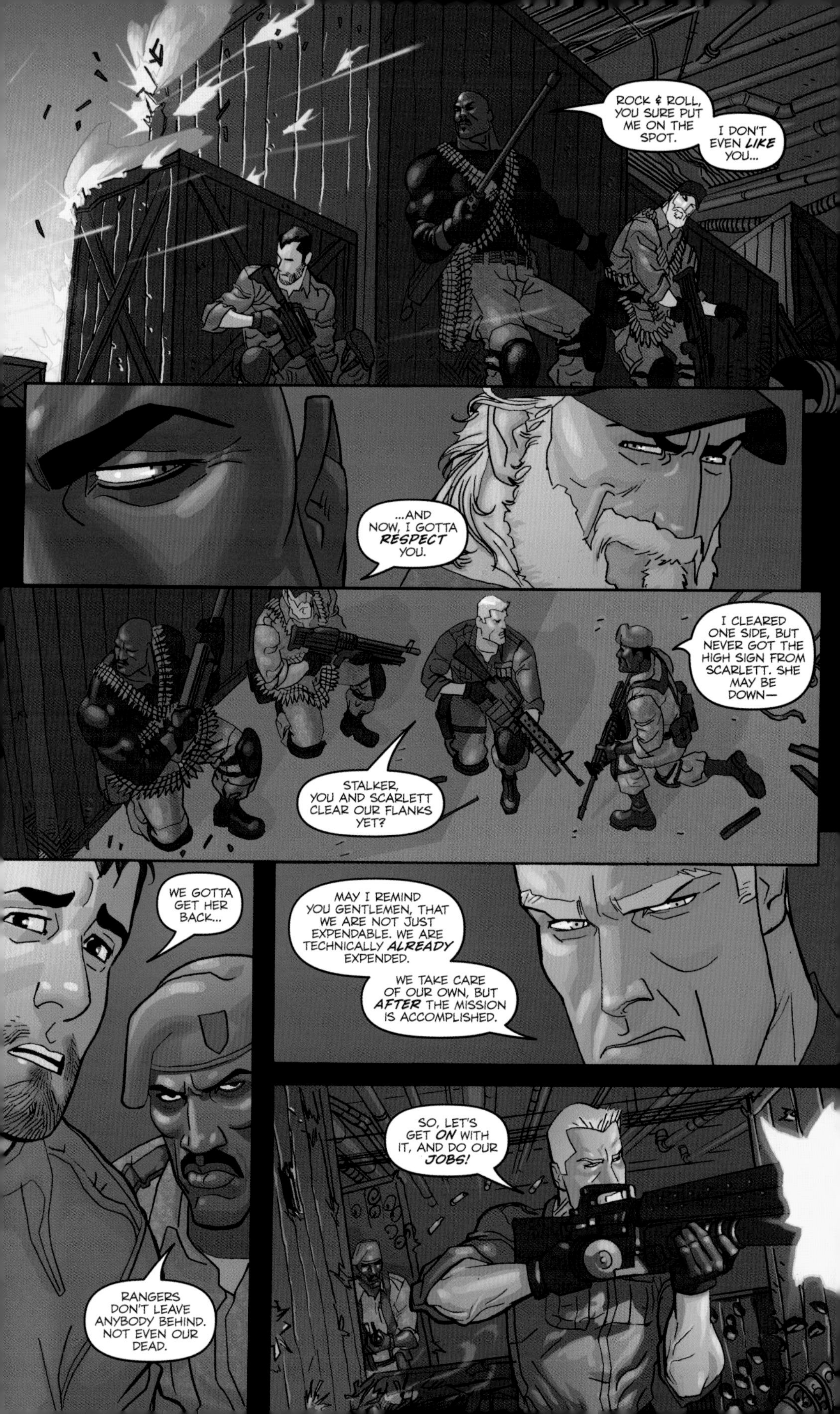
ROCK & ROLL, YOU SURE PUT ME ON THE SPOT.
I DON'T EVEN LIKE YOU...
...AND NOW, I GOTTA RESPECT YOU.
STALKER, YOU AND SCARLETT CLEAR OUR FLANKS YET?
I CLEARED ONE SIDE, BUT NEVER GOT THE HIGH SIGN FROM SCARLETT. SHE MAY BE DOWN—
WE GOTTA GET HER BACK...
RANGERS DON'T LEAVE ANYBODY BEHIND. NOT EVEN OUR DEAD.
MAY I REMIND YOU GENTLEMEN, THAT WE ARE NOT JUST EXPENDABLE. WE ARE TECHNICALLY ALREADY EXPENDED.
WE TAKE CARE OF OUR OWN, BUT AFTER THE MISSION IS ACCOMPLISHED.
SO, LET'S GET ON WITH IT, AND DO OUR JOBS!

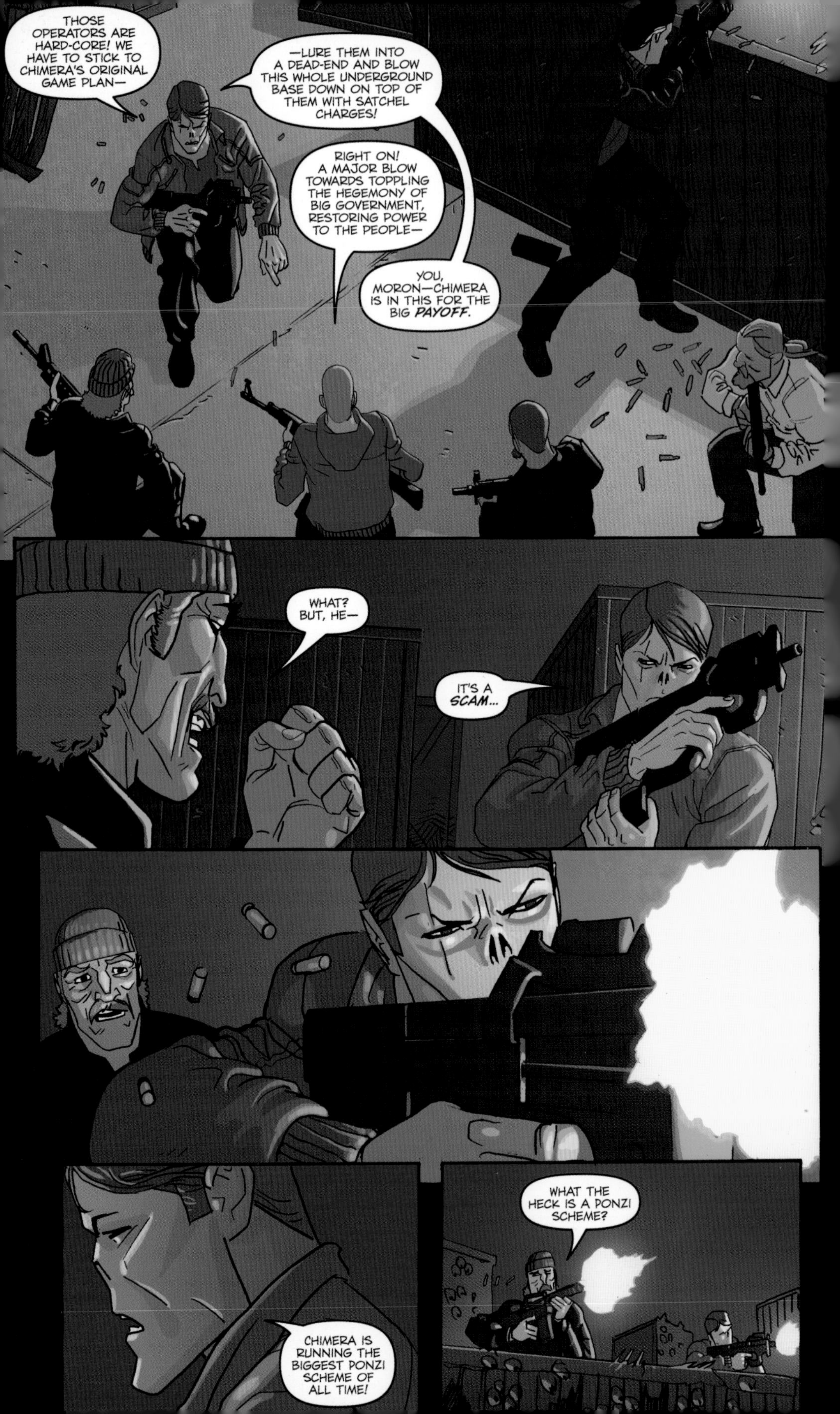
THOSE OPERATORS ARE HARD-CORE! WE HAVE TO STICK TO CHIMERA'S ORIGINAL GAME PLAN—
—LURE THEM INTO A DEAD-END AND BLOW THIS WHOLE UNDERGROUND BASE DOWN ON TOP OF THEM WITH SATCHEL CHARGES!
RIGHT ON! A MAJOR BLOW TOWARDS TOPPLING THE HEGEMONY OF BIG GOVERNMENT, RESTORING POWER TO THE PEOPLE—
YOU, MORON—CHIMERA IS IN THIS FOR THE BIG *PAYOFF*.
WHAT? BUT, HE—
IT'S A *SCAM*...
CHIMERA IS RUNNING THE BIGGEST PONZI SCHEME OF ALL TIME!
WHAT THE HECK IS A PONZI SCHEME?

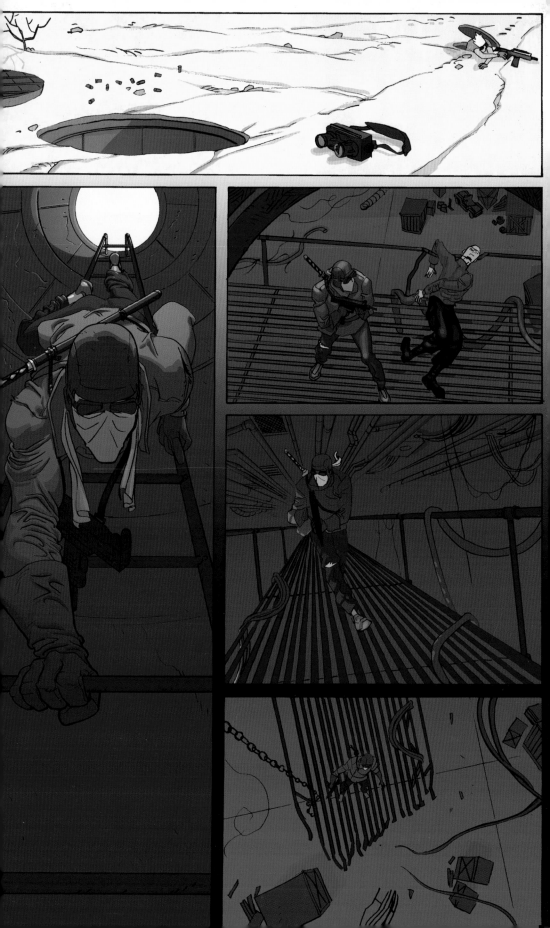

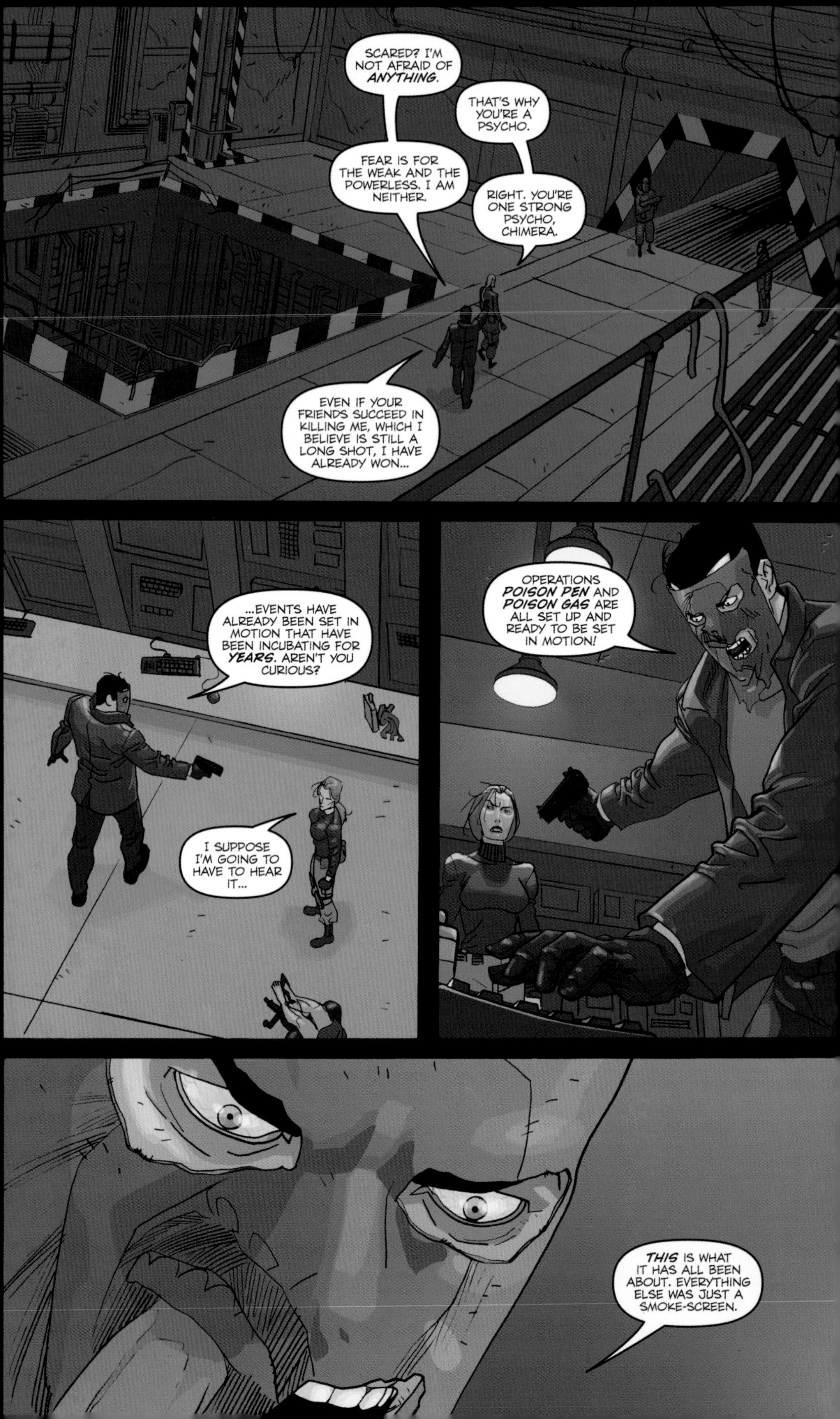
SCARED? I'M NOT AFRAID OF ANYTHING.
THAT'S WHY YOU'RE A PSYCHO.
FEAR IS FOR THE WEAK AND THE POWERLESS. I AM NEITHER.
RIGHT. YOU'RE ONE STRONG PSYCHO, CHIMERA.
EVEN IF YOUR FRIENDS SUCCEED IN KILLING ME, WHICH I BELIEVE IS STILL A LONG SHOT, I HAVE ALREADY WON...
...EVENTS HAVE ALREADY BEEN SET IN MOTION THAT HAVE BEEN INCUBATING FOR YEARS. AREN'T YOU CURIOUS?
I SUPPOSE I'M GOING TO HAVE TO HEAR IT...
OPERATIONS POISON PEN AND POISON GAS ARE ALL SET UP AND READY TO BE SET IN MOTION!
THIS IS WHAT IT HAS ALL BEEN ABOUT. EVERYTHING ELSE WAS JUST A SMOKE-SCREEN.

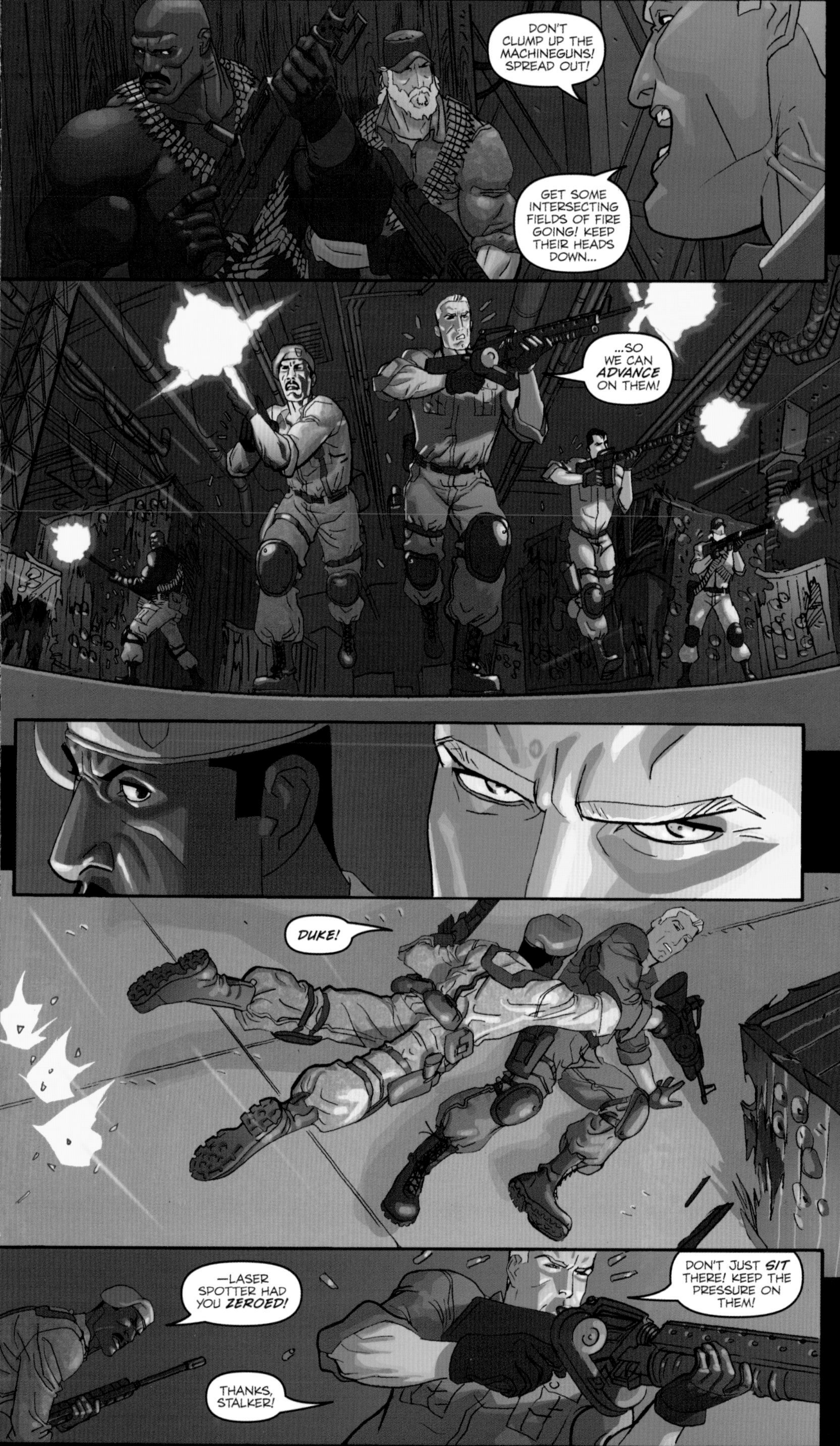
DON'T CLUMP UP THE MACHINEGUNS! SPREAD OUT!
GET SOME INTERSECTING FIELDS OF FIRE GOING! KEEP THEIR HEADS DOWN...
...SO WE CAN ADVANCE ON THEM!
DUKE!
—LASER SPOTTER HAD YOU ZEROED!
DON'T JUST SIT THERE! KEEP THE PRESSURE ON THEM!
THANKS, STALKER!

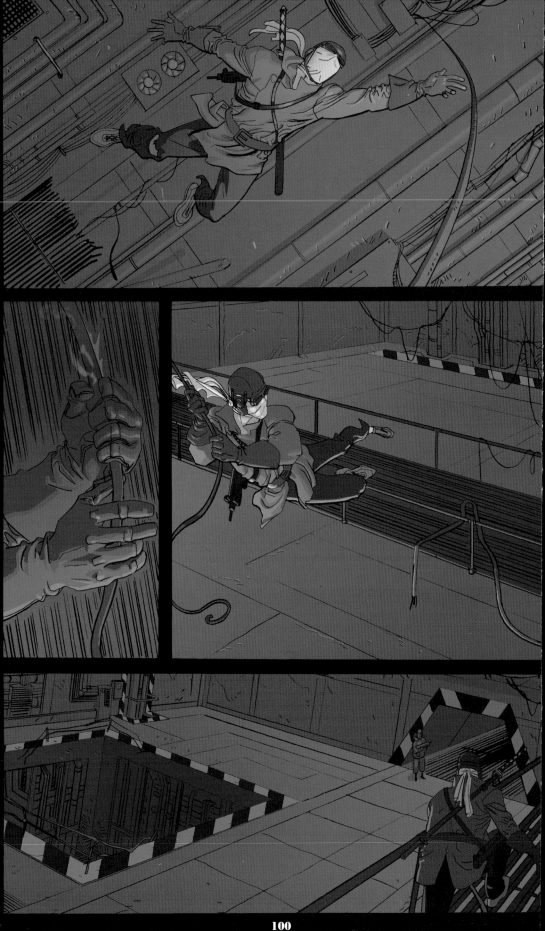

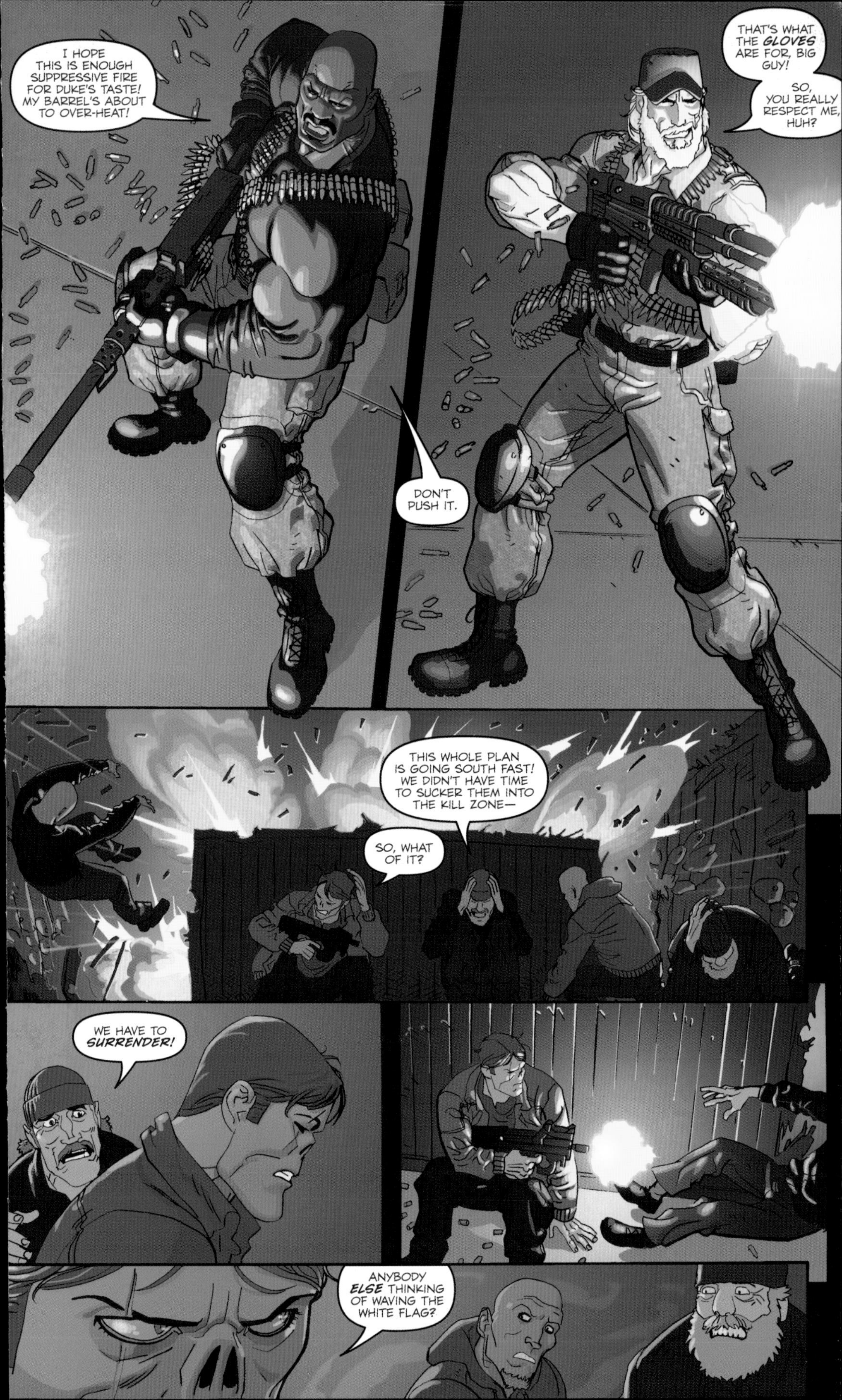
I HOPE THIS IS ENOUGH SUPPRESSIVE FIRE FOR DUKE'S TASTE! MY BARREL'S ABOUT TO OVER-HEAT!
THAT'S WHAT THE GLOVES ARE FOR, BIG GUY!
SO, YOU REALLY RESPECT ME, HUH?
DON'T PUSH IT.
THIS WHOLE PLAN IS GOING SOUTH FAST! WE DIDN'T HAVE TIME TO SUCKER THEM INTO THE KILL ZONE—
SO, WHAT OF IT?
WE HAVE TO SURRENDER!
ANYBODY ELSE THINKING OF WAVING THE WHITE FLAG?

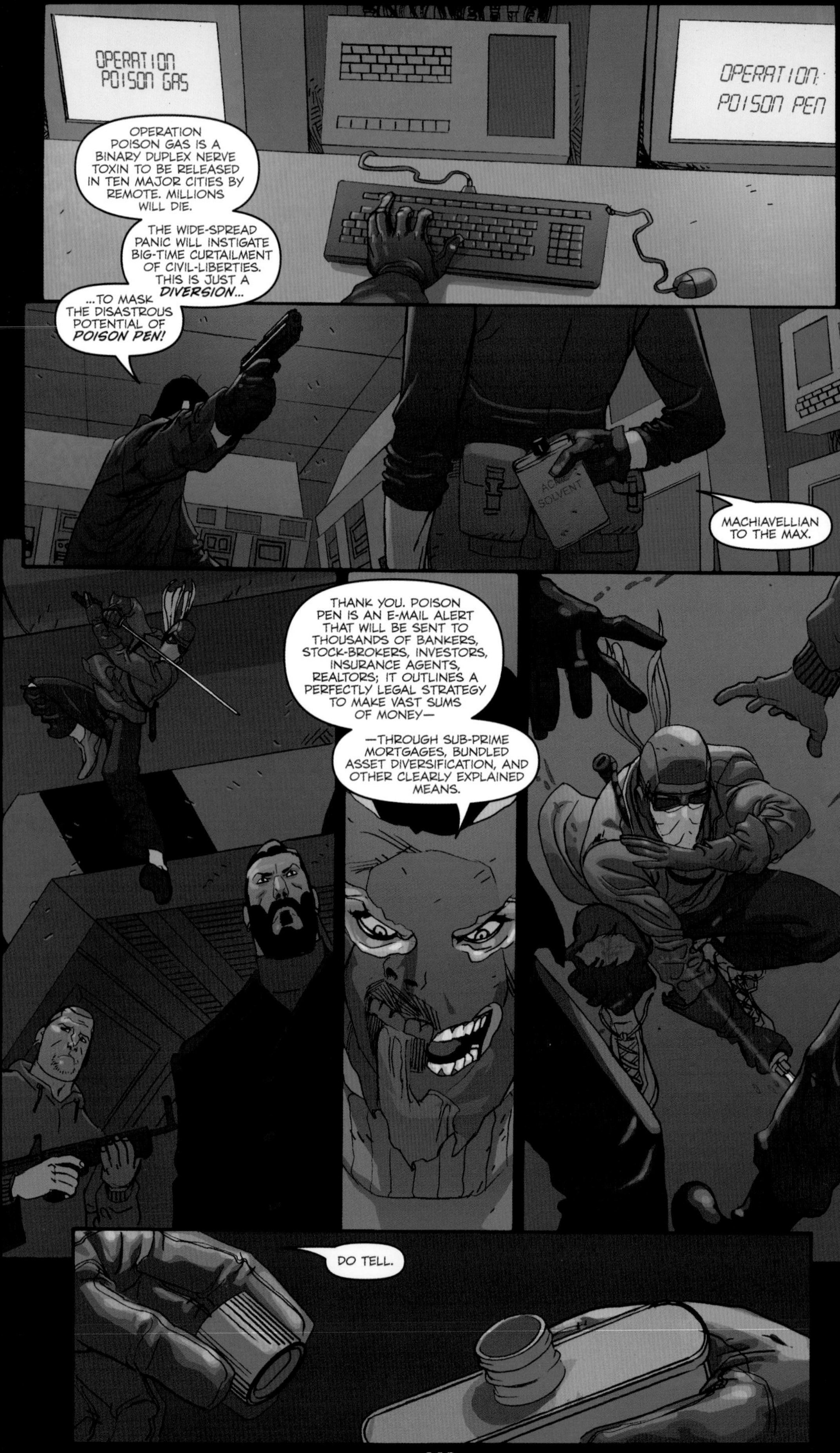
OPERATION POISON GAS
OPERATION: POISON PEN
OPERATION POISON GAS IS A BINARY DUPLEX NERVE TOXIN TO BE RELEASED IN TEN MAJOR CITIES BY REMOTE. MILLIONS WILL DIE.
THE WIDE-SPREAD PANIC WILL INSTIGATE BIG-TIME CURTAILMENT OF CIVIL-LIBERTIES. THIS IS JUST A *DIVERSION*...
...TO MASK THE DISASTROUS POTENTIAL OF *POISON PEN!*
MACHIAVELLIAN TO THE MAX.
THANK YOU. POISON PEN IS AN E-MAIL ALERT THAT WILL BE SENT TO THOUSANDS OF BANKERS, STOCK-BROKERS, INVESTORS, INSURANCE AGENTS, REALTORS; IT OUTLINES A PERFECTLY LEGAL STRATEGY TO MAKE VAST SUMS OF MONEY—
—THROUGH SUB-PRIME MORTGAGES, BUNDLED ASSET DIVERSIFICATION, AND OTHER CLEARLY EXPLAINED MEANS.
DO TELL.

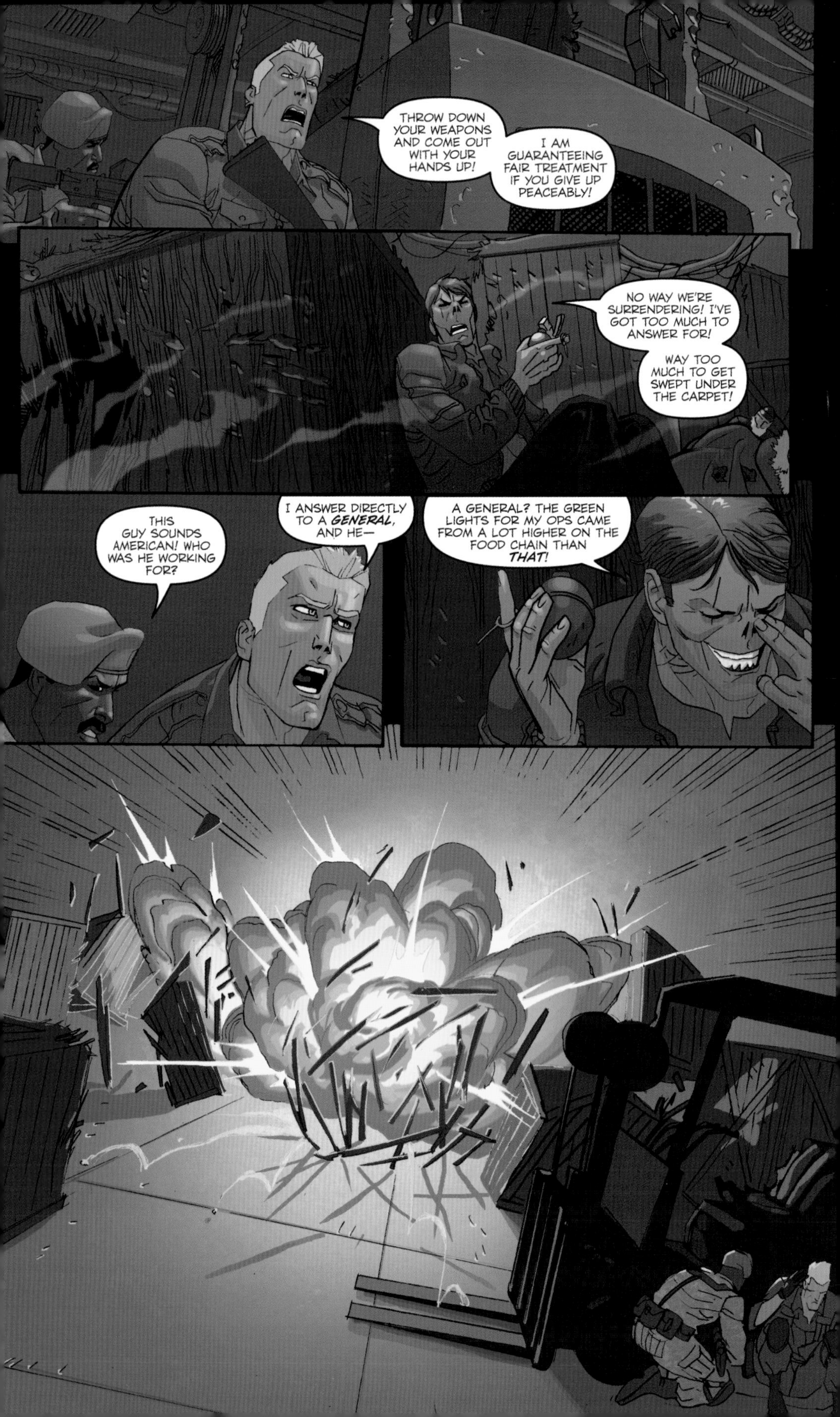
THROW DOWN YOUR WEAPONS AND COME OUT WITH YOUR HANDS UP!
I AM GUARANTEEING FAIR TREATMENT IF YOU GIVE UP PEACEABLY!
NO WAY WE'RE SURRENDERING! I'VE GOT TOO MUCH TO ANSWER FOR!
WAY TOO MUCH TO GET SWEPT UNDER THE CARPET!
THIS GUY SOUNDS AMERICAN! WHO WAS HE WORKING FOR?
I ANSWER DIRECTLY TO A ***GENERAL***, AND HE—
A GENERAL? THE GREEN LIGHTS FOR MY OPS CAME FROM A LOT HIGHER ON THE FOOD CHAIN THAN ***THAT***!

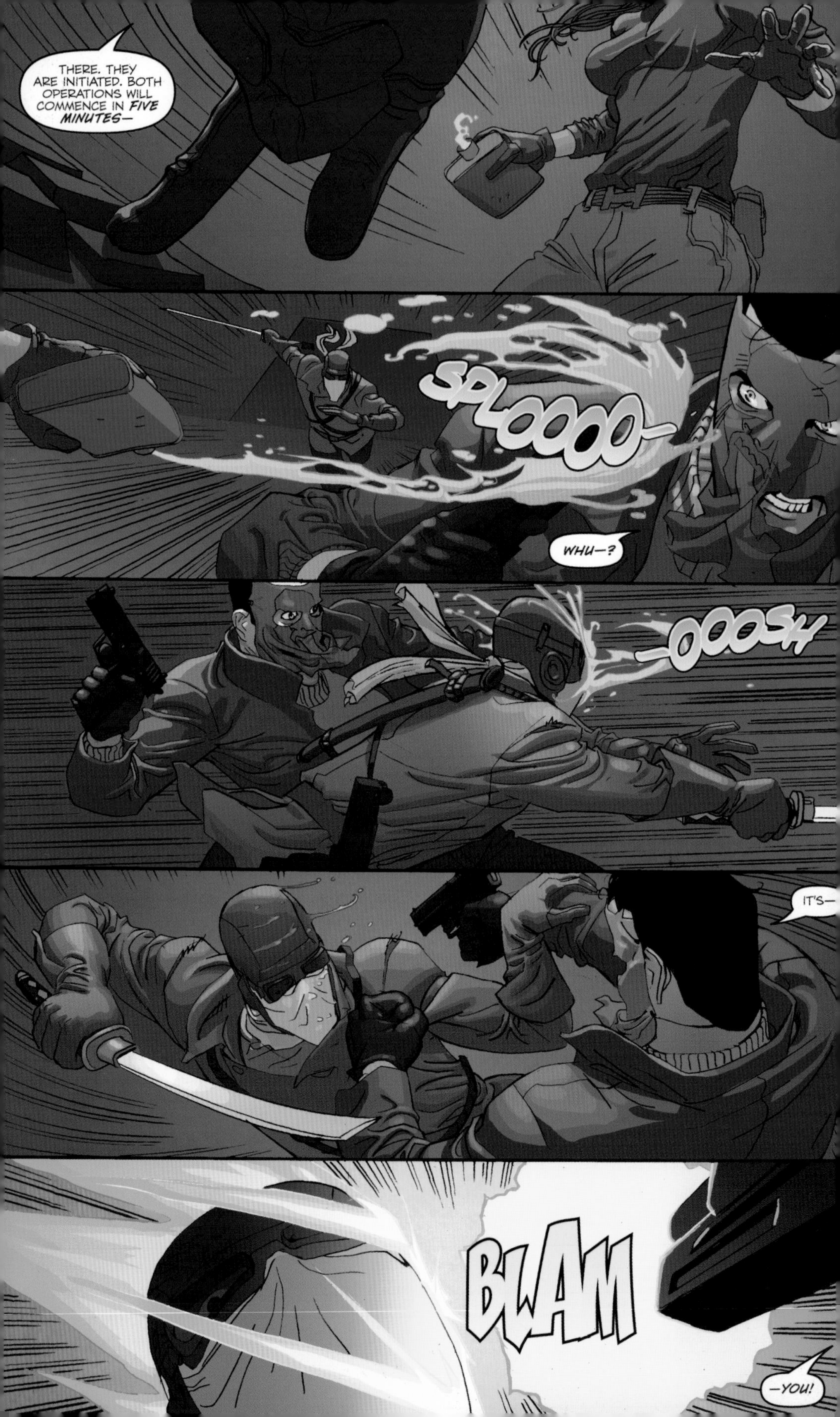
THERE. THEY ARE INITIATED. BOTH OPERATIONS WILL COMMENCE IN *FIVE MINUTES*—
SPLOOOO—
WHU—?
—OOOSH
IT'S—
BLAM
—YOU!

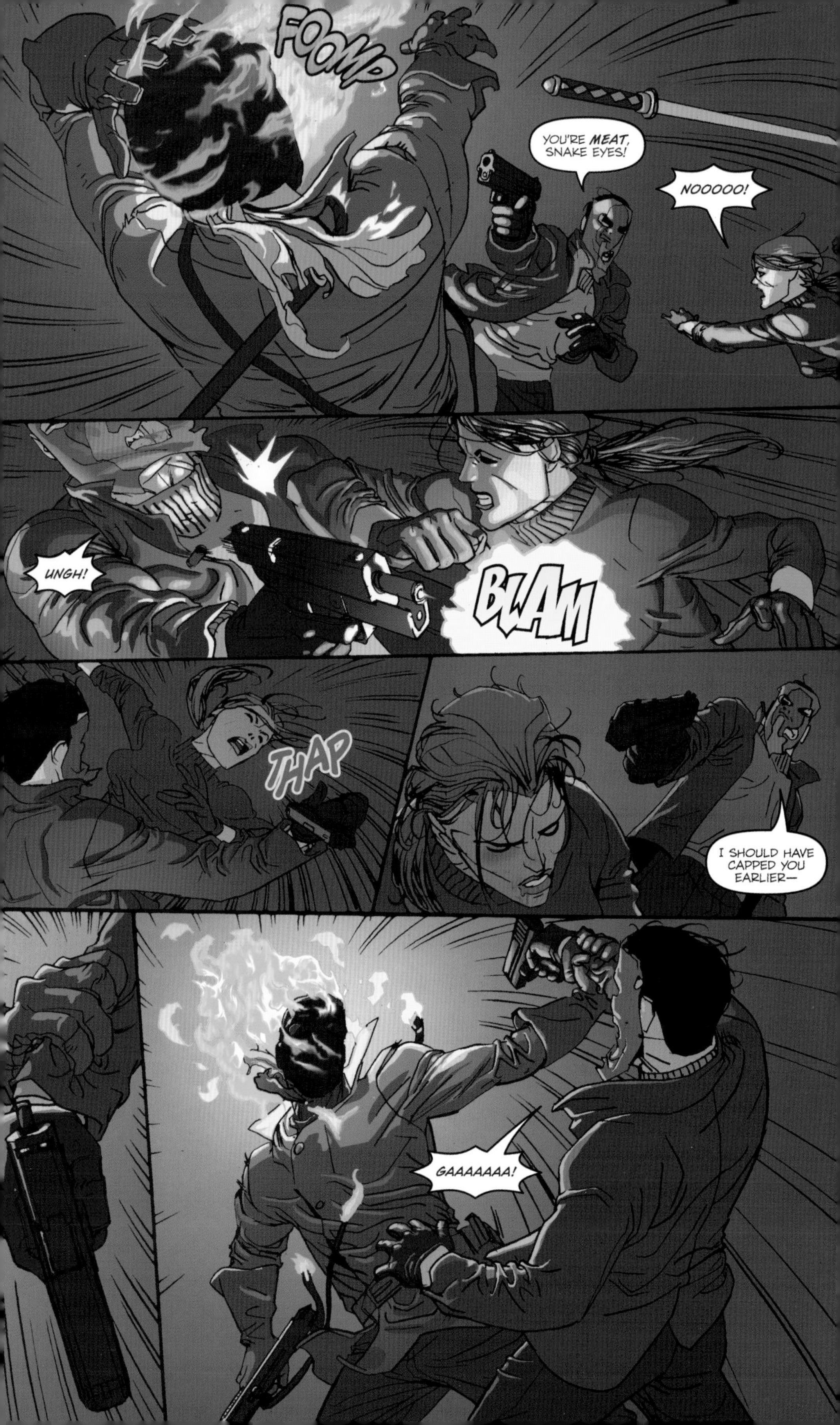
FOOMP
YOU'RE MEAT, SNAKE EYES!
NOOOOO!
UNGH!
BLAM
THAP
I SHOULD HAVE CAPPED YOU EARLIER—
GAAAAAAA!

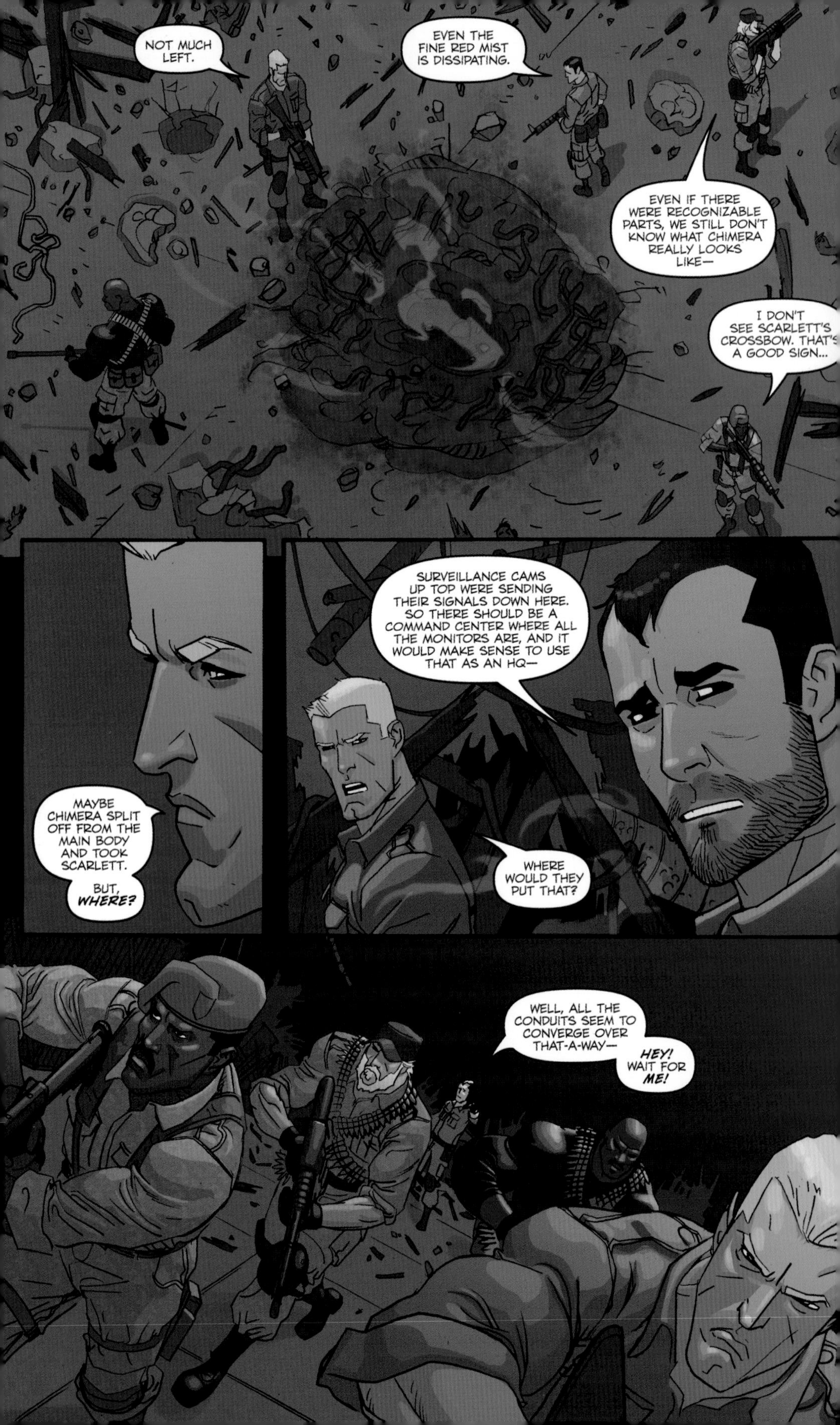
NOT MUCH LEFT.
EVEN THE FINE RED MIST IS DISSIPATING.
EVEN IF THERE WERE RECOGNIZABLE PARTS, WE STILL DON'T KNOW WHAT CHIMERA REALLY LOOKS LIKE—
I DON'T SEE SCARLETT'S CROSSBOW. THAT'S A GOOD SIGN...
MAYBE CHIMERA SPLIT OFF FROM THE MAIN BODY AND TOOK SCARLETT.
BUT, *WHERE?*
SURVEILLANCE CAMS UP TOP WERE SENDING THEIR SIGNALS DOWN HERE. SO THERE SHOULD BE A COMMAND CENTER WHERE ALL THE MONITORS ARE, AND IT WOULD MAKE SENSE TO USE THAT AS AN HQ—
WHERE WOULD THEY PUT THAT?
WELL, ALL THE CONDUITS SEEM TO CONVERGE OVER THAT-A-WAY—
HEY! WAIT FOR *ME!*

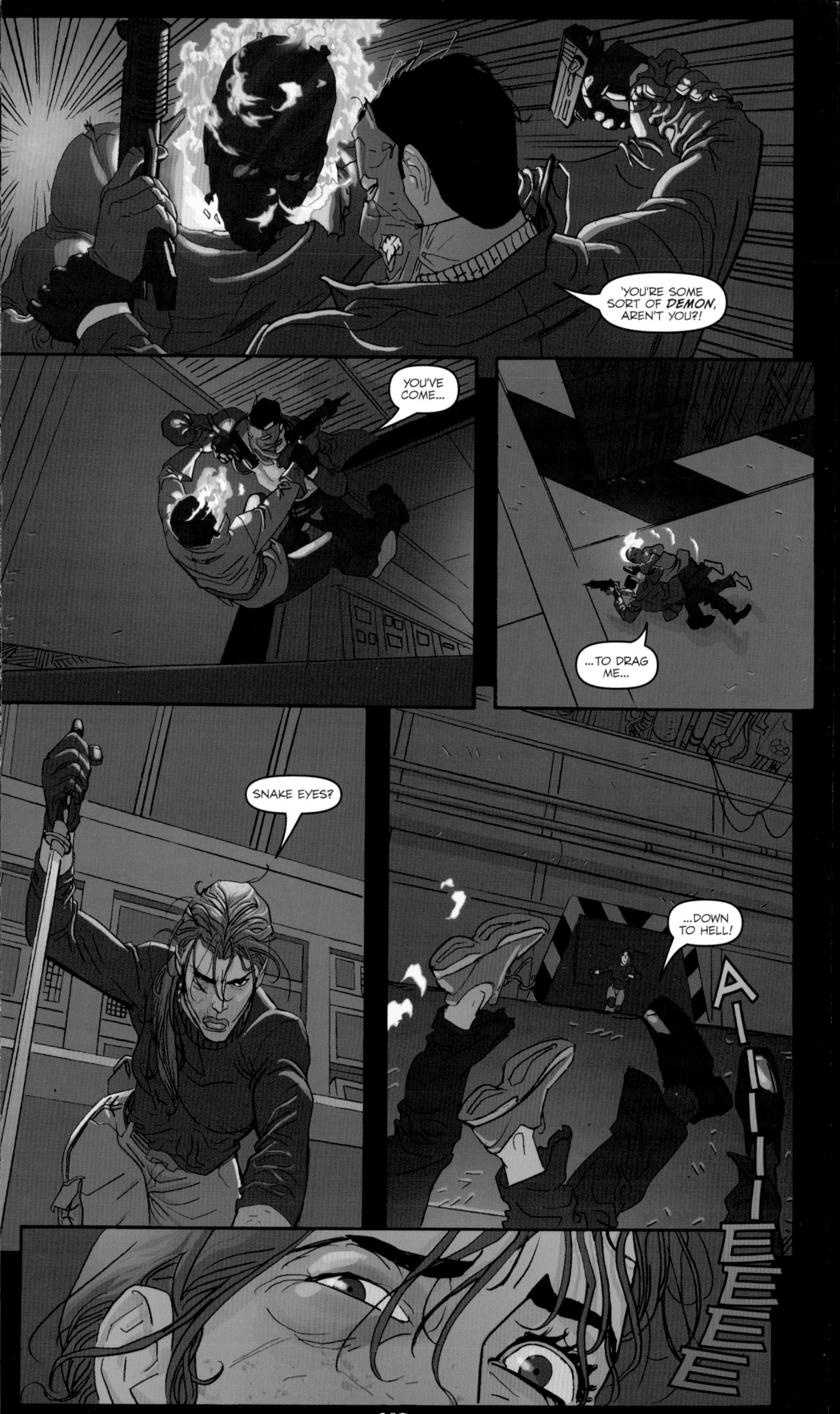
'YOU'RE SOME SORT OF DEMON, AREN'T YOU?!
YOU'VE COME...
...TO DRAG ME...
SNAKE EYES?
...DOWN TO HELL!
AIIIIEEEEEE

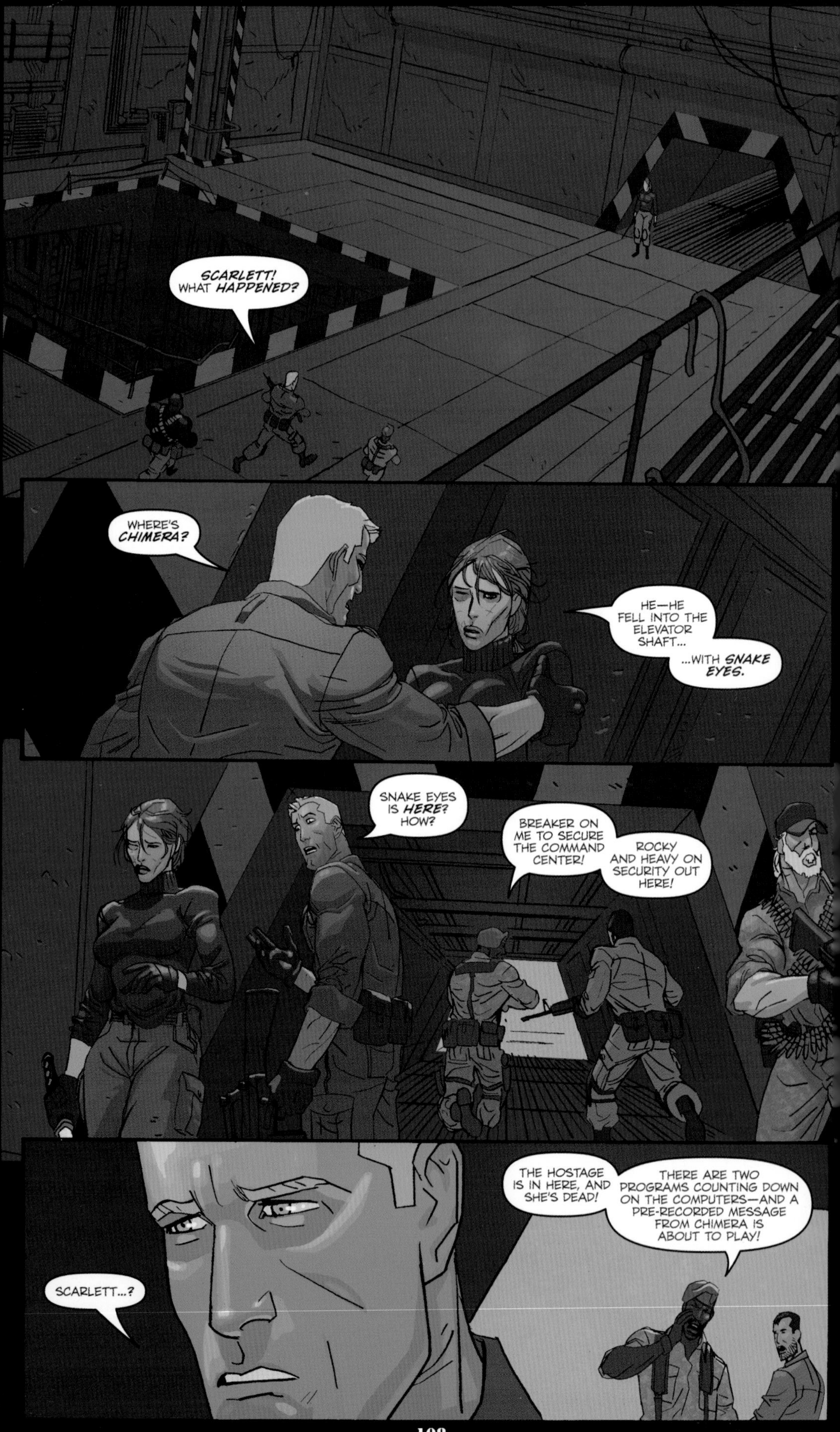
SCARLETT! WHAT HAPPENED?
WHERE'S CHIMERA?
HE—HE FELL INTO THE ELEVATOR SHAFT...
...WITH SNAKE EYES.
SNAKE EYES IS HERE? HOW?
BREAKER ON ME TO SECURE THE COMMAND CENTER!
ROCKY AND HEAVY ON SECURITY OUT HERE!
THE HOSTAGE IS IN HERE, AND SHE'S DEAD!
THERE ARE TWO PROGRAMS COUNTING DOWN ON THE COMPUTERS—AND A PRE-RECORDED MESSAGE FROM CHIMERA IS ABOUT TO PLAY!
SCARLETT...?

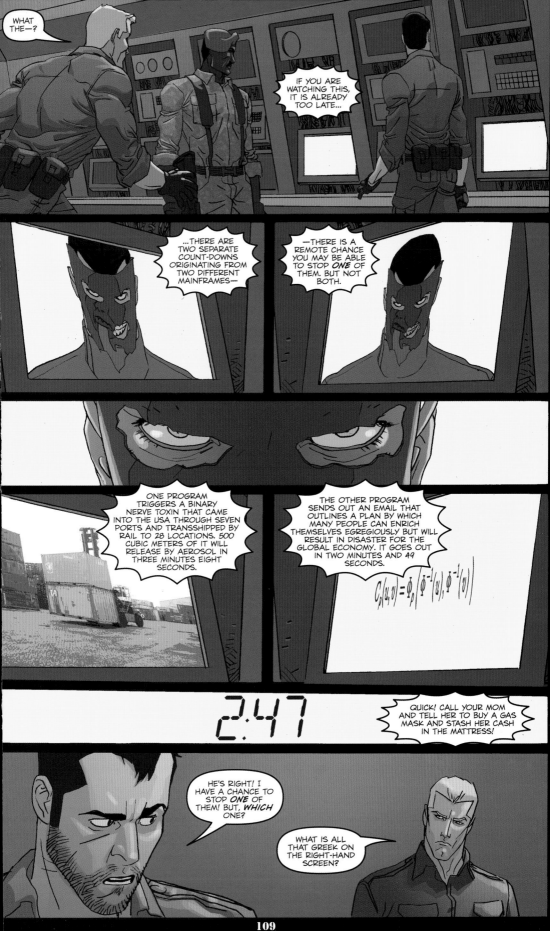

WHAT THE—?

IF YOU ARE WATCHING THIS, IT IS ALREADY TOO LATE...

...THERE ARE TWO SEPARATE COUNT-DOWNS ORIGINATING FROM TWO DIFFERENT MAINFRAMES—

—THERE IS A REMOTE CHANCE YOU MAY BE ABLE TO STOP *ONE* OF THEM. BUT NOT BOTH.

ONE PROGRAM TRIGGERS A BINARY NERVE TOXIN THAT CAME INTO THE USA THROUGH SEVEN PORTS AND TRANSSHIPPED BY RAIL TO 28 LOCATIONS. 500 CUBIC METERS OF IT WILL RELEASE BY AEROSOL IN THREE MINUTES EIGHT SECONDS.

THE OTHER PROGRAM SENDS OUT AN EMAIL THAT OUTLINES A PLAN BY WHICH MANY PEOPLE CAN ENRICH THEMSELVES EGREGIOUSLY BUT WILL RESULT IN DISASTER FOR THE GLOBAL ECONOMY. IT GOES OUT IN TWO MINUTES AND 49 SECONDS.

$$C_p(u,v) = \Phi_p\left(\Phi^{-1}(u), \Phi^{-1}(v)\right)$$

2:47

QUICK! CALL YOUR MOM AND TELL HER TO BUY A GAS MASK AND STASH HER CASH IN THE MATTRESS!

HE'S RIGHT! I HAVE A CHANCE TO STOP *ONE* OF THEM! BUT, *WHICH* ONE?

WHAT IS ALL THAT GREEK ON THE RIGHT-HAND SCREEN?

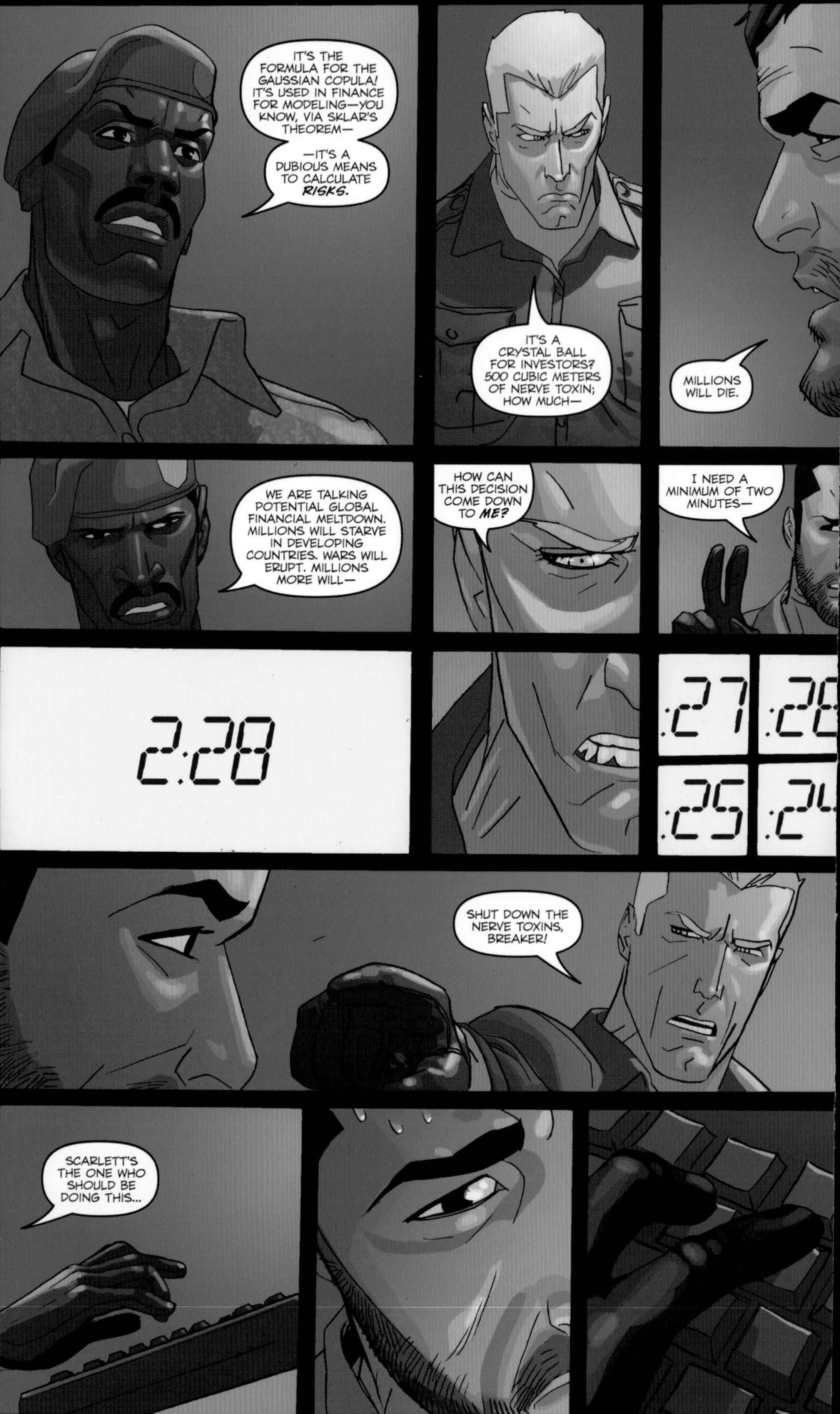
IT'S THE FORMULA FOR THE GAUSSIAN COPULA! IT'S USED IN FINANCE FOR MODELING—YOU KNOW, VIA SKLAR'S THEOREM—
—IT'S A DUBIOUS MEANS TO CALCULATE RISKS.
IT'S A CRYSTAL BALL FOR INVESTORS? 500 CUBIC METERS OF NERVE TOXIN; HOW MUCH—
MILLIONS WILL DIE.
WE ARE TALKING POTENTIAL GLOBAL FINANCIAL MELTDOWN. MILLIONS WILL STARVE IN DEVELOPING COUNTRIES. WARS WILL ERUPT. MILLIONS MORE WILL—
HOW CAN THIS DECISION COME DOWN TO ME?
I NEED A MINIMUM OF TWO MINUTES—
2:28
:27
:25
SHUT DOWN THE NERVE TOXINS, BREAKER!
SCARLETT'S THE ONE WHO SHOULD BE DOING THIS...

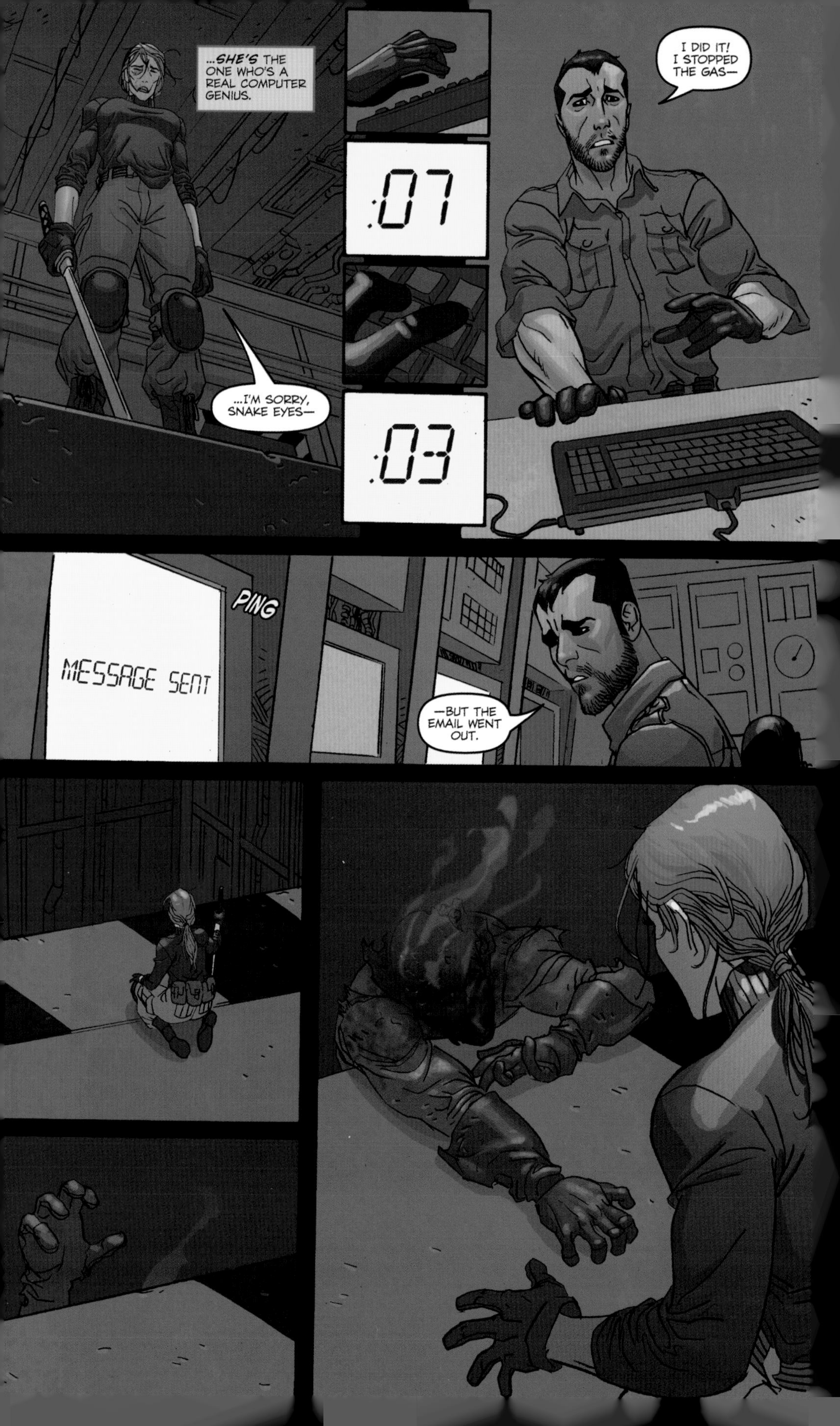
...SHE'S THE ONE WHO'S A REAL COMPUTER GENIUS.
...I'M SORRY, SNAKE EYES—
:07
:03
I DID IT! I STOPPED THE GAS—
MESSAGE SENT
PING
—BUT THE EMAIL WENT OUT.

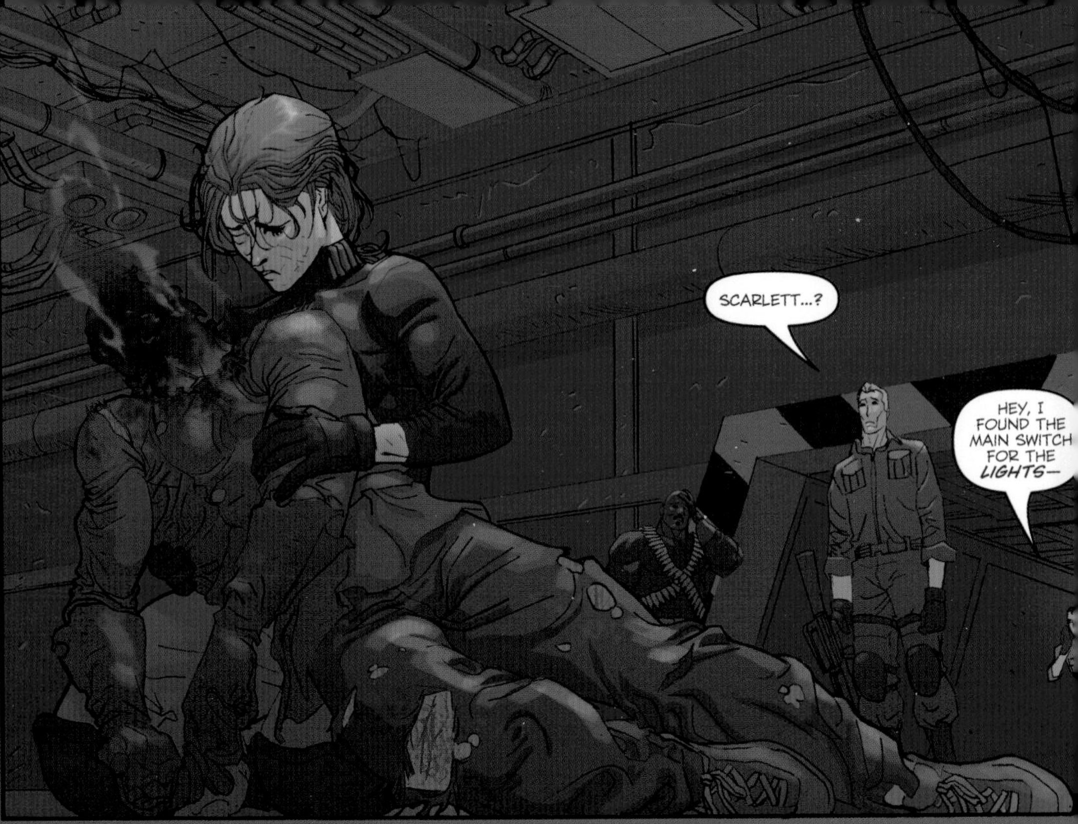
SCARLETT...?
HEY, I FOUND THE MAIN SWITCH FOR THE *LIGHTS*—

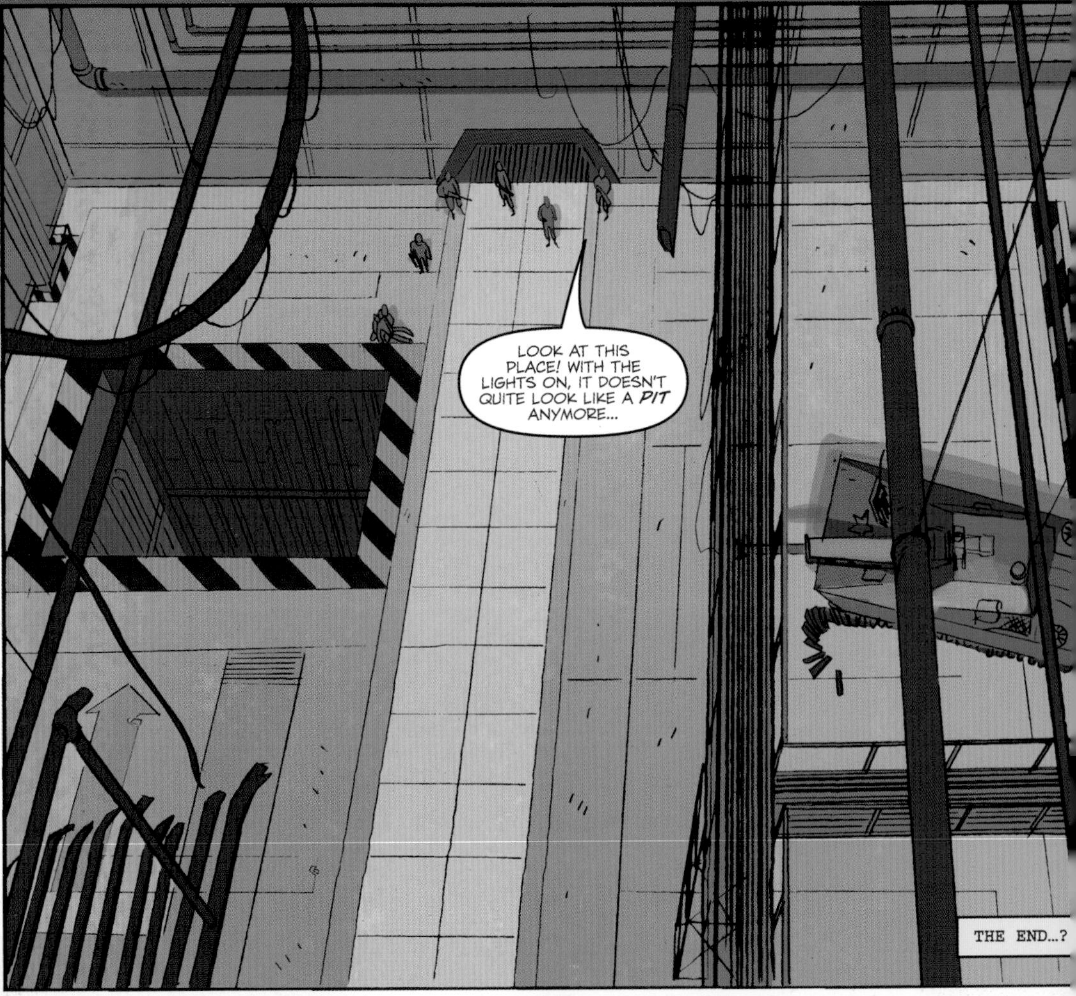
LOOK AT THIS PLACE! WITH THE LIGHTS ON, IT DOESN'T QUITE LOOK LIKE A *PIT* ANYMORE...
THE END...?

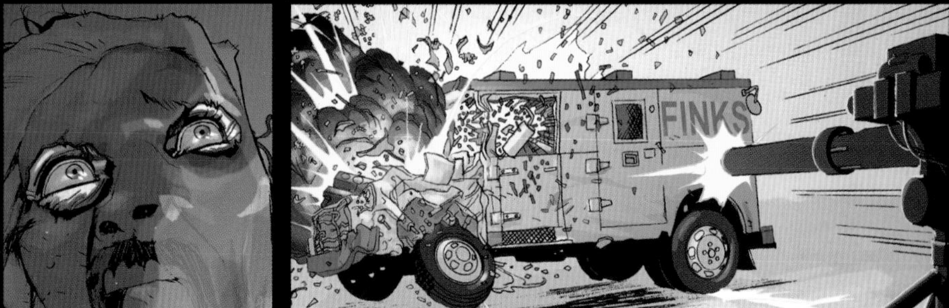
FINKS

ART & SKETCH GALLERY

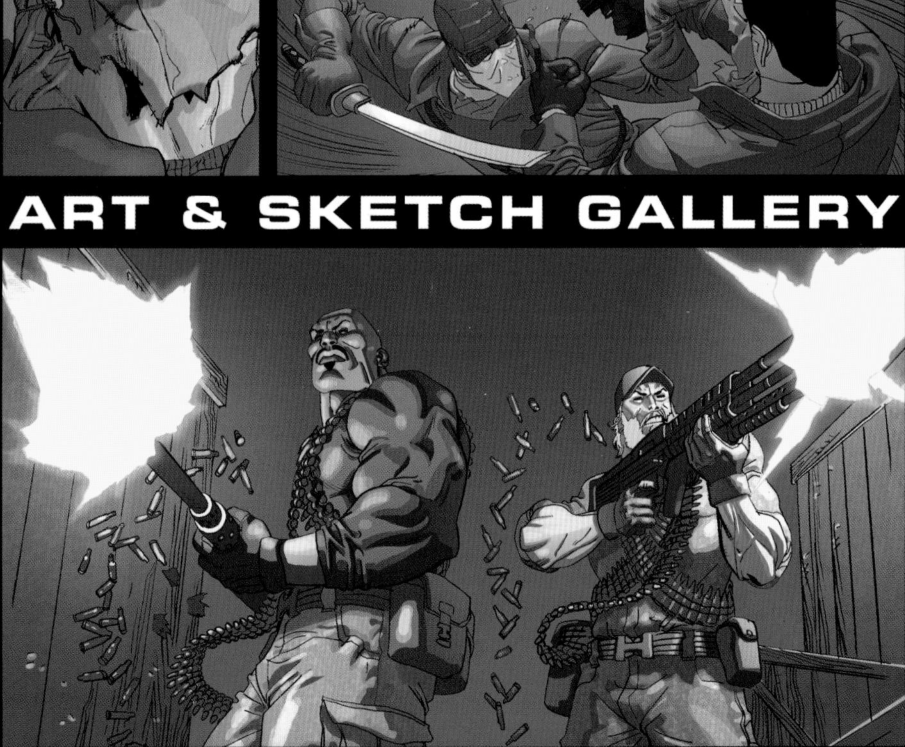

ART BY ANDREA DiVITO, COLOR BY CHRIS SOTOMAYOR

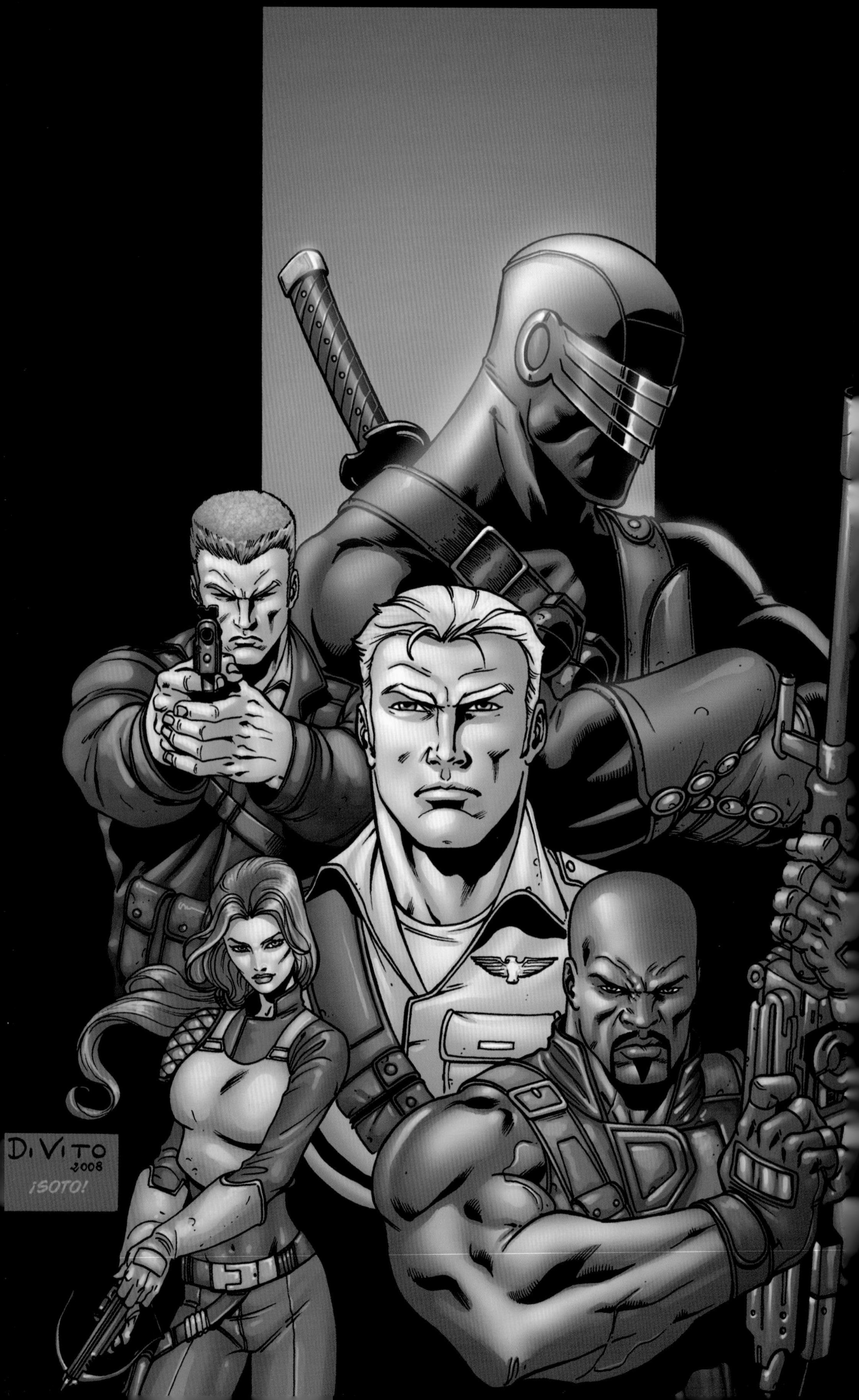
DiVITO
2008
¡SOTO!

ART BY TOM FEISTER

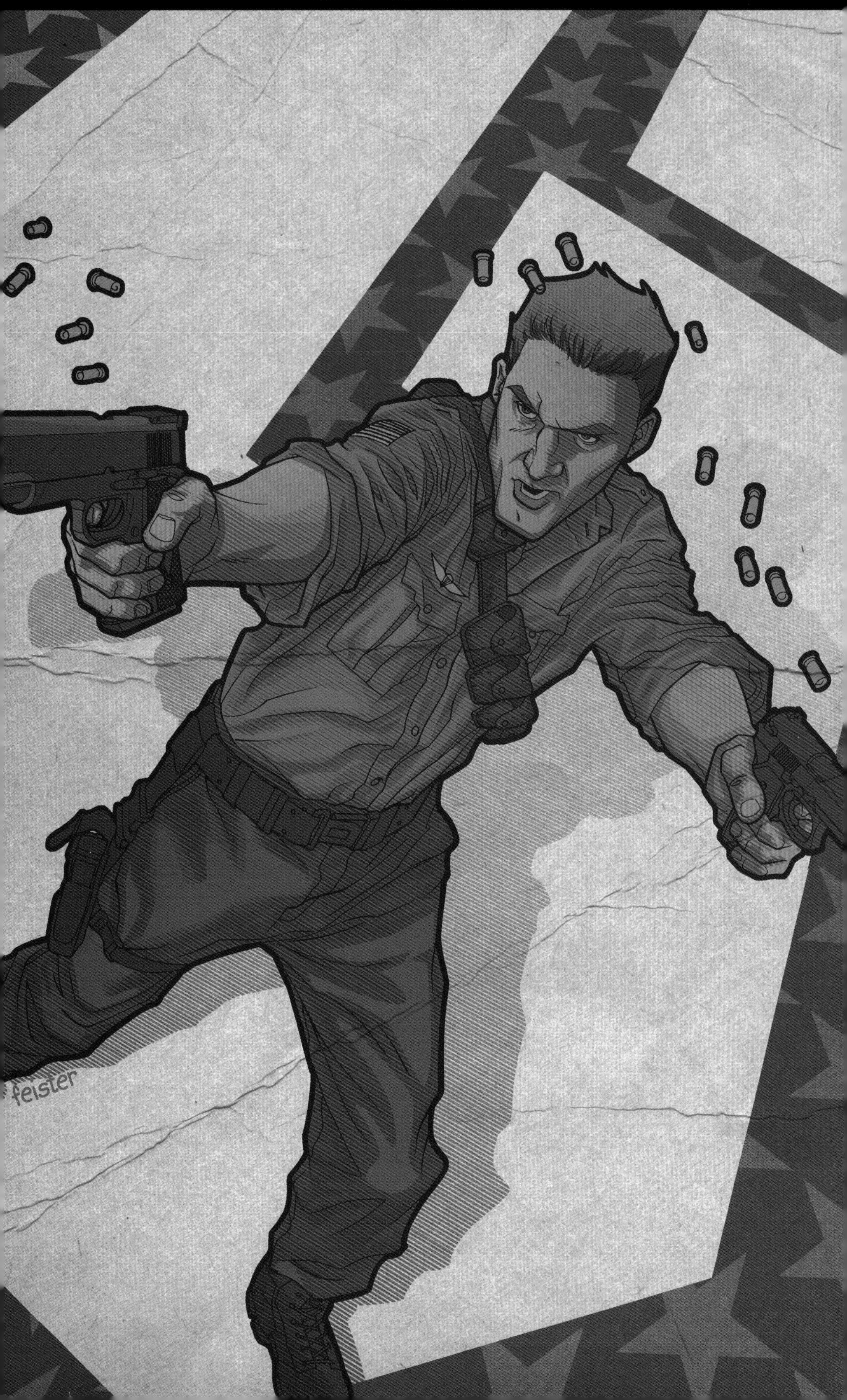
feister

ART BY ANDREA DiVITO, COLOR BY CHRIS SOTOMAYOR

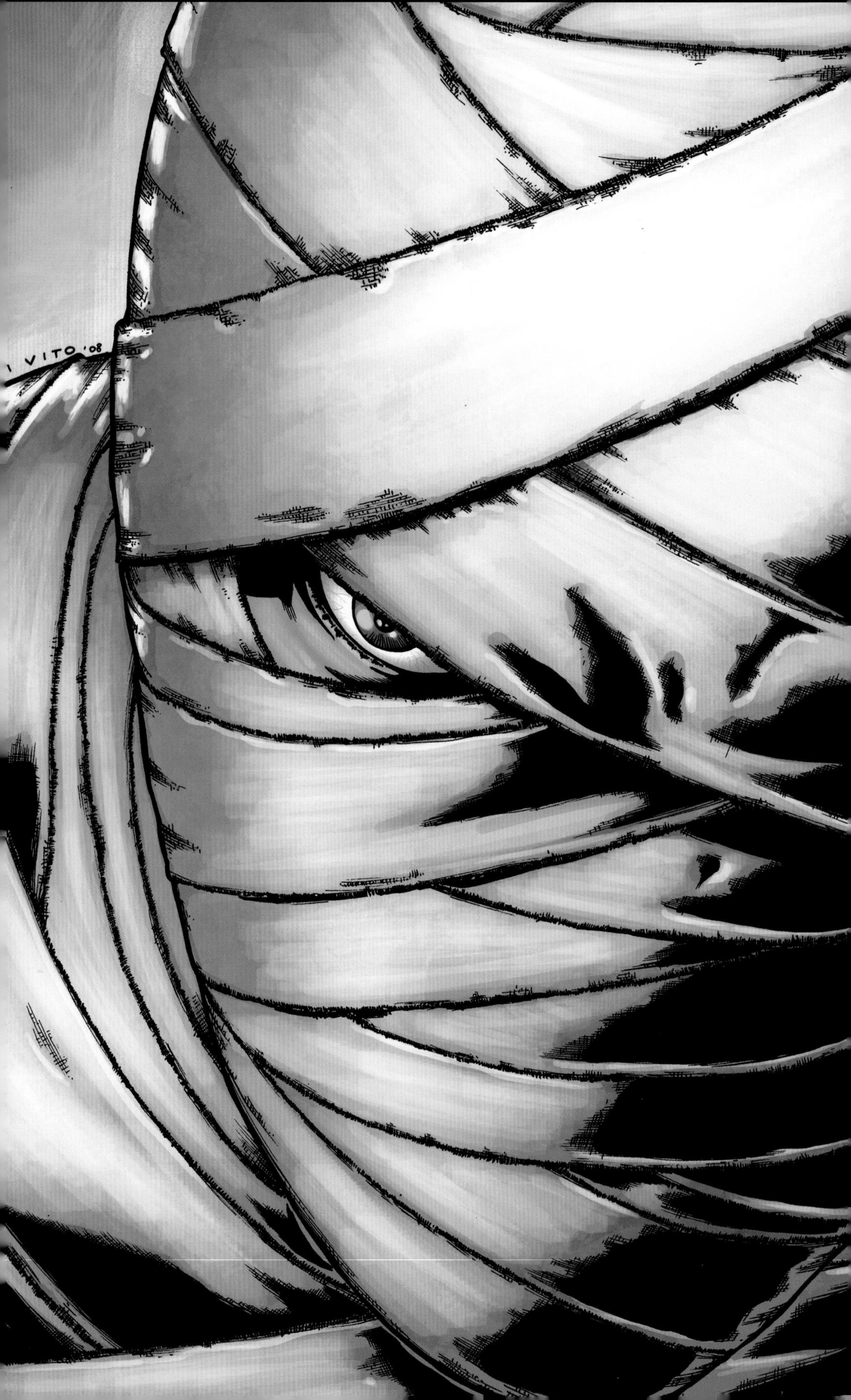

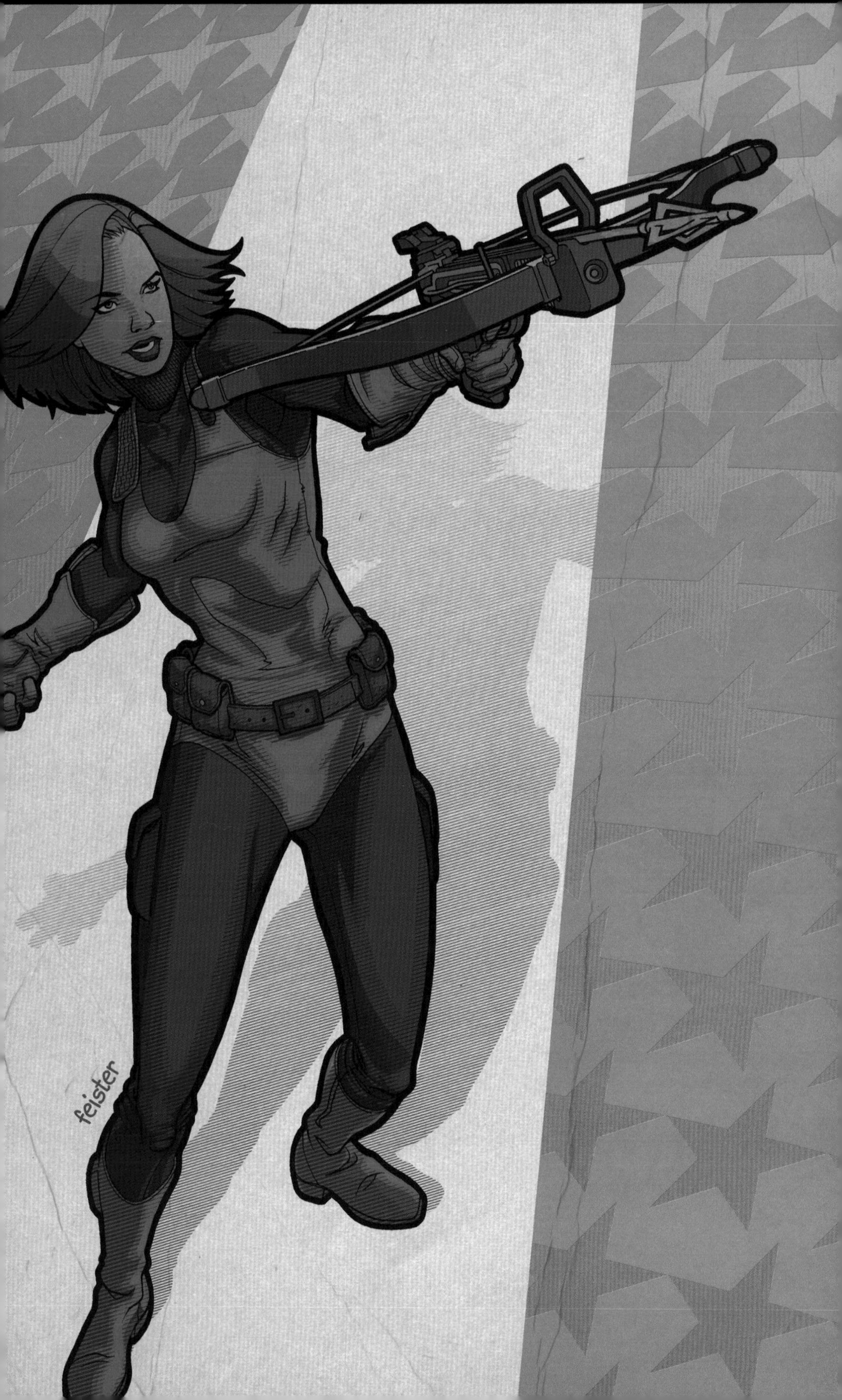
feister

ART BY ANDREA DIVITO, COLOR BY CHRIS SOTOMAYOR

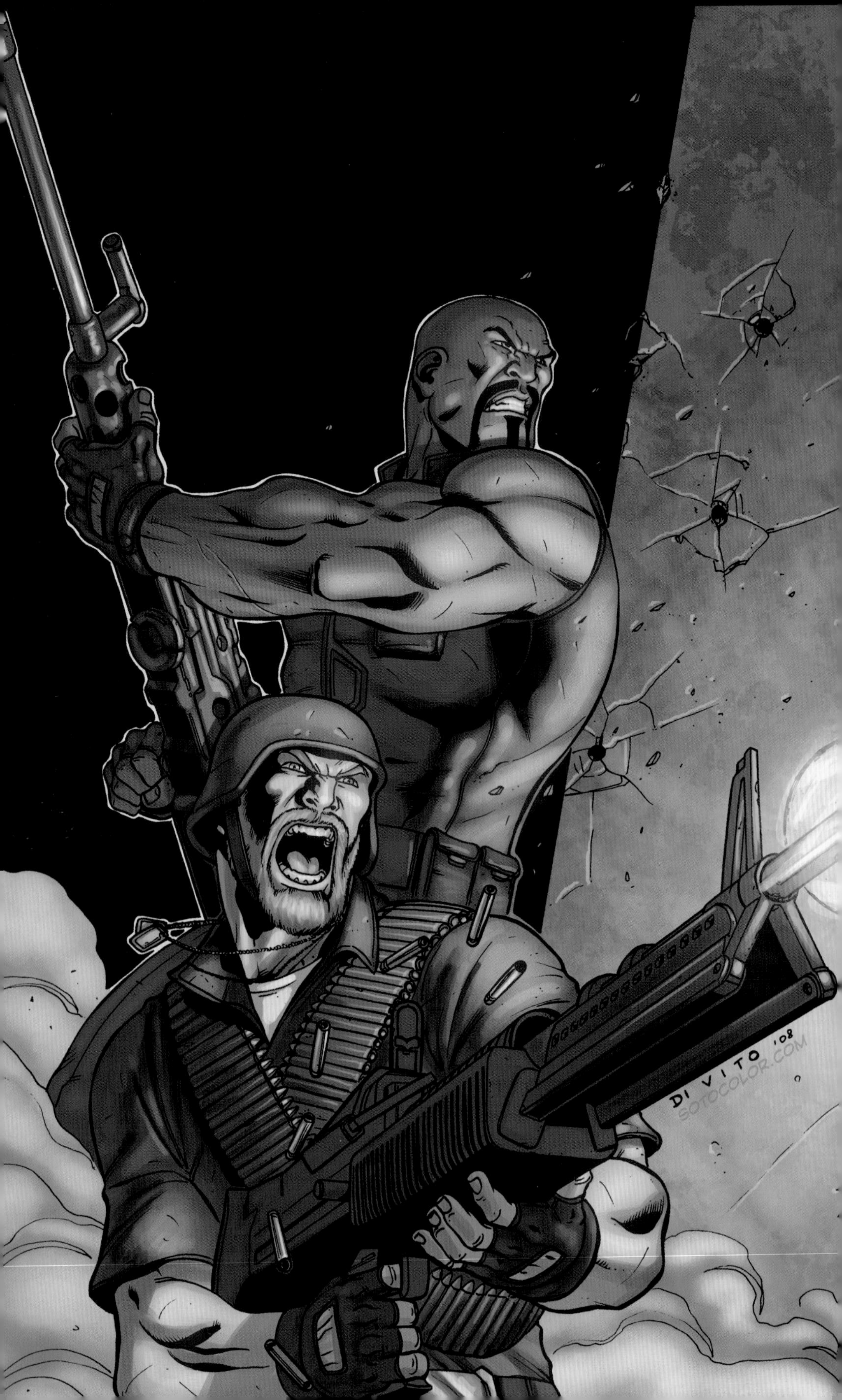
DI VITO '08
SOTOCOLOR.COM

ART BY TOM FEISTER

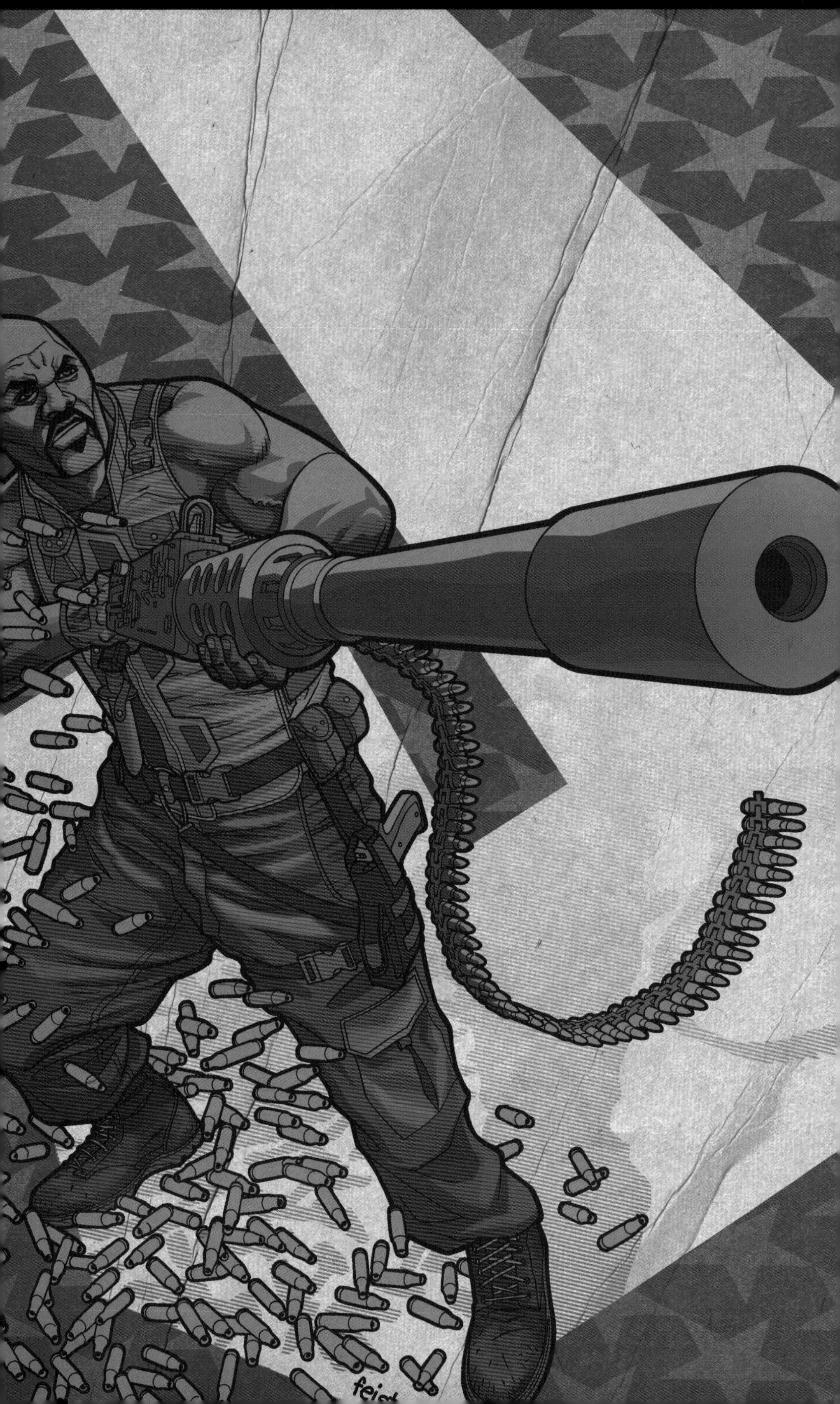
feist

ART BY ANDREA DIVITO, COLOR BY CHRIS SOTOMAYOR

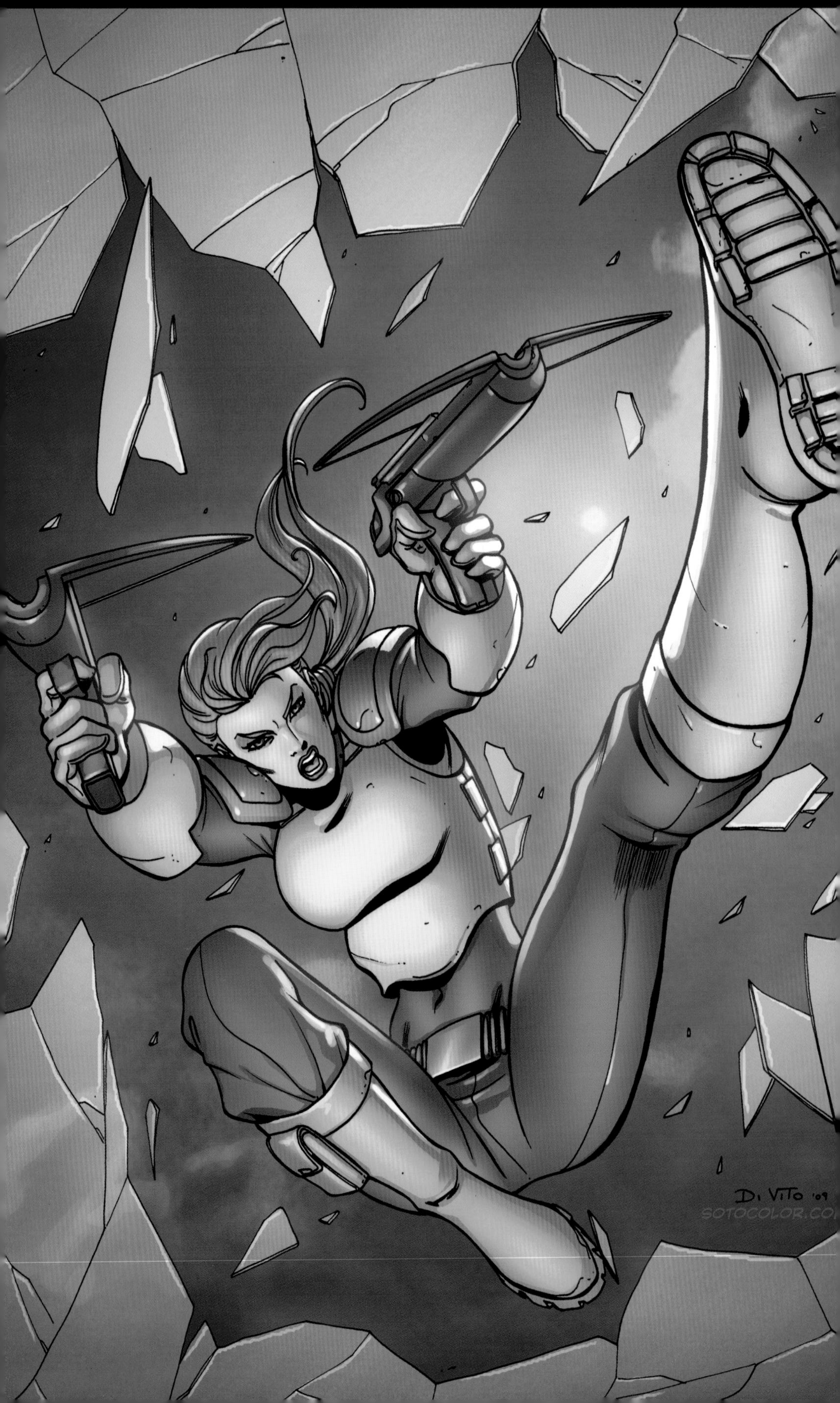
DI VITO '09
SOTOCOLOR.CO

ART BY TOM FEISTER

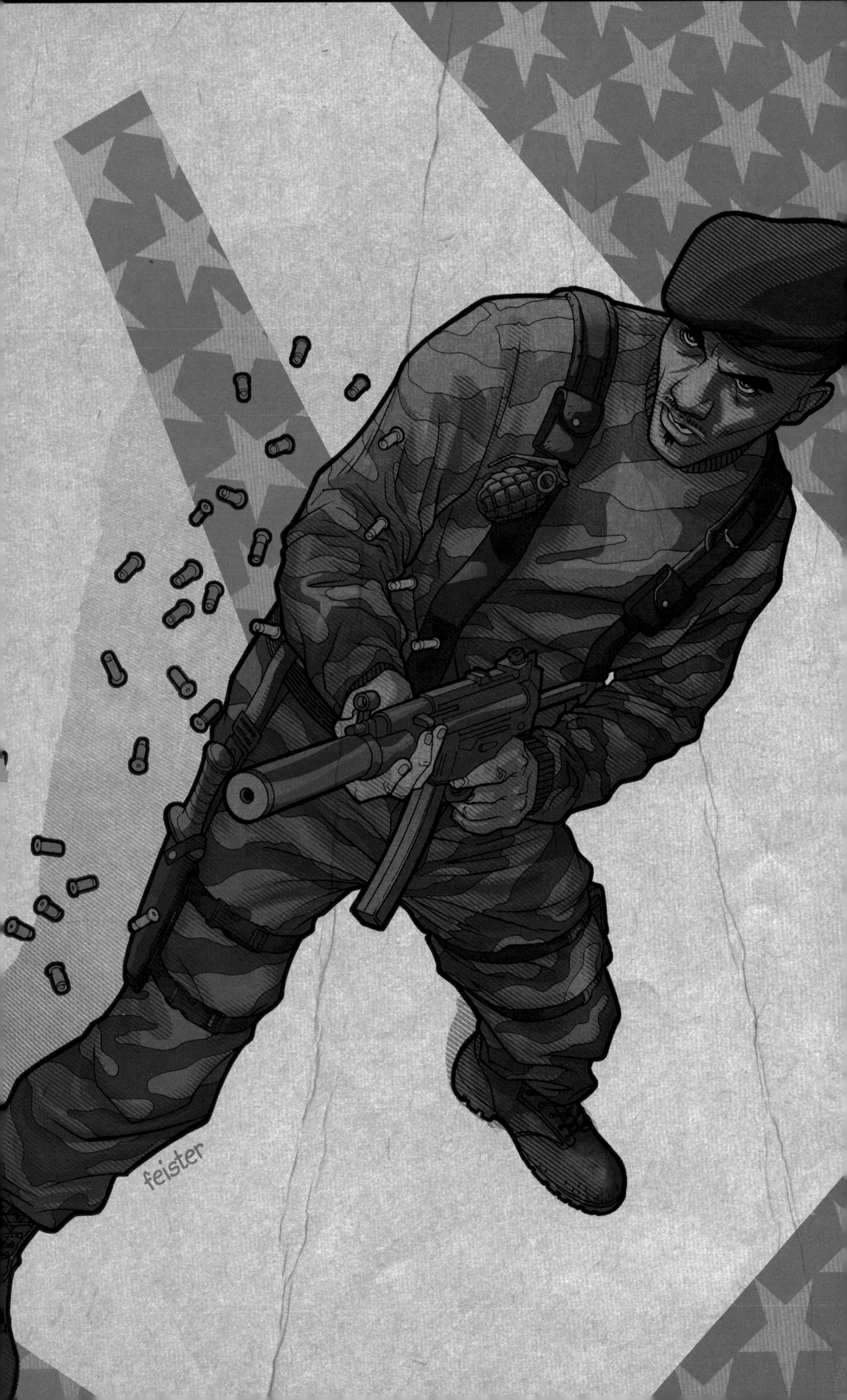
feister

ART BY ANDREA DIVITO, COLOR BY CHRIS SOTOMAYOR

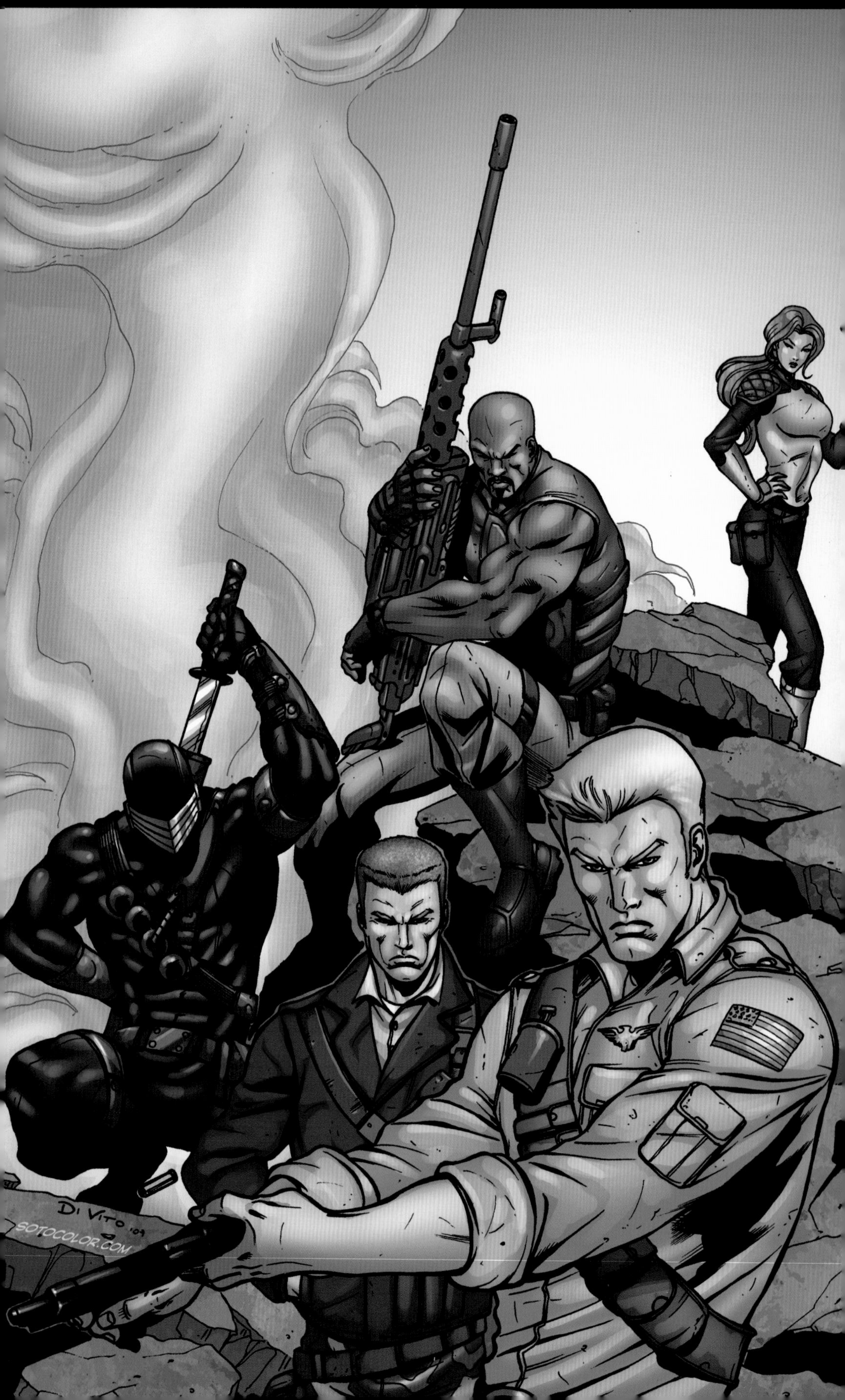

ART BY TOM FEISTER

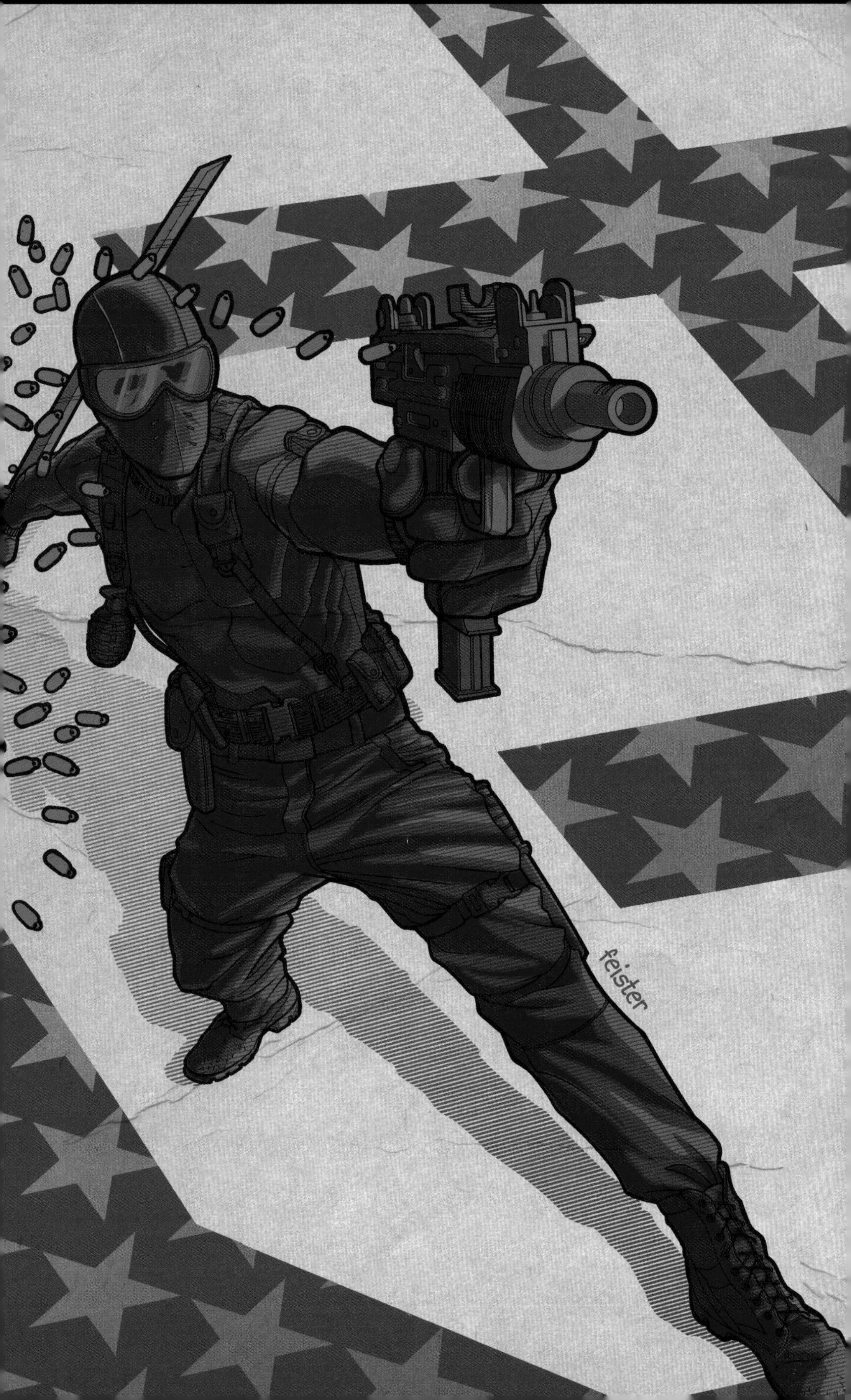
feister

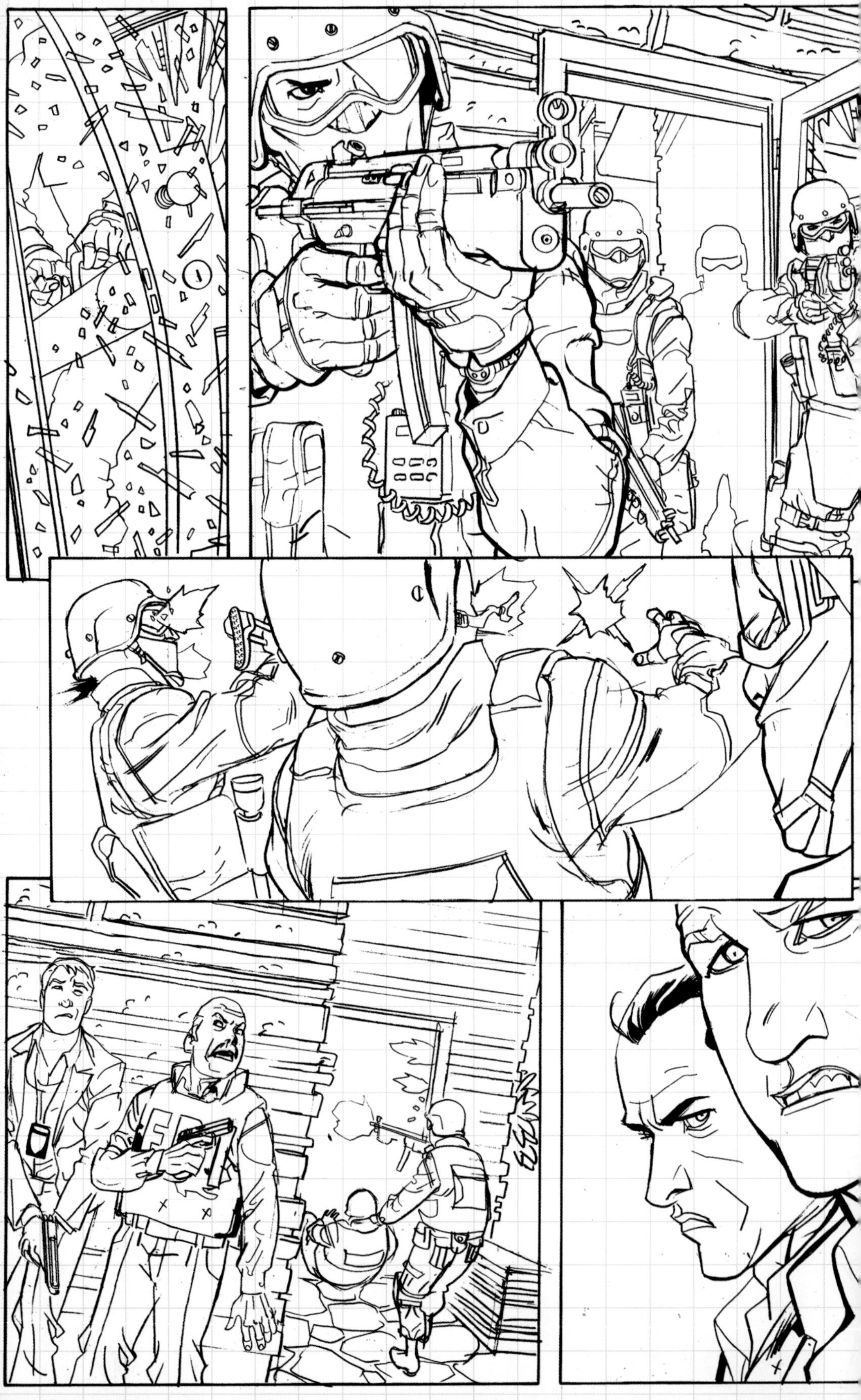

INKS BY MIKE HAWTHORNE

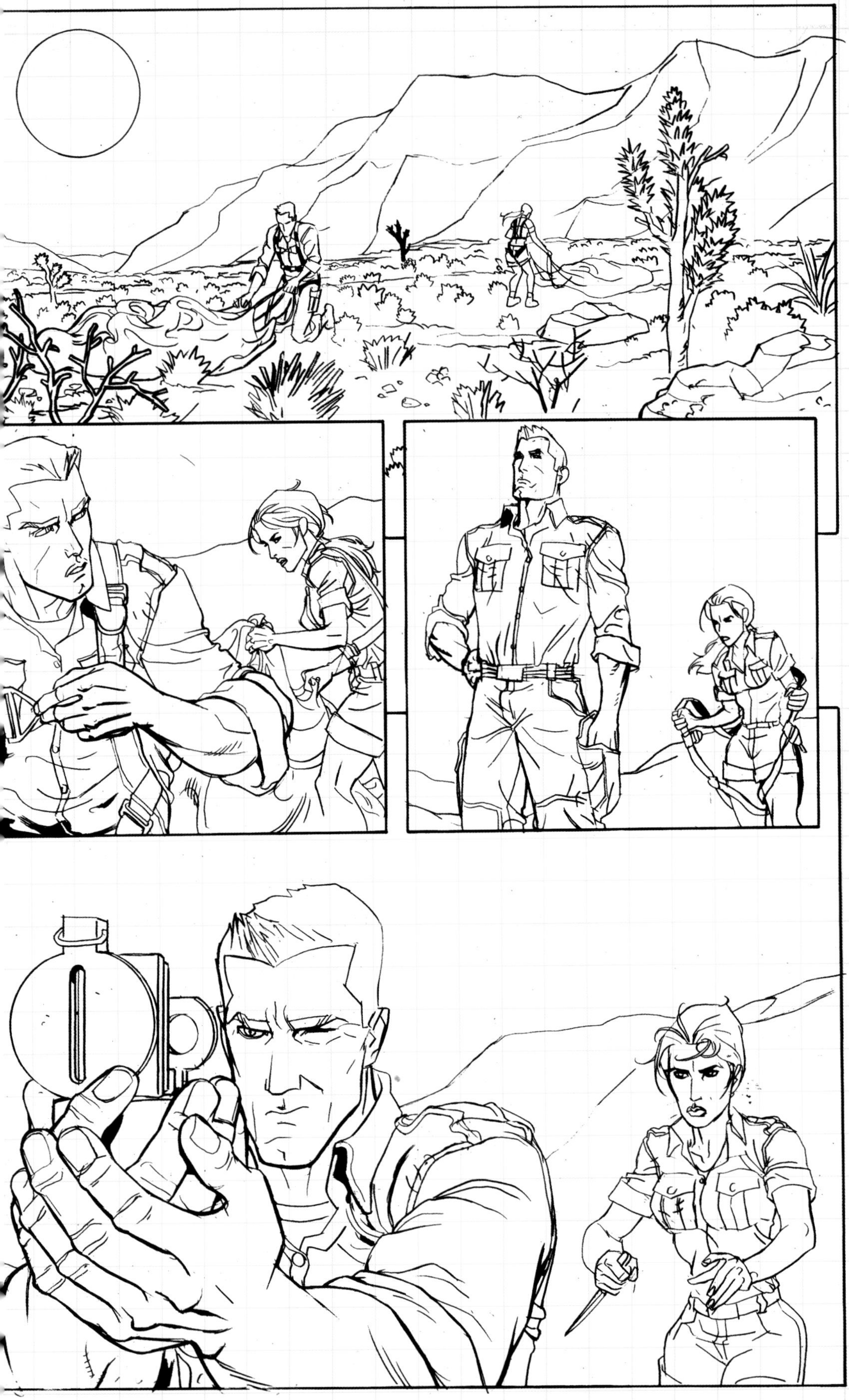

INKS BY MIKE HAWTHORNE

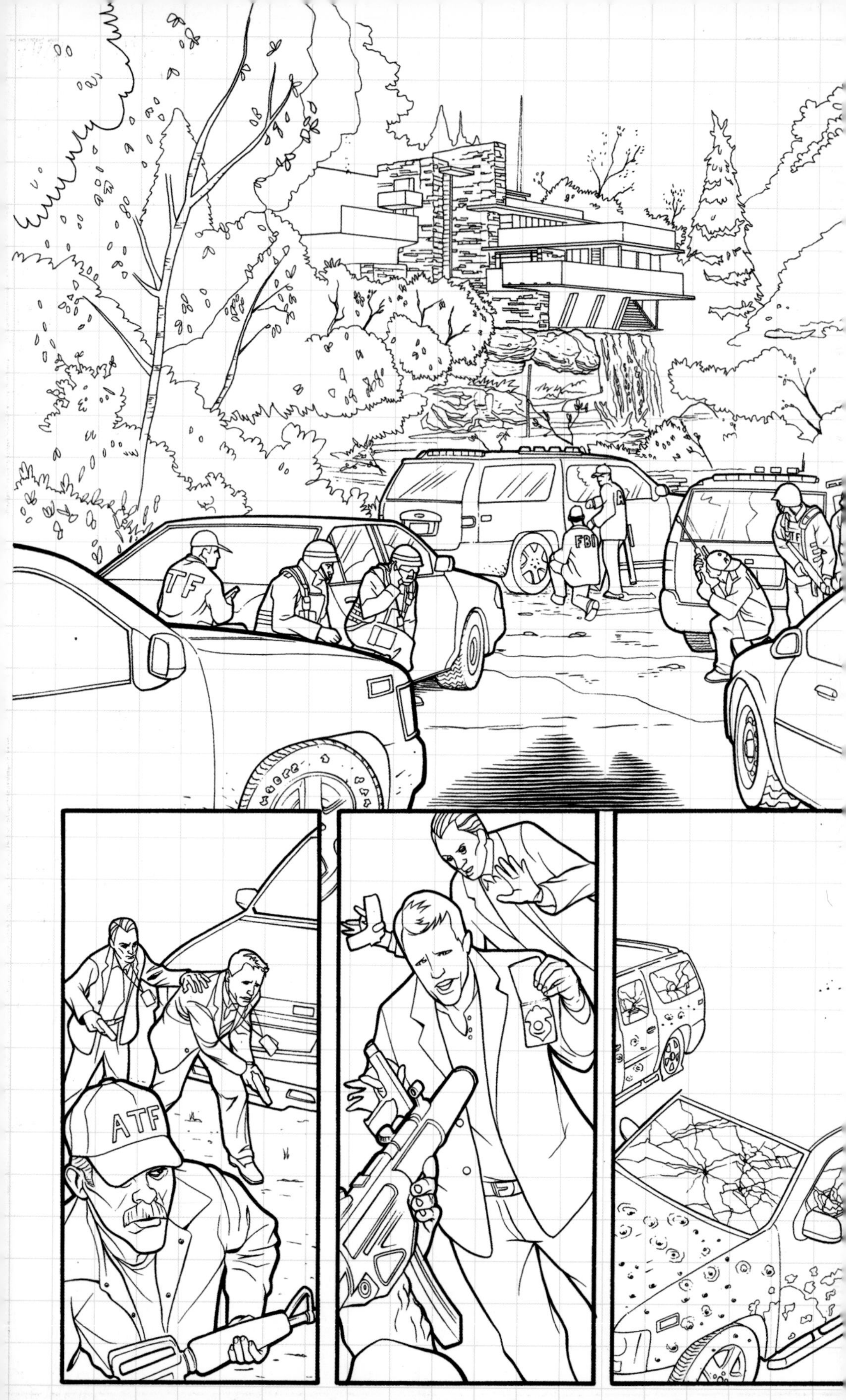
FBI
ATF

INKS BY MIKE HAWTHORNE

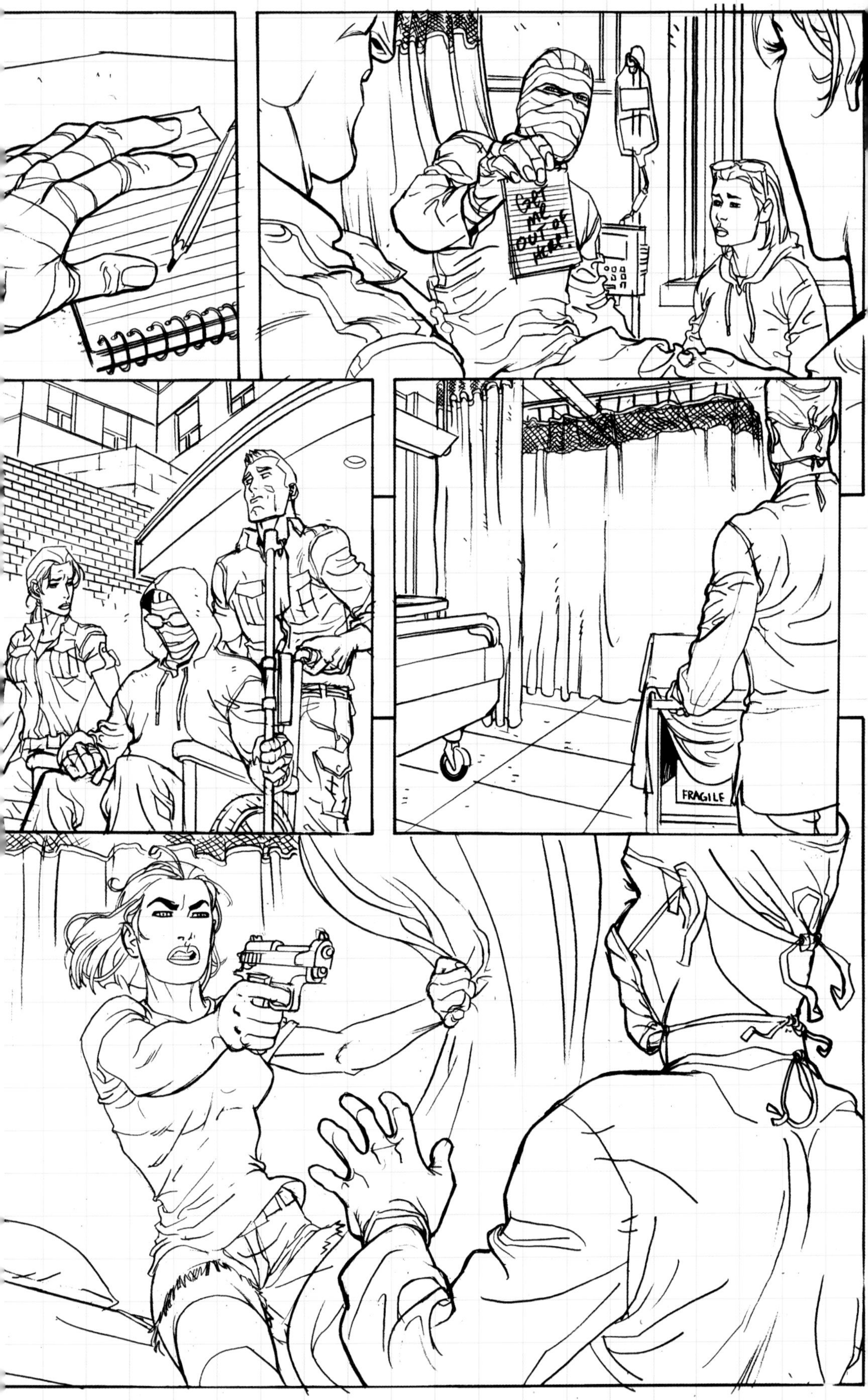

GET ME OUT OF HERE!
FRAGILE

INKS BY MIKE HAWTHORNE

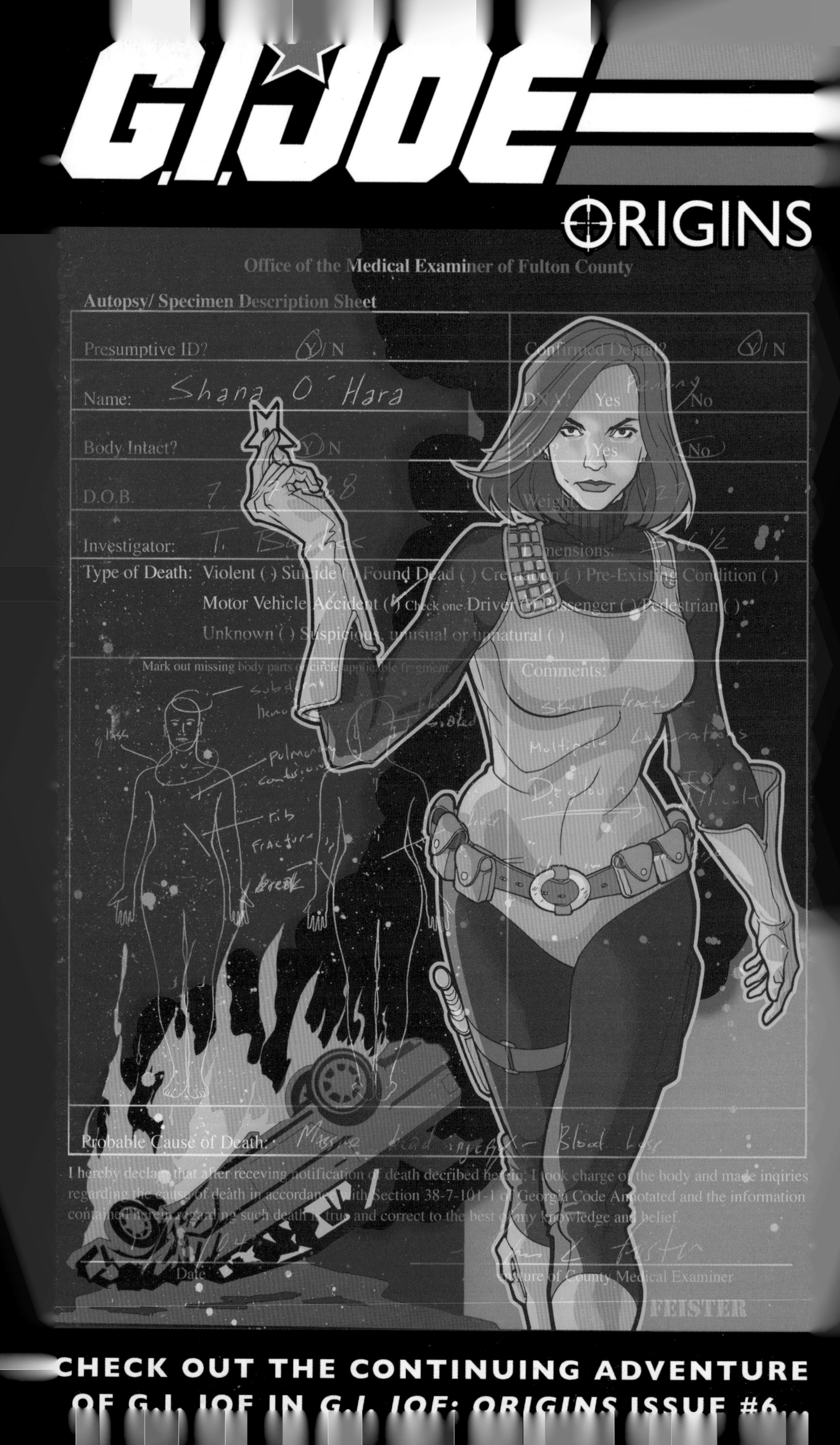
G.I. JOE
ORIGINS
Office of the Medical Examiner of Fulton County
Autopsy/ Specimen Description Sheet
Presumptive ID? Y / N
Confirmed Dental? Y / N
Name: Shana O'Hara
DNA? Yes No
Body Intact? Y / N
Tox? Yes No
D.O.B.
Weight:
Investigator:
Dimensions:
Type of Death: Violent ( ) Suicide ( ) Found Dead ( ) Cremation ( ) Pre-Existing Condition ( )
Motor Vehicle Accident ( ) Check one Driver ( ) Passenger ( ) Pedestrian ( )
Unknown ( ) Suspicious, unusual or unnatural ( )
Mark out missing body parts or circle applicable fragment.
Comments:
Skull fracture
Multiple Lacerations
pulmonary contusions
rib fracture
break
Probable Cause of Death:
I hereby declare that after receving notification of death decribed herein, I took charge of the body and made inqiries regarding the cause of death in accordance with Section 38-7-101-1 of Georgia Code Annotated and the information contained herein regarding such death is true and correct to the best of my knowledge and belief.
Date
Signature of County Medical Examiner
FEISTER
CHECK OUT THE CONTINUING ADVENTURE
OF G.I. JOE IN G.I. JOE: ORIGINS ISSUE #6...